After the Party

Lisa Jewell was born and raised in north London, where she lives with her husband and two daughters. Her first novel, *Ralph's Party*, was the bestselling debut of 1999. She is also the author of *Thirtynothing, One-Hit Wonder, Vince & Joy, A Friend of the Family, 31 Dream Street* and *The Truth About Melody Browne* all of which have been *Sunday Times* bestsellers.

Lisa Jewell

After the Party

C

CENTURY · LONDON

Published by Century 2010

2 4 6 8 10 9 7 5 3 1

Copyright © Lisa Jewell 2010

First published in Great Britain in 2010 by
Century
Random House, 20 Vauxhall Bridge Road,
London SW1V 2SA

www.rbooks.co.uk

Addresses for companies within The Random House Group Limited can be
found at: www.randomhouse.co.uk/offices.htm

The Random House Group Limited Reg. No. 954009

A CIP catalogue record for this book
is available from the British Library

ISBN 9781780891644

The Random House Group Limited supports The Forest Stewardship Council®
(FSC®), the leading international forest certification organisation. Our books
carrying the FSC label are printed on FSC® certified paper. FSC is the only forest
certification scheme endorsed by the leading environmental organisations,
including Greenpeace. Our paper procurement policy can be found at
www.randomhouse.co.uk/environment

Typeset in Palatino Light by Palimpsest Book Production Limited,
Grangemouth, Stirlingshire
Printed and bound in Great Britain by
CPI Group (UK) Ltd, Croydon, CR0 4YY

For Jascha, Amelie and Evie

Acknowledgements

This time round thanks are due almost entirely to Kate Elton. Thank you for taking huge chunks out of your precious maternity leave to read and re-read and re-read again, to thrash it into shape and thank you, even, for the eighteen pages of painstaking (10pt font, single-spaced) edited notes which I would quite happily have doused in petrol and set fire to the first time I saw them. I appreciate every single moment of your time and effort. It's the hardest I've ever worked on a book post-delivery and I'm so glad you made me do it.

Thank you to everyone who said: 'Ooh, a *Ralph's Party* sequel. I can't wait!' during the writing of it. It simultaneously spurred me on and terrified me, but ultimately I'm just delighted that people still remember and still care. I really hope I haven't let you down.

Thank you to Jascha for being completely unfazed by me writing a book about a Completely Fictional Relationship That Bears No Resemblance Whatsoever to Anything That Has Happened to Us – for the SECOND time. Since you haven't read any of my books since *Vince & Joy*, I feel fairly confident that you'll never get round to this one.

Thanks to the usual behind-the-scenes people; the amazing team at Random House: Louise, Claire, Rob, Oliver, Georgina, Louisa and everyone else. Thanks to Jonny Geller and to everyone at Curtis Brown. Thanks to booksellers and readers and library workers the length and breadth of the land without whom it would all be a little bit pointless. And thanks, as ever, to my dear friends on the Board, for being there inside my computer whenever I need you.

'A successful marriage requires falling in love many times, always with the same person.'

Mignon McLaughlin

Prologue

The twelfth anniversary of Ralph and Jem's first kiss falls upon a cool, paper-dry Wednesday at the beginning of March. The wisteria outside Jem's office window has yet to yield its cascades of perfumed lilac blooms and the hydrangea by the front door is stubby and only just turning green – spring feels a long way off although it is just round the corner.

At about three fifteen, Jem leaves her office, heading for an appointment in Battersea. She takes with her a small manila folder, her mobile phone, her handbag and a loaf of brown bread. Before she leaves she turns to her assistant, Mariel, who is making tea in the kitchenette, and says, 'Off to see the recluse.'

'Oh,' says Mariel, 'God. Good luck.'

'Thanks,' says Jem. 'I'll need it. I'll be back in an hour.'

Mariel smiles sympathetically, and Jem closes the door behind her. The sad irony of a trip to Almanac Road on such an auspicious date is not wasted on her. She is painfully aware of it as she walks the fifteen minutes from the office on Wandsworth Bridge Road. When she gets there, she glances down, as she always does, into the basement pit of the house at number thirty-one.

Terracotta tiles gleam, newly laid and freshly mopped. Three small trees carved into pom-pom balls of varying sizes sit in shiny cobalt-blue pots. The front door is thickly painted in a matt shade of mushroom and dressed with nickel-plated knobs and knockers. Through the window she can see more mushroom paint on walls hung with black-and-white photography. Suddenly, two small hands and a baby's head appear over the top of the sofa. Jem smiles. The baby smiles, then disappears again.

Someone else lives here now. A young family, a house-proud family with enough money to renovate the run-down flat they'd bought a year ago, and enough foresight to have done it when the lady of the house was four months pregnant with their first child, unlike Jem, who had spent the last night of her first pregnancy on a mattress in the dining room of her sister's flat, her possessions piled around her in gigantic cardboard boxes, like a township, waiting for a woman in Camberwell to sell her flat to a man in Dulwich so that the owner of their new house in Herne Hill could sign the completion forms and hand them their front door keys.

Before the very neat and well-organised family lived here, a scruffy woman with a deadbeat teenage son and three obese cats had lived here. And before the scruffy woman with the fat cats, a young couple with matching bikes and cagoules had lived here. And before the smug, outdoorsy couple with the bikes, a man called Smith had lived here, alone, having an existential crisis that led, eventually, to him retraining as a reiki teacher and relocating to San Francisco. And even longer ago than that, years before the man called Smith had lived here alone having an existential crisis, Smith's best friend, Ralph, had lived here with him. And so, for a very short while, over twelve years ago, back in 1996 when Oasis were the most famous band in the country and football was, supposedly, coming home, when she was a child of only twenty-seven, had Jem.

Jem can feel it, even now, as she stands on the pavement, peering through the window at strangers' mushroom walls – she can still feel the electric jolt of sudden promise, the thrill of new beginnings. She feels it for just a moment, and then it passes, because for some strange reason things have not worked out how she thought they might during those long-ago days and now it's just a dull echo of a moment in her life when fate, chance and destiny all came together and took her somewhere quite remarkable.

She sighs sadly and pushes her hair behind her ears. Then she looks up, her attention taken by the clatter of a sash window being pushed open and then a loud male voice:

'Intercom's broken!'

A small shiny object leaves his hand and hurtles towards her, catching the light as it falls, landing on the pavement within an inch of her toes.

'Let yourself in!' The large hands slide the noisy window back into place. Jem tuts and picks up the keys. She climbs the front steps and prepares herself, mentally, for the next half an hour of her life. She picks her way through the debris of Karl's life: forgotten T-shirts, a broken guitar, a carrier bag full of recycling, and, oh God, a pair of underpants. She finds him on the sofa, eating a ham sandwich and watching an old episode of *Murder She Wrote*.

'I thought you said you needed bread?' she says, waving the loaf of Warbutons Malted she took for him from her own kitchen cupboard that very morning.

'I do,' he says, 'that's the end of it. Had to scrape some spores off it, make it, you know, edible.' He takes the fresh loaf from her and smiles, gratefully. 'Thanks, Miss Duck.'

'You're welcome,' says Jem, lowering herself on to the very furthest edge of a grubby yellow armchair. 'What happened to the cleaner?' she asks, looking around the room.

Karl smiles, his catch-all, 'forgive-me-for-I-know-not-what-I-do-but-oh-I-am-lovely-aren't-I? smile. It is a good smile, a smile that has seen him through a ten-year career in B-list television presenting, but not quite a good enough smile to stop him killing that career stone dead after a terrible episode in the Australian jungle last autumn, in front of six million viewers. 'I kept forgetting to pay her,' he replies in his smooth Irish croon. He shrugs. 'Who can blame her?'

'How've you been?' Jem squints slightly as she asks the question, almost not wanting him to answer it.

Karl rearranges his large form on the sofa, so that he's facing her. 'Oh, you know, the parties, the premieres, the hot dates, it never ends.' He looks old. Not a line on his face, not for a man of forty-seven, but his face looks dead, like someone has taken a sheet of sandpaper to him and scoured away all the gloss, all the glitter.

'It doesn't have to be like this, you know,' she says, opening up the manila folder. 'Everyone's ready to forget.'

'What you got in there?' he asks, eyeing the folder sceptically.

'Well, it's not money, that's for sure.'

He winks. 'Maybe I need a new agent,' he jokes.

Jem sighs. Jem is Karl's agent, and Karl's joke (this is not the first time he has made it) is not funny any more. She takes out a letter that arrived this morning, printed on sky-blue paper. It is confirmation of a phonecall that she had last week with a production company who are filming a series of interviews with 'controversial' celebrities.

Karl takes it from her and scans it, rapidly, with a furrowed brow. 'Jeez,' he says, 'what is this – the Last Chance Saloon for Battered B-listers? Christ. You're going to make me do it, aren't you?'

Jem shrugs. 'I can't make you do anything, Karl. But it's money in the bank –'

'How much?' he interrupts.

'Five thousand. And if you handle it well, if you paint yourself in a good light, it'll open all those doors again.'

Karl puts the paper down on the sofa and picks up his sandwich. He stares at it disconsolately for a second.

'If that's what I want,' he says, so quietly that Jem only just hears him.

'Yes,' she replies, 'if that's what you want. But here's the thing, Karl.' She pauses. She didn't come here to give Karl a piece of paper. She could have put it in the post. And she certainly didn't come here to replenish his breadbin. 'Here's the bottom line: if you don't do the interview, I'm letting you go.'

The words are gone now, the words that Jem has been carrying round in her head for days, for weeks. She's imagined this conversation a thousand times and every time her heart has raced, her skin has flushed. *Letting a client go.* And not just any client, but her first client, the one who started it all, twelve years ago. And not just a client, but a friend. It's harsh, but it's for his own good, she reminds herself – without the threat he wouldn't do the TV interview, and without the TV interview there is no career for her to manage.

'Jesus fucking Christ,' he drawls. 'That's bribery!'

'Well, yes, though more gentle bullying, I would have said.' Jem pauses and stares at the sleeves of Karl's jumper, which are encrusted with some kind of beige paste. 'I only want what's best for you, and I think this,' she points at the sky-blue paper, 'is what's best for you.'

'I know,' says Karl, 'I'm not stupid. It's fine. I hear you loud and clear. And yeah, OK, I'll do the show. But if it backfires in my face, I reserve the right to sack *you*.' He winks at her, smiles, and then sighs. 'I'm sure life used to be simple,' he says. 'I'm sure there was a time.'

Jem smiles, thinking of a night, exactly twelve years ago, when for a while life had felt far from simple. Exciting, romantic, crazy – yes, but not simple. She thinks again about the way she'd felt when Ralph had proclaimed his love for her, when she realised that she loved him too, when the gates to the Rest of Her Life had swung open and she'd taken her first tentative steps on to the open road.

5

And now she is here: separated, a single parent, inhab-
iting a desperate, heartbreaking place that she never
expected to be. She swallows a swell of tearfulness and
smiles. 'No,' she says, 'it's never been simple. Did you
know, for example, that it is precisely twelve years to the
day since you beat up Siobhan's boyfriend outside an art
gallery?'

Karl smiles. 'What, really?'

'Yeah. Really and truly.'

'You have a very good memory,' says Karl.

'Well, it is also twelve years to the day since Ralph and
I first . . .'

'What, shagged?'

'Yeah,' she laughs, although she doesn't really feel like
laughing. 'It's our sexiversary! Well, it *was*,' she adds sadly.

Karl nods knowingly. 'How is he?'

'Ralph?' Jem still finds it strange saying his name now
that the syllable no longer belongs to her. Once she hadn't
noticed the word leaving her lips, now it feels like something she's borrowed from someone, something she needs
to give back. She swallows another lump of sadness and
says: 'He's all right. I think.'

Karl raises an eyebrow.

'No, he's fine. I just haven't really talked to him lately,
that's all. It's always such a rush whenever I see him.' Jem
has begun to hate the weekly handover of the children.
She hates it when he's in a hurry and doesn't have time
to talk and then hates it when he isn't and he spills over
into the new order of her life with his familiarity and his
beautiful hands that she is no longer permitted to touch.

'Here,' says Karl, getting to his feet and feeling around
the bookshelf beside the TV, 'talking of blasts from the
past, look at this.' He hands Jem a photograph. It is of a
small child, possibly a baby, but hard to tell because it
has lots of long dark hair. The baby appears to be Asian,
probably Chinese.

6

'Siobhan's baby,' says Karl, resuming his slouch on the sofa.

Jem's eyes open wide. 'She's adopted a baby?'

'Adopt*ing*. She just got back from China. I think there's still a long way to go, a lot of red tape, y'know?'

'Right,' says Jem, staring at the photo, at the little soul somewhere on the other side of the world, a tiny person without a family, whose whole destiny is about to turn on its axis. 'Very brave of her,' she says, 'adopting on her own.'

'Yes,' says Karl, 'I know. That's Siobhan, through and through.'

'How old is she now?'

'Siobhan? She's, God, she must be forty-eight, I guess.'

Jem nods and hands the photograph back to Karl. 'Good on her,' she says, 'good on her.'

'Yeah,' he agrees, 'she always wanted a baby and life didn't give her one so she's gone out and made it happen.' He pauses and stares at the photograph of the baby for a moment. 'There's a lesson in there for us all.'

'Yes,' says Jem, drawing herself up, readying herself to leave, 'yes, there really is.'

Jem pushes open the front door. She has mixed feelings about Wednesdays. Wednesday is handover day, the day that Ralph takes the children for the weekend, or at least until Sunday morning. That is how their week is split. Jem gets the kids Sunday to Wednesday. Ralph gets them Wednesday to Sunday. They both live in the same post-code and equidistant from Scarlett's school and Blake's childminder, and the children barely notice the difference. But Jem does. It is both liberating and depressing in equal measure when the children are away. The house feels both full of potential (Books to read! E-mails to catch up on! Clothes to sort through! TV shows to watch! Even, possibly, nights out to be had!) and devoid of life. Her existence feels both joyful and futile. And whether her children are with her or not, the sheer loneliness of living apart from Ralph can sometimes take her breath away.

She stops in the hallway and peers at her reflection in the vast rococo mirror that hangs behind the front door. It is a beautiful mirror, pockmarked and musty and still holding the scent of the distempered walls of whichever lost French palace it was rescued from. It is exquisite, flawlessly tasteful, but it is not Jem's mirror. Neither is it Jem's wall nor Jem's front door. The mirror was picked up from a Parisian flea market, not by Jem in some uncharacteristic moment of extravagant good taste, but by her sister, Lulu, whose house this is and whose house Jem has been living in for the past four months, while she and Ralph wait to see what will become of them.

Jem and her sister see themselves as a modern-day Kate and Allie, but with a few more kids and a husband between them. Or the Brady Bunch, but with one extra adult. Lulu has her two boys, Jared and Theo, and her husband's three older boys from his first marriage, who live here most of the time because their mum lives in Grenada. It is a remarkable house, Tardis-like, with unexpected mezzanine floors and rooms off rooms and secret roof terraces. It is an odd-shaped building, thrown together in the nineteen sixties. It used to be a pub. They bought it ten years ago as a set of flats and are still only halfway through converting it back into a house, so Jem and the kids have their own floor: a set of three rooms, a small terrace and a kitchenette. It is more than enough.

Jem puts down her briefcase and starts to unbutton her tartan jacket. The woman in the mirror gazes back at her – she looks preoccupied, she looks tired. She is about to sigh loudly when a noise distracts her. It is the unmistakable sound of her first-born clattering down the stripped floor-boarded stairs in her pink Perspex Barbie Princess slippers.

And there she is, her Scarlett, a vision in mauve nylon net and fuchsia polyester. But instead of sweeping this raven-haired, Mattel-attired lovely into her arms and squeezing her with every ounce of every moment she has spent thinking about her today when she wasn't there, she looks at her aghast and says, 'What on earth are you doing here?'

'Daddy's not coming,' says Scarlett, throwing her embrace at Jem's lower hips and almost knocking her over.

'What?'

'He just called. He's not coming.'

To her credit, Jem's first reaction is concern. Ralph has never missed a Wednesday. Ralph lives for Wednesday evenings in the same way that Jem lives for Sunday mornings.

'Is he all right?' she asks, picking Scarlett up and heading for the big kitchen at the back of the house where she knows her sister and her husband will be.

Scarlett shrugs and runs her hand through the curls at the nape of Jem's neck.

'Did you speak to him?'

Scarlett shrugs again.

Lulu is cleaning poster paints off a small vinyl-topped table and her husband, Walter is sautéing potatoes over the hob.

'Yeah,' Lulu begins, before Jem is even through the door. 'He didn't show up at six so I phoned and left messages on his voicemail – nothing – then I got through to him just now, literally about three minutes before you walked in.'

'And?' says Jem putting Scarlett down and heading towards Blake, who is sitting on his knees in front of *In the Night Garden* with a finger up his nose.

'He sounded . . .' Lulu mouths the next word, silently, '*weird.*'

'*Weird?*' Jem mouths back and Lulu nods.

9

'Anyway,' she continues, audibly, 'he said he had to go away for the weekend; he said he won't be able to have the children this week.'

'And he said this an hour *after* he was due to collect them?'

'Yes,' says Lulu. 'I know.'

It is clear now that this is a conversation that needs to be had away from small ears, and Jem follows Lulu into the den, which is a small painted concrete box of a room off the kitchen, where they keep their computer.

'What?' says Jem.

'I don't know,' says Lulu, twirling a heavy silver ring round and round her third finger. 'He just sounded . . . *desperate.*'

'Oh God, what do you mean by desperate?'

'Just, like, like he was going to cry. Like it was all too much. And he said . . .' Lulu pauses, twirls the silver ring one turn in the opposite direction. 'He said to me, "Do you know what day it is today?" And I said, "It's Wednesday." And he just kind of went, "Humph." And hung up.'

'Shit,' says Jem, putting the pieces together. 'Our anniversary.'

'What, your first date?'

'First shag,' says Jem, distractedly. 'First kiss. First, you know, *us*.'

'The night at the art gallery?'

'The night at the art gallery, yes.'

'Shit,' says Lulu. 'Is that what it is then, you reckon?'

'Must be,' says Jem. 'Should I be worried?' she asks her sister, feeling that it's already too late to be asking that.

Lulu frowns. 'Possibly,' she says, 'though at least he hasn't actually got the kids with him.'

'Oh, stop it, don't even joke about it. God, what shall I do? Shall I go round there?'

'Well, he did say he was going away.'

'Yes, but maybe he meant *away*.'

'You mean . . . ?'

Jem sighs and pulls her hair away from her face. 'No, of course not. I mean he's been a bit weird but not, you know . . .'

'Suicidal?'

'Exactly.' She sighs again, feeling the weight of things she needs to do now that she has the children for the next few days: baths to run, stories to read, clean clothes to sort out. Plus a baby-sitter to arrange for Friday night when she and Lulu had planned a night out at the theatre. But behind all that there is a terrible, gnawing sense that *something is wrong with Ralph*, that he is in some kind of peril. She remembers a terrible conversation she had with a woman on the street just the week before. She remembers the woman's words. 'Imagine if there was no second chance. How would you feel?' the woman had asked. *'How would you feel?'*

Immediately, Jem knows exactly how she would feel. *Devastated. Finished. Dead.* 'OK,' she says decisively, 'I'm going to give him a ring. Upstairs.'

'Good,' says Lulu, standing aside to let her pass, 'I'll keep the kids out of your way.'

Upstairs, in the tiny room that she and the kids use as a living room, Jem pulls her phone out of her bag and calls Ralph's home number. Her hands shake slightly. It goes to the answerphone and Jem clears her throat: 'Hi,' she says, 'it's me. Just got home. Erm, don't worry about the kids, that's OK, I'll cover it, but just wondering . . .' she pauses, tries to picture the inside of Ralph's flat, who might be there listening to her plaintive, slightly pathetic voice. 'Actually, I'm going to try you on your mobile. Bye.'

She calls his mobile number and is surprised and over-whelmed with relief when he replies after five ring tones.

'I'm sorry,' he says, before she's even spoken. His voice sounds soft and childlike.

'It's cool,' she says, caring about nothing other than that he is not dead. 'We've got it covered. Are you OK?'

'I'm OK,' he says, and it sounds to Jem like the kind of thing you'd say if you'd just been asking yourself the same question.

'Where are you?'

'In the car.'

'Right. And where are you going?'

'Er . . .' He pauses and Jem can hear the swoosh of other cars passing his, the blast of wind through an open window. 'I was on my way, halfway there, to your place, then something came up.'

'Something came up?'

'Yeah, I'll explain it all when I see you.'

'And when will I see you?'

Ralph exhales softly down the phone; 'I'll come for the kids next Wednesday. I'll be there. I promise. I just need to . . .' The line fills up with cracks and bangs and shards of interference. Then it dies.

PART ONE

One Year Earlier

Chapter 1

Jem felt curiously light, unfettered, almost limbless as she headed down Coldharbour Lane towards the tube station. She was wearing shoes with heels. This was the first time she had worn shoes with heels since the previous spring. It was also the first time in three months that she had left the house without a child either in a pram, strapped to her front, hanging off her back or gripped to her by the hand. The sun reflected her mood, neither bright nor gloomy, neither warm nor cold. Jem had just said goodbye to her tiny baby for the first time since he was born. She'd left him in the care of her big sister, a woman who'd given birth to and successfully raised two of her own children and been a mother to a further three belonging to her partner, but still, he was so small, so used to her, such a part of her, so . . . she stopped the thoughts, considered the afternoon ahead. Back to work.

It amazed her that the people she passed on the street were unaware of the existence of her baby, had no idea that she had another one too, a small girl with long, string-thin legs and curls of ebony and the haughty demeanour of a fifteen-year-old It girl. Scarlett and Blake. Beauty and Innocence. Her children. It alarmed her that a stranger might see her and consider her a woman alone, without attachments and dependants or responsibilities beyond the job she was clearly headed towards in her smart black drainpipe trousers, tartan jacket and carefree shoes. She thought about wearing a T-shirt, emblazoned with the images of her offspring, so that people would know that she was more than just this, more than just a woman going to work, and it was while she was thinking this that she saw him.

He was also without his child, also wearing a jacket, also, she assumed, going to work. She caught her breath, feeling suddenly unguarded and stripped naked. She had never before seen him without his child; he had never before seen her without hers. They were not friends, merely two people occupying the same small square of London, pushing their children on the same swings, eating at the same child-friendly cafés, wheeling prams along the same grimy pavements. Their daughters were the same age and had once played together in the small timber house in Ruskin Park. Ever since then she and this man had exchanged nods, smiles, hellos, the occasional how-are-yous. His name was Joel (she'd overheard him answering a call on his mobile) and he was the sort of man who made no first impression at all but climbed his way slowly inside your consciousness, grew outlines and texture and colour like a photo in a tray of developing fluid. And at some unknown point over the past three years Jem had begun to notice him in a way that made her blush at the sight of his rounded back over a buggy on the street ahead of her, his pale, unremarkable hair behind a hedge in the playground, his odd, shuffling walk in soft leather loafers, his daughter's hand in his, emerging from the nursery across the road. But she was safe from the way that he made her feel because of them, the children. The children made them occupied, distracted, hurried. But here and now they were two adults, alone, coincidentally headed the same way at the same time, in matching work attire, hands free, heads free.

Jem slowed her pace and let him walk ahead of her. She realised she was slightly breathless, a fluttering of panic in the pit of her belly. He'd seen her, she knew that. He knew that she'd seen him. They were now ignoring

16

each other. Maybe he felt it too, she wondered, maybe he felt the danger of the two of them being free to . . . Free to what, exactly? She was as good as married. They were parents. What was she afraid of? She stared at the back of his head on the escalator and tried to imagine what would happen if she caught up with him at the bottom. What would she say? 'Hi! Look at us! No kids!' Then what? A train had just pulled in as she approached the platform and she ran for it, forgetting momentarily about the man called Joel ahead of her and there he was, as she shot through the doors, glanced around for a spare seat. He was already seated, surrounded by spare seats, but she turned the other way, squeezed herself between two men, pulled a paperback out of her handbag, pretended to read it. It was a stupid book; her sister had forced it on to her just now. On the cover was a photograph of a young woman in flimsy clothes, lying in long silky grass, looking forlorn and possibly recently abused. It had a silly title too. *Forgetting Amber*. Still, it was better than staring at the adverts, or the ridges in the floor. She glanced surreptitiously at Joel. He was reading a freebie paper. He knew she was there. She knew he was there. They were still ignoring each other.

She imagined another conversation, the one they'd have at the swings, or outside Pizza Express in a few days' time. 'So,' he'd say, 'I saw you on the tube the other day. How come you didn't say hello?' And she would blush and then decide to be truthful. 'I didn't say hello,' she'd say, 'because I find you attractive. And if I'd said hello, we might have started talking and if we'd started talking I might have found that you were dull, or stupid, or un-appealing in some way, and then I wouldn't be able to find you attractive any more. Or worse still, we might have started talking and discovered that we didn't want to stop talking. We might have made a connection and I am not free to make a connection. Do you see?' 'Oh,' he would smile, his cheeks colouring slightly. 'Yes. I see.' And hopefully that would be enough to explain, to ensure that he never spoke to her again.

The man called Joel did not, as she'd predicted, get off at Victoria, nor at Green Park, nor at Oxford Circus. The spaces between stops felt interminable. She read the opening line of the silly book around twenty to thirty times. *Please get off this train*, she chanted to herself, *please get off, I need to breathe.* But the longer he stayed on the train the more convinced she became that this meant something, this coincidence, this proximity, and when the tube pulled into Warren Street and the man called Joel rolled up his freebie paper and sauntered towards the doors, Jem knew it. This was her stop. It was also his stop. Something was going to happen. She slid the silly book into her handbag and got to her feet.

Chapter 2

Ralph felt the emptiness of the house and it chilled him. This wasn't the same emptiness that he felt when Jem and the kids were out, this was a different emptiness. Today, for the first time in a very long time, his family was disparate. Scarlett was at nursery, Blake was at Lulu's and Jem was off to a business meeting somewhere in central London. She'd left the house half an hour ago in heels and tailoring, her scruffy curls tightly secured in clips and bands, her lips painted vermillion. It was her, the other Jem, the Jem who didn't wander in and out of the house all day in well-worn skinny jeans and scuffed Converse trainers, lugging shopping-laden buggies behind her, smelling of milk and Johnson's wipes. He'd watched her and the baby leave from the studio window, and it looked like she was stealing their baby, that petite, elegant woman in tartan and heels an inch too tall for her. And then they'd turned the corner and suddenly he was alone.

Rather than feeling liberated by this open expanse of solitude, Ralph felt distracted by it and immediately put down his paintbrush and headed for the tiny balcony off his studio to smoke a cigarette. The balcony had been added when the previous owners had converted the loft into a studio space and it had always seemed unpleasantly flimsy to Ralph, a few pieces of metal bolted together with oversized wing nuts, barely seeming strong enough to withhold his weight. Whenever he stood on it he subconsciously held on to the wall with his left hand, as if, in the event of the balcony finally giving way under his feet and hurtling three storeys to the patio below, he would somehow be able to embed his fingers into the brick-work where he would dangle, Harold Lloyd-like, until his rescuers arrived.

The balcony overlooked the garden, a typical south London patch of land the shape of an A5 envelope and not much bigger. The beginning of March was not a happy time for gardens. The grass was mulchy, the neglected plastic toys that littered the decking and the lawn were tinged green and the swing under the apple tree swung forlornly back and forth in a chilly breeze. Beyond their small garden, Ralph could see more terraces, more sad gardens, a school playground and the fire escapes skirting the roofs of the parade of shops around the corner. He could be anywhere, he thought desolately, absolutely anywhere. He might as well be in the suburbs. All that effort, all that money, all that saving and searching and financing and settling and this was it: a three-bed terrace in the back end of Herne Hill, a view of nothing, a scrap of grass, a dangerous dangly balcony.

He sucked the last dregs from the end of his cigarette and brought it back inside, where he let it drop into a jar of brown water on the windowsill. The e-mail was still open on his computer. It had arrived this morning, from California, from Smith, his oldest friend.

'It is 81 degrees today and I am off to the beach. Wanna come??'

It was meant as a joke, just a throwaway line to rub Ralph's face in the fact that while he was trapped in a loft in south London on a dreary Wednesday morning, Smith, tanned and lean, was jogging past girls with augmented breasts and minimal pubic hair along vast expanses of creamy beach. It wasn't supposed to be an invitation, but every time Ralph looked at it, it seemed more and more as if it should be. And now, seeing Jem leaving the nest, taking her baby bird to be looked after by someone else, wearing high heels, it seemed a phase of his life had just drawn to a close. They could be separate now. They could be apart. For the past seven years Ralph and Jem had been bound together by trying to get pregnant, by miscarriages, by more trying, then, finally, by babies and breastfeeding schedules and now that glue was starting to unstick. They'd finished. They were fragmenting. He could go. *He could go.*

He paused, questioning the quiet euphoria that suffused his body as he thought of escape. Did that mean he was unhappy? *Could* he be unhappy? He had it all. He had Jem, he had two beautiful children, a house, a career.

He looked at himself in the mirror that was bolted above the paint-splattered sink in the corner of his studio. He looked OK. Considering he was forty-two. Considering he barely saw the sun these days. Considering he hadn't had a holiday in two years. Considering he smoked thirty cigarettes a day. Considering he hadn't had sex for nearly seven months. He looked OK.

What had he thought forty-two would be like? How had he pictured it? He'd assumed there would be a wife, that there would be children. And he'd assumed that both the wife and the children would be beautiful, of course he had; who dreams of an ugly family? He might not have predicted, though, that he would still be painting. His career had always been precarious, a little like his balcony; a funny, rickety old thing, not to be trusted. The fact that he would be making a living from oil and canvas would have been surprising to him. Less surprising would have been the extent of that living: enough for mortgage repayments, for nursery fees, for car repairs and Ocado deliveries, enough for birthday dinners in smart restaurants, enough for Diesel jeans and Monsoon baby clothes and proper cigarettes and a cab home after a night out.

But still, not enough.

Eleven years ago Ralph's star had risen. Eleven years

ago all his dreams had come true one icy March night, in an art gallery in Notting Hill. Ralph had declared his undying love to his soulmate and been acclaimed a star. Eleven years ago Ralph had felt it – something that most people never get to feel – the sharp punch of success. The girl of his dreams! His! The respect of his peers! Goal!

Now he was just a man with a family who painted pictures for middle-class people who couldn't afford real art.

He heard the stillness of the house again; it came to him ominously, like the barely audible rumble of a far-away train. He looked around his studio, at the half-finished canvases, the uninspiring still lifes of poppies and daisies and hands and faces, the same safe ground, trodden over again and again because it paid the mortgage.

He sighed and decided to go to the gym.

The gym.

This was not a place that Ralph ever imagined he would have cause to haunt.

But he was here today, not for calorie-burning or muscle-toning, just for the background noise. He wanted to move among other human beings, in a coolly detached way, wanted to smell their smells and overhear their mobile phone conversations and watch their bodies moving in time to some unheard music. He wanted to be part of something, even if it was just mid-morning at a slightly grubby gym in south London.

He picked a treadmill that was comfortably apart from other exercisers and hung his towel over the handle. He typed in the settings, stumbling for a moment as he always did over the number 42 when asked to input his age – really, it seemed so unnaturally old – and then he started to walk. He'd forgotten his earphones so had to make do with watching the screens overhead silently. Screen one showed an R&B video; three sphinx-like women in red hotpants and bandeau tops, gyrating, pursing full lips, passing hands across taut bellies. Ralph watched for a while, wondering why every time he came here a woman under the age of thirty wearing hardly any clothes was gyrating unsmilingly on that screen. Every single time. Ralph thought of Scarlett, imagined her here beside him watching that screen, her pale jaw hanging slightly open as it always did when she watched TV. What would her small, sponge-like brain make of these women, impossibly engineered, humourless, characterless, thrusting, shining statues, imploring the world to buy some man's music with every flick of their hips? And if Scarlett was to watch her, and women like her, all day long, what would she learn of womanhood, what would she think of musicianship, what would it say to her about fame?

Ralph shook his head sadly and glanced at the next screen. A real-life action show: paramedics prising a middle-aged man out of a concertinaed car. His head was held in place with a plastic neck brace, his nose and mouth covered with an oxygen mask. His eyes flicked from side to side as he allowed a man in a fluorescent jacket gently to pull him away from beneath his bent steering wheel. A few moments before, he had been a bloke driving somewhere, who knew where; to buy cigarettes, to work, to pick up a new bit for his power drill? Now he was trussed up inside a written-off car, about to spend the day, at the very least, in hospital, all the while being filmed by a man with a camera, to be broadcast on national television. How much more surprising and unsettling a turn could a normal day take? Ralph knew that the man was alive and well because they kept cutting to clips of him in a studio, reliving his nightmare to an off-screen interviewer, but still, thought Ralph, an ordinary life, touched for ever, never to be the same again.

In contrast, screen three showed a series of slightly over-weight models parading up and down a tacky TV studio in 'outsize' clothes. Ralph wasn't sure where he stood on the subject of overweight models. Or overweight women in general, really. Try as he might to be piously PC about the whole thing, he couldn't quite get beyond thinking that women that shape generally looked better in basques and camiknickers than they did in tailored trousers and natty waistcoats. But he did know that the pompous little man officiously directing the big women up and down the studio floor as if his job was on a par with oncology would probably have benefited from an unforeseen car crash and a little new perspective on his existence.

On the fourth screen there was a news report from somewhere in middle America, square-faced men and women with placards, lambasting pissed-off looking people in cars for not adhering to some scripture or other that governed their lives. Their faces were hard with blind belief, their mouths were oblongs of disregard for other people's values. The people in the cars batted them away as if they were wasps bothering their lunch. How could the people with the placards possibly believe that these actions would lead to any more believers? How could they not know that all they were bringing about with their shouting and their bombasting and their ugly talk of Christ and saved souls was repulsion?

Ralph looked around him at the sparsely occupied gymnasium. Were there believers in here, he wondered. Were any of these normal-looking men and women likely to pick up a placard on a Saturday morning and yell at people for not seeing the world the same way they did? He glanced again at the screens overhead, at the thrusting women in red, the broken man in the broken car, the larger ladies in the frumpy clothes and then once more at the angry Americans with their placards, and for a second it hit him, somewhere round the side of his head, a shocking thought: *What if they were right?*

What if those Americans were right?

What if there was a God? What if his son had saved all our souls? What if religion were true? Would it make sense of all the nonsense in the world? All the flukes, all the coincidences, all the miscarriages and car crashes and people worrying about being fat? Where, he wondered, did all that belief come from? It had to come from somewhere? It had to have some substance, surely?

Ralph left the thought suspended outside his consciousness like a spoonful of something he wasn't sure he could put in his mouth. And then he shut the door on it.

God was for freaks.

Christ was for idiots.

He turned his attention to his heart rate and brought it, as quickly as possible, up to 160.

Chapter 3

Jem scooped her baby boy into her arms and felt relief suffuse her body. 'How was he?' she asked, secretly wanting her sister to say, 'Oh, you know, devastated to be apart from you.'

'He's been great, haven't you, little man?' said Lulu, running her hand across his cheek and smiling at him fondly.

'How much milk did he have?'

'He had about three ounces just after you left, and then another three just now. He's slept most of the time.'

'Typical,' smiled Jem, sliding the bridge of her nose across Blake's cheek and inhaling the scent of him as though he were a flower.

'How'd it go?' asked Lulu.

'Oh, great, fine, it was just a preliminary meeting, nothing scary.' She carried Blake to the sofa in Lulu's kitchen, laid him across the cushion and unstrapped her high heels, kicking them off triumphantly. 'Those,' she said, pointing at them where they lay on the floor, 'were a mistake.'

'Yeah, you should have worked your way back up the heel scale a bit more slowly. Converse to skyscrapers in one swoop, not good for the calf muscles.'

Jem stretched her aching legs out in front of her and examined her feet. What would he think now, she wondered. What would Joel think if he could see her here, flopped ungainly, feet in damp tights, a squelchy baby at her side? She could feel curls escaping from the pins she'd trapped them with three hours earlier. Her left breast was leaking warm milk. She was halfway between the two states, halfway between ragged mother and desirable woman, a changeling. She unbuttoned the Vivienne Westwood Red Label jacket that she'd won in a fevered eBay auction three weeks ago and peeled it off, shedding her layers. Then she picked up her baby and held him over her shoulder and let his warmth and stillness soothe her back into being.

'The funniest thing happened,' she said to Lulu.

'Oh, yes?'

'Yes, it was like something out of a novel. There's this man –'

Her sister's face registered her surprise.

'No, nothing like that, just this man, a dad, I see him around, he's cute, but it's nothing . . . it's not *significant*. Just, you know, something to do.'

Her sister smiled knowingly. Silly crushes on men they weren't married to was something of an ongoing joke between them, a way of maintaining some sense of girlishness.

'Anyway, he's always with his little girl, I think he's a house-husband, never seen the mum, we smile and stuff and he's cute and then today he was there, on the tube, without his little girl and it was a bit . . .'

'Oooh,' smiled Lulu.

'Well, yes, a bit oooh, and we were, I think you could say, *studiously* ignoring each other and then he got off at my stop, at Warren Street, and I thought, oh my God, this is it, one of those moments, like something from inside your head has escaped, gone feral, you know, doing its own thing.'

'And so, what happened?' urged Lulu.

Jem shrugged, and moved Blake on to her other shoulder. 'Nothing,' she said, 'nothing happened. *Of course*. He went off to the Northern Line, I went to the exit.

I watched his back disappear from view. I breathed a sigh of relief . . .'

'Because you don't really want anything to happen?'

'Exactly,' said Jem. 'I don't really want anything to happen. It's just sometimes you get the feeling that something was supposed to have happened, you know, that a door was left open deliberately for you and you have to wonder why.'

'The "sliding doors" thing.'

'Yup,' said Jem, sitting Blake up on her lap and smiling at his little floppy head. 'Timing is everything. And maybe, you know, if me and Ralph had been going through a bad patch or something then –'

'You'd be in a wine bar with Mystery Dad right now, banging on about how your husband doesn't understand you.'

Jem smiled at her sister. 'Something like that,' she said. 'Oh, look at him, he's knackered.' She appraised her baby son. 'I'd better get him home.'

'No time for a cup of tea?'

'No, honestly, I'm knackered and so's this one and if I time it right, I might just get a lie-down when we get home.'

Her sister gave her Blake's coat and sat down next to her, helping her to thread his floppy arms through the sleeves. 'So everything is all right, is it, with you and Ralph?' She sounded concerned, as if it was a question she'd wanted to ask for a while.

'Yes,' answered Jem, slightly too abruptly. 'Well, as all right as things can be when there's a baby in the house. And we did have a bit of a row yesterday –'

'Oh, yes?'

'Yes, about me going back to work, about the fact that he was "too busy" to look after Blake for a few hours today. You know, it's just ridiculous, he's there all day, in that house, nowhere to go, nothing planned, this is *his* son, *his* baby, yet I've had to bring him all the way over here so just so I can go into town for a few hours.'

'Yes,' said Lulu, circumspectly, 'I did wonder about that. What was his excuse?'

'Oh, you know, *deadlines*, always deadlines, deadlines that miraculously disappear when there are things going on that he actually wants to do. He just couldn't hack it, that's the bottom line, just couldn't hack the thought of being stuck with his baby for half the day, all on his own. Plus, of course, he thinks my job is some kind of *joke*. He's never taken it seriously. Maybe if I was a lawyer, or maybe even an artist, like him, maybe then he'd be more supportive of me trying to find my way outside the home. But as it is . . .' She paused, and then she sighed. There was no point, she reminded herself, no point whatsoever getting herself worked up about all this stuff. It was just the way things were, not only for her but for nearly every woman she knew. At some point in the last few years Ralph had turned his back, stuck his metaphorical hands in his metaphorical pockets and allowed her to become a housewife. And somewhere deep down inside she hated him for it.

She sighed again. 'Anyway, it's fine, it's sorted, for now. And yes, generally things are OK. We just need to get through the next nine months, just need to get to Blake's birthday, and if we get there intact, we'll be fine.'

She glanced down at Blake, bulky and squashy now in his winter coat, and smiled at him. 'We'll be fine, won't we, little man?' she asked him in a softer voice. 'We always are.'

Chapter 4

Ralph watched Jem return. Her hair was looser, but she was still resplendent in her tight jacket and high heels. He watched her negotiate the pushchair up the footpath, he could see the rotund form of his son slumbering in his fat winter coat, his outstretched legs cocooned in a thick soft blanket the colour of sky. Jem looked great, he thought, trim and tiny and back to her pre-pregnancy weight already. She was, he thought to himself, a very yummy mummy. He smiled at the thought. And then he thought that he wanted her. He wanted this Jem, *his* Jem. He wanted her out of that jacket, naked, except perhaps for the extraordinary heels. He wanted to breathe in her breath, taste her mouth, be a part of her again, not this useless adjunct, this separate floating particle. He wanted to drift back to port, slot himself in, anchor down. He wanted to be wanted and he wanted it now.

He smiled at her from halfway down the stairs. 'Welcome home,' he whispered, 'how'd it go?'

'Good,' Jem whispered back, wheeling the pushchair into the alcove underneath the stairs.

'And how'd it go with the baby at Lulu's?'

Jem smiled. 'Really well. I don't think he missed me in the slightest.'

'See,' he said, descending the stairs, 'I told you it would be fine.'

'Hm,' said Jem.

Hm.

Ralph, with an agenda that didn't involve tedious

bickering about whose turn it was to plonk themselves down triumphantly at the top of the moral high ground and stick their flag in it, decided to let it pass.

'I watched you coming back just now,' he said, 'from the window.'

'Oh, yes?' Jem unlooped Blake's nappy bag from the back of the pushchair and pulled out two empty milk bottles.

'You look amazing,' he said, somewhat breathlessly, as if Jem were some hot stranger in a bar, not the woman he'd lived with for eleven years, not the woman he'd watched give birth to his two babies.

Jem glanced at him, half suspicious, half pleased.

'No, really, I looked at you and I thought, if I were to walk past that woman in the street, I'd want to . . .'

Jem frowned at him.

There it was, the knee-jerk rebuke. Ralph thought about giving up – it would be easier. But then he glanced down at Jem's feet, so small, so feminine, in those heels. He thought about the dull ache in his chest, the empty space in his soul where *they* had once resided. He saw his son, still slumbering; he saw an opportunity slipping through his fingers. 'Reckon we could squeeze in a quickie?' he said, a hint of apology tingeing the edges of his words.

Jem looked at him in horror. 'What,' she said, 'now?'

'Well, yes, why not? Blake's sleeping, the house is empty . . .'

'I thought you were busy?'

'No. I mean a real quickie. You know, three minutes, tops.'

Jem blanched. 'Jeez,' she muttered. 'I mean, *no*.'

'Right,' said Ralph. 'I see.'

'No, it's not that, it's not . . . it's just I have to express some milk, look, I'm leaking.' She pulled her tartan jacket out of the way to show Ralph the damp patch on her blouse.

31

'And then I was going to have a lie-down. I only got five hours' sleep last night.'

Ralph nodded. He couldn't argue with that. How could he argue with that? How could he argue with breast milk? How could he say that she shouldn't be tired when it was she who had woken three times in the night to feed their hungry baby? How could he even begin to make a case for his own needs and wants? He couldn't. Which was not to say that there wasn't a case to be made. There was a very strong case to be made indeed.

Jem and Ralph had not had sex for nearly seven months.

If there were such a thing as a court of sex law, Ralph's case would be open and shut. He was being starved of sex at the very same time as being expected to remain faithful. It was a little like being cut with a knife and told not to bleed.

'Sorry,' he said, trying his hardest not to sound cross and hurt, 'bad timing.'

'No,' said Jem, 'I'm sorry. I'm really sorry. It's just, you know, everything's all over the place, I'm just a mess, it's –'

'Honestly, it's fine.'

'No,' said Jem, 'it's not fine. I know it's not fine. I just can't think about it right now.'

Ralph breathed in. He wanted to shout. He wanted to say, 'How come you can get yourself all dolled up for work, how come you can put on heels and make arrangements for the baby and be away from him for half the day and sit in a hotel lobby with a stranger and discuss their career with them, and get on tubes and make notes and be prepared to think about all that *right now* but you can't even slip upstairs for a few minutes just to be with me?' Instead, he breathed out slowly and forced a smile. 'I know,' he said, kissing the top of her head, smelling the underground and the city in her hair, 'I know. We'll get there. It's cool.'

She smiled at him apologetically, kissed the top of his hand. 'I love you, you know,' she said.

'Yeah,' he said, 'I know.' And then he turned and took the steps back to his studio at the top of the house.

This wasn't the first time that Ralph and Jem had experienced a sexual drought. The last few years had seen their sex life take more than a few knocks. Four pregnancies. Two miscarriages. Two babies. Ralph wasn't stupid. He knew that that was the way of these things. He hadn't expected all-night sessions, he hadn't expected Jem to be crawling all over him two minutes after losing a baby at twelve weeks' gestation, demanding her conjugal rights, he hadn't really expected anything at all. But four years was a long time for a man to be flung back and forth between being the Absolutely Crucial Supplier of Sperm and being the Utterly Redundant Non-producer of Milk. Four years was a long time to be expected to pretend that you didn't want something that you wanted really, really badly.

And four years was a long time to wonder if the woman you loved actually even wanted you any more.

Chapter 5

Jem went to bed at nine thirty that night. Blake woke up at ten thirty for a feed. Ralph joined Jem in bed at eleven. At one fifteen Scarlett crawled into their bed, pressing her small warm body up against Ralph's back, the plush fur of her polar bear tickling the crook of his neck. Jem left the bed at two twenty to settle Blake and came back at a quarter to three. Unable to fall into a proper sleep with the thick breath of his daughter thundering past his ear, and the ball of her foot thudding him in the thigh at intervals, Ralph took his pillow, tiptoed from the room and stretched himself, not entirely luxuriously, upon Scarlett's toddler bed, threw her toddler-sized duvet across himself, and finally succumbed to a deep and fruitful sleep. It was only when he awoke a few hours later and surveyed the new day through Scarlett's lipstick-pink curtains that it occurred to him that the previous day had been the anniversary of the first time that he and Jem had slept together. Eleven years ago today, he mused, he and Jem had awoken together for the first time, had found each other instinctively, pulled themselves together, made themselves one. Eleven years ago today the air had been full of wonder and tenderness, passion and potential. Eleven years ago today, Ralph had felt his life beginning.

Today, his head clogged with tiredness, his body aching with loneliness, the thought of his unfinished, uninspiring canvases awaiting his attention overhead and the sound of his baby boy screaming for his mother across the hallway, Ralph felt that it had come to a premature end. And it was with that thought in his head that he stepped into the new day with a sense that something had to change.

Chapter 6

'I beg your pardon?' Jem looked up from the sausage she was dissecting into discs for Scarlett's tea and hoped for a hint of joke in Ralph's facial expression. But there was none. He was being serious.

'California,' he said again, his face colouring slightly. 'Next month. Just for a week.'

Jem felt something extraordinary happen to her brain at these words, like a piece of elastic snapping inside it. The disbelief she was experiencing was so pronounced that it almost physically hurt. 'Just for a week,' she repeated, almost like a mantra.

'Yes, it's his birthday.' Ralph hopped nervously from foot to foot, whilst squeezing his left fist with his right hand, as though he were nursing sore knuckles.

'Right. So it's Smith's birthday. And you want to travel all the way to California to celebrate it with him?'

Ralph nodded, and stalked across the kitchen to the fridge to get himself a glass of orange juice.

'And me and the kids stay here?'

Ralph stopped what he was doing and sighed. Jem threw a look at his back, which was slumped and facing towards her. The reality of what Ralph was saying to her was so at odds with anything that she could reasonably have expected him to be saying that it seemed to warp the very air she breathed.

'You are kidding, right?'

Ralph turned to face her. He looked peeved. 'I know it's not ideal . . .'

'Oh, and what makes you say that?' she asked, sparing not an ounce of sarcasm.

'Look, it's not just a holiday, it's –'

'It's a holiday, Ralph.'

'No!' he shouted. Ralph never shouted. He collected himself. 'No,' he repeated in a more measured tone, 'it's not. I need ... I've lost my ...'

Jem dropped the plate of sausages and mash in front of Scarlett, who was too busy watching *LazyTown* to notice. Jem spun round and glared at Ralph. 'Your what? Your *mind*?'

'No. Well, yes. Maybe. I've lost ... whatever it is that makes me want to make art, create. You know, my mojo. It's gone.'

'Right. And you think you're going to find *your mojo* with Smith in California, do you?'

Ralph grimaced. 'I don't know,' he muttered. 'I don't know.'

'And you think now is a good time to be doing this? You think now, with a three-month-old baby, when I'm trying to get back to work, this is a good time to piss off to the other side of the world to get drunk with Smith?'

'No!' he shouted again. 'It's a bloody shit time. I'm not stupid, I know that. But I'm feeling like if I don't do something now, if I don't *change* something now, my whole being, my existence is just going to come to a grinding halt. I feel like I'm almost paralysed ...'

Jem poked the sharp bit of a plastic straw through the foil hole on top of a strawberry smoothie and handed it to Scarlett. She took a deep breath. She let a moment pass while she tried to find a way to form a reasonable response to what, it was now clear, was a genuine cry for help. But even as she tried to reason with herself – *he's a human being, he's the man I love, he's calling out to me, I must at least consider his request as I would a request from any friend in need* – her less fair-minded instincts rose to the surface, bashing reason out of their way. *What about me? What about everything I've been through these past few years, what about the toll on my body of four pregnancies, two births, what about all the sleep I've lost doing the night-time wake-ups, what about the endless, thankless cleaning and cooking and sorting and clearing and arranging and fixing and remembering that is my sole responsibility all day every day from before I even open my eyes in the morning? Where's my holiday? Where's my break?*

She felt herself begin to bubble over with rage and had to turn away from Ralph for a moment to calm herself down. 'Fine,' she said, turning back to him, 'fine.' The words felt the wrong shape in her mouth; they weren't the words she wanted to say. But she pulled the alien words from her mouth, like stray hairs, and decided that now they were out that she quite liked the sound of them. They sounded like the words of a sane and endlessly patient woman, a woman who was marching briskly up the moral high ground, flag in hand, leaving her selfish, useless husband floundering at base camp. 'If that's really what you need to do,' she continued, 'then do it. If you're really feeling that bad about everything then how the hell can I tell you that you can't?' She paused and then smiled as something like relief flooded through her. *A week without Ralph.* A week without his uselessness being felt in every bone in her body. A week without feeling guilty for not wanting to have sex with him. A window of fresh air and possibility. *An opportunity.*

'You so owe me.'

Ralph's face relaxed into a smile. 'Are you sure?' he asked.

'Don't spoil it for yourself,' she snapped. 'I've said yes. But seriously, I will make you pay for it.'

'What, in sexual favours?' He threw her his wonky smile, the wonky smile that used to make her feel like the luckiest girl in the world, that now just made her think, yeah yeah.

'Ha. Ha. Ha.'

'You never know,' he grinned again. 'You might miss me so much that by the time I get back you'll be gagging for it.'

She looked at him and blinked.

'You never know,' he said.

She blinked again. 'Go away from me now,' she said.

He grinned at her and turned to leave, but at the kitchen door he turned back. 'Did you know that it was the anniversary of the art gallery yesterday?'

She pulled a piece of paper towel from a roll and gazed at him. 'Was it?'

'Yeah,' he said, 'eleven years ago yesterday.'

'Christ,' said Jem, 'last of the great romantics, aren't we?'

'Not right now, we're not,' said Ralph, his voice tinged with regret. 'Not right now.'

Ralph and Jem's relationship was, it was agreed by anyone who knew them, a yardstick by which all relationships should be judged. From unconventional beginnings – Ralph and Jem had met whilst sharing a flat, after Ralph had spent weeks reading her diaries and snooping round her bedroom and while Jem was going out with Ralph's best friend, Smith. It was not an auspicious start. But then, how many relationships really begin with eyes meeting across rooms? How many marriages are predicated upon pink roses and blushed cheeks and the right words whispered at just the right moment, while the perfect song plays serendipitously in the background? They'd made up for it, though, for the first three years of their relationship. Jem's sister had put it like this: 'Whenever I'm with you both, I'm smiling.' Being together had felt so obvious, like something that they'd been half expecting to happen all their lives, that when they finally did find each other on a damp March evening at an art gallery in Ladbroke

Grove, when Smith showed himself to be a poor excuse for a boyfriend and Ralph glowed with pure, unsullied love, when they'd rushed home, giddy with it all, and shared their first kiss on a blue sofa, it had felt like the last, breathy page of a novel.

They'd built on the perfection of that moment, let the magic they'd sparked that night grow and multiply and not been afraid of it. They rented a flat in Battersea, they sat in pubs and curry houses, they let in the other bits of their lives – the parents and sisters and best friends and bosses – they went to Bruges, they went to Cornwall, they bought a kitten and called it Smith, they trusted each other, they liked each other, they had couple time, they had friend time, their lives rolled out before them, day by day, like lovely bolts of fabric, glimmering and soft, full of splashes of colour and blocks of mellow beige. Life was sweet.

Until they had a baby.

Ralph had *quite* wanted a baby. Jem had *really* wanted a baby. They talked about it every now and then and each time they'd decide to wait, wait until they could afford a house, wait until Ralph's terminally ill mother was dead, wait until the big order came in for ten poppy paintings, wait until the housing market slowed up, wait for the right moment. Eventually, as Jem approached her thirty-second birthday, she decided that the right moment had come and gone a dozen times and that they could play the waiting game indefinitely. She was not old, but certainly not young if she wanted the option of having a big family, and certainly not young if it turned out for any reasons that conception didn't happen and that they would need a helping hand.

It was the first decision in their relationship that hadn't been reached mutually. Jem, uncharacteristically, but knowing she had no option, had forced the issue.

'I mean it, Ralph,' she'd said, one night over a Thai on

Battersea Park Road, 'I don't want to wait any more. I want to start trying.'

'Is that an ultimatum?' Ralph had said nervously.

'Should it be?' said Jem, suspiciously.

Ralph had shrugged noncommittally.

'You've said all along that you want children,' she said. 'It's not as if we haven't talked about this.'

'Yeah,' Ralph poured the end of his Tiger beer into his glass, 'I know, but what's the hurry?'

Jem had laughed, in exasperation. 'Ralph, we've been together for four years! You're thirty-five! What exactly are you waiting for?'

He'd shrugged again. 'I don't know,' he said. 'To feel ready, I suppose.'

'Well,' Jem had said, 'I feel ready and that will just have to do, as far as I'm concerned.'

Ralph, a gentle soul, and something of a realist, accepted his fate. Three months later Jem was pregnant.

Chapter 7

'Smithy,' Ralph began the e-mail, 'the missus says yes! I told her you were having a birthday party so if you happen to talk to her, which obviously you won't, but just in case, go along with it. And if you did actually fancy organising yourself a birthday bash, so much the better. Looking into cheap flights now. Will let you know as soon as I've booked them. See you in a few weeks!'

Ralph pressed Send and felt a strange cocktail of dread and euphoria sitting in the pit of his belly. He hadn't really expected Jem to say yes. He'd been ready for a fight, ready to really lay it on thick, and she'd acquiesced, rolled over like a soppy cat, just like that. He was slightly unnerved and it occurred to him that maybe she'd been inside his head, knew the strange and unexpected machinations that had led him to making the decision to go away. Maybe she was sending him away to test him. In what way, he didn't know, but he could definitely feel something untoward beneath the surface of things.

But it wasn't just the unexpectedness and peculiarity of Jem's acceptance of his trip abroad that was unsettling him, it was also the fact that it meant that he was actually going. In just over three weeks' time he would close the door on his studio, kiss his family goodbye, climb on to a Boeing 747, close his eyes and wake up in America. Alone. Ralph had not been anywhere alone since 1996. He felt simultaneously excited and scared. This trip was so important to him, without it he could see himself going down under the pressure of work, family, his own feeble-mindedness.

But the week of his visit also felt like a large white void. He had no fixed mental image of Smith's abode, his lifestyle. Smith was a secretive bugger, his e-mails terse and to the point, never more than a line or two. It was almost as if he felt that he was still here, still sharing a flat with Ralph, that he didn't need to expound on the detail of his existence or his circumstances, his e-mails the equivalent of passing Ralph outside the bathroom and throwing him a vague, 'All right?' He didn't even know if Smith lived on his own or with friends.

Ralph pulled down the lid of his laptop and exhaled. This was good, he thought, this was good. To get away from this room, this house, this world in which he'd become less and less essential, more and more ordinary, just a bloke at the top of the house painting flowers, changing the occasional shitty nappy and annoying his partner. Whatever happened in California, whatever kind of a trip he had, things would change when he got back, change for the better, he would make sure of that.

And with that thought, instead of heading downstairs to help Jem tidy up after tea, instead of sitting on the sofa with his baby boy in his arms, instead of admitting to himself that the paintings could wait, that his presence up here was not so vital, that there were better things going on downstairs and that the time to make a change could be right now, he picked up his Marlboros and a green Bic lighter and headed for his balcony where he smoked a cigarette in contemplative and solitary silence.

Chapter 8

Jem saw Joel again three days later. It was a blustery morning and she was taking Blake and Scarlett to Brixton library for parent and toddler story time. Blake was strapped upon her chest, small heels flopping back and forth against her abdomen in leather booties, his head covered with a blue fleece-lined deerstalker that kept twisting around and covering his eyes. Scarlett was in the buggy. Scarlett was too big to be in a buggy but due to a combination of her own indomitable spirit and the reality of how long it would take for her to walk there without it, Jem had acquiesced with a weary 'OK then' when she'd come upon her daughter in the hallway, jaw set with determination, already strapped in.

Jem's hair was loose, apart from a small diamanté clip to the side of her parting which she'd contemplated momentarily before leaving the house – at what age should a woman stop wearing things in her hair, particularly sparkly things? – but decided, on balance, that she wasn't forty yet and that maybe one day when she was forty she'd wish she'd worn more sparkles in her hair when she was thirty-eight.

She was glad of the diamonds in her hair now, as she approached the man called Joel walking towards her, his girl, Jessica, careering towards them determinedly on a small pink scooter. Jem had made little effort with her wardrobe this morning: skinny jeans, zip-up hoodie, sheepskin boots and a huge knitted scarf. The fact of a small baby attached to her body added little to her overall allure, she imagined, but maybe, just maybe, the touch of glamour in her hair would provide enough of a distraction.

She questioned her need to look pretty for a strange man. And then she questioned her lack of physical interest in Ralph. Did it mean that she didn't love him any more? Did it mean that she wanted to be with someone else? She considered the question for a second or two and decided that no, it just meant that she wanted someone to notice her and see her for what she used to be rather than what she'd become.

The gap between the two sets of people was growing smaller and Jem needed to decide how to approach the oncoming moment. Should she acknowledge their close encounter of last week by being extra fulsome with her greeting, or just revert to her old-style nod and fifty per cent smile? She stole a look at him and then made a show of rearranging Blake's hat. Joel really was a most unspectacular-looking man, almost bland, but clearly, if the rapid pulse of her heart beneath Blake's warm body was anything to go by, he had a certain something.

Joel and Jessica closed upon them. There was, in Jem's opinion, too much space between father and child, especially as the pavement had a slight downward camber to it. She would not feel comfortable if that was her small child looping side to side across the paving stones, inches from the kerb on occasion.

She could see concern start to etch itself on to Joel's face and for a moment felt a flicker of relief: there would be no encounter, he would pass them by, distracted by his daughter's reckless scootering and Jem would be able to breathe properly again. But instead Jessica, looking up and seeing her small friend Scarlett, broke out an enormous smile, cried out, 'Scarlett! *Scar*-lett!' lost all concentration and came off the pavement between two parked cars.

'Oh, Jesus!' Joel abandoned his usual soft-shoe shuffle and broke into a long-legged gallop. 'Oh my God!' Jem ran forwards, forgetting that she had fifteen pounds of baby on her chest. An oncoming car swerved gently to avoid the pink scooter, which had rolled into its path. Jessica wailed.

Joel scooped her up from the gutter with one strong arm, hoiked back the errant scooter with the other. He held her on his lap and pulled her fine blonde hair from her cheeks. 'Jessie, Jessie, Jessie, what were you thinking? What were you *doing*?'

He glanced up at Jem, his expression a mix of relief and embarrassment.

'Is she all right?' asked Jem.

He pulled back her fringe and looked into her eyes. 'Are you OK, pops?'

She wrinkled her nose and sniffed. 'My knee hurts,' she cried.

Jem breathed a sigh of relief. A hurt knee, considering the alternatives, was a glorious thing indeed.

Joel was flustered, making too much of the hurt knee, avoiding Jem's gaze. She could tell he was mortified, not just by what had happened, but by the fact that Jem had witnessed it; all dads knew that their parenting skills were being judged constantly, not only by their own wives but by every mother they passed on the street, in this case quite literally. Men spent much less time imagining their children dying than women, which was, Jem felt, both a good thing and a bad thing, but on this occasion, clearly, he could have done better.

He looked up at her and smiled. 'Oops,' he said.

Jem smiled back. 'I have to say, I was half expecting that to happen.' She smiled again, not wanting to come across as hectoring.

'Yup, well . . .' he tailed off, gently bringing Jessica to her feet.

'Let's have a look at that knee, shall we?' said Jem.

Jessica rolled up the leg of her jeans and Jem and Joel peered at it. It was scraped and raw and showed the beginnings of a bruise, but was not bleeding.

'That's not a very big ow,' Scarlett interjected haughtily from her pushchair.

Jessica looked at her crossly, her cheeks streaked with tears. 'But it *hurts!*' she wailed, throwing herself against her father's legs and howling into them. Jem and Joel threw each other a look of bemusement.

'OK, pops,' he soothed, stroking her hair, 'let's get you home. Let's go home and make you a nice big cup of hot chocolate, eh? Would you like that?'

Jessica nodded her head up and down against his legs and Joel smiled at Jem again.

There was a moment's silence. Joel touched his dry lips with the tip of his tongue. 'I saw you,' he said, 'the other day.'

Jem flinched slightly, feeling exposed. 'Oh, yes . . . ?'

'Yes, on the tube.'

'Ah, yes,' she feigned a slow dawning memory.

'You were . . .' he made a gesture with his shoulders and arms that Jem thought might have been suggestive of a jacket.

'Smart?' she asked.

'Well, yes, smart, not that you're not always . . .'

'No, actually, I'm not always, very rarely, in fact.'

'Oh, I see.'

'Yes,' she continued, knowing that it was very much time to say goodbye and be on her way, but wanting him to know something about her anyway. 'It was my first day back at work.'

'Oh,' he replied, his eyebrows raised, 'maternity leave over then?' He gestured at the wriggling Blake.

'Kind of. I'm only doing the odd day, just here and there, when I can squeeze it in. And what about you?'

'Oh, kind of the same really. The odd day, here and there, when I can squeeze it in. And a kind of rolling, ongoing maternity leave the rest of the time. Heh.' He smiled and rubbed the back of Jessica's head again.

Jem wanted to ask him more, find out what he did for a living, *here and there*, why he looked after his daughter, if he had a wife, where he had been, where he was going, but her daughter, with more sense than she had, saved her from herself.

'I want to go now, Mummy, can we go now, Mummy, now, Mummy?'

They smiled at each other apologetically. 'Well, yes, you're absolutely right, of course,' Joel said to Scarlett, who looked mildly embarrassed to be spoken to by a strange father. 'Time for us to go too. Time for hot chocolate. And Barbie plasters.'

Jessica gripped his hand and smiled up at Jem. 'What's your name?' she asked.

'She's called Jem,' Scarlett called from her pushchair, like a cantankerous old lady in a Bath chair. 'Jem is her name.'

'That's a pretty name,' said Jessica.

'Why, thank you, Jessica, and so is yours.'

Jessica smiled shyly and then they both turned to leave, father and daughter, hand-in-hand, homeward bound, for hot chocolate and soothed knees.

'Can we go now, please?' moaned Scarlett.

'Yes, sweetheart, we're going now,' she replied.

'Did that Jessica nearly die?' she asked thoughtfully.

'Well,' said Jem, 'she was going a bit too fast on her scooter and her daddy wasn't really paying enough attention but it could have been a lot worse.'

'Is he a bad daddy, then?'

Jem smiled. 'Yes,' she laughed, 'he's a rubbish daddy.'

'Not like mine, then?'

'No,' Jem sighed, 'no. Not like yours.'

'Cause my daddy's the bestest, bestest, bestest daddy, ever, ever, ever.'

Jem smiled again. And then, as she walked, as the distance between them grew out again and the length of time she would have to wait until she saw him again increased, the smile fell slowly from her lips.

When she was younger, Jem had had a recurring dream. In this dream she walked down a quiet street, alone, under a full moon. In this dream she stopped outside a house and glanced down into a window just below street level and through that window she saw a man with a neat skull, facing away from her, smoking a cigarette. It was, though she didn't know it at the time, a glimpse of her future, it was a glimpse of the man she would meet and fall in love with and live happily ever together with. It was a glimpse of Ralph. She had dreamed him before she'd met him. What more assurance could a girl want that the man she was with was the right man than to have a string of vivid precognitive premonitions?

These sorts of things had happened to her when she was young, when her head was light with indefinites and nebulas, when her world was floaty and haphazard and totally lacking in any form of ballast. She'd been able to open her mind and imagination to the foibles of the future, she'd had time to analyse her dreams, and her life had been unstructured enough to allow for fortuitous meetings and romantic serendipities. Not now. From the moment Scarlett had been handed to her in the hospital three years ago her life had been firmly pinned down, like tiny weights inserted into the hem of a flyaway dress. It was still a pretty dress, but it no longer flipped out wantonly at the edges, it didn't ruffle in the wind, it hung straight and serious, a grown-up dress, a modest dress. Jem didn't mind this sudden straitening of her existence. She'd been expecting it. She was ready for it. If anything,

49

she'd expected motherhood to curtail her essential spirit more than it actually had.

But now it was time to search inside the fluff of her head again, see what her unknowing mind had to say about dream men who turned into unsupportive partners who mocked your job, left you with all the cruddy chores, pestered you for sex and then thought it OK to disappear to America for week-long birthday parties, what it had to say about innocuous crushes on strangers who made you blush and how you squared the whole cycle of falling in and out of love with the reality of a three-year-old in a pushchair telling you how much they loved their daddy, because she was, she suddenly realised, faced with finding an answer to a terrifying question: *If Ralph and I can't find a way to reconnect with each other, then what the hell happens next?*

PART TWO

One Year Later

Jem turns the key uncertainly in the lock of Ralph's front door. She has never used this key in this lock before, although the key has been hanging from a peg in her kitchenette for months. The kids are with Lulu, thoroughly exhausted after a birthday party in a soft play centre in West Norwood. Lulu is giving them lentils, beans and brown rice for their supper, the only dish that all four of them will eat, mainly so that they can have a farting competition afterwards.

Jem pushes open the main door to the house and feels a chill against her skin. The communal hallway is large and under-furnished, piles of unclaimed junk mail sit on a crude MDF shelf nailed into the wall, a bike, divided into two parts and folded in on itself, rests against the wall, tethered to a water pipe. The front door of the ground-floor flat is painted turquoise and has a 'Beware of the Dog' sign taped to it. Jem can hear an animal growling ominously from behind it.

She takes the dun-coloured steps up to the first floor and inserts the next of the two keys into the white door there. The door has four dimpled glass panels in it and a vertical chrome letterbox. She inhales greedily before she pushes open the door, taking in extra air to see her through the next moment or two of her life. She has only been to this flat on three other occasions and each time it was full and alive with her children and their father. Now it is

53

empty, and Jem is not entirely certain of what she will find on the other side of the door.

It is seven days since she last spoke to Ralph. It is seven days since he was in his car, headed somewhere dark and mysterious, and it is two hours since he was due once more at Lulu's house to collect Scarlett and Blake. Jem has been oscillating crazily between anger and fear. She is angry in the moments when she looks at her children and tries to imagine what there could possibly be out there in the big wide world that is more alluring, more compelling than being with them. And then she is fearful in the moments when she knows there is nothing and that the only thing that could be keeping Ralph from his children is foul play, madness or tragedy.

Ralph has not been answering either of his phones, he has not been in touch with his father and he has not been in touch with his friends. This morning Jem was even moved to e-mail Smith, in California, to see if he knew anything about the whereabouts of the errant Ralph. She has yet to hear back from him.

Ralph gave her his keys a few months ago, *not* so that she could let herself in in the event of him disappearing off the face of the earth, but in her capacity as his nearest neighbour, in the event of him locking himself out. It was Lulu's idea to use it. 'Go,' she said, as the hour of Ralph's promised reappearance and collection of his children came and went, 'go now. Leave the kids here. It's lentils and farting tonight – they'll be fine.'

Jem peers into the hallway and moves a large pile of mail to one side with her foot. The flat smells bare and unlived in, slightly damp. Ralph's shoes and trainers sit in a row on a wooden plinth outside the living room. She glances at them and feels a wave of tender sadness. *Ralph's shoes*. She's always had a thing about Ralph's disembodied footwear. When they'd shared the flat in Almanac Road, she would anthromorphise his shoes when he was out.

Shoes were such intimate things when they were discon-nected from their wearers. When she was younger, Jem had used the 'empty shoe' test to judge whether or not she would want to sleep with a man. She would look at his shoes then imagine them empty by the side of her bed the next morning. More often than not, this would be suffi-cient to extinguish any misplaced sexual interest. It had been the opposite with Ralph's shoes. Every time she saw them she felt a glow of warmth and desire, and when she'd awoken the morning after their first night together and seen them there, his shoes, separate from him, the insides worn smooth with the imprint of his socked feet, she'd felt complete.

But now, not only are those shoes empty, but their owner is lost and Jem's heart is aching for him. She fails to under-stand how their perfect love story could have come to such an abrupt and almost incomprehensible pass.

Jem walks into Ralph's living room and sees a room left in a hurry. There is a pile of crinkled cotton sheets draped halfway between the tumble drier and a basket. The sink is full of plates and mugs. Assorted newspapers, magazines and etchings have been piled haphazardly into the middle of the coffee table and a pair of Ralph's socks sit in unfurled coils on the carpet.

It is clear that Ralph knew he was going away, but that he possibly imagined he'd be back fairly soon. There is a bad smell coming from the fridge and Jem reveals a piece of unwrapped Cheddar and an old packet of smoked salmon to be the culprits. She tips the lumpy dregs of a plastic bottle of milk down the sink and wrinkles her nose at the rank sourness, and then she finds a carrier bag and empties the contents of Ralph's fridge into it. She pulls open the door beneath the sink, where Ralph keeps his bin and is about to drop the bag into the bin when some-thing catches her eye. It is a note, crumpled up, with Ralph's handwriting on it. It has been torn into numerous pieces and some of the pieces are discoloured where an old teabag has soaked into the paper. Jem tries to reassemble it and ends up with a message that reads:

> You are so beautiful. I will take your beauty with me . . . You are a pure and sweet and perfect human being . . . coming to me last night. I will never ever forget it . . . I have to go now . . . There is something I have to do . . . and start the whole thing all over again . . . I'll be gone for a while . . . You are an angel . . . Ralph x

Jem gasps and feels the room start to spin slightly. She feels she might faint and slams her hands against the table's edge to steady herself. There is a love note in Ralph's bin, a love note that has been ripped into pieces and screwed up in anger. Who was it written to? It must be Sarah. Jem feels suddenly filled with rage and hatred. Whoever this Sarah is, she has Ralph's heart and for that, she despises her.

She goes into Ralph's bedroom. She has never been into Ralph's bedroom before. It is smaller than she'd imagined. It is not airy and white and full of billowy curtains and soft sheepskin rugs, as she has imagined, but small and cramped, with an unmade bed in one corner, a cheap teak-effect wardrobe in the other and a rather small window overlooking the side return, which is where the household keep their wheelie bins. One of Ralph's paintings hangs over his bed. It is not one of his 'Jem' paintings, the famous collection he painted while he was aching with unconsummated love for her. Those were all sold a long time ago, for vast amounts of money, save for one that Jem keeps above her own bed. Rather it is one that he painted just after he got back from California, after his ill-fated trip to see Smith last year. It is a dove, painted in thick scrapings of off-white paint, its wings outspread, its oversized beak wide open as if in a silent scream. Below the disturbed dove lies the footprint of a city, painted in black, brown and scarlet squares. It is not clear whether the city is alive, on fire or razed, post-apocalyptically, to the ground. The expression on the dove's face would suggest the latter.

The painting is ugly. She hates the stuff that Ralph has been painting lately. It makes her feel sad. Jem turns her head from it and looks around for clues. The first thing she sees is a bracelet, on the bedside table. It is silver with small blue and rose-pink beads hanging from it. She picks it up. It is very light, cheap, probably cost a few quid from River Island. She holds it to her nose and breathes in – it smells of skin. Her skin. Sarah's skin.

Jem knows nothing about Sarah. Blake and Scarlett have never met her. Jem has seen only her car, a neat Ford Fiesta in a strange shade of lime green, with a pair of sage-green Wellington boots and a large umbrella on the back shelf. A year ago, Jem could have pictured the sort of girl that Ralph would want to be with if he wasn't with her. A year ago she could have described a thin, wispy blonde with a difficult personality and a fondness for black eyeliner. But now . . . all she knows is that Sarah has Hunter Wellingtons in the back of her car, that she wears cheap, flimsy, not especially stylish jewellery. And now, clearly, that she has shared a bed with Ralph.

Jem puts the bracelet back on the table. She feels shivery with distaste and sadness. Ralph. Her Ralph. With another woman. She aches for him. She misses him.

Jem returns to the living room and heads for the answer-phone. She sees it flashing and presses play.

'You have five new messages.'

Two of the five messages are from Philippe, Ralph's agent, wondering how he is and if he has anything new he would like to show him. His voice is slightly high-pitched and laced with barely concealed frustration. The first message is Jem's, the one that she left last week when he didn't come for the children. The fourth is from Ralph's dad, saying that he'd just spoken to Jem and that everyone was a bit worried about him, and the last is from her, from Sarah.

She is American.

'Hi Ralph, it's Sarah. Sorry not to have been in touch, things are crazy round here. Anyhoo,' Jem wrinkles her nose at the 'anyhoo', *'would be gorgeous to see you. Give me a ring. See ya!'*

Jem shudders. But then she has a thought. The message was left yesterday. But if Sarah is the same woman who was in Ralph's bed last week, the recipient of the love note, she seems very upbeat about things, all of a sudden. How did she go from tearing up love notes into bitter shreds to leaving jaunty answerphone messages? Is it possible, she wonders, that Sarah is not his lover? Is it possible that the woman with the bracelet is someone else altogether?

She presses 1471 and takes down the last number to have called Ralph's. Maybe this Sarah, whoever the hell she is, might be able to help her find her missing partner.

Chapter 1

Ralph felt himself re-forming as he took his seat on the plane and tucked his rucksack under the chair in front of him. He had a window seat and the flight was half empty so he stood a good chance of not having to sit next to anyone.

Saying goodbye had been tough. Tough and unsettling. Jem had been tight-lipped, clearly resigned to his going but not about to let him go without letting him know how lucky he was that she'd let him. Which he was. He was a bright man. He knew he was pushing his luck. He knew that he hadn't done anything to deserve this break. He knew that in the bank account of their relationship, Jem was very much in credit. But still, the force of whatever strangeness lay within him had been strong enough to propel him away from a sobbing Scarlett and a resentment-storing Jem and on to the Heathrow Express with a rucksack and a cheery farewell. He'd felt sad for about forty-five seconds and then he'd felt euphoric. The image of his small son stayed longer in his consciousness than those of Jem and Scarlett, maybe because he knew that Blake was the only one of the three who would be markedly different when he came back or maybe because he felt the most guilt about leaving him. His son, so new he barely knew him, and yet he was running away from him, glad to be gone from him, happy not to have to think about him or consider him for the next seven days. He felt relieved. Yet he didn't know why. It wasn't as if Blake was his responsibility anyway. Jem did everything for him. But still Ralph found his presence vaguely oppressive. Maybe, he mused, it was not because of what he needed from Ralph now, but what Ralph knew he would expect from him in the future.

Ralph enjoyed the flight to LA. He got slowly and pleasantly drunk, he read half a David Baldacci novel, he ate something with chicken in it and an actually quite nice raspberry trifle, he listened to some music and watched an episode of *The Office* and a not particularly brilliant film called *Forgetting Sarah Marshall*, which had that weird Russell Brand bloke in it who Jem seemed to think was incredibly funny. And then he had a little sleep. An undisturbed, indulgent and completely guilt-free sleep.

Ralph liked to fly.

He didn't like to take-off, which always felt somewhat unlikely, and he didn't like to land, which always felt somewhat rash, but the bit in between he enjoyed very much. He and Jem had flown to Italy when Scarlett was two. It was the first time either of them had flown with a child and it was the last time he would do it for a good long time.

As they'd dismounted the plane at Pisa airport Jem had said, 'Well, that wasn't so bad.' Ralph had raised an eyebrow and said, 'Define bad.'

But this, just himself, nobody wanting to be taken to the toilet, nobody constantly dropping crayons underneath the seat in front, nobody spilling orange juice all over themselves and nobody screaming when their ears popped on landing, not to mention nobody giving him filthy looks when he attempted to flick through the in-flight magazine and hissing, 'You think you're going to *read*? Are you *serious*?' at him – this was good.

Smith was there when he left Customs.

He was wearing a black suit, a grey T-shirt, black

sunglasses and was holding a sign that said: 'MR DICK SMALL'.

Ralph smiled when he saw him. 'A-ha ha. And ha,' he said, bringing Smith to him in a one-armed man-hug. 'Good to see you.'

Smith patted him back solidly. 'Bloody good to see you too,' he said. 'It's been bloody ages.'

'Four years and three months to be precise. New Year's Eve 2003.'

'Oh, yeah, that's right, we went out in Croydon, didn't we, trying to recapture the old days?'

'Yeah, and ended up feeling like we were about sixty.'

'Yeah, well, you may as well be sixty if you're over thirty in Croydon on New Year's Eve. Christ, that was a shit night.'

'Totally,' said Ralph. 'You're looking good.' And he was. Smith had always been a good-looking man, but in a care-worn way. He'd always looked like he was in need of the love of a good woman, to feed him properly and make him smile. Now he was fit, his skin glowed, his hair shone. He looked well, very well.

'Thanks, mate, not sure I can return the compliment.'

'What!'

'London boy.' He punched his arm affectionately.

'I've just spent ten hours on a fucking plane, what do you expect?'

'Yeah yeah. You just need some sunshine and some exercise.'

Exercise? Ralph smiled mockingly. When he and Smith had lived together in Battersea all those many years ago, the concept of exercise had been about as alien to the two men as the concept of vegetable carving. Or indeed the concept of reiki therapy, the discipline that Smith now practised for a living.

'Come on,' he said, taking hold of Ralph's hand-luggage, 'let's get back to mine.'

*   *   *

Smith lived in a very small but well-furnished apartment in Santa Monica, three blocks back from the sea. The building was quite scruffy, painted white and a sickly apricot and centred around a dull-looking swimming pool, but Smith had done a good job with the interior. It wasn't minimalist and blokey, it was tasteful and comfortable, and remarkably tidy.

'Do you always live like this,' asked Ralph, lowering his rucksack to the floor, 'or is this on my account?'

'Bit of both, really,' said Smith dropping his front door keys into a large glass bowl. 'It's easy to keep the place tidy when it's just me. And I've got a cleaner.'

Ralph raised his brow in surprise. It seemed odd to him that Smith was functioning out here, alone, without him. He couldn't imagine Smith sauntering around a department store picking out glass bowls and velvety cushions. He couldn't see how he'd have found a cleaning lady, how he'd have engineered a conversation with someone about how often he'd like his toilet bowl cleaned and how much he would pay her to do it. None of it made any sense. Ralph had always been the practical one when it came to domestic matters. He was the one who'd remember to buy bleach and hoover under the sofa and get the windows cleaned once a year. Smith had just coasted along, paying his way, offering the occasional 'cheers' when he could sense that Ralph had put himself out.

'It's a nice place,' he said. 'What's the rent like?'

Smith blew out his cheeks. 'You don't want to know. Too much.'

'So, you're doing all right then, with the old ...' he waggled his fingers, 'reiki business.'

'Yeah,' Smith ran his hands over his hair, 'not bad at all.'

'So, where shall I ... ?' He pointed at his rucksack.

'Oh, sure, yeah, you're in here.'

Smith led him through a narrow corridor, painted white and hung with panels of patterned glass.

'Bathroom here,' he said, opening a door and pulling on a light switch to reveal a plain white bathroom, clean and fragrant, equipped, Ralph was impressed to note, with more than one bath towel. 'Your room here,' he opened a door at the end of the corridor, revealing a small white room filled with a large white bed, a pale ash console table with a flat-screen TV on it and a wall of fitted wardrobes. Over the bed was a large canvas of a small hand holding three fat peony blooms.

'Ha!' Ralph said, putting his rucksack on to the bed. 'One of my Jem paintings.'

'Yeah,' said Smith, his hands in his pockets. 'I've hidden it in here.'

'Yeah, charming, I noticed.'

'Well,' he said, 'it's a great painting but it's a bit, you know . . .'

'Yeah, whatever.'

'No, really, I wouldn't have paid a thousand fucking quid for it if I didn't like it. It's just a bit girly, that's all. And I think it goes in here . . .'

Ralph nodded and smiled, rubbing his chin sceptically.

Smith smiled. 'Anyway,' he said, 'it's five o'clock, what do you want to do? Take a shower?'

'*Have* a shower.'

'What?'

'*Have* a shower, not *take* a shower.'

Smith rolled his eyes. 'Have a shower? Have a sleep? Hit the town?'

Ralph considered the weight of his eyelids against the dryness of his eyeballs. He thought about the grimy film that covered his entire body and the stickiness of his scalp. But then he thought about trying to locate his wash bag inside his badly packed rucksack, finding a whole clean outfit to change into afterwards and the fact that by the time he took his clothes off he'd probably just want to collapse in bed and that this was his first night in LA. Away from his family. That he only had six more nights before he had to go home again. That he wasn't here to shower and sleep, but to live and breathe.

'The town sounds good,' he smiled.

'Cool,' said Smith, 'let's go.'

Chapter 2

Smith drove.

He had a swanky little Chevrolet, in forest green. It was very clean. Ralph thought about his car at home. He thought about the empty Pom-Bear packets stuffed into the storage panels in the door, the lumps of rock-hard chocolate brownie in the footwell, the sticky orange juice cartons wedged between the back seats and the cluster of tiny plastic toys that seemed to reside nowhere in particular. He thought of the back seat, once a spacious bench for the ferrying around of friends or paintings or trays of pansies from the garden centre, now home to two large and ugly child seats. It wasn't his car, it was his *family's* car. How luxurious, he felt, to have a car of your own.

He stared out of the window at the scenery. Low-level shopping arcades, wide pavements, thirty-foot palm trees, men and women in beachwear, unfeasibly small dogs, rollerblades, baseball caps, frozen yogurt, car parks, parasols, beach clubs, whitewashed walls overhung with golden Angel's Trumpets, tessellated paving, potted cacti, a spangle-fronted cinema, Mexican food, Spanish food, French food, food from the Pacific Islands and acre after acre of soft white sand.

For a moment it struck him as bizarre that he willingly lived in a damp corner of Herne Hill in a house the colour of fag butts. Why would he do such a thing when this place existed? Had he chosen to live where he lived, was it a decision he'd ever consciously made? And if so, what was he thinking? London had its charms, it had pubs (which he rarely visited), it had a magnificent river (which he rarely saw), it had cultural diversity and tradition and elegance and beauty. It had trees and parks and a trillion restaurants. But of what use were any of these things to Ralph when all he experienced of it was a dank loft room, a treadmill at the gym, the occasional half-decent take-away and even more occasional beer and meal out with Jem? They had gyms here. They had children's play-grounds. They had good restaurants and places to drink beer and people to talk to and things to do.

And they had a beach.

And they had the sun.

And they had palm trees thirty feet high.

Ralph folded his arms and looked once more out of the window. He considered the sky, so clear, so expansive, so distinct from the landscape. He let the blueness and simplicity of it wash over him for a while and then he watched a small white-tipped wave hit the soft caramel sand.

Smith glanced at him and then smiled. 'Ha!' he said, 'you're wondering what the fuck you're doing in London, aren't you?'

'Just a bit.'

'Yeah, I know. Why d'you think I never come back?'

Smith took them to an Asian fusion restaurant called Pacifique. It had a wide terrace at the front where they took a table looking out towards the sea. A very cute girl with a name badge on that declared her to be called Avril took their orders for tequila-based cocktails and mixed hors-d'oeuvres, the latter of which arrived on rough-hewn crockery the same colour as the sky, with numerous dipping sauces in various shades of red and brown.

Ralph watched Smith take a sip from his cocktail. 'I thought they were really tight on drink-driving out here?' he asked.

'Yeah, they are. I'm leaving my car here; Rosey's borrowing it.'

'Rosey?'

'Yeah, the other half.'

'You have an other half?' Ralph asked in flattened surprise.

'Yes. A girlfriend, you know.'

'Yeah, I know what an other half is. I'm just surprised, that's all.'

'What,' snorted Smith, 'surprised that anyone would want to go out with me?'

'No. Not that. Just that you've never mentioned anyone.'

'No, well, there's not much to say.'

'Well, God, I don't know, how long have you been seeing her? How old is she? Where did you meet? Et cetera.'

Smith threw him a puzzled look. 'Do you really want to know?' he said.

'Yeah, of course I do, you're my mate. I mean, were you even going to mention her to me?'

'Of course I was. You'll meet her tomorrow when she brings the car back. It's not a secret or anything.'

'So, tell me.'

Smith rolled his eyes. 'Well,' he sighed, 'she's thirty-three, she's from Melbourne –'

'Australian?' interrupted Ralph.

'Ye-es. She's a dental hygienist. She's got blonde hair, like this –' he made the shape of a blunt bob with the side of his hand against his jaw – 'and she lives over there.' He pointed at a small block of flats above a mall, painted deep coral with sky-blue balconies. 'Oh, and we met here –' he tapped the tabletop with the heel of his hand – 'eight months ago.'

'Ha, so this is your special place then?'

'No,' Smith sighed impatiently, 'this was already my favourite place. I come here all the time. Here, have one of these.' He passed Ralph a plate of tiny tempura soft-shelled crabs, sprinkled with slivers of chilli and burned garlic, 'they're amazing.'

Ralph popped one of the crabs into his mouth and instantly decided that it was his favourite dish in Santa Monica. It was, he mused, the sort of thing that would cost twenty quid in Nobu, and that in order to eat it you'd have to book a table three months in advance and then pay a taxi driver twenty-five pounds to take you there, yet here this was just a relatively inexpensive snack in a local neighbourhood restaurant. 'That's fantastic,' he said, licking the oil from his fingertips.

'Good, isn't it? Everything here is good.'

'So, this Rosey, is it serious?'

Smith shrugged and finished his cocktail. 'Yeah,' he said, 'I guess.'

'Wow, so this could be it then? This could be the one?'

Smith shrugged again. 'Depends what you mean by The One?'

'I mean, the one you marry, the one you have a family with.'

Smith laughed, scoffing at him. 'A family?' he repeated.

'Yeah, you know, kids, children, genetic offspring.'

'No way.'

Ralph frowned. 'Why not? You're forty-one, mate.'

'Yeah. I'm forty-one and I've got a fucking amazing life. What the fuck would I want to go and have kids for?'

Ralph paused. He picked up another little crab and ate it. What could he say to that? That was exactly how he'd felt seven years ago when Jem had first started talking about having kids. Life was good. It didn't need improving, it didn't need changing, it didn't, in fact, need anything, let alone helpless, needy, extremely short human beings who depended on you for everything and woke you up when you were sleeping and didn't take lie-ins and didn't want to do anything that wasn't their idea and didn't know how to use a toilet and didn't understand anything what-soever about the world or how it worked. He knew exactly why Smith would balk at the suggestion.

But then . . . it would be odd to get to the end of your days without having done something as fundamental and basic and utterly human as procreating. It would be like dying without having read a book or gone for a swim or eaten an orange or trimmed your toenails or had an argument or fallen in love. It would be like having not lived at all.

Ralph gulped. He found the thought alarming and he certainly wouldn't share it with Smith. It would mean nothing to him, it would sound smug and trite and it would make Smith even more determined never to cross to the other side. It was exactly the sort of sentiment that had put Ralph off the idea of kids for so long. And it was exactly the reason why he had had no desire to have another baby after the arrival of the precious and remarkable Scarlett.

One child was enough for him. He was a dad. He was a parent. He'd crossed over, and he'd loved it. And it wasn't that he didn't love Blake, it was just that he couldn't quite see the point of him, beyond taking his life back to the same stage it was at four years ago, without any of the thrill of new beginnings.

He shrugged. 'Fair enough, I suppose, I can't say I was that wild about the idea myself, but now, you know. What I do think is this: depending on your outlook, having kids is either much better than it looks, or much worse.'

'And your outlook was?'

'Let's just say, I've been pleasantly surprised.'

'Family man, eh?'

'Through and through.' Ralph laughed, knowing that this was far from the truth, unless the definition of a family man was a man who spent his whole life smoking in a garret, who had changed only two of his new son's nappies since his birth, hadn't taken his daughter to the playground for over a month and was currently eating

69

soft-shelled crab five and a half thousand miles away from his partner, daughter and four-month-old baby.

'So, you've got two now?'

Ralph could tell Smith was just being polite. He had no interest in Ralph's kids, not in a belligerent way, just in the same way you might have no interest in a friend's rare stamp collection. 'Yup,' he said, 'Scarlett and little Blake.'

'Great names.'

'Thanks.'

'Any more?'

Ralph snorted. 'No. Way. No no no no no. I am done.'

Smith smiled knowingly. 'Anyway, cheers.' He raised his empty glass to Ralph's and clinked it lightly. 'Great to see you.'

'Great to see you, too.'

'And how is . . .' Ralph could sense Smith forcing out the words, 'little Jem?'

'Oh, she's fine, you know. Jem is always fine.'

'Good. What's she up to?'

'You know, breastfeeding, shouting a lot, being exhausted – all that usual new mum stuff.'

Smith, who had clearly never had a close encounter with a new mum, nodded vaguely. 'Is she still, you know, agenting?'

Ralph nodded. 'Yeah, she's on a cushy number there. They gave her her own division after Scarlett was born – the "Celebrity" division. Which consists of two clients. One of whom is Karl Kasparov.'

'What, Karl Kasparov who used to live upstairs at Almanac Road? The DJ?'

'Yeah, except he's not a DJ any more. He's a "TV personality".'

'What! No way!'

'Yeah, he crops up on panel shows and those *Five Hundred Greatest Bollocks* shows. And he even read out a bedtime story on CBeebies the other night, which freaked us all out.'

'Christ, so he made the most of his fifteen minutes.'

'Well, that was Jem's job, to capitalise on it. I mean, he gets around, but he can't be earning that much money because he's still in the same flat.'

'What, Almanac Road?'

'Yeah. Weird thought, huh, to still be there, all these years later?'

'It feels like a lifetime ago. You, me and Jem.'

Ralph thought back briefly to those days and experienced one of those rare moments when a memory leaps out of itself and grows a third dimension and suddenly he could feel the carpet beneath his bare feet, smell the under-rim toilet block in the freshly flushed lavatory just opposite his room, hear Jem cooking in the kitchen, see the fat blooms of a peony in a vase on the dining table. He was wearing long johns and a thermal top. He had all his hair. He was young. He was there. In the moment. And then it was gone.

'We had a laugh, didn't we?'

'Yeah,' said Smith, 'on occasion. I can't say I was in the same place as you back then. You were, you know, on the brink of stuff. I was just shuffling along, trying to find my way.'

That's right, thought Ralph, that's exactly right. At the time it had seemed like Smith was the sorted one. He had the City career, the flat, the Thomas Pink shirts, while Ralph just slouched about the house in old underwear, earning enough money to pay his rent and for his Marlboro Lights. But under the surface there had been a different story: Smith struggling with his career, hopelessly in love with a woman who didn't know he existed, going out with a girl he didn't care about, no idea where he was headed. Ralph, on the other hand, had been just a whisper away from his destiny: it was there, in front of him, on a plate; all he had to do was reach out and grab it.

'And look at us now,' he said, 'bloody fortysomething, and you, the reiki, I mean, I still cannot *believe* that you touch people for a living.'

'Ha, well, I don't, that's the whole point. It's all about *energy*. Not flesh. Not bones. I don't actually touch anyone.'

Ralph laughed. 'Yeah,' he said, 'except for their hard-earned dollars.'

'Well, yes, there is that.' Smith smiled. 'But it works, you know. Believe it or not, I am actually really good at what I do.'

Ralph smiled and shook his head. 'Christ,' he said, 'who'd have thought it?'

'Yes, indeed. You a dad. Me a hippy. Heh.'

They both sat for a moment in contemplative silence, until Ralph realised that the silence had passed through contemplation and into awkwardness and then it struck him that he and Smith had never had so little in common.

'Come on,' he said to Smith, draining the diluted dregs of his cocktail from the bottom of the glass, 'let's get some more drinks in. I've got a bit of a thirst on.'

'What? In LA? You know that'll never do,' teased Smith.

'Fuck it,' said Ralph, 'let's show LA how to party like an Englishman. Two more of these please,' he said to Avril, 'and can you make them doubles?'

Chapter 3

Jem quite liked the feel of the house without Ralph in it.

It was odd, because when he was there, but not there, when he'd gone into town for a drink or down to Shirley to see his ageing father, when he was due back, she missed him a lot. And when he was here, but not here, when he was upstairs in his garret, when she could hear his bare feet pad-pad-padding around above her and all the domesticity, she willed him to come down and join in. But now that if there was no imminence of his presence, she felt more relaxed. She tried to analyse this and got as far as thinking that it had something to do with the fact that if he wasn't there then he couldn't fail to help her with the tea/look after the kids while she went to the gym/put Scarlett's shoes on before they left the house/empty the dishwasher or pop out to buy nappies. Neither could he secrete half the household's collection of mugs in his garret, permeate the lower floors of the house with the smell of old cigarettes or huff and puff when Blake woke him up in the night in the manner of someone who has an early flight to catch the next day followed by a performance of open heart surgery, rather than a man who was just going to potter around all day splodging paint on to canvas, untroubled by any form of appointment or intellectual challenge.

Yes, life was less irritating without Ralph. But there was more to it than the simple removal of a source of friction. She was enjoying more than Ralph's absence, she was enjoying also her own presence, the sense of being herself.

She felt more capable, more open to new things, more spontaneous and more confident.

And it was with this newfound sense of increased substance that Jem set off for the playground the following afternoon with both her children, a bag of chocolate croissants and an umbrella.

It was not the ideal weather for a visit to the playground. The air was viscous and the sky laden with clouds as thick as lagging. But this was her first afternoon as a single mother and she needed to be out and about doing something that would make coming home feel extra nice. She also thought it might be quite nice to bump into Joel.

Bumping into Joel.

It seemed to be happening more and more frequently.

Which is not to say that she was stalking him, because she most definitely was not. They were purely chance meetings. And that is also not to say that anything of any significance was happening during these chance meetings, because it was not. They smiled. They said hello. They waved at each other across the street. Sometimes days lapsed without a chance meeting. Sometimes they met twice in a day. It was all entirely innocent and meaningless. But strangely magnetic.

And she'd felt it just now, as she was pulling on Scarlett's Wellington boots: *He'll be there.*

And he was.

There, on a bench, reading the *Observer* (of course) in a thick blue overcoat, his breath making a cloud around his head. On the bench next to him was a paper cup of something hot with a corrugated cardboard jacket, and Jessica's pink mittens. Jessica herself was halfway across a wooden bridge, high enough up that if it had been Scarlett up there, Jem would probably not have been absorbed in the Sundays, but hovering around on the woodchips below, ready to catch her should she miss her footing. Jessica stopped when she saw them and threw her arms in the air: 'Scarlett!' She turned to her father. 'Look, Daddy, Scarlett!'

Joel looked up over the top of his newspaper and smiled when he saw them. 'Oh, yes,' he said. 'Hello, Scarlett.'

Scarlett stared at him icily for a moment, before dropping Jem's hand and running towards the climbing frame to join Jessica.

'Say hello!' Jem called out after her, but it was too late, she was gone. She smiled apologetically at Joel. 'Sorry,' she said, 'she seems to have a phobia of polite conversation.'

Joel shrugged and started to close his newspaper. 'Don't worry,' he said, 'they're all different. That one hugs the bin men.' He pointed at his daughter.

Jem smiled and absent-mindedly stroked the hair of the baby currently sleeping on her chest.

'He looks happy,' said Joel, smiling at Blake.

Jem glanced down at his head and smiled again. He was zipped into a padded snow suit and his right cheek was squashed up against the top of Jem's left breast. He was fast asleep and warm as toast. 'Good to be a baby, eh?' she said.

'I'd say.'

Jem kissed Blake's head and turned to check on Scarlett. She was on the wobbly bridge with Jessica and they were making it rock back and forth, giggling at each other. She had no idea what to do next. Joel had closed his newspaper. He hadn't just lowered it, he'd closed it. That had to mean that he'd rather have a conversation with Jem than read his newspaper. Which would also make it rather rude of her to walk away now and sit on another bench, which was exactly what a sizeable part of her wanted to do. She glanced back at him. He smiled at her. She glanced down at his shoes. They were nice. She was paralysed.

She was about to move away, when Joel said something.

'How old is he now?'

Jem had to think for a moment to whom he might be referring and then remembered her son on her chest. 'Oh, he's, er, fifteen weeks, coming up to.'

Joel squinted. 'Oh, right, that's nearly four months.'

Jem nodded.

'Yes, you forget what the weeks mean when you haven't had a small baby for a while. Have to revert to months.'

Jem laughed and turned again to watch her daughter, vaguely hoping that she might be doing something terribly dangerous that would necessitate an immediate sprint across the playground, thus ending this curiously painful exchange. Instead she observed that she and Jessica had commandeered the wooden playhouse from a very small boy and were sitting safely at its internal table, playing tea parties.

No. It was clear. She was going to have to have her first conversation with Joel. She breathed in deeply and sat down against the arm of the bench.

'Oh, here, here.' Joel moved the paper cup and the mittens out of the way.

'Oh, no, honestly, this is fine. If I sit down properly he'll get all scrunched up and wake up and then I'll be on walkabout.'

Joel smiled at her. 'So,' he said, 'are you back to work tomorrow?'

'No, no,' she shook her head. 'No. I'm full-time mum for a week. My partner's away, so . . .'

'What, your business partner?'

'No. My, ah, life partner, I believe that's the correct, rather awful term.'

'Oh, I see, so he's . . .' He paused for a brief moment and looked at her questioningly and it suddenly occurred to Jem that he was seeking clarification that her life partner was indeed a he. She nodded encouragingly. 'He's away on business, is he?'

Jem laughed, louder than she'd intended. 'No. Not really. He's away finding his mojo.'

'Ah.' His eyes widened to register his surprise. 'And where might it be, this missing mojo?'

'In Santa Monica, apparently.'

'I see.' Joel nodded, once and definitively. It was clear that he was completely aware of the liberty that Ralph was taking, not to mention Jem's feelings about it.

'Hmm,' agreed Jem, forcing her hands down into the pockets of her large downy coat and resting her chin on Blake's crown.

'So what does he do, your, er . . . ?'

'Life partner.'

Joel laughed. 'Yes, your life partner.'

'He's an artist.'

'Oh,' Joel's brow rose. He looked impressed. 'What sort of an artist?'

'Oil, canvas, quite traditional.'

'Oh, right, so he's gone off to top up his creative juices?'

'Er, no,' said Jem, 'he's gone off to get away from us.' Jem gulped. She really had not intended to say that. Saying that was practically tantamount to saying: my partner is a crud, I'm sick of him, would you care to have an affair with me?

Joel looked from Jem to her daughter and back again. 'Oh,' he said, 'I'm sure he hasn't.'

'No, really, honestly. He has. I promise.'

'Well,' said Joel, kindly, 'I think that sounds pretty unlikely.'

'In his defence, I would say it's more that he wanted to get away from him.' She pointed at the blissfully ignorant Blake. 'I think he was quite happy before he came along.'

Joel nodded. 'I see,' he said, in his gentle, measured tone. 'Sleepless nights getting to him?'

'Yes. The sleepless nights, the dilution of attention paid

to him, the –' Jem stopped herself. She was moving into an unattractive anti-Ralph rant. She didn't know this man and this man did not know Ralph. It was unfair to discuss him with a stranger, with someone who had never had a chance to know the Ralph that she'd known, the sweet, gentle, attentive, talented man she'd spent over a third of her life with. 'Anyway,' she smiled, 'it's fine. I really don't mind. It's quite nice to have a bit of space . . .'

Joel glanced at her, looking as if there was something he wanted to say, but he wasn't quite sure if he should. 'You know,' he began, 'I thought you might be a single mum.'

'Ha!' Jem threw her head back, delighted with the delicious irony of Joel's observation.

'Yes. It's just I've only ever seen *you* with Scarlett, never your partner, but then when I realised you were pregnant, and when this one came along I thought, well, clearly there's someone else involved here,' he laughed, gruffly. His laugh was warm and deep. 'And now I know. Your life partner. An artist.'

'Ralph.'

'Ralph,' repeated Joel. 'Currently hunting down his mojo in Santa Monica.' They both laughed then and turned then to watch their girls, now sitting on their haunches in the sandpit, digging some kind of hole.

'And what about you? Are you a single dad?'

He smiled wryly. 'Yes,' he said, 'I suppose I am.'

Jem waited a moment to see if he would elaborate. He did.

'My, er, *life partner* didn't really manage the "life" bit of the arrangement very well.'

Jem left a silence.

'Yes, my wife, Paulette, that's her name, she's got some issues, shall we say. It's better for her not to be around us. So, on the whole, she isn't.'

Jem nodded and stared into the middle distance. 'I see,'

she said, though she absolutely didn't see at all. But she could tell that Joel had gone as far as he was prepared to go down this particular conversational avenue, so she subtly changed route. 'And Jessica, she's your only child?'

He smiled and shook his head. 'No. I've got a son too. He's twenty-four.'

'No!'

'Er, yes!'

'But you don't – I mean, how old are you? If that's not a rude question.'

'Well, clearly it's a very rude question,' he teased, 'but since you asked, I'm forty-four.'

'So you had him when you were twenty?'

'I did indeed.'

'With the same woman? With Paulette?'

'No, no,' he laughed and shook his head as if the very notion was hugely comical. 'No, Lucas was a mistake, a casual girlfriend, nothing serious, but she wanted to keep him and so she did and I played as big a part in his life as I possibly could given that he lived in Doncaster and I lived in London. We're close now, though. He lives down here now, not too far away, Clapham, so I get to see him a fair amount.'

'Wow,' said Jem. 'Well, it just goes to show, nobody's what they seem.'

'Why,' he laughed, 'what did I "seem"?'

'Oh, I don't know. I suppose just the kind of conventional bloke who waits until they've run out of excuses before starting a family. A 2.4 kids kind of guy.'

'Boring, you mean?'

'No! Not that! Just not the sort of guy to have a grown-up son.'

'Well, a grown-up son was really rather *thrust* upon me. It wasn't exactly a life choice. And, you know, there's a very thin line between most sexually active twenty-year-old men and a twenty-four-year-old son.'

79

Jem laughed.

He smiled. 'And you,' he said, 'are you what you seem?'

'That depends,' she said, aware as the words left her lips that those words, *that depends*, were rarely used in a context that wasn't at least mildly flirtatious, 'on what you think I seem?'

Joel laughed again and folded his arms across his chest, his legs outstretched in front of him and crossed at the ankles. 'Well,' he began, 'you *seem* thoroughly normal in every way.'

'Well, in that case I am exactly what I seem. I am. Totally normal. Really. In every single way.'

'Well, how refreshing. Very rare thing, a normal person.'

'I suppose it is,' sighed Jem, feeling very strongly that she was making an impression on Joel, that he was *thinking* things about her, that after they went their separate ways she would be in his mind while he prepared his daughter's tea, while he sat at his computer, while he brushed his teeth. She knew all this for sure and the thought terrified her. No more. Time to walk away from the door and go back to the safety of Scarlett and Blake and their empty house.

'Mummy!' called Scarlett, blessed Scarlett. 'Mummy, I need to do a poo!'

Jem laughed and stood up. 'I think I might just take this as my cue to go home.' She looked up. 'Those clouds are looking pretty ominous.'

He looked up too. 'I see what you mean.' And then he glanced at his watch. 'But, God, that leaves a lot of left-over Sunday afternoon.'

Jem hitched her bag over her shoulder and smiled. 'Ah, yes. Killing the time,' she said. 'And then the next thing we know they'll be twenty years old, never call us and we'd give anything for a long, damp Sunday afternoon in the park with them again.'

'Very wise words.' He rearranged his body into the shape

of a person no longer engaged in conversation and smiled. 'I'll see you soon.'

'Yes,' she said, 'see you soon.'

She met Scarlett on the path in front of her. She had her hand wedged up between her butt cheeks. 'I really, really, really need to poo!' she cried again.

'Yes, I know, baby, that's why we're going home.'

'But *I don't want to go home!*' she wailed.

'Well, then,' said Jem, in the slightly lobotomised voice she used to talk to her daughter when resisting the urge to scream, 'shall we go and dig a hole in the sandpit and you can do a poo in there, like Smith the cat?'

Scarlett smiled slyly and nodded.

Jem groaned. 'Well, unfortunately you're not allowed to poo in sandpits, so unless you want to do it in your pants, I suggest we go home.'

'But argh, Mummy, *we're playing!*'

'I know you're playing, my darling, but you're going to have to stop playing. There'll be other times to play. Jessica will be here on other days, won't you, Jessica?'

Jessica nodded enthusiastically. 'Tomorrow, probably,' she said, 'and the day after that. And the day after that. And the day after that.' She pulled a pink button out of her pocket and gave it to Scarlett. 'That's my button,' she said, 'off my favourite cardigan. You can keep it, if you want, and then you can give it back to me next time.'

Scarlett looked at the button in awe, as though it were the Koh-i-noor.

'Oh, look at that, Scarlett, look at the beautiful button Jessica gave you. Are you going to say thank you?'

'Thank you,' Scarlett muttered, flatly.

'Yes, thank you, Jessica. That's very kind of you. I'll make sure Scarlett looks after it.' She beamed at her and Jessica beamed back and Jem wondered what it must be like to have a child who smiled that fulsomely at strangers.

She took Scarlett's hand and began to lead her towards

the gate, when she felt someone behind her. It was Joel. 'Look,' he was saying, 'you know, they get on so well, maybe we should get them together one afternoon?'

'Oh!' said Jem, over-brightly. 'Right. Yes! That's a great idea.' It wasn't a great idea, she realised, even as the words left her mouth. It was a terrible idea. It kicked the door of their passing acquaintance wide open and let the possibility of growing intimacy walk right in.

'Here's my card.' He slipped a sliver of blue card into her free hand. 'Text me. Maybe one afternoon this week, seeing that you're a full-time mum. We could kill an afternoon together?'

'Cool,' she said, staring unseeingly at the card, stultified by the potential magnitude of this development. 'Yes, I'll text you. Great.'

She smiled, one last stiff smile, then waved and headed home, not just for the urgent lavatorial relief of her wriggling daughter but also for her own peace of mind.

Chapter 4

Ralph heard a voice, a female voice. It was quite a long way away and it sounded happy.

He tried to open his eyes but they appeared to have been soldered together, so he turned on to his side and attempted to drift back into sleep for a few moments.

It was then that he became aware of a dull pounding across his brow and a thick coating of something on his tongue and slowly he remembered every single one of the double-measure Margaritas and numerous bottles of what he'd referred to at the time as 'piss-weak Yank lager' that he'd imbibed the night before. He also remembered that he'd only landed on American soil the previous day and that his head, his blood and most of his internal organs were convinced it was either the middle of the night or lunchtime, he couldn't remember which, and that he should probably get out of bed, face the day and hit the hangover and the jet lag head on.

The female voice broke into a laugh. It was a gutsy laugh, though simultaneously very feminine. It was the laugh of a fresh-complexioned person, a person who had not been drinking the night before, someone wholesome and healthy, someone who'd probably had a nutritious breakfast, a jog on the beach and had flossed between their teeth, rigorously.

Ralph's curiosity – what little he could currently muster – was piqued.

This must be Rosey.

He dragged himself from the bed and pulled a crumpled

83

T-shirt – the same T-shirt he'd been wearing since early the previous morning – over his head, searched for his wash bag in his rucksack, failed to find it and then remembered vaguely having taken it out and put it in the bathroom the night before in one of those inexplicable drunken bursts of efficiency.

In the bathroom the extent of his drunken burst of efficiency was clearly evident in the neat line of toiletries lined up on the glass shelf above the sink. He ran the tap, reached for his toothbrush and then glanced at himself. What was it Smith had said yesterday? *London boy.* That's right. And yes, in this light, that's exactly what he looked like. He looked like tube stations and pavements and pigeons and slush and grubby smudged pages of *The Times.* Grey, lifeless, not far off dead, really.

He heard another delicious chime of laughter coming from the living room and decided that before he could possibly face the hearty source of this mellifluous sound, he would have to do something dramatic about his appearance. He found something inside Smith's shower cubicle called Super Strong De-Scaling Scrub, which sounded like exactly the thing for fish, kettles and grimy-looking Englishmen. He applied it generously to his face and neck and then soaped his entire body with a shower wash scented with limes and mandarins and then stepped into the soft embrace of one of Smith's luxurious and freshly laundered bath sheets. By the time he had rehydrated his sour London skin with something green and slightly herbal in a white pot and then put on an outfit consisting solely of unworn clothes (pants and socks included) he felt almost human. He sauntered towards the living room and prepared himself for his first look at Smith's girlfriend.

Except he could never have quite prepared himself for his first look at Smith's girlfriend because she was, quite simply, one of the most exquisite women he had ever seen in his life.

'Ralphy!' Smith got up and patted Ralph matily on the back. 'Good morning. Or should I say, good afternoon?'

Ralph failed to register the fact that he'd slept through lunch and smiled blankly at him. 'Morning,' he said.

Rosey stood up too. She was wearing a loose cream sundress with straps that tied up in bows on her honeyed, angular shoulders. On her feet were plain white flip-flops. Her hair was thick and blonde and, as Smith had described last night, cut off into a chin-length bob, with a thick fringe that swept sideways across her forehead. Her jaw was on the square side of things, but very fine-boned, and her nose was dead straight with a slight upwards slant to it. But it was the eyes that skewered him, a deep greeny-blue, which, if he were to equate it to a shade in the set of Schmincke Mussini oil paints in his studio at home, would be called Chromium Oxide, framed with fans of thick lash and appraising him confidently, intelligently from beneath the heavy fringe.

'This is Rosey,' said Smith. 'And this is Ralph, the only person I'm not related to who's known me since I was a child.'

'Wow,' said Rosey, her smile steady and strong. 'So I can get all the dirt off you, then?'

'Oh, yes, definitely,' said Ralph. 'And if Smith had let me know that he actually had a girlfriend, before I got here, I would have been able to bring along some pretty embarrassing photos too.'

'Why d'you think I didn't tell you?' interrupted Smith.

'Oh, shame,' said Rosey, fiddling with a heavy silver chain on her left wrist. 'I would *love* to see photos of little Smith.'

'Less of the little,' said Smith, and Rosey and Ralph laughed politely. 'Coffee?' he asked Ralph.

'Oh, yeah. A coffee would be great.' Smith left them there and headed for the kitchen. Ralph glanced at Rosey.

He felt strangely shy, almost as though he'd found himself alone at a bus stop with the hottest girl at school.

As well as the heavy silver bracelet, Rosey had a row of small silver studs in her left ear, a tattooed laurel wreath around her ankle and a small silver cross around her neck, set quite high on the chain so that the cross rested in the dip of her throat. The cross itself did not register in Ralph's subconscious in quite the same way that the curve of her throat did. It was magnificent; long and taut and just precisely the sort of brilliantly designed instrument that a laugh of that quality would require.

'So, Smith tells me you've just had a baby?'

The question picked Ralph up off the wooden floor by the scruff of his freshly scrubbed neck and hurled him against the wall. It took him a moment to recover and when he did he saw Rosey staring at him unblinkingly with her Chromium Oxide eyes, awaiting a response.

'Yeah,' he said, a beat too late, 'well, not me, my, er, girlfriend, partner, you know. But yeah. A little boy.'

He watched her response. He could spot a broody woman at ten paces. Something happened to a broody woman when you mentioned the word baby, something raw and animal behind the eyes. The animal thing wasn't there with Rosey, just a kind of, aw, babies, cute wrinkle of the nose and an indulgent smile, no different from if they were talking about tiny little kittens or watching newborn lambs gambol around a field. She seemed, to Ralph, much younger than thirty-three.

'What's he called?'

'Blake,' he said, clearing his throat, which felt suddenly thick with the sound of his son's name. 'Yeah, Blake.'

'That's cool,' she said, 'like Amy Winehouse's fella?'

Ralph grimaced. Blake was *his* name. When they'd first started discussing baby names, four years ago, when Scarlett was still a gender non-specific ball of cells in Jem's womb, when Amy Winehouse was still at stage school, he'd said: Blake. If it's a boy. Blake. Blake for Peter Blake and William Blake and Quentin Blake, not to mention for *Blake's 7*. But not for Blake whatever his name was, who was in prison for beating someone up in a pub. They'd gone ahead with the name anyway, safe in the assumption that by the time their Blake was at school, no one would remember the one in the pork-pie hat.

'Yes,' he sighed, 'but not named for him. Named for some people of actual substance. Named for some geniuses.'

'Ah,' she said, her eyes widening with understanding. 'Peter and William? And Quentin, too?' And Ralph saw it, a flash of something bright and frightening and exceptional. She knew all the Blakes, the rancid tabloid Blakes and the genuine substantial Blakes. He threw her a look of respect and she smiled at him. 'I studied History of Art,' she said, 'well, for a year, anyway – I dropped out.'

Ralph was about to ask her about her course and why she'd dropped out but she sensed the question coming and dodged it. 'And is he your first, this Blake of yours?'

Ralph shook his head. 'No,' he said, 'we've got a girl too. Scarlett. She's three, four in September.'

'Another cool name, she said appreciatively. 'You and your wife –'

'Girlfriend,' he interjected, quickly.

'Girlfriend,' she corrected herself, with a knowing smile, 'you have very good taste in names. Any pictures?'

'Of the kids? Erm, yeah, I do actually. Jem made me bring some, to show Smith.'

'Oh. Let's see them,' she cajoled.

Ralph went back to his room and delved around in his rucksack, looking for the shiny wallet Jem had forced on him when he was packing on Friday night with the words: Smith will want to see your kids. 'No he won't,' Ralph had countered, 'he won't have the slightest interest.'

'Of course he will,' Jem had said, 'and even if he

doesn't, won't you want them for yourself, just to, you know, look at?'

Ralph hadn't replied, just taken the wallet and stuffed it into his bag, wondering why it was that women always thought you should feel the same things they felt and care about the same things they cared about. But now he was glad he had them. He wanted this amazing woman to see his stunning daughter, his dinky son, to see what he'd produced. Although he was forty-two years old, at heart Ralph still felt as unformed and insubstantial as a teenager. The existence of his children gave him the stature of a man.

He took the wallet back into the living room and passed it to Rosey.

She held it unopened for a moment, eyeing Ralph like he was delicious sport. Ralph felt his temperature rise. This woman was amazing. Everything about her was amazing. The more he looked at her the more beautiful she became. The more time he spent with her the more he wanted to know about her. Ralph was not a man with a roving eye or a weak heart. Ralph was a loyal and faithful man and he was unnerved to find himself feeling a deep attraction to another woman for the first time since he'd fallen in love with Jem.

'So, Smith tells me you're an artist?' She pulled the wallet open and took out the photos, her eyes still on Ralph, waiting for his response.

'Yup,' he said, glad for a line of questioning that would take his mind off his feelings.

'What sort of stuff do you make?' she asked, glancing at the top photo.

'Oil on canvas. Still life. Smith's got one of my paintings in his spare room.'

'Ah! The flowers in the hand! I LOVE that painting. I keep telling him he should put it out here, soften the place up. Wow, that's one of yours?'

'Yeah. It's an old one. Very old. But it's kind of the same vein as what I'm working on now. It was supposed to be my "floral period" and it's turned into ten years of churning out the same stuff.'

'Well, you know, if that's what you're good at, and you clearly are . . .'

'Yeah, I suppose. Though I could do with testing myself a bit more. That's one of the reasons why I'm out here.'

'Oh, nice, and I thought you'd come to see me,' mocked Smith, returning with a mug of coffee and a croissant on a plate.

'That too,' Ralph smiled. 'Just needed to get a fresh perspective on things, see things in a different light – literally.'

'Good on you,' said Rosey, approvingly, 'good on you. And this must be Scarlett?' She turned a photo round to show him. It was Scarlett, last month, black curls in a cloud around her pale face, almond eyes squinting into the camera, in a white dress and big net fairy wings, her hands green with felt tip pen and a splodge of something orange on her dress.

Ralph nodded and felt a brief burst of adoration at the sight of his perfect girl.

'Wow, she's beautiful,' said Rosey, 'and she looks just like you.'

'Er, that doesn't make sense,' joked Smith. 'Let's have a look.'

Rosey passed him the photo and he examined it, looking from the picture to Ralph and back again. 'Nope,' he said, 'looks nothing like you, she's all Jem.'

'Ah, yes,' said Rosey, looking at the next photo in the pile. 'This must be Jem.' She turned it to show him. It was Jem, her face still plump with pregnancy, a newborn Blake held against her cheek, her eyes bright with the euphoria of new life, her hair a mass of black curls. It was typical of Jem to have chosen a photo of herself that did her no justice whatsoever. For Jem this photo was an advertisement for parenthood. Look, it said, look at the sheer unadulterated joy in my eyes. *Nothing else in the world could make you feel this good*. It was a look of utter triumph, of Olympian achievement, of world domination. And of total and utter bliss.

Jem was weirdly evangelical about procreation. Ralph didn't get it. He loved his kids, he enjoyed being a dad, but he could see that it wouldn't be for everyone. He could see that it was the sort of decision you could only make if your heart was really, really in it and that if you weren't that keen no number of breathless conversations with besotted parents or ecstatic post-birth photos would change that.

'Let's see.' Smith took the photo from Rosey. 'Cute baby,' he said. 'And Jem looks . . . well.'

'That's quite old now,' said Ralph. 'Just after Blake was born. She's lost all the weight already. She's looking really good actually.'

'Er, mate, there's no need to be so defensive. I meant it. Jem looks good. She looks the same. Hard to believe she's almost forty.'

Ralph smiled, slightly embarrassed by his outburst. It was still there, still the sense that he'd taken Smith's girl, even after all these years. Except Smith wasn't bothered and he was.

They left the apartment a few moments later and headed for a late lunch on the sea front.

The early afternoon sun glittered off the feathery ridges in the sea and the beach was full of flesh. Ralph, his belly still in GMT, ordered scrambled eggs on toast and an orange juice. Smith and Rosey shared a grilled spatchcock chicken and roasted vegetables.

'So, you do teeth?' he opened, smiling at Rosey across the table.

'Yes, I do teeth. Lovely, shiny American teeth.'

'And how did you go from History of Art to teeth?'

'Well, I wanted to come and live in La-La land and there wasn't a great call for art historians so I thought, hmm, what does America really want, and I thought, aha! People to make their teeth look pretty! So I dropped out of uni and signed up for a dental hygiene course. And here I am, ten years later. Knee deep in American plaque.'

'And you enjoy that, do you?'

'Well, enjoy is not quite the word, no. But it pays well, I live on the beach in the coolest place in the world. And I have my band.'

'Your band?'

'Yeah, I do vocals with a band.'

'What kind of band?'

'Rock. Well, kind of rock-cum-pop, I guess. With a hint of emo, except I'm way too old to say I play in an emo band.'

'They sound like the *Dawson's Creek* soundtrack,' added Smith drily.

'Fuck you,' said Rosey, thumping Smith affectionately on the arm. 'Smith's just jealous because he has no creative outlet in his life.'

'Pah!' countered Smith. 'Creative schreative. I've got plenty of outlets. I've got spiritual. I've got emotional. I've got sexual . . .' He counted them off on his fingers.

Ralph looked at him askance. 'Spiritual?' he said. 'Emotional? Er?'

'Yes,' sighed Rosey, leaning her head into the crook of Smith's shoulder, 'just because he is skilled in the ancient art of reiki massage, Smith seems to think he's got all his spiritual bases covered.'

'Look,' he said, 'I'm happy. Isn't that what it's all about? Isn't that the bottom line? Who cares about whether or not anyone's written a book about it, called it something? Whatever. I wake up every morning and I feel good. End of story.'

He folded his arms across his chest and then smiled, before leaning in towards his beer and lifting it. 'To happiness, without all the bollocks.'

Ralph picked up his orange juice and lifted it to Smith's beer. 'Indeed,' he said, thinking actually, he would go for happiness any way it came, with or without the bollocks. All he wanted was someone to show him where to find it.

'Hey!' said Rosey, suddenly alert. 'Ralph could come to see me play, Tuesday!'

Smith gave her a questioning look.

'Yeah. Why not? You're busy on Tuesday. Ralph could come and see us play. What do you say, Ralph? Fancy a night out? It's a nice venue, a community hall. Free entry. Beer. You'll be in bed before midnight. I'm driving, I'll get you home. Eh?'

Ralph nodded, slowly, numbly. 'That sounds great,' he said, 'I'd love to. Thank you.'

Chapter 5

Jem awoke the next morning and stared into the dark blinking eyes of her infant son. He had shared the bed with her all night and had awoken not hungry, as he had fed on demand like a grazing cow all night long, but fully rested and ready for the day to begin. Jem, on the other hand, was drained, her sleep having been disturbed at horribly regular intervals by not just her greedy baby but also her overactive imagination.

She had spent wakeful hours in the night mentally wording her text message to Joel.

Hi, it's Scarlett's mum, how are you fixed for Wednesday?

Hi, Joel, this is Jem, Scarlett's mum. Still up for a play-date this week?

Hello! Which afternoon would you like to kill off this week? I'm free most days.

She'd also spent wakeful hours in the night mentally playing out the detail of the as yet unplanned meeting. Whose house? What to wear? Would she drop Scarlett and run? Would she stay and roll a glass of wine between her hands whilst making gentle and revealing conversation with Joel?

She'd then spent wakeful hours in the night wondering why any of this was happening in the first place. Why had this pale, unassuming man about whom she knew absolutely nothing suddenly jumped into three dimensions and taken over part of her brain? Why was she seeing his smile in her dreams? Why was she courting intimacy with him?

She had only just had a baby. When she had started trying to conceive that baby she had thought of it as the next step in the evolution of her life with Ralph. Blake hadn't been created on a whim, by mistake; he'd been deliberately and specifically manufactured in order to complete their family. Now he was here, in her bed, staring at her, smiling at her, delighted to see her. He was real and becoming more real by the day. They were four. Ralph, the love of her life, Scarlett, the daughter she'd always dreamed of, Blake, this curious boy in her bed, and her. Wasn't this the point at which one drew a line underneath one's existence? Wasn't this the point at which one could say, well done me, I have come in on schedule, I have one of each, I have a house, I have a good man, now I can sit and revel in all the work and the wonder and the growing yet to come, I am home?

This surely wasn't the point at which one started making glad eyes at single dads and fantasising about stolen moments on play-dates.

An ego boost. That's what this was, she'd concluded at some time around 4.30 a.m. She was nearing forty. Her partner had run away from home. She didn't feel pretty any more. She wanted someone to make her feel pretty. And that man could be anyone. Joel just happened to be the only one she knew who looked like he might want to.

That was it. That was all. It was nothing more. It was just an ego boost. It was just a play-date. On Saturday Ralph would be home and somehow they'd find a way to fix themselves, and when that happened this thing with Joel would diminish into perspective like a rock falling into a chasm.

She gathered the gurgling Blake into her arms and rested him on top of her chest so that they were nose to nose. 'As if,' she whispered into his ear. 'As if I would do anything to make your life anything less than perfect.'

The door opened then and Scarlett stood in the doorway, her polar bear hanging from her hand by the paw, her curls in flaming disarray around her head, her pyjama trousers round her ankles.

'I just did a bit of wee in my pyjamas,' she said, her teeth catching her bottom lip as she said it.

Jem pulled herself up to sitting and rested Blake on her lap. 'Why?' she asked.

'It just came out,' she said, 'when I was trying to take my trousers off.'

'That's all right,' said Jem. 'Happens to me sometimes. Take 'em off.'

'Where shall I put them?'

'Just there,' she said, 'leave them. Are you coming into bed with us?' She lifted the duvet.

Scarlett nodded, kicked off her pyjama bottoms and leaped on to the bed, nearly squashing Blake in the process.

'Careful!' cried out Jem.

One of the more unexpected aspects of Blake's arrival into their family was how utterly gigantic Scarlett immediately appeared to be. Her hands, previously the hands of a small girl, looked like shovels, her fingernails seemed as big as roof tiles. She seemed man-sized, a vast threatening figure, big enough to squash and maim and knock the life from Blake in a single blow.

Scarlett crawled across Jem's lap and kissed Blake on the lips. Blake looked at her in surprise. 'Is it time to go to nursery yet?' she asked, rolling on to Ralph's half of the bed and pulling the duvet up under her chin.

Jem glanced at the time on the clock radio on Ralph's bedside table: 6.45 a.m. She groaned inwardly.

'No,' she said, 'not for ages. Shall we just all snuggle for a while?'

'Yes,' said Scarlett, 'let's all snuggle.'

For a short moment the three of them lay there like that, still figures beneath the duvet, the only noise the slight ruffle of Egyptian cotton as Scarlett adjusted the cover below her chin. Jem smiled. This was good. This felt complete. This felt – it shocked her to realise – absolutely fine without Ralph. She thought of the previous night, the luxury of being able to fuss over Blake without the accompanying tuts and sighs and exaggerated flounces from the other side of the bed. She closed her eyes and imagined that her children might just lie here, might just let her sleep for a few more precious minutes, but a second later Scarlett was out from under the duvet, bouncing up and down, and Blake was fidgeting on top of Jem and trying to climb on to her head, and she gave up.

'Come on,' she said, 'let's go and have breakfast. Let's start the day.'

Chapter 6

Jem took Blake to her sister's house after dropping Scarlett at the nursery. Jem had two sisters: Isobel, who lived in Rotterdam with her Dutch husband and twin daughters, and Louisa, or Lulu as she was known universally, who lived just round the corner in a massive converted pub with her partner, Walter, a statuesque fifty-three-year-old dermatologist from Ottawa. Lulu was only a year older than Jem and not just her sister but, over the last few years, as they'd both grown into motherhood, her best friend too. Walter earned enough as a consultant dermatologist to mean that Lulu did not have to work, and since the birth of their first son, eight years earlier, she had been a full-time mother.

Jem loved coming to Lulu's house. It was always warm and it was always on the right side of messy, and her sister always made her tea like their mum made and Jem never had to apologise for her daughter's behaviour or for her baby's screaming or for being late or being scruffy or not having anything interesting to talk about. Lulu's house was her sane place, the place where everything made sense and nothing really mattered as much as she'd thought it had before she got there.

'Hello! Hello!' Lulu greeted her at the front door with a brush of her warm cheek and a snuffle of Blake's head and a pile of paperwork in her hands. 'How was your weekend? I can't believe you didn't pop over!'

Jem shook her head and unfurled her neck scarf. 'No, I know. I thought I would but then suddenly it was

Sunday night and I'd got through the whole weekend on my own.'

'So it was cool?'

'It was cool. It was actually . . .'

'. . . quite fun?'

'Yes, quite fun.'

'I know,' said Lulu. 'I love it when Walt's away, when it's just me and my babies and my own rhythm, but it's all about the fact that Walt's coming back, you know, not like I'd actually want to be a single mother or anything, heaven forbid, they should all be awarded something, OBEs or something. Come in.'

The house was empty, Theo and Jared and the older children all at school. Lulu had clearly been in the middle of doing the household accounts. The big oak table in the kitchen was spread thick with bills, letters, Post-its and a calculator. 'You've come just in the nick of time actually, just as I was about to hang myself. Look at this.' She pointed at the table. 'How can one small-ish family produce so much paper? I mean, it's like we're a small nation or something, a flipping principality. Plus I've just worked out that we can't actually afford to eat any more. I'm afraid,' she blinked at Jem with pursed lips, 'I'm going to have to charge you for your tea.'

Jem laughed and began to unpop the straps on the Baby Bjorn. 'Christ,' she said, 'is it that bad?'

'Yes,' she said. 'It's that bad. I might have to get a job.'

'But I don't understand,' Jem handed Blake to Lulu while she took off the baby carrier. 'Walter's still earning the same, yes?'

'Yes, but we're spending more. Simple as that. It's my fault. I just don't know when to stop. I keep saying the same things to myself over and over to justify it, you know: well, at least I'm not paying for childcare. Well, at least we're not paying for school fees. Well, at least we're not gadding off on expensive holidays. Well, at least we're not driving an expensive car. But you know me, it's all the, you know, *extras*. The posh shampoo. The eBay habit. The not-even-looking-at-the-prices in Waitrose. You know, I picked up a packet of organic blueberries from there the other day and didn't notice until I got home that they were £3.99. For nineteen blueberries; 21p each.'

'You worked it out?'

'Yes, I worked it out. And I also worked out that I will not be buying organic blueberries from Waitrose again. Party Ring?' She offered her a plastic tub of pastel-coloured biscuits. Jem took two. 'Anyway, apart from not missing Ralph, how are you?'

'Yeah, I'm fine.' Jem sat Blake on her lap and let him suck the edge of one of her Party Rings.

Lulu had the kettle under the tap and turned to glance at Jem curiously. 'Are you going to tell me?' she said.

'What?' said Jem.

'What's going on.'

'With what?'

'With you and Ralph.'

'Nothing.'

She put the lid back on the kettle and put it on its base. 'Right,' she said. 'Have you two had sex yet?'

Jem shook her head.

'How long has it been now?'

'Six months,' said Jem, 'maybe longer.'

'Right, so it's been EIGHT MONTHS.'

Jem started to protest, but Lulu talked over her. 'It's been eight months and you need to do something about it.'

'Oh God.' Jem let her head drop into her chest. 'Just the thought of it. Just the idea of having to be all . . . sexy.'

'You don't have to be sexy, you just have to open your legs.'

Jem sighed. Talking about this stuff with Lulu was always unedifying because Lulu loved sex. She'd loved it even more when she was pregnant and then been up

99

for it again within mere days of giving birth to both her sons. For Lulu sex was on a par with drinking champagne or eating cake or buying things in nice shops. For Lulu sex was a salve at the end of a stressful day. For Lulu sex was fun. 'I know,' sighed Jem. 'And when I think about it I can just about imagine it. I can just about imagine myself saying yes and going for it. But then the minute he asks, it's like, it's like he's just suggested going roller-blading. Or, *skiing*. Or even, you know, going for a jog. All things that I quite enjoy but don't particularly want to do at nine at night when I've been looking after chil-dren all day.'

'Well, then, don't do it at night. Do it during the day.'

'Right, just ask the kids to entertain themselves for an hour –'

'No,' Lulu interrupted, 'when Scarlett's at nursery, when Blake's sleeping.'

Jem thought back to Ralph's request a few weeks earlier, just after she'd got back from her meeting in town. What had been her excuse that day? Sore feet. Leaking breasts. Lack of sleep. But beneath all of that just really, really not wanting to have sex. Because Lulu must also have had sore feet, leaking breasts and a lack of sleep when her babies were small but she had also still enjoyed the notion of taking all of her clothes off and bouncing up and down naked on top of her husband. These things were reasons but they were not an explanation.

'Do you still fancy him?' Lulu asked bluntly.

'Fancy him?'

'Yes. Think he's handsome. Think he's *gorgeous*. Want to touch him. Want to squeeze him.'

She conjured up an image of his face. It was a beautiful face. She thought about his long strong arms, the hardness of them, his elegant legs, his perfectly shaped skull, his angular hands and feet. Ralph was gorgeous by any measure, slightly older, slightly greyer, slightly balder and

100

slightly less defined around his middle, but still undeniably a very attractive man. For years she had found him irresistible, had slept with her body entwined around his, had breathed in the scent of his scalp as if it were the meaning of life. Her physical love for him had been desperate, overwhelming, exhilarating. And then it had just stopped. Not gradually but almost overnight.

'I still think he's gorgeous,' she replied, 'totally. But I just don't want to have sex with him. A bit like, you know, I think *you're* gorgeous but . . .'

'Right, so you fancy him platonically, like he's your really hot brother or something.'

'Er, yeah, I guess so.'

'And while you're not having sex with him, what do you expect him to be doing about it?'

'I know,' Jem hissed. 'I'm not stupid. I know what I should be doing.'

'Then do it,' said Lulu. 'When he gets back on Saturday, have a bottle of wine . . .'

'I can't! I'm breastfeeding!'

'OK then, have a small glass of wine, take him to bed, it's been so long he'll be over and done with in thirty seconds, you'll lie there thinking, actually, that was more fun than roller-blading, he'll lie there thinking, hurrah, my wife let me have sex with her, onwards and upwards, your future secure for your children.'

Jem nodded decisively. 'Yes,' she said, 'you're right. I know you're right. I think it's just – I do everything, and having sex with Ralph just feels like yet one more thing I have to do, just to keep everyone happy, just to stop everyone moaning, and that's all I do all day, stop people moaning.'

'So, if Ralph did more about the house you'd be more minded to boff him?'

Jem considered this. Was it that simple? If he emptied the dishwasher more often and got the kids ready to leave the house without asking, would Jem feel a sudden return to carnal longing? It was a very pertinent question and the answer, Jem felt, lay at the root of everything. Was she fed up with Ralph because he was unsupportive and didn't help around the house or was she fed up with Ralph because, well, because they were nearing their conclusion?

'I don't know,' she said, 'maybe.'

'And you're clearly not dead from the waist down,' said Lulu, 'given that you've been having meaningful brushes with strange men on the tube.'

'What strange men?' asked Jem, feeling slightly unnerved that her sister had remembered their conversation.

'You know, the one that was like something out of a novel. The single dad.'

'Oh, *that*.' Jem tried to look insouciant. 'That wasn't about sex. That's just me and my old destiny thing, you know, imagining too much into scenarios, thinking that stuff has to, you know, *mean something*. And besides, I've kind of got talking to him lately and honestly, there's nothing there.'

'Nothing there?'

'No. Nothing. He's nice. That's all.' Jem smiled tightly, unsure as to whether or not her words held the truth.

'So you don't want to boff him?'

'I don't want to boff him. I don't want to boff anyone. I just want to be left alone.'

Lulu smiled and passed Jem her tea. 'Be left alone to have a deep and meaningful love affair with your baby,' she said.

Jem looked at her baby. She inhaled the smell of his scalp. She ran her finger around the inside of his trouser hem, tracing the silk of his delicious new skin. She brought his fist to her lips and kissed it.

'Yes,' she whispered.

'There's nothing like it,' said Lulu, watching her. 'But don't leave Ralph out in the cold for too long. For all your sakes. Christ, at least give him a BJ, that'll buy you a few weeks' grace!'

Jem looked at her sister and her sister looked at her and then they both began to laugh uproariously.

Chapter 7

In Santa Monica the sun was surrendering itself over the Pacific Ocean in roily ribbons of peach and copper. Ralph sat in the passenger seat of Smith's car and watched it in awe. On his left, Rosey held the steering wheel loosely with one hand whilst tuning the radio with the other. Unlike Smith, she drove with the windows down and the air conditioning off, and the early evening breeze swept thick licks of her hair across her cheeks, which she would occasionally push back behind her ear with two fingers. She wasn't making any attempt to converse with Ralph. 'I can't talk before a gig,' she'd explained, 'I'm too sick with nerves.' But Ralph was glad. All he'd done since he arrived in California was talk. He wanted some silence, just a moment or two, to absorb his surroundings, to taste his aloneness, to wonder how he was feeling.

His family seemed a long way away. He'd spoken to them three times since he'd been here, including a Skype chat with a web cam last night that had left him feeling a little unsettled, watching the luminous, ghostly image of his daughter, resplendent in a pink hoodie and bunny ears, bobbing up and down restlessly in his swivel chair, showing him things she'd made that day at nursery, happy to talk to him but clearly not missing him in the slightest. Blake had been presented to the camera as a furled-up ball of sleep, his new hair glowing in the light of the monitor like a halo of fur. Then Ralph had spoken to Jem, who'd looked tired and pale, and underwhelmed by the experience of speaking to her three-day-absent partner. It was as though they'd communicated across a galaxy. It was as though the air between them had been sucked away into a black hole the moment the computer was turned off, like waking from a dream and swiftly losing the sense of substance, the detail. They were there. He was here. Between them was just endless space.

'You hungry?' Rosey broke into his reverie.

He contemplated his stomach. 'Yeah,' he said, 'a bit.'

'Taco?'

He smiled. Taco. The last notion a peckish person in Britain would conjure up out of hunger. 'Yeah,' he said, 'why not?'

She drove them into a drive-thru Taco Bell and ordered for the two of them. A moment later she handed him a large cup of Coke and something in a box. On inspection it was a crispy shell the shape of a flattened hedgehog, sprouting spikes of red pepper and frills of lettuce and weighted down with a brown sludge of mince and creamy sauce.

'It's better than it looks,' said Rosey, 'honest.' She herself had a much more discreet-looking pancake roll stuffed with something yellow. 'I don't normally eat this sort of shit,' she said, watching his expression with amusement, 'just a treat to calm my nerves before a show, you know. Go on, get stuck in.'

He worked his way through the taco silently and in as businesslike a fashion as he could manage as they continued on their way out of town. He wanted to appreciate the experience of eating a taco in a car in California with a beautiful woman he barely knew. This would never happen to him again.

'So,' said Rosey, a few moments later, 'what's it been like, catching up with Smith after all these years?'

Ralph rubbed his face with a cheap paper napkin and

considered the question. 'Yeah,' he said, 'it's good. It's great to see him so happy, you know.'

'Wasn't happy in London then, eh?'

'No. Not really. It wasn't really coming together for him then. He was, well, kind of pretending to be something he wasn't.'

'Whilst all the while secretly yearning to be a laidback California reiki dude?'

Ralph laughed. 'Yeah,' he said, 'something like that.'

'You must have made the odd couple, back then, you the artist and Smith all stiff in his City suits?'

'I guess we did.'

'So how did you get together in the first place?'

Ralph pressed the napkin into a ball inside the palm of his hand and related a story from a lifetime ago, a story of two grammar school boys with nothing in common except a foreign exchange student from the States called Sherelle. She'd been lodging with the Smith family but had taken a shine to the sooty-eyed, soap-stiff-haired Ralph and pursued him into a frenzied sexual relationship, mainly within the confines of the guest bedroom in Smith's liberal house. Smith, who'd always assumed that the gangling, slightly fey Ralph was gay, looked upon him with newfound respect and Ralph, stultified by his life as an only child with two ageing parents, began to look forward to the time he spent in the loud, messy and easy-going Smith abode. They'd found themselves starting jobs in London at the same time and within a year Smith had put down a deposit on a flat and asked Ralph to move in with him. They'd spent ten carefree years barely conversing, getting stoned and watching too much telly. And then, just as it had taken a girl to bring them together, it had taken another girl to pull them apart. Their flatmate. Jem.

'You mean Smith was dating your wife?'

'Girlfriend.'

'Girlfriend?'

'Yeah. I came home from a party one night, she was in his bed.'

'No way!' Rosey's eyes were alight with the scandal of it. 'And you were in love with her at this point?'

He nodded. 'Totally,' he said.

'Oh my God, you must have been gutted. And did he know, did Smith know that you had the hots for her?'

'No. In his defence, no, he had no idea, but it was extra galling because he didn't even really like her that much. He was . . .' He was about to tell her about Cheri. He was about to tell her how Smith had been almost psychotically in love with the girl who lived on the top floor of their house, a girl called Cheri, a dancer with hair the colour of expensive Sauvignon and a total disregard for anyone who couldn't immediately improve her situation. He'd been obsessed with her for the best part of eight years, even whilst sharing a bed with Jem, and there was a story, a terrible story, that Ralph would love to share with Rosey, the story of how Smith had humiliated himself in front of strangers and lost his real girlfriend and his imaginary girlfriend within the blink of an eye, but as much as it was one of Ralph's favourite ever stories and as much as it would have brought joy to his heart to be able to retell it to this stunning girl sitting to his left, Ralph found himself feeling curiously loyal to his oldest friend and left it there, untouched, untold, maybe something to bring out on another day. 'He was in love with somebody else,' he finished circumspectly. 'He was just using Jem, really, using her to make himself look more unattainable. But it didn't work.'

'Yeah,' said Rosey, clicking the indicator on to left, 'that shit rarely does. Us women aren't as stupid as we look. Well, here we are.' She brought the car into a space outside a building that looked curiously like a church hall. 'And there are the guys.' She got out of the car and waved at a bunch of young men, all wearing grey T-shirts and faded jeans, all fresh of face and long of hair and bright of teeth. There was something about them that reminded Ralph of an advert from the early nineties, possibly for chewing gum. Or possibly for a fizzy drink. He couldn't quite remember which.

She wandered towards them and kissed them each in turn. 'Hey,' she said, turning towards him, 'this is Ralph. He's a buddy of Smith's, from London.' Ralph shook various hands and smiled and said hi and then followed Rosey and 'the guys' through the church hall and into a small room at the back where the band proceeded, in their own words, to hang out. Rosey disappeared without a word and someone handed Ralph a bottle of beer and he perched himself against a low bookshelf, feeling vaguely awkward amongst all the camaraderie and easy banter.

'So, what is this place?' he asked, during a quiet moment.

'This?' said a guy whose name was Ryan. 'It's just the community hall for this neighbourhood. We've played here before – it's cute. You know, it's a good chance to do something intimate for our fans, but really, we prefer to play the big festivals.'

'What are you called?' Ralph asked.

'We're called Pure & Simple.' Ryan said this without a trace of embarrassment.

'Oh,' said Ralph, resisting the urge to grimace and say: shit, that's the worst band name I've ever heard. 'Cool,' he managed.

'Yeah, it's good. And you, what do you do?'

'Oh,' said Ralph, 'I paint. You know. Art.'

'Cool,' said Ryan, nodding appreciatively. 'And you make a living with that, do you?' He smiled apologetically and laughed. 'If that's not too personal a question?'

Ralph smiled. 'No,' he said, 'it's fine. And yeah, I do. Not a lot, but you know, just enough.'

'That's cool,' said Ryan again, 'that's my goal. You know, make this pay, give up the day job.' He finished his beer from the bottleneck and slammed it down on the tabletop. 'Right,' he said, 'I think we're on. I'll see you out there.' He winked at Ralph and picked up his guitar before leaving the room followed by his identikit band members. Ralph sighed. He had a strong and un-assailable feeling that Pure & Simple were not going to be quite his kind of thing. And as the playing field behind the community centre began to fill up it soon became clear to Ralph that neither were their fans going to be quite his kind of people.

There was something peculiar in the air, something intangibly wrong. It was impossible to define, just a feeling that the people surrounding him were there for something other than the rock and roll, a feeling that he was not amongst like-thinkers. There was an eagerness in the air that he had never before encountered at a gig, a fervour that went beyond excitement. He stood towards the edge of the gathering and he sipped his beer and he waited for what he was now quite sure was going to be a revelation.

The band wandered on to the stage. Rosey was lumi-nous in a white sequined slip, her blonde hair pushed behind her ears, her lips painted rose pink. 'Hello!' said Rosey.

A hundred fans shouted hello back. 'It's good to see you all!' she shouted again. 'We're all gonna have a great great GREAT night!' The band built up a riff behind her and she tapped out the rhythm with her white Converse sneakers against the stage, the audience whistled and hollered and clapped their hands in the air above their heads and then Rosey sang. At first Ralph was so mesmerised by the vision of Rosey, the light from three lone spotlights catching the white sequins and turning her into something celestial and divine, her mouth wide with words and song, her hair swinging back and forth with the rocking of her body that he failed to notice the content of her lyrics. In fact, he failed to notice the content of the lyrics of the next three songs until a man next to him, whipped up into some state of frenzied joy, took to a chair, cupped his hands around his mouth and yelled out, 'Hallelujah! Hallelujah! Christ ROCKS!'

A woman to his side turned and beamed at the man on the chair and hollered, 'AMEN!'

Ralph blinked, slowly and calmly.

OK, he thought to himself. OK. This is FINE. They're only Christians. Do not panic. Do not panic.

He looked once more at the quintet on the stage. Pure & Simple. Did that mean that they, then, were a Christian rock band? And did that in turn mean that the edgy, husky, slightly dangerous Rosey was also a Christian? He looked at the cross around her neck. It was so small, so innocuous, nothing more than a pretty piece of silver, an adornment for her pretty neck. He mentally replayed the few brief conversations they'd enjoyed over the past forty-eight hours and at no point did he recall a mention of Jesus, of Christ, of prayer, of conviction or faith. At no point had she appeared wide-eyed with love for Our Lord or quoted the Bible or tutted at a casually uttered word of blasphemy. In fact her language was far from gentle, it was laced with Gods and Christs and even the occasional Jesus fucking Christ. She oozed something both cool and carnal, some-thing fundamentally in control. She did not seem like someone who needed the crutch of organised religion in her life.

The rest of the gig passed in a blur. Beyond the occa-sional Jesus- and love-related hollers from the crowd, there was nothing to suggest that he was listening to Christian rock. They were good songs, on the whole, the band played well, Rosey sang with guts and soul.

Not, as he'd suspected, his kind of music, but really not too awful.

After the show, Ralph found Rosey on a deck chair behind the church hall, sipping water from a plastic bottle and chatting with a fan. He waited for the fan to slink away before taking a seat next to her and saying: 'Congratulations. That was excellent.'

'You liked?' she said, wiping a lick of water from her upper lip in the manner of a weary cowboy.

'Yeah,' he said, 'I liked. You sing very well.'

'Why, thank you!' she smiled at him, languorously, her tone set as it always was, somewhere non-specific between cynical and bullet-straight upfront.

'Christian rock?' he said a moment later, having tried and failed to find a less direct way of asking about the genre.

'Hah!' she slammed her beer bottle down against her lap. 'Yeah! Christian rock! Woo!'

Ralph glanced at her, trying and failing to gauge her inference.

'I guess so,' she said eventually. 'I guess if you had to give us a "tag",' she made the quotes with her finger-tips, 'then, yeah, that would be it. But, you know, it's not as clear-cut as that. I mean, I'm not even a Christian.'

Ralph felt something hard and abrasive inside his chest melt to liquid at these words. Such relief, but he had no idea why. 'Oh,' he managed.

'Yeah. I believe. You know. I believe in, you know, the spiritual, like, completely. I go to church. I say my prayers. I have a relationship with God. And I guess I have a very Christian outlook on life. But Christian with a small c. If such a word even exists.'

'So, how come you're in this band. How come –'

She interrupted him. 'Saw an ad. Applied. They liked me. I liked them. They were prepared to overlook the fact that I don't live my life according to some screwed-up words in a really weird old book. I was prepared to overlook the fact that they are a bunch of cheesy Jesus-loving old fucking virgins. We hooked up. We made it work. And yeah, now I'm on the Christian rock circuit. Woo!' She wound her fist in the air and then rolled her eyes.

He looked at her, unsure what to say next.

'Are you shocked?' she asked.

Ralph shrugged.

'Yeah, you Brits, you're so scared of God, aren't you?'

He scratched the back of his neck. 'It's not that I'm scared of God,' he said, 'I just don't believe he exists. Therefore I'm scared of people who believe in him. It's like . . . it's like being with someone who believes in leprechauns or believes in the tooth fairy. It makes them seem a bit mad.'

Ralph inhaled sharply. That last sentence had just slipped from his lips inadvertently.

But Rosey laughed out loud. 'I know,' she said, 'I know exactly what you mean. It's tough having a God thing, knowing that most of the people you come into contact with think you're a loon, and I do question the God thing.'

'You do?'

'Yeah, constantly. All the time. I mean, I am a bright girl and I know that logically, rationally, there is nothing to suggest that the big man exists. I've tried the Bible and frankly it just goes over my head. But still, it's there, when I talk to him, I can feel him listening. When I'm in a church I can sense him watching. And I like having him around. You know.'

'And Smith . . . ?'

'Smith has his own spiritual shit going on.'

'He does?'

'Yeah, he does. Not in the conventional sense, but yeah, he has a relationship with something bigger than himself.'

Ralph blinked.

'You are freaking out right now, aren't you?' she asked with a twinkle in her eye.

'Just a bit,' he replied.

She smiled, almost fondly. 'You shouldn't, you know. It's just another way of living. It's just another way of making sense of it all. It's nothing to be scared of.'

'Hmm,' said Ralph, rubbing his chin, 'try telling that to the fundamentalist, terrorising, murdering nutters of the world.'

'Oh, come on,' she rolled her eyes, 'if they weren't doing it for God they'd be doing it for something else. It's just a pretext.'

They fell silent for a moment. Ralph picked at the paper around the neck of his beer bottle and stared into the dark trees. Cicadas chirruped in the shadowy grass, someone was plucking at a guitar round the corner and the air was honey warm. He wasn't in the mood for a shouty discussion about organised religion. 'Yeah,' he said, 'you're probably right. A nutter's a nutter's a nutter.'

'So, you want to come to the pub with us?'

'Us?'

'Yeah, me and the guys. It's tradition. After a gig we go to the pub. I get drunk. They get tipsy and call me a heathen. It's a hoot.'

'But what about the car?'

'The pub's right next to my apartment. I'll park up and we can walk.'

'And how will I get back to Smith's?'

'Cab. I can lend you some cash if you need it?'

'No, it's cool. I've got plenty.'

'Great, I'll call Smith, see if he wants to come along when he's finished his class. He won't, but it's only polite to ask.' She winked at Ralph and Ralph smiled. There was something flirtatious in the wink. And there was something dangerous in the invitation. Ralph felt too

113

strongly attracted to this woman to be spending any more time with her away from Smith. But on the other hand, there were still a million things he didn't know about her that he wanted to find out.

'Cool,' he said, 'let's go.'

Chapter 8

It had come almost as no surprise at all to Jem that when she left her sister's house that afternoon the first person she'd seen was Joel.

But of course, her subconscious had whispered to her, like a conspiratorial friend.

'Hello,' she'd said, feeling awkward, as if their relaxed conversation at the weekend had never happened.

'Hello,' he'd replied, looking at her curiously.

'You're off the beaten track around here,' she'd said, more as a question than as a statement.

'I was about to say the same to you.'

'And no Jessica?'

'She's with my son.' He nodded, as if that should be enough information for now.

'My sister's place,' she'd said, pointing behind her to the large house.

'Ah,' he said, sounding strangely relieved to have been given a plausible reason for Jem's presence in this precise spot.

He was clearly not about to elaborate on the reasons for his own presence in this precise spot, and Jem didn't like to ask. There was something shifty about him, as though he'd been caught out in some way. She smiled at him, reassuringly. 'I've been meaning to text you,' she said, 'arrange something for the girls.'

'Yes,' he lifted his head, as if consulting somebody taller than himself. 'Yes, that would be great. Actually,' he looked down and into her eyes for the first time, 'we're free tomorrow afternoon, if you are ... ?'

Jem pretended to think, although she really wasn't thinking at all, more just reacting to yet another unnerving development. 'Er, yeah,' she said, lightly, 'we are free actually.'

'Good, good. Come to us. Come for tea. Does Scarlett like the normal things?'

'Yes. And she also likes some of the abnormal things.'

He smiled. 'Well, Jessica unfortunately sticks very much to the normal, so it'll be pasta or something. You've got our address?'

'Yes!' said Jem, over-brightly. 'Yes! It's on your card. And I know where it is.'

'Behind the Thai place.'

'Behind the Thai place. What time?'

'Four? Ish?'

'Great. See you then.'

'Great.' He smiled then, a tight, distracted smile and tapped the face of his watch absent-mindedly. He looked like he was about to say something else, but he didn't. Jem watched him for a moment as he shuffled away from her, his hands deep inside the pockets of his big blue overcoat. She felt sure he wouldn't turn back to look at her. And he didn't.

The following day was Wednesday. It was overcast and drizzling intermittently, and Jem thought of Ralph in California, sleeping, she assumed, though maybe he was not. Maybe he was sweating in a nightclub full of twenty-year-old girls, maybe he was frantically mating with a stranger, expunging himself of eight months' worth of pent-up sexual frustration. (She felt, in retrospect, that it might have been prudent of her to have had sex with him at least once before letting him escape to America, though really, she doubted very much that Ralph had either the skill or the inclination to persuade women into bed with him. It had never been his style, even when he was single. He'd always ended up with predatory women.) Maybe he was in an open-topped car, driving through the night on some adventure, she mused, but whatever he was doing, he was doing it in a temperate climate and that, even more than the thought of writhing females and thumping nightclubs, made Jem want to punch the wall with resentment.

She took Scarlett to nursery and then she and Blake went to Tesco.

As she was unloading her shopping on to the kitchen counter fifteen minutes later, her mobile rang. As always, her phone lurked somewhere mysterious and unknown in the bottom of her bag: through handfuls of crumpled tissues, old receipts and spare nappies Jem waded until, finally, she extracted it, dusted off some crumbs and pressed answer.

'Hello, Jem, it's Stella. How are you?'

Jem raised her head to the ceiling and breathed in deeply. She knitted together a smile and a matching tone of voice and said: 'Oh, hi, Stella. I'm *fine*, thank you, how are you?'

'How's little Blakie?' Stella butted the irrelevant question about herself firmly out of the way. Stella never answered questions about herself. Stella was the office manager-cum-receptionist at Jarvis Smallhead, Jem's agency. She had been working at Jarvis Smallhead since she was eighteen years old. She was now somewhere in the vicinity of fifty. She was unmarried and nobody knew where she lived or who she lived with or what sort of things she did when she left the office in the evenings because Stella was only interested in other people.

'Oh,' said Jem, fake sunshine in her voice, 'he's fantastic, he's here now, in his bouncy chair, looking right at me.'

'Ah,' simpered Stella, 'that's nice, and how's beautiful Scarlett?'

'Scarlett's fine, she's at nursery today, so it's all nice and quiet here.'

'Oh, yes,' Stella gushed, as if she herself liked nothing more than a quiet day at home with a baby. 'I'm sure it is. And Ralph? How's he?'

'Well, he's in California, right now.'

'*Really*?' Stella's voice filled with glee, as if the fact of Ralph's presence in California were a special gift, just for her. 'How wonderful! Is he there to paint?'

'No,' smiled Jem, through teeth clamped tight, 'just a holiday. Seeing old friends.'

'Oh, lovely! How lovely. What I wouldn't give for a bit of Californian sun right now.' She sighed and Jem inhaled, waiting for her to get to the point.

'Well, anyway, here's some news!' she opened. 'We've just had a call from ITV. They wanted to talk to someone about Karl. Didn't say what it was about, but it must be, mustn't it?'

Jem wiped a slick of posit from Blake's chin with a slightly crispy muslin cloth and moved the phone to her other ear. 'God, yeah,' she said, 'I guess it could be. What was their name?'

'I've got all the details here. Have you got a pen? I said you were at home with your baby today and that you'd call back when you got a chance. They said it wasn't urgent, any time this week would be fine.'

Jem took down the details and a moment later, thanks in the main to some unprovoked crying from Blake, managed to extricate herself from the grip of Stella's conversational vice. She pulled Blake out of his bouncy chair and he looked at her pathetically. Then he yawned, the vast, toothless, honey-scented yawn of a newborn. His translucent lids started to lower and Jem knew that in less than a minute he'd be asleep. She nestled him into her shoulder and very gently carried him to his room above the kitchen. She laid him in his basket, and then tiptoed backwards from his room, taking care to avoid the squeaking floorboard near the door and she fled downstairs, empty of arms, light of foot, ready to seize her precious half-hour, possibly more, of freedom.

She tended to panic at these moments. Suddenly the mountain of undone jobs and tiny snatched luxuries seemed to loom above her, insurmountable, as though someone had just clicked on a stopwatch and said, 'GO!' She needed to put a wash on, she needed to sort out a pile of Scarlett's clothes that had been sitting on the landing outside her bedroom for four days, she needed to write out a cheque for the nursery fees for this term, a fox had shredded a bin bag two nights ago and left flotsam and jetsam strewn across the small patch of grass in front of the house, which would require squelching about in the rain in rubber gloves with an empty carrier bag, and now she had this phonecall to make, too. Plus she really wanted to have a little nap. And sit down with a cup of tea and flick through the glossy property magazine that had been dropped on to her doormat this morning while she was at the shops. And decide what to wear this afternoon to Joel's place. And return a long overdue phonecall to her mother.

She was paralysed with options, the clock was ticking. Eventually she decided to do the thing that would take the least time and make her feel the most like she'd achieved something. She picked up her mobile and the piece of paper with the ITV contact details on it and she dialled.

Jem was unable to get hold of Karl. He was not answering his mobile phone or his home line. It was not a matter of urgency, rather that Jem wanted to tell someone and if she didn't tell Karl there was a real danger she might tell Joel. Or the first person she walked past on the street. Who, on recent evidence, might well be Joel. The call from ITV, had, as Stella had suspected, been from the *I'm a Celebrity . . . Get Me Out of Here* casting office, and they did indeed want to know whether or not Karl Kasparov – famously and publicly regretful adulterer (working as a DJ on a London station, he had spilled his emotional guts live on air, after Siobhan, his long-term love, had uncovered his indiscretions with the leggy blonde on the top floor and left him), slightly chubby, rather shambling and the kind of TV personality who engendered not so much fervent adoration as a kind of oh-yeah-that-Irish-guy-whatsisname fondness – would consider the possibility of going into the jungle for eighteen days to eat grubs, pee in a dunny and possibly, maybe resurrect his career, earning an amount of money for the same that was, for now, specified only as 'negotiable'.

But until Karl answered his phone she had no one to share the news with and she was more or less bursting with it.

For the first time since he'd gone on Saturday, Jem missed Ralph.

She calculated the time in LA and then she called him.

He sounded husky. He sounded like a man who'd spent all night shouting and smoking. He didn't sound overly pleased to hear from her. She swallowed a bubble of annoyance and carried on regardless.

'Guess what,' she said.

'I don't know,' said Ralph.

'ITV want to put Karl on their long list for the next series of *I'm a Celebrity . . .*'

'What, the jungle one?'

'Yes. The Ant and Dec one.'

'Wow,' he said, although his voice did not reflect the sentiment of the word.

Jem felt her excitement wane a degree. 'Prime-time telly,' she continued, 'major pay cheque. Possibly a big career move.'

'Yeah,' said Ralph, his voice still hollow and dull. 'I guess it could be. What did he say?'

'I haven't spoken to him yet. He's not answering his phone. I'm not supposed to tell anyone, but you know that never includes you.'

'Yeah, well, I don't think he'll do it.'

'Oh.' Jem was momentarily winded by the bluntness of this pronouncement.

'Well, it's just a piss-take, isn't it? Who the hell would want to go on telly and make a tit of themselves in front of the world?'

Jem drew up her shoulders. Having just spent the last four hours persuading herself that this was the Best Thing That Could Possibly Have Happened, she wasn't about to let Ralph pour water all over it. 'It will be good for him,' she countered. 'Not just professionally, but on a personal level. Get him out of his rut. He hasn't even been on a plane this millennium.'

'Yeah, and there's probably a reason for that.'

'Laziness. That's all. And there nothing like the promise of a big fat cheque to cure someone of laziness.'

'OK,' said Ralph, dismissively, 'whatever. He's your client. It's your job. You know best. I just personally think he'll laugh in your face. That's all.'

Jem inhaled. She'd called Ralph in a burst of pure, childlike excitement, because he was her best friend and because he was always the first person she wanted to talk to when something important happened to her, but everything about his attitude and tone of voice suggested that he wished she hadn't called.

'Right,' she said, circumspectly, 'OK. Well, anyway, I just thought you'd like to know. Obviously if it comes off it means I'll be bringing some proper money into the house. It could even cover the kitchen extension.' She hoped that waving some cash in Ralph's face might awaken some enthusiasm.

'I thought we'd decided against the kitchen extension,' he said.

'Er, no. *You* decided against it because we couldn't afford it. But if this deal comes off, we will be able to afford it.'

She heard Ralph sigh. 'Look,' he said, 'I had a late night. It's early. I can't say I'm in the right frame of mind to be talking about extensions.'

'Oh, God, I'm SO SORRY,' said Jem, lacing her voice with uncontrollable sarcasm. 'Of course, you're on HOLIDAY. I forgot. I'm really sorry to have disturbed you with my stupid news. I'll let you catch up on your beauty sleep. While I trudge through the rain to collect your daughter from nursery.'

'Oh, Jem, come on . . .'

'No, come on what? I let you go on holiday and leave me at home with your children and the very fucking LEAST you could do is make the effort to be pleasant and conversational when I call you and not wind me up with talk of late nights and early starts. OK?'

'I am not winding you up, it's just –'

'I don't want to know. Really. I don't. I have to go now or I'll be late for Scarlett.'

Ralph sighed again. 'Jem.' There was a long, brooding silence. 'This is . . . Christ, something's got to change, something . . .'

'Too bloody right,' said Jem. And then her finger hit the End Call button and suddenly she was in her silent kitchen, staring at her baby son, her head spinning with adrenalin, her heart racing with emotion, tears threatening.

Ralph had been right about one thing. Something had to change. It really, really did.

And with that thought she forced back the tears, painted on a smile, dressed her baby for the rain and headed off to a strange man's flat for the afternoon.

Chapter 9

Ralph left the phone by his ear for a moment, not because he hoped that Jem would suddenly come back on the line but because he didn't have the energy to move it. He had conducted his entire conversation with Jem in a prone, semi-foetal position, the phone a few centimetres from his head, her voice like smashing glass to his delicate ears. He groaned and licked his lips.

He'd only answered the phone because somewhere deep down inside his addled thoughts it had occurred to him that it might be an emergency, that something might have happened to the kids. But once he'd realised that Jem had only called to talk to him about some stupid TV show and the bloody kitchen extension that she was so obsessed with, he'd lost the awakeness of potential disaster and fallen back into the dark corners of his half-conscious state. For a moment he was cross with Jem, for waking him up when he'd had only four hours' sleep, for giving him grief about his tone of voice, for making him feel guilty yet again for the fact that he wasn't as perfect as she was. But then, as the light kept him from dipping back into sleep, as noises outside the apartment entered his consciousness, and as he remembered the rather surprising conclusion to his night out with Rosey, so did the truth.

He was a shit.

He really was a shit.

He'd known it for months, he'd felt the knowledge of his own fecklessness eating away inside him like a tumour.

He should have spoken kindly to Jem. He should have been pleased for her. He should have said, 'Wow, hon, that sounds great, fingers crossed that Karl will go for it.' He shouldn't be here, in Smith's spare room, he should be in his home, he should be offering to go out in the rain to collect Scarlett from nursery, he should be popping into Tesco on the way back to pick up some groceries, cooking something good for supper, insisting that Jem go out for the evening, take some time, that he would be *fine* with the baby, with *his* baby. He should not let his family exist in a different plane, he should not keep making excuses for his own absence, he should start to make friends with his baby boy and he should take more responsibility for his ravishing daughter and not just flourish her like a trophy.

He knew all of these things. He knew them intensely and deeply, in vivid shades of awareness. But he had no idea how to change his patterns of behaviour. They were so profoundly etched into his being. And he was still so unflinchingly cross with Jem for her physical rejection of him, for her aloofness, for just forging on through life like a human plough, forwards and onwards with her jobs and her schedules and her own throbbing rhythms, never turning back to look at him with a fond smile, *are you there, are you keeping up, do you want to hold my hand?*

He knew it was his own doing, he knew that since Blake was born he'd retreated from family life, he knew that the onus was probably on him to pull up his socks and get stuck into things without too much fuss. But he was stuck, suspended in a pit of resentment and fear.

He felt the top of his bedside cabinet with his left hand, brought down the slim package of photos that Jem had packed for him. The first photo he pulled out was of Blake. He rubbed his eyes and he stared at the image, his gaze taking in every detail of the baby's face, his wide dark eyes, his pale ruff of hair, his neat ears clipped to the sides of his head like cashew nuts. Who was he, this boy? Where had he come from? What did he want? Ralph had never wanted a son. He'd assumed after making one girl that the next would follow suit. The sight of Blake's clearly boy-shaped genitalia on the ultrasound screen all those months ago had taken Ralph by surprise. He felt sure there'd been a mistake. 'Are you sure?' he asked the sonographer. 'Oh yes,' he'd replied, happily, 'One hundred per cent. That's a boy.'

The sonographer had seemed so happy for Ralph. 'One of each,' he'd said, as if he'd imagined Ralph to be desperate for a boy to complete his life. But Ralph had not been desperate for a boy. He'd wanted another Scarlett. Well, he hadn't wanted another baby at all, but if he was going to have one thrust upon him, the only palatable concept of babyness he could conjure up was one exactly the same as the one he'd already grown to know and to love.

He'd hoped right up until the very last moment, right up until Blake had slithered from between Jem's open thighs on to the bloodied hospital bed that there'd been a mistake, that the midwife would look at them both in surprise and exclaim, 'Well, I never, it's a girl!' But instead Ralph had seen immediate evidence that his second child was indeed a boy, and not only that, a boy red of face and wide of mouth and angry of expression, a boy who appeared not to want to be here, a boy from perhaps another species. Ralph had been hoping for the moment to carry him swiftly away from his misgivings, waiting for his heart to fill with paternal pride, *my boy, my boy*, he waited for the first thirty-six hours in a state of suspended animation, thinking: now, now I will get him, now he will enter my heart. But days and weeks and months had passed and Ralph still felt as though a stranger was in their midst. And not only that but a stranger who slept with his partner, who drank from her body, who occupied most of her waking thoughts.

He ran his thumb across the glossy skein of the photo-graph. He stared at the baby again, waiting for something to soften his heart. Just a baby, he thought to himself, just a tiny baby. But nothing gave. He was still stone.

He sighed and slid the photo back into the pocket. He was lost. Lost in his marriage. Lost in his career. Lost in his role as a father. And now he was lost here, too, lost in California.

But the weirdest thing had happened to him last night. There'd been a moment. When was it? About three in the morning, he supposed, halfway between the bar and Rosey's apartment block. He'd been ripe with beer, his head a soft sponge of cheer and joy, the warmth of the balmy Californian night wrapped around him, sleepless cicadas scratching a lazy rhythm in the bushes. They'd meandered across the busy ocean-side drive, loosely together but not quite apart, bare arms occasionally brushing against each other. The boys from the band had left hours earlier, their pleasure curtailed by the prospect of early starts for day jobs and long cab rides home, but Rosey didn't work on Wednesday mornings and Ralph clearly had no reason to want to head home so they'd carried on, into the early hours, talking about things that Ralph had no recollection of this morning, the conver-sation like a high-speed train, a streak of words that had left no mark on his consciousness. But there was one moment he remembered vividly, just as they reached the other side of the road, the moon hanging heavy behind a palm tree. Ralph had stopped, looked at the moon, looked at Rosey, looked behind him at the ocean and suddenly been overcome with emotion. Every beautiful moment of his life flooded through him. Every grand emotion he'd ever experienced came at him all at once and left him fighting for breath.

Was this it? he thought. Was this where it all stopped? All the sensation, all the joy, all the giddy delight of simply being? He was, he feared, too old to feel like this any more. He thought about the first few years with Jem, how every single day had felt like a gift, when these moments had come thick and fast, when he'd barely had a chance to register one joyful moment before another had come hurtling up behind it. Was that youth? Was it love? Was it just a sugar-coated chemical fuelling his brain? What was it? Where had it gone? And did he really have to run away, get drunk and flirt with another woman to feel it again?

Rosey had turned and smiled at him. 'You OK?' she'd said.

He'd stared at her for a silent moment. 'You're so beautiful,' he'd said (he felt sick with himself at this memory).

She'd looked at him quizzically. 'That's what all the drunk guys say.'

'No, but really. You are so beautiful. Not in a "I want to fuck you" kind of way,' (had he really said that, had he really said 'fuck you'?) 'just in a perfectly symmetrical, flawless bone structure kind of a way. I'd love to . . .' (God, this was probably the worst of it all) 'I'd love to paint you.'

'Ha, well, feel free,' she'd said, though his muffled memories prevented him from being sure about her tone of voice; had she been flattered or embarrassed or quietly, sweetly condescending? He had no idea. He just knew that he'd said those things because he'd meant those things, because for the first time in a long time he was feeling like a fully functioning human being with a core and a purpose.

They'd moved on then, through a small shopping complex, past the restaurant where he'd had dinner with Smith that first night and into a courtyard apartment block. 'This is me,' she'd said, 'and you're sure you're OK getting a cab?'

He glanced about, feeling absolutely certain that he would be OK getting a cab and that even if he couldn't get a cab he'd be more than happy to walk on this perfect night.

He nodded. 'I'll be fine,' he said.

'OK, well, look, thanks for coming to see the band and thanks for letting me stay up late. It's been cool.'

'Yeah,' he'd said, steadying himself against saying anything else he might later regret, 'it's been fun. I'll see you . . . I guess . . . ?'

'Tomorrow night? I think I've arranged to meet up with Smith, and since you are officially Gooseberry of the Week,' she smiled, 'no doubt I'll see you then.'

He smiled, happily, relieved that he would only have to wait a few more hours before seeing her again.

'And listen,' she continued, 'if you were really bored, I'm going to church tomorrow, six-ish. You could come along, see if you and God can, you know, hook up?' She laughed at the ludicrousness of the suggestion.

But Ralph didn't laugh. He nodded firmly. 'Yeah,' he said, 'yeah. Why not?'

She looked at him in surprise. 'Great!' she said, her face breaking open into something soft and glad that Ralph hadn't seen before, 'I'll pick you up. Five-thirtyish.'

'Excellent,' he said, forcing his hands down deep into his pockets and backing away from her. 'See you then.'

She gave him a wave and a small smile, her face still washed over with the new softness, and it was then that it happened, a small, shocking moment that still reverberated around his sore head today. Rosey had leaned in towards Ralph, her lips had touched his, not in a kiss – it was too dry and too soft to be a kiss – but not a peck either – it had been too gentle to be a peck – but something more like a caress. They'd pulled apart, not fast, but leisurely. 'Oh,' Rosey had said, confirmation in that one syllable that something significant had just happened.

She'd put her fingers to her lips and laughed. And then she'd slipped between her front door and the frame and disappeared.

Ralph didn't even look for a taxi that night. The straight gridlines of the seaside town and the distinctive landmarks of restaurants and bars made it simple to navigate his way back to Smith's apartment. He breathed the warm, briny air into his lungs, knowing that the opportunities to walk alone through a balmy night in a strange land were waning with every moment. He didn't feel like a forty-two-year-old man; he felt ageless, timeless, almost born again.

Was he in love? He had no idea.

For now, all Ralph knew was this: it was so late it was early and he felt like he was walking on sweet, sweet air.

Chapter 10

By the time Jem had collected Scarlett from nursery and found her way to Joel's flat, her sheepskin boots had lost a large percentage of their former waterproof quality and the heels of her socks were damp. The unpleasant sensation of damp socks, added to the sense of having shiny, but not exactly well-arranged hair, and a three-year-old daughter who had done nothing but complain since her collection from nursery about the fact that they were not going straight home and that she 'did not want to go to Jessica's house – I HATE Jessica's house,' led her to think that really, she may as well have just given into Scarlett's terrifying will and headed straight home, possibly to break her No Wine Before 6 p.m. rule. But a date was a date and, she reasoned with herself, it would be good for Scarlett to have a local friend, especially as she had failed to provide her with a sister for regular girl play on rainy afternoons.

Jem made it up the last damp leg of the walk, to a sharp hill that ran up the side of Thai Dreams on Herne Hill and round a tight corner into a funny little mews that Jem had never even noticed before. The mews was modern, probably thrown together in the 1980s, and facing fairly rudely on to the rear ends of the shops in front. The lower floors of the boxy little houses were garages, with open concrete staircases leading to the upper floors. Joel's house was the second one along. Parked outside was a squat Austin Mini in an indistinguishable shade of sludge, a car that looked like it had not been driven in many a year.

'I don't like it,' said Scarlett, backing away. 'It's scary.'

Jem had to agree that it was far from salubrious, the sort of place that put you in mind of drug deals, and swaying drunks pissing up walls, and sociopaths hiding out in squalid solitude, sticking news cuttings of celebrities to their walls and playing with hunting knives. It did not look like the kind of place where you would bring up a child, especially not one with the sunny disposition of the fragrant Jessica.

Jem pressed the bell and waited for the crackle of the intercom to acknowledge her request.

'Hello!' It was a small voice. It was Jessica.

Scarlett looked at Jem gloomily as if her last possible avenue of salvation from the hellish prospect of the afternoon ahead, the possibility that Joel and Jessica *might not really live here*, had just been cruelly snatched from her.

'Hello!' chimed Jem. 'It's Scarlett and her mum!'

The door buzzed and Jem and Scarlett gingerly stepped through into the hallway.

Scarlett crushed herself against Jem's waist whilst Jessica ran towards them, arms windmilling in their sockets, strawberry-blonde hair hanging down her back in unkempt tangles. 'Yay!' she hollered and then threw her arms around Scarlett in a fulsome embrace.

Jem felt Scarlett's small body stiffen and recoil. Jem felt the same mixture of emotions she always felt at these moments: pride that she had a child who did not throw herself like a treat at anyone who cared to have her, and concern that in not wishing to cuddle other more affectionate children she might give people the impression that she was possibly unused to affection because she was given none at home.

'Come into my room! Come into my room!' Jessica

hopped from one foot to the other, holding Scarlett's stiff, still-cold fingers in hers.

Joel appeared in the doorway at the top of the corridor. 'Now, come on, Jess, give poor Scarlett a chance to at least take off her coat.'

Jem glanced up. There he was. Joel. He was wearing a grey lambswool crewneck and blue chinos. His feet were socked and he was wearing glasses. He looked like a geography teacher. 'Find us all right?' he asked.

'Yeah,' smiled Jem, 'just behind Thai Dreams. Couldn't really miss it.'

She glanced around the flat quickly, taking in unpapered walls, cheap blinds, bicycles, washing hanging on radiators. It was very much the home of a single dad.

Joel offered Jem a cup of tea. 'Yes, please,' she said, 'it's miserable out there. I'm cold to the bone.'

He disappeared into a small galley kitchen that peered out into the living room through a rectangular opening. 'You know, you can hop off in a minute, if you like. I'd be happy to oversee if there were things you needed to get done?'

Jem glanced down at the three-year-old girl wrapped around her left thigh and laughed. 'Maybe I'll hang around for a bit,' she said lightly, 'wait and see how these two hit it off.'

'Now! Now!' pleaded Jessica. 'Will you come now? To my room?'

Scarlett looked at Jem beseechingly.

'Maybe Scarlett would like some juice first, and a muffin?' He directed this question at Jem.

Jem nodded enthusiastically.

'Is it a chocolate muffin?' Scarlett whispered in her ear.

'I don't know,' said Jem. 'We'll have to ask Jessica's dad, won't we?'

Joel smiled and looked down at Scarlett. 'It is indeed a

133

chocolate muffin,' he said, 'with extra chocolate chips inside.' He pulled apart the Cellophane wrapping of a pack of four from Tesco. 'Why don't you take off your coat and sit down and I'll bring it in in a minute.'

Jem could feel Scarlett's body starting to relax under her arm. She leaned down to help her with the fastenings of her parka and slipped it off her shoulders.

'So,' she said, 'how long have you and Jessica lived here?'

Joel shrugged and poured boiling water from a white plastic kettle into a chipped brown teapot. 'Well, I've been here for about ten years. It was my dad's place. He used to have a stand at the antique market on Northcote Road ... used this place for storage. When he died I had to sell off everything else he owned to pay off his loans. This was all that was left. So now we call it home.' He smiled tightly, suggesting that he would not have chosen such a place to live if he'd had more options. 'Sugar?'

Jem shook her head. 'But your dad – I thought you were from up north?'

'No,' he replied simply, 'why did you think that?'

'Your accent, I suppose,' she said, 'there's a hint of something, and the fact that your son was brought up there?'

'No.' Joel piled cheap mugs, muffins and the teapot on to a tray and carried it into the living room. 'I was at university in Sheffield. I was up there for five years in the end, it must have rubbed off a bit, but, no, I'm a south London boy, through and through, born and bred in Clapham Junction.'

'Really?' Jem brightened. 'Whereabouts?'

'Just off Northcote Road. Lovely little house. I was gutted when I had to sell it after my dad went.'

'Ha! I used to live there. Do you know a little road called Almanac Road?'

'Yes!' Joel placed the tray on the coffee table. 'I was in the next road up. When were you there?'

'Oh God, about ten years ago, I was in a flatshare. It's where I met Ralph, actually.'

'Ah yes, Ralph of the missing mojo. You met him in a flatshare?'

'Yeah,' she smiled. 'We were flatmates. It was an interesting way to get to know someone.'

'Well, I was long gone by the time you were living there then. In fact, yeah, I'd just moved in here. Me and Jessica's mum, starting our *new life*.' He smiled wryly and poured tea into mismatched mugs with business logos on them. His hands were pale and angular, his knuckles were slightly red and dry. From this angle Jem could see that his pale hair was thinning at the crown. There were moth-holes in his lambswool jumper and his glasses were slightly crooked on the brow of his nose. Jem wondered once more at her feelings for this man. What was it about him that kept him in her thoughts? Why had she even noticed him? Was it, as she had concluded a few nights ago, simply an ego boost or was it that she was reading too much into his recurrent appearances in her life, or did she actually want to have an affair with him? No – she threw the thought violently from her mind – she did not want to have an affair with him, she was just impressed by him, that was all. She found the sheer novelty of a man who could look after his own child without a woman enthralling. But somehow she had blurred the boundaries in her head between respect and attraction. He was a nice-looking man, nothing special, but compared to Ralph he was surely a god.

Blake began wriggling in the sling and she unpopped the fastenings. Then she took a handful of small toys from her handbag and laid him on the floor where he stared in awe at the rather ugly mother-of-pearl lightshade over the central light, rolling gently from side to side in his fleecy all-in-one.

The girls ate in silence, occasionally lifting plastic cups of juice to their lips, gingerly, with two cupped hands. Jem sipped her tea, which was very good, and wondered if it was her turn to speak.

'So,' said Jem, looking at the monitor screen behind him, 'what is it that you do, exactly?'

Joel turned and glanced at the screen. 'Oh, that. That's not work, that's household accounts. Just been working out if we can afford to eat next month.'

'And?' Jem asked.

He took a sharp intake of breath and smiled drily. 'Just about,' he sighed. 'Just about. So really, I need to spend more time working and less time working out our household accounts.'

'And working is . . . ?'

'Well, working is the problem. Because really I don't. I do some work for a youth centre on Electric Avenue. I get paid for it, but not really enough to live a proper life. And I do some research here and there for think tanks, about youth and drugs and crime, and a bit of stuff for the *Brixton Times*, but it's all very piecemeal. I've just sort of put everything on hold for this one,' he gestured towards Jessica. 'I need to sort myself out. She'll be starting nursery full time in September. Then it's school. Then, well,' he smiled sadly, 'my work here will be done.'

'No it won't!' rejoined Jessica. 'You still have to give me baths. And brush my teeth. You still have to carry on being my daddy!'

Jem and Joel laughed. 'That is very true, munchkin,' said Joel. 'Very true indeed. I will have to carry on being your daddy for a very long time indeed.'

'Good,' said Jessica, 'that's good.'

'But,' continued Joel, 'once you're at school all day, your

daddy will need to start thinking about ways to earn more money, so that you and I can have all the things we need.'

'Like pink paint in my bedroom?'

'Yes, like pink paint in your bedroom.'

'Whoo-hoo!' Jessica got to her feet and performed a victorious air thump. 'Come on, Scarlett. Let's go an' PLAY!'

Scarlett looked at Jem beseechingly but Jem just blinked at her reassuringly. 'Go on,' she said, 'I'm just in here.'

For a moment it seemed as though Scarlett were on the brink of one of her magnificent and immovable refusals, but after a moment she allowed herself to be pulled forcibly from the room by her hand and suddenly Jem and Joel were alone.

'I didn't offer you a muffin!' said Joel, getting to his feet, slightly panicked.

'Oh, no, honestly, it's fine. I'm sort of off the muffins for now.'

'Oh.' He looked at her for a moment, clearly not sure how to respond to a comment plucked from the murky pond of women and their weight issues. 'More tea?'

'No,' she waved her half-full mug at him, 'I'm fine. Thank you.'

They both smiled at the sound of Jessica's shrieking laughter coming from elsewhere in the house. Jem was glad of the diversion from the slightly awkward fact of their aloneness. 'She's such a lovely little thing,' she said, 'your Jessica. So full of life and so friendly.'

'Yeah,' he smiled proudly, 'I know. No idea where she gets it from!'

Jem laughed.

'Yes, she's had a tough start in life – not easy, you know – but here she is, mad and glorious and just full of wonder. I thank God for her every minute of every day. I really do. Without her . . . well . . .' He tailed off and smiled weakly at Jem. His eyes were glossy with tears. Jem looked away, surprised and shocked. This sudden show of emotion in a man whom she had previously imagined to be rather cool and steely was the last thing she had expected. 'I tell you what,' he said, getting to his feet again, 'I know it's early, but it's raining, we're killing time together, I think it would be perfectly acceptable to have a glass of wine, don't you?'

Jem breathed in sharply. There it was. The offer of wine. There was a sense of inevitability about it. And the moment was pivotal. Say no and it would be tantamount to saying, 'This is just a play-date, back off, buddy.' Say yes, and, well, it wasn't tantamount to saying, 'Sex? Now? Oh, yes please!' but it certainly left things a bit more open. 'Well,' she said, 'I'm still breastfeeding so I can't really go to town, but a small glass would be nice.' She sighed with relief. She felt she'd made a sound compromise.

'Good. Good.' He clapped his hands together and headed for the kitchen. 'Red? White?'

'Whatever you're having,' she said.

'And what about you?' he said, appearing from the fridge with a bottle of something white. 'How long have you lived round here?'

'About four years, I suppose. We were in the flatshare in Almanac Road for about a month after we got together, then things there got a bit awkward so we got a flat in Lurline Gardens, you know, the mansion flats just behind Battersea Park. Then we bought here when I was pregnant with Scarlett. Only place we could afford a proper house.'

'The classic manoeuvre,' said Joel, inspecting two wine-glasses for smudges. 'What is it about us English and our need for *stairs*. Seriously. Don't you think they're overrated?'

Jem laughed. 'I guess so. But it's not just about stairs, is it, it's about gardens.'

'Yes, there is that, although I have raised my own child quite happily without a garden for nearly four years. That's the beauty of London: green stuff everywhere; you don't have to walk too far. And Lurline Gardens, wow, right on Battersea Park.'

'One-bedroom flat,' she said.

'Ah,' he conceded, 'fair enough.'

He placed the glass of wine in front of her and she picked it up.

'Cheers,' said Joel, 'here's to killing time.'

'Yes, indeed, killing time.'

The first sip of wine seemed to bypass all the usual channels, hitting her somewhere around the left side of her head like an affectionate punch. She smiled at Joel. He smiled at her. 'All quiet on the girl front,' he said.

'So far, so good. She's a funny one, my Scarlett. A big fan of her own company. A big fan of home. Makes her easy to manage in some ways – she can just spend hours pottering around doing her own thing – but socially, she can be a bit awkward.'

'And where does she get that from, do you think?'

Jem shrugged. 'No idea. I'm pretty sociable. So's Ralph. Well, he *used* to be!' She laughed and rubbed her forearm.

'Before he lost his mojo?'

'Yes, indeed, before he lost his mojo.'

'Will you ever forgive him?' he asked abruptly.

'Excuse me?'

'Ralph. Will you ever forgive him?' He was staring at her, not as intently as the question he'd just asked might have suggested, but rather in fond concern.

'For what?'

'For buggering off to California and leaving you on your own with two kids?'

Jem put her glass down and got to her knees to pluck the increasingly complaining Blake from the carpet and consider the question. Should she be offended? Outraged?

Perturbed? She didn't know. She just knew that she felt relieved that he'd asked it.

She brought Blake to the sofa and sat him on her lap. 'Interesting question,' she said. 'And you know, I'm not sure I will. Although I will say that I have enjoyed some time to myself. I think I needed a break too. Though I would quite like it to have been me having the break in paradise!'

'Hmm.' Joel tented his fingers and appraised her over them.

'Hmm, what?' she smiled.

'I just find it really interesting.'

'What?'

'The whole set-up. You, your single-mother persona, your artist partner, the mojo-hunting. It just makes me wonder about stuff, that's all.'

'What kind of stuff?'

'Well, the nuclear family, the truth of it. I suppose I've always seen myself as set apart from that kind of normality, I've always been the outsider, the single dad. And I've made assumptions about the people I've seen doing things the conventional way, that they've had it easier than me, that they're somehow, not superior, but just kind of elevated from me. The dichotomy, that life would be easier if I lived with the mother of my child, but that also it wouldn't be as challenging, as interesting, that somehow my experience of parenting is more *valid* than yours because I've got all these issues. But you're making me question all that. You know, you've got the house, the two kids, the nice little family-of-four thing going on. Except it's not as perfect as it looks, is it?'

Jem smiled. 'No,' she said, 'it's not. And there are times when I wonder if it wouldn't be easier if I did it by myself. I mean, this week, for example. It's been a revelation. It took approximately twenty-four hours to get used to him not being around. Because really, and this is a hard thing to say, but really, even when he is there, he's not. You know?'

Oh, my husband doesn't understand me. Jem checked herself. That was enough personal stuff. She was giving this stranger too much. It felt dangerous and strangely disloyal.

'You mean, he's not there, emotionally?'

'Oh,' she tried to shrug it off, 'it's not that. It's just, men, you know, they always manage to find ways of being busy that don't involve doing anything remotely useful. I don't suppose he's much different from anyone else, just that when there's a new baby around it sort of *magnifies* everything. All the discrepancies. You know.'

Joel smiled knowingly, having clearly picked up on her sudden defensiveness. 'All men are useless,' he intoned.

'No. No, it's not that. I don't subscribe to that, just that there is this weird thing that happens when two people who are equal in every way except their gender procreate. There's this sort of primal separation, this kind of caveman thing that kicks in, and the man just suddenly thinks it's OK to let the woman do eighty per cent of the work.'

'Oh God, now you're making me wish I was married!'

Jem laughed. 'No, but it's true and it's not just me. It happens to nearly everyone I know and, as my sister said, you either fight it or get used to it. I suppose I've got used to it. But this week apart, it's been, well, it's been interesting. I think things are going to have to change when he gets back.'

'Well, maybe he'll have changed when he gets back. Maybe that's part of the reason he went?'

Jem shrugged. 'We will see,' she said, 'we will see.'

'And when is that? When is he coming back?'

'Saturday morning.'

Joel nodded. 'So, two more days of solitude.'

141

'That's right. Two more days of coping on my own without hating anyone for it.' She glanced at Joel, who smiled at her questioningly. 'I guess you're used to that then?' she asked.

'Yes. But then, I've only got the one. And I've been coping on my own since day one, pretty much, so never had to hate someone for not being more helpful.' He smiled and Jem laughed.

Blake was growing increasingly wriggly on her lap and as much as Joel had just offered her the perfect opportunity to ask about Jessica's mum, Jem really had to deal with her baby and, dealing with her baby, she increasingly recognised, would require giving him a feed. She'd been expecting this, she'd known that at some point while she was here Blake would get hungry and that she would have to reveal a naked breast in the presence of a strange man, but now that it was actually turning into a reality she was losing her nerve.

Breastfeeding had been a revelation to Jem, something she'd never envisaged herself doing, something she'd undertaken purely because as a middle-class mum in a certain London postcode it was somehow *expected* of her, and something she'd taken to so naturally that she'd never questioned it for a moment. Before she'd had children she'd been of the opinion that breast-feeding was something very personal and, like other bodily functions, should be conducted somewhere private. But from the moment she'd taken the infant Scarlett out in public for the first time she'd known that unless she wanted to spend her entire life in a branch of John Lewis, that was neither practical nor desirable, and anyway, she felt utterly unselfconscious about it. But this, this was awkward. There was sex in this room. Not blatant sex, but quiet, surreptitious sex, twitching and tugging at the corners of their conversations, ruffling the still air like gentle fingertips through a calm pond, and now, at the prospect of an unclasped bra, an unleashed breast, the sound of her young son taking from her body, Jem froze.

'I, er, I need to feed him. Is that OK?'

Joel gazed at her for a moment, not sure what she was asking. A second later he worked it out. 'Ah, right, yes, of course, go ahead. I'll go and check on the girls, give you some privacy.' He smiled and left the room.

By the time he came back five minutes later, Jem was neatly arranged with a baby at her breast, her scarf covering the top of her breast, her baby covering the bottom, and Blake was fast asleep.

She smiled at Joel. 'How are they getting on?'

'Brilliant,' he said. 'Something to do with stickers and reward charts. I *think* Jessica might just have tried to put Scarlett in the naughty corner but she wasn't having any of it.'

'That sounds about right,' laughed Jem.

'More wine?' he asked.

Jem looked at her empty glass and her sleeping baby. She wouldn't have to feed him again now for a couple of hours, she *could* have one more, and suddenly she really, really did want another one. Her baby was asleep, her big girl was playing happily, the sun was going down and there was no rush to get home, nobody waiting for her, nobody to explain to where she'd been and what she'd been doing. She could relax. She could get to know this shabby, bright, mysterious and oddly attractive man in an adult, slightly reckless way. She could even flirt and get pink-cheeked and let him tease her. They could talk into the early evening. Maybe he would move from his eyrie on the old swivel chair across the room and share the sofa with her. Maybe they'd accidentally touch. Maybe they'd start to reminisce about their youths, about their half-travelled lives, their histories, their mistakes, their goals, their dreams. Maybe she'd have a third glass of wine.

And maybe something would happen here today that could never be physical but could be something even more powerful. And it all hinged on another glass of wine.

'Yes,' she said, holding out her empty glass. 'That would be lovely.'

Chapter 11

The last time Ralph had been in a church was, predictably, for a friend's wedding. Churches tended to lose some of their 'churchness' when filled with non-believing thirty-somethings and their offspring. They felt more like holding centres, departure lounges, somewhere to wait awhile before escaping, somewhere stripped of anything godly or ethereal. It was almost as if, sensing the approach of a wedding party, God packed a small bag and left through the back door, muttering something about coming back when it was all over.

As a child Ralph had been taken to church every Sunday, 10.45 a.m., the same vaguely sticky pew, the same indigo-blue hymn books, the same overlarge family to their left, the same baggy-faced man in a cassock talking about the same improbable parables and biblical anecdotes in the same slightly camp voice. Ralph had never felt anything but boredom and resentment in church as a child. This was the first time he had been, willingly and for no good reason, to a church since he was fifteen years old.

Rosey's church was out of town, along the coast, a small clapboard building that wouldn't have looked out of place on a prairie. The car park was empty. There was no service. 'I don't like services,' she explained. 'I just like to sit there. On my own.'

Ralph shrugged awkwardly. 'You should have said . . .' he began.

'No, I don't mean *all on my own*, I just mean not as part

of a crowd, all that standing up and sitting down and standing up and sitting down. And then, Christ, even worse, all that singing and hallelujah-ing and Jesus-ing. Not to mention the God-awful *clapping*.'

'Listen,' he began tentatively. 'About last night. I'm really sorry. If I embarrassed you.'

'Embarrassed me?' she asked.

'Yes,' he said. 'I was very drunk and I think I might have been, well, overly complimentary, let's put it that way.'

'Christ, yeah,' said Rosey, turning to smile at him. 'There's nothing I hate more than getting too many compliments.'

'No, I mean, I shouldn't have. It was . . . *inappropriate*.'

'It was fine, Ralph,' she said, opening the car door. 'Really. It was sweet. And if you did want to paint me, well, I certainly wouldn't say no.'

Ralph smiled. 'I wish I could,' he said, 'but only two more days.'

'True,' she said, swinging a tanned leg out on to the gravelled forecourt, 'but hey, you could do me from memory.' She winked, and Ralph smiled.

Ralph followed her through into a small sunny entrance hall. The walls were painted white and hung with brightly coloured paintings and notices about yard sales and Bible meetings and sewing circles. Two huge patchwork quilts acted as partitions into the main body of the church, each patch hand-crafted by a parishioner and illustrating some small detail about the area. Inside the church, the sun pushed through wide stained-glass windows on to pews carved from pale honey-coloured wood and strewn with multicoloured cushions in shades of green, red and blue. A large gold and red banner hung behind the small altar, embroidered with an image of Jesus holding his hand to his bleeding heart, his other hand held out towards a dove. There was no gloomy organ music, no dry coughs, no gluey stench of incense and burning candles, just the sun, light and clear, the salty whisper of a sea breeze through the open door, the sense of something living and breathing.

'Can you see why I make the journey out here?' Rosey asked him. 'It's a cute little place, eh? Got something a bit special about it.'

Ralph sat down next to Rosey and, without even thinking about it, he closed his eyes. He let the background noise come to him. Small birds. Early evening cicadas. A moped turning a corner. The ocean. Rosey's steady breathing. The blood going through his head. And somewhere out of sight, to the side of the altar, a man clearing his throat, the chink of a coffee cup. He glanced at Rosey, took in her remarkable profile. Her eyes were closed and her head was slightly bowed. He remembered her touching her fingertips to her lips after their kiss last night. He wanted to touch her lips too, to echo her gesture and bring it back to life, but he knew deep inside that he wouldn't and that he couldn't. He ached for the need to hold her and explore her but he never would. There was too much at stake.

Instead he let his chin drop into his chest and then he found himself doing something remarkable; he found himself praying. It seemed so obvious all of a sudden. He was a man with issues, a man feeling lost and directionless and here he was in a place, small, bright and still, where he could not just dwell on his state of mind but almost open a tiny door in his head and see what happened. And what happened was quite extraordinary.

As the silence drew out and Ralph's contemplation expanded into reverie, Ralph found himself talking to someone. It was not a conventional conversation, mainly because it was happening inside his head and because there were no words involved, but it had all the cadence and rhythm of conversation, the speaking and the listening, the pauses and the intonations. There were no questions and answers, just needs and silent reassurance. It was like having a massage, as though someone were silently kneading all the knots out of his psyche. It was a strange, gentle, overwhelming catharsis and through this odd jumble of emotions and sensations he felt something else: Rosey's hand curling around his on the pew between them. He opened his eyes and stared first at their entwined hands and then at her in surprise.

'Are you OK?' she whispered.

'Yeah,' he nodded.

'You sure?'

He nodded again and then realised, as he felt a wetness around his nostrils, that he was crying. He breathed in deeply, keen to take away the unexpected tears, but it was too late.

'You wanna talk about it, or would you rather just be?'

He smiled, pathetically, gratefully. 'I'm OK,' he said. 'I'm just, you know, it's OK. It's OK.'

She squeezed his hand one more time and then moved her hand back into her lap.

He glanced at his hand and then he shut his eyes, squeezing back deeply against the tears that he couldn't control. He tried to analyse this sudden onset of emotion, tried to work out where it had come from. What had been the trigger? And then he realised. It was just now, while he was praying, communing, contemplating, whatever the hell it was he'd been doing, he'd suddenly realised that everything was going to be all right. It was easy! All he had to do was to take himself out of the centre of absolutely everything. All he had to do was to surrender. Surrender himself to Jem, surrender himself to his family and surrender himself to his existence. But, in order to do all of that, first of all he needed to surrender himself to something else entirely, and he wasn't sure what that was, but he'd felt it just now and he thought, yes, he really did think, he could barely bring himself to formulate the

148

concept, but it was there, it was real and he thought it might be God.

No! Not God! He shook the idea from his consciousness the second it started to implant itself. Not God. But something. Something bigger than just a one-syllable word, or a stupid bearded icon. Something wider and heavier and lighter and kinder and deeper and just better. He opened his eyes and stared into the eyes of Jesus Christ, picked out in lustrous silk stitching above the altar. No, he thought. It wasn't him. He turned to look at the images on the stained-glass windows, the birds and the butterflies, the trees and the faces of children. It wasn't even them. It was almost as if a voice that had been living deep inside him all his life was finally making itself heard. It was almost like discovering the truth of himself.

He turned to look at Rosey and realised with a start that she wasn't there, that he was all alone. He looked behind him and was about to leave the church when he noticed a row of votive candles on a wooden stand. Like everything else in this quirkily unconventional church, they were brightly coloured, flickering like jewel-coloured fireflies trapped in glass jars. There was a money jar on the stand and Ralph felt inside his jeans pockets for a handful of loose change. He dropped the coins, clink, clink, clink, then lit a candle for himself. He chose a blue jar, because the candle was for Blake. He stared into the dancing blue light of the candle and he thought about his boy. He imagined the smell of him and the unformed feel of him in his arms, and for the first time he felt something primal inside him start to unfold its arms and its legs and slowly make itself known. For the first time he felt like Blake's dad.

Suddenly there was a man in the room. He'd appeared from behind the altar, clutching a mug of coffee. He was small and wiry, dressed in a turquoise Hawaiian shirt and three-quarter-length trousers. Even though he wasn't wearing a dog collar it was entirely without question that he was a priest. He smiled broadly at Ralph and then stopped for a moment. Ralph smiled back at him.

'You got everything you need?' the man asked.

Ralph shrugged. And then he smiled. 'Yes,' he said, feeling the full meaning of the question and of his answer. 'Yes. I have. Thank you.'

'Great.' The priest winked at him and then carried on through to a door on the other side of the altar.

Chapter 12

'No,' said Karl. 'No fucking way.'

Jem sighed. She was halfway through a ham and mustard sandwich, which she'd been thoroughly enjoying, but at his words she let it fall to the plate. She wished that Karl were her child, she wished that she could just say, 'Because I said so,' and that that would be the end of it. But Karl was not just an adult, he was also an incredibly stubborn adult, an adult who did not know what was best for him and had no interest in anybody else's opinions on the matter. She sighed again and turned to face the back door.

'Karl,' she said, in her best agenting voice. 'I know it has certain . . . *negative* associations, but you have to think about the bigger picture. Think about Tony Blackburn . . .'

'Well, *exactly*,' he boomed. 'I mean that fucking comparison has been haunting me for long enough as it is. The last thing I want to do is to draw attention to it yet again.'

Jem didn't like to say that she doubted anyone remembered the brief flurry of press reports about his public meltdown on the airwaves of All London Radio all those years ago and that actually it was unlikely that anyone remembered that Tony Blackburn had ever been on *I'm a Celebrity* now anyway, and that really Karl's fame was so ephemeral and so indefinable that it barely mattered either way.

Instead she said: 'We won't let that happen. It was a long time ago. The world's moved on. You are more than just the bloke who did a Tony Blackburn. The public do not see you that way any more.'

'Yeah, and that's half the problem. How do they "see" me?' And will being bombarded with me and my big fat hairy arse on the telly for two fucking weeks make them want to see me ever again? I don't think so.'

Jem tried to push the image of Karl's big fat hairy arse from her mind and concentrate on the job in hand. 'Look,' she said, taking her voice down a notch from businesslike to friendly, 'I personally think that, a) you will actually enjoy it, and b) it will do wonders for your profile. You're a great guy. You're likeable. You could even win it, you know?' And this she actually meant, because Karl, for all his faults, did have a very agreeable demeanour and a gentle vulnerability that drew people to him.

'Pah!' he guffawed disdainfully. 'Yeah, *right*. Look, anyhow, let me think on it. I have to say, I fucking *hate* the idea, but just for you, my little duck, I will think on it. OK?'

'Fine,' she said, her eye drawn back to her ham and mustard sandwich. 'Thinking. That's a good start. But don't think too long, OK, we don't want them to go off the boil.'

'I'll be in touch,' he said, and then he hung up, not because he was rude, but because Karl was partly 1940s tobacco-chewing, plaid-shirt-wearing maverick cowboy, and Jem didn't suppose that they ever said goodbye in the Westerns.

Jem exhaled, glad that that was over and that, all things considered, it had gone rather well. If he had agreed that readily to giving it some thought then there was a higher than average chance that he would say yes. She picked up her sandwich and finished it with a renewed appetite.

* * *

When Blake awoke from a nap thirty minutes later, Jem looked out of the window and decided that since, for the first time in more than twenty-four hours, it was not raining, she would celebrate by going for a walk. She changed him and zipped him into his fleecy suit and strapped him to her front, with his face fronting forwards instead of into her bosom, as he would be watching, not sleeping. Jem had a peculiar aversion to prams or buggies or pushchairs or whatever it was that she was supposed to call them nowadays but could never quite be sure. They were such cumbersome, unattractive pieces of equipment, even when tarted over by famous fashion designers, and they just lent something dowdy and beaten-down to her whole demeanour.

She pulled on her parka, grabbed an umbrella, just in case, and headed for the nearest shops. One of the things that Jem liked best about the high street where they lived was that there was absolutely nowhere for her to spend her money. Unless she were to develop a serious plantain habit or an addiction to cheap plastic storage boxes, her hard-earned cash was safe. So heading for the shops generally meant bypassing a couple of dozen entirely unappealing retailers on her way to Tesco. But today, with a spring in her step and a rush of something youthful and rather silly to her head, she decided to venture further afield. She decided on a whim and fancy and a spritz of spontaneity to go to Sainsbury's instead. They had just refitted it and it had reopened last week with a bit of a fanfare so it almost but not quite constituted a treat. She smiled as she walked. The sun was low in the sky, lighting the tops of the shops and the buildings she passed like a thick layer of golden icing. Where it fell on the road between the parades it sparkled off hubcaps and windscreens and rippled across this morning's puddles. The sudden cessation in the rain seemed to have cheered everyone she passed, and she and Blake were the recipients of at least eight separate smiles as they walked down the road.

Jem had not felt this happy in a long time. In fact, feeling this happy now had made her suddenly and startlingly aware of how not happy she had been feeling before. She could not quite pinpoint the precise source of this happiness. She knew she'd come upon it yesterday at Joel's flat and she knew it had something to do with him, and with the way the light had fallen in the room and the way her head had softened with wine and the way Joel had smiled at her, his mouth half-covered with his hand and the way she'd felt when she looked at his feet.

His feet.

She tried not to think about his feet.

But there it had been, something gentle and magical, something almost, but not entirely, unexpected.

The girls had played among them after tea and the conversation had not quite returned to the earlier more intimate subjects. They talked about the area, about which schools they were hoping for for their girls and about Jem's job. It was neutral, it was safe but it was also the nicest time Jem could remember having in over a year. This, she'd thought, this is what it should be like in my house. A family, sitting together, talking kindly, in sweet harmony. When had she and Ralph stopped talking nicely to each other, she'd wondered. She was equally to blame as Ralph for the poor levels of general communication in their home. More so, perhaps, as she often felt the need to express her frustration with the status quo obliquely, in the way she assembled her responses and in her tone of voice, wanting Ralph to feel constantly aware of his shortcomings. She also felt, subconsciously, that if she spared the time to talk to him nicely she might mistakenly give him the impression that she had the luxury of time. She did not want Ralph to think that she had time.

154

If he thought she had time to be nice to him, he might think that her life was not over-burdened with mind-numbing domesticity and that he was not doing anything wrong in allowing the situation to continue unchecked. This realisation had strengthened her suspicion that yes, at its roots, everything really was Ralph's fault, even her own bad behaviour. He had created her. He had made her this way.

She'd had one more small glass of wine and then at nearly seven o'clock they'd finally pulled on their coats and headed towards the front door. And it was while she was standing there that Jem noticed a photo, pinned to a cork board. It was a black-and-white shot of Joel and a very thin, very pretty woman, both gazing into the eyes of a tiny newborn baby.

'Is that? . . .'

'Yes,' said Joel, 'that's Paulette, and that's Jessica, when she was, oooh, about ten days old. My son took it.'

'It's lovely,' she said.

'Yes.' He looked at it for a moment and his face took on an unsettling hardness, as if he was holding something back; sadness, anger, it was impossible to tell.

Jem gazed at the photo a moment longer than was strictly polite. She was trying, subconsciously, to get a handle on this woman, to work out how she had gone from this clearly besotted young mother to someone who had so many problems that she could no longer be a part of her daughter's life. 'Does she live locally?' she asked.

'Yeah,' said Joel, 'not far.'

'But you don't see her much?'

'No, not really. It's, well, it's complicated.' He smiled apologetically, as if he wished he could tell her all about it, but not here, not now.

Their parting had been rushed, neither of them clearly having given any thought as to how they were going to conclude their shared afternoon. Jem had said something vague about the possibility of returning the favour some time, and then they'd left. Jem had walked her two children home through the dark wet night, thinking that motherhood plus slight inebriety was always a perfect mix.

Sainsbury's was all aflutter with orange balloons, and a small jazz band fronted by a black woman in an evening dress played outside. Blake's feet twitched against her abdomen in excitement at the sound of the music and she stood for a while with him, letting him watch. And it was while she was watching that she had an idea. Tomorrow night was her last night alone. On Saturday Ralph would be back, and once Ralph was back she needed to start finding answers to her dilemma. Did she want Ralph to change? Did she need to change? And even if both of them changed, would they ever be able to get back to the place they'd once been? And if it turned out that they couldn't, that they were stranded for ever in this uncomfortable, uncompanionable place, then would she maybe find happiness with another man? Or was that just a silly, immature fantasy? She was fairly certain that she didn't want to have an affair with this man but needed one more chance to be sure of that.

She pulled her phone out of her pocket and began a text message.

'Hello! Thanks so much for yesterday. Scarlett had the best time EVER and won't stop talking about Jessica! It's my last night of single motherhood tomorrow, wondered if you wanted to help me celebrate with a curry and some beers at our place. Maybe 6ish, keep the girls up late? Let me know and I'll give you the details. J.'

She was about to press the Send button when she drew in her breath and paused. Now, she thought to herself, this is no longer a story of fatal attraction. There is no longer some inexplicable force beyond my control dictating the rhythm of this thing. If I press Send then I am being utterly proactive, if I press Send then anything that happens after this point will be something I created and something that I will have to take full responsibility for.

She breathed in again and then saved the message in her drafts folder. She wanted to think through the possible implications of her actions for a while longer, be sure she was doing the right thing.

Sainsbury's had been turned upside down, at right angles to its former self. It was most disconcerting and as much as Jem did not want to be the sort of crotchety middle-aged woman who complained when the layout of her local supermarket was tampered with, she did think turning an entire shop upside down was a bit uncalled for. But as she wandered the aisles she began to see the benefits. Cookware. Babygros. T-shirt bras. Quality toys. Books. A whole aisle for stationery.

In the food aisles she noticed new lines, more choice and there, the sign she always felt, for some unknown reason, of an impeccably stocked supermarket – a Thai Curry Kit.

She picked it up and gazed at it in wonder. It was all there, neatly compartmentalised. Two sticks of lemongrass, already truncated into stumps and starting to brown slightly at the ends, but lemongrass none the less. And a fan of glossy lime leaves. A small bunch of coriander. Bald, peeled shallots, pink and translucent as newborn mice. And five shiny chillies in red and green.

There had been a time in her life, before Ralph, before babies, when Jem had spent an inordinate amount of time in Asian supermarkets. Her agency's offices were in Soho and her lunch hours were more often than not spent in Chinatown exploring the aisles and the counters for weird and delicious things with which to concoct weird and delicious meals. Back then she'd have spat on this sterile, film-wrapped parody of authenticity. Back then she'd have felt nothing but pity for a person picking this up and paying for it and thinking that they were doing something somehow exotic and daring in doing so. Back then she'd sooner have had a plain cheese sandwich than have cooked a meal with one of these. But now, her horizons were smaller, her life was confined to her London village. The thought of buggies and nappy changes and buses and children and tubes and the hustle and bustle of Chinatown, well, it was not an appealing prospect. On the rare occasion that Jem ventured into town these days it was either on business or to meet friends, never just to idle away the time, never just to absorb the city. Jem was a very different sort of Londoner these days.

She sighed, silently, and placed the pack in her basket. She and Ralph had bonded over food. To be more precise, she and Ralph had bonded over the making of a curry. Jem had taken pity on the high-salt, low-flavour, extremely expensive ready-meal diet of her flatmate and one night had shown him how to cook a simple chicken curry. There had then followed a slightly drunken, slightly stoned encounter with a packet of raw chillies, which had ended with Ralph's head in the freezer and both of them high on the adrenalin of burning mouths.

If Jem were to look back on her eleven years with Ralph, as though it were a bullet-pointed timeline, that night would have been one of the key and utterly pivotal points. If that night hadn't happened then it is very likely that none of what came afterwards would have happened either. If it hadn't been for the cooking of that curry and the eating of those chillies, there would have been no Ralph and Jem, no Scarlett and Blake and no festering, mouldering, dysfunctional long-term relationship to fix. Ralph had not phoned since their terse phone conversation the previous morning and his last words to her 'something has got to change' still rang in her head. *Something's got to change.*

Yes, something *did* have to change. Starting with her.

Jem decided there and then that she would cook a curry for Joel. Not to impress him and not to seduce him but just to remind herself of the girl she'd once been. She positively rampaged from aisle to aisle then, filling her basket with chicken breasts, with cans of coconut milk, with miniaturised aubergines and with clutches of Tiger beer. In her absolute certainty about what she was doing she failed entirely to add a much-needed roll of tin foil to her basket, or the two-pack of kitchen roll or the four-pint bottle of organic full-fat milk that she actually needed. In her slightly unhinged mood of urgency she sailed past the Shreddies and the fresh bread and the Dove deodorant. She was growing an evening in her shopping basket. It was all there from the Red Thai Curry flavoured Kettle Chips to snack on while she prepared the meal, to the chocolate truffles she would bring out afterwards as though her larder always held a spare box of chocolate truffles.

Before anything happened to defuse her conviction, she pulled out her phone, opened up the draft message and pressed Send. There. It was done. The ball was officially rolling, and it was rolling straight towards his court.

She headed towards the brand-new self-serve checkouts, thinking that it might be fun, thinking that Blake might enjoy the sparkling red laser light, the chirruping of the scanner over the barcodes. *Beep* went the chicken, *beep* went the coconut milk, *beep* went the Kettle chips, but as she passed the Thai curry kit across the glass panel there was no *beep*. She checked the screen: 'Unexpected item in bagging area.'

She smiled to herself. It was almost as if the machinery knew.

Unexpected was an understatement.

Chapter 13

Ralph spent his last day in California on the beach. Alone. Smith would be joining him here at four o'clock, after his last appointment of the day. But for the next four hours it would be just him, a beach towel, a book and the sand. Ralph felt slightly self-conscious as he sat there, his pale English body glowing like a silver-birch in a forest of glossy teak.

Ralph sat for a while, his arms wrapped around his knees, and stared into the ocean. It glittered beneath the midday sun as if it had been laced with fairy lights. In the distance he saw small white boats and the trailed foam of jet skis. To his left was the Santa Monica pier, gaudy and loud, even from this distance. He contemplated the last six days. He remembered his thoughts before leaving home, what felt like a month ago now, how little he knew about Smith and his lifestyle, how hard he'd found it to imagine being right here. And now here he was, on the beach, a person in Santa Monica, a person who had been here, who knew it, who could navigate their way round town, who could picture the inside of Smith's apartment, who had felt the rhythm of his days, been inside his car, got to know his girlfriend, eaten from his fridge. The experience was complete. The nebulous concept was now fully upholstered. And what could he take from these strangely peaceful, uneventful few days?

Well, for a start he could go home safe in the knowledge that the only thing now keeping the long and unillustrious connection between himself and Smith alive was purely that – the sheer length of their association. There was the fact of Ralph's state of semi-conflicted fatherhood and Smith's state of happy and enduring childlessness. And there was the fact that Smith and he simply didn't have much to say to each other, a state that is fine when sharing a home, but awkwardly jarring when trying to socialise, and Ralph knew that things would settle back into the pattern of occasional two-line e-mails about nothing in particular the moment he returned to English soil.

But this trip had never been about him and Smith having a Good Time Together, this trip had been about something much more tenuous than that. It had been about finding answers and even before that it had been about finding questions, because before he got here he really had had no idea at all what it was that he needed to know.

For a moment on Tuesday night he'd thought he'd found what he needed. He'd thought it was Rosey. He'd thought that if he could make a beautiful young woman with creative rather than reproductive preoccupations fall in love with him, if he could be set free to start life over again with someone fresh and sharp and bright and cool, someone like Jem used to be, then maybe he would remember what it was all about. But that had been a red herring. He had very strong feelings for Rosey. He wanted to have sex with Rosey. If he was going to run away and have an adventure and leave all his commitments behind then Rosey would be just the woman to do it with. She was beautiful and bright and fresh, and all those other things, but she wasn't the mother of his children. Ralph didn't need another woman, he just needed to work out how to make the one he already had like him again. And now, he knew how to do it.

He hadn't spoken to Jem since their fractious phone conversation on Wednesday morning. When he was awake she was either asleep or looking after children, and trying to talk to Jem about anything of any importance when there were children in the room with her was completely impossible. And besides, this was not a conversation he wanted to have on the phone from five and a half thousand miles away, this was a conversation for the two of them on Saturday night, face to face over the kitchen table and possibly a bottle of wine.

The day passed dreamily for Ralph. He knew it would be a very long time indeed before he could sit on a beach alone again. He read his book, he lay on his back in the sun, letting the hot beach play its auditory tricks with the sounds around him, the hazy drone of strangers' words, the dreamy hum of traffic on the road behind him, the occasional shard of laughter or the horn of a car.

At four o'clock Smith joined him and they passed the early evening in gentle talk, about nothing in particular. Rosey didn't join them that last night. She was out with friends, and Ralph was glad. He wanted to keep his head clear on this, his last night away from home. He wanted to empty his head of everything except his determination to make things better at home. He felt alive and clean, he felt ready to do whatever it took to be a better husband and a better father.

They moved from the beach to a casual beach bar where they sat with their shoes full of sand and their skin sticky with the last application of sunscreen. Ralph's face felt tight and rough, his hair felt like straw, and for the first time since he'd arrived six days ago, Ralph felt completely relaxed with Smith.

'You should marry that girl,' he said, a propos of nothing much.

'What? Rosey?'

'Yeah, you should marry her. If you don't, someone else will.'

'Nah,' said Smith, turning a beer mat round on the table-top against its edges. 'She's not the marrying type.'

'I wouldn't be so sure,' said Ralph.

Smith threw him a puzzled look. 'Oh, yeah,' he said, 'and what have you two been talking about behind my back?'

'Nothing much,' said Ralph. 'I just don't think she's as unconventional as you think she is. I think,' he continued, 'it's all a bit of an act. That's all.'

'Well,' said Smith, letting the beer mat drop to the table and lacing his fingers behind his head. 'I am most certainly not the marrying type, so that kind of puts an end to that. And anyway, you're a fine one to talk – what about you? And Jem?'

Ralph smiled. 'I think that bringing two children into the world is quite enough of a commitment to be going on with, but you never know, maybe one day . . .'

Smith studied him for a moment. 'Don't you ever worry?' he began.

'Worry about what?'

'I don't know. You're not married. She's a good-looking woman. Don't you ever worry she might, you know . . . ?'

'What – Jem?'

'Yeah.'

Ralph almost snorted. 'No way!' he said. 'She doesn't even want to have sex with me, let alone someone else. Besides, she's stuck at home all day with two kids. The only people she sees outside the home are her sister, her gay boss and Karl Kasparov. Even if she wanted to . . .' he shrugged, conclusively.

'You need to sort that sex thing out,' said Smith.

'Yeah,' said Ralph, squinting across the beach into the brilliant gold of the lowering sun. 'Yeah,' he said again. 'Lots of things to sort out when I get back. Loads of stuff to do. But thanks,' he held his beer bottle out to Smith, 'thanks for letting me take some time out, thanks for

164

giving me some space to breathe. It's been really . . . useful.'

Smith smiled at him, slightly sceptically. 'Glad to have been of service,' he said. 'And next time you should bring Jem. And the kids.'

Ralph laughed out loud. 'Yeah, right,' he said. 'You'd love that!'

'Why not?' said Smith, simply. 'Just because I don't want kids of my own, doesn't mean I don't want to meet yours.'

'Seriously, mate,' Ralph continued, 'your lifestyle, and my kids . . .' He drew his finger across his throat. 'Not a match made in heaven. But next time you come home, come over. You can see them in their own environment.'

Smith smiled. 'Yeah,' he said, 'I'd like that. That'd be good.'

They both leaned back then, their beers held in their laps, their faces lit by the evening sun, two decent men, no longer best mates, but at peace with themselves and with each other for the first time in eleven years.

And tomorrow, Ralph's life would start afresh.

Chapter 14

Hours before this perfect Californian moment, and over five thousand miles away, Jem had not been giving much thought to tomorrow. Her thoughts were mainly of the next few hours, specifically between *now* (5.55 p.m.) and *then* (roughly 8 p.m.? Possibly even later).

She had had second, third and fourth thoughts about this arrangement from the moment Joel had replied in the affirmative to her text message fifteen minutes after she'd sent it.

She dressed herself carefully in clothes that said, 'Just because I've invited you here under the dark cover of night it does not necessarily mean that I wish to have extra-marital adventures with you,' but would also make him hope that she did. She chose a loose grey tunic, thick black tights and her rip-off Uggs. She looked cute, not foxy. And everyone knew that there was not a man alive who found Ugg boots sexually alluring.

Her hair, on the other hand, she paid more attention to. She pulled it back to reveal the nape of her neck and then plucked curls from the bun with her fingertips, and it was while she was standing in the hallway, distractedly pulling curls from her bun with her fingertips that it occurred to her that maybe she was insane.

Really.

Was this the behaviour of a sound-minded woman? She had only just given birth. She was sharing her bed every night with a tiny suckling babe. She hadn't had sex with her partner for eight months. And her stomach turned into a tongue when she leaned over.

The only rational explanation for any of it was that she was mad. She contemplated herself in the mirror. Did she look mad? She looked tired, but that was normal these days. And she looked pale, but it was April and her skin had not seen the sun for seven months. Her hair looked reasonably controlled. She was dressed in a very pared-down restrained style. She had no food on her, no holes in her tights. She stared deeply into the green-grey strata of her irises. Was there a sign there? Was there an answer in there to the imminent arrival at her own home of a strange man the night before the arrival home of her long-term partner? No, there were no answers in there, just a soft, faded sadness, just a slightly confused woman looking back at her, wondering what the hell she thought she was doing.

She sighed and was about to head towards the kitchen when her phone rang. She picked it up from the hall table and read the ID. It was Karl. So typical of him to phone her exactly one minute before the official end of the working week. She was tempted to let it ring through to voicemail, but then remembered that Karl never left answerphone messages.

'Karl,' she said, smiling at her own reflection in the mirror as if she were smiling at her client.

'Miss Duck. I've had a beer and it's decided me.'

'Oh, yes?'

'Yes. I'm going to frigging well do it.'

Jem watched her face burst into a sunbeam of pure delight. 'Yes!' she said, punching the air with a fist.

'I thought that'd make you happy.'

'God, yes, Karl, that really has. That's brilliant. And I think absolutely the right decision. Not just financially, although obviously, that'll be a boon, but for you, for your career. Well done!'

She heard him laugh wryly. 'I'm still not convinced about any of it, I'll tell you that, and Christ, if they try and make me eat anything that some animal has shat out of I'll be out of there in a flash, but yeah, what the heck, it's a free holiday. And they usually put someone easy on the eye in there, don't they?'

'They do, Karl,' smiled Jem, little knowing as she said it how the words would come back to haunt her, 'they do. So I can phone them, then? Tell them you're a yes?'

'You can do that, Miss Duck. Yes you can. And now you can relax and enjoy your weekend.'

Jem smiled ironically at her reflection. 'Yes,' she said, 'yes. I will. You too. And I'll speak to you next week after I've told the ITV people.'

'That'll be grand. I'll speak to you then.'

And then the line went dead.

Jem smiled and then broke into a spontaneous and rather peculiar happy dance. Scarlett watched her with concern from the kitchen doorway. 'What are you *doing*?' she asked in horror.

'I'm dancing!' she replied. 'Because I'm happy!'

'I don't like it,' said Scarlett.

Jem laughed. 'Why not?'

'Because I don't. It makes me feel wrong. When's Daddy coming home? I want Daddy to come home. Then you won't do funny laughing and dancing any more.'

Jem laughed again, amused by her daughter and her buttoned-up persona but slightly saddened by her inadvertent declaration of the poignant truth of the thing.

'Come on,' she said to Scarlett, 'let's go and put some crisps in bowls for our guests.'

But as she said it the doorbell rang and there was a shadow through the dimpled glass of the door and the sound of excitable girl-child from somewhere out of sight and they were here, their guests, the next paragraph in this slightly odd chapter of her life.

Joel smiled at her diffidently in the doorway. 'I thought, curry, it should really be beer,' he began, handing her a thin blue carrier, 'but then I thought, wine is a nicer thing to bring to a person's home. So I brought both.'

She took the bags from him and let him in, helping him with Jessica's coat, taking his jacket, hanging them against her own family's coats on the coat pegs behind the door.

'Nice road you live on,' he said, rubbing his cold hands together.

'Yes,' she said, 'we like it. Come in, come in.'

Jem had expressed three bottles of milk so would not need to breastfeed Blake until at least tomorrow morning. Jem was not a big fan of expressing (it made her feel like something very slightly less than human, somewhere between woman and cow) and Blake was not a big fan of being bottle-fed. It was not a perfect arrangement and Jem had felt guilty for a moment about making her infant son suckle from a rubber teat just so that she could let her hair down with a man who wasn't his father, but then she'd thought about Ralph, his week of lie-ins and days on the beach, his nights out drinking freely and staying out late, and stopped feeling guilty immediately.

'Can I get you a beer?' she said, emptying Joel's bag of bottled Becks and £8.99 Chablis into the fridge.

'That would be great, thank you.'

She opened two Tiger beers and handed one to him.

The radio in the kitchen was tuned to Xfm which was playing something bouncy and feelgood by Jack Johnson, and there was still some early spring sunshine left in the sky, and the window was open a crack to let the curry smells out. Smith the cat lay curled up on the sofa and in this light, with that soundtrack, with a cold beer in her hand and good news still lifting her spirits, Jem felt something like youthful euphoria pass through her like a seltzer. Yes, she thought to herself, yes, this is all right. This is good. I am glad he came. I am glad he is here.

She smiled and lifted her beer bottle to his. 'Cheers,' she said.

'Cheers,' he said. 'Thank you for having us.'

'It's a pleasure,' she said. 'And I hope you don't mind but I got a bit inspired in the new and improved Sainsbury's and thought I'd cook rather than order out. Are you OK with Thai food?'

'I love Thai food,' he smiled.

'Great! And what about Jessica?'

'Oh, she's eaten already.' He leaned down and smiled at her and she smiled back. 'Hey,' he said, 'why don't you go and say hello to Scarlett?'

She looked up at him and smiled again. 'OK,' she said, losing her uncharacteristic shyness and bouncing over to where Scarlett was still skulking in the corner.

Jem watched as they bonded gently over the cat, both taking it in turns to stroke him very slowly and very seriously.

'So,' said Joel, turning back to Jem, who was slicing up chicken breasts into thin slivers. 'You must be looking forward to seeing your partner tomorrow then?'

Jem smiled grimly. 'Yes and no,' she said. She didn't look up to see how he'd responded to this admission, carried on slicing the pink meat. Realising that she didn't have a clue how to explain her response to Joel she softened. 'No,' she smiled, 'I am looking forward to seeing him. Definitely. It's been a good week, but it's a bit lonely, you know. Well,' she said, slightly apologetically, 'obviously . . .'

'Yes, I think I know what you mean.' He laughed. 'It is lonely living alone, even when you have a child. Lonelier in a way, because you can't get out and find some life to live, you know. You're tied to your child, tied to your home, tied to the routines. And you're just *desperate* for an adult to have a conversation with, even if it's only about getting the drains cleared. You're lucky,' he said, 'lucky to have built-in company.'

170

Jem poured some crisps into a bowl and boiled the kettle for the rice.

'So,' said Joel. 'This is a very nice house you have here.' He glanced around. 'Ralph is not your typical impoverished artist in a draughty garret then?'

Jem smiled. 'Not quite. He was when I met him, and quite literally, in fact. He spent two weeks living in an unheated studio in east London, finished twenty paintings, came home emaciated and feverish. Which of course makes him sound like some kind of tortured genius. Which he isn't. He was just . . . *in love.*'

'With you?'

'Yes. With me. Ha.'

'Wow,' said Joel, 'that's quite something. What girl could resist?'

'Quite,' said Jem. 'I could not. I knew nothing about it until the day the exhibition opened, and there I was, in a room in Notting Hill, surrounded by paintings of myself.'

'Seriously? He locked himself in a garret for two weeks to paint you? Exclusively?'

'Uh-huh. It seems unthinkable now. It seems so long ago, another world, another lifetime, and of course children bring so much to your life, so much joy, so much magic, but they take stuff away too. They take *that* away, you know, that passion that you had for each other. That *madness.* It's like, before the kids were born, the worst thing I could possibly imagine happening to me would have been losing Ralph, you know, getting that phonecall in the night, the knock at the door: "We're so sorry, it's your partner, he's been knocked down, there was nothing we could do . . ." Just the thought of it,' she shuddered. 'And then you have a baby and suddenly you think, Christ, there is something *much much* worse than losing Ralph. My sister said to me, before I had Scarlett, she said: you know once you have a baby, Ralph won't be your baby any more? And I said: rubbish, he'll always be my baby. And she shook her head, very slowly, said: no, he won't. And she was right. It really is just a matter of him having to look after himself now. It's not my job any more. And I think he hates me for it.' She looked up at Joel and smiled sadly. 'Sorry,' she said, 'way too much information.'

'No, no, not at all,' he reassured, 'I suppose if he went away to find himself, he was probably hoping that you would do some soul-searching too.'

'Yes,' Jem nodded. 'Yes. I hadn't thought of that. You're absolutely right. I suppose he did. I've been so busy being cross with him for going and then so busy unexpectedly enjoying him not being here that I hadn't really considered the depths of my soul. I've just been kind of, well, waiting for him to come back, I suppose. Waiting to see what he'll have to say for himself. Anyway,' she continued over-brightly, 'how are you with spicy food?'

'Average,' he said.

'Average?' she repeated.

'Yes. For example, when I'm eating at Nando's I tend to order it medium.'

'You do not!' she exclaimed.

'I do!' he laughed. 'Why, what's so funny about that?'

'Nothing. I just never met anyone who ordered medium in Nando's before! I always wondered why they even bothered making a medium sauce. I thought everyone had it extra hot.'

Joel folded his arms across his chest and eyed her defensively, but with a smile. 'Well, now you know. It's me! The phantom medium peri-peri eater of south London.' He pretended to unmask himself and Jem laughed.

'Well,' she said, 'in this house we like our food very, very hot. So, are you up for the challenge?'

He rubbed his hands together. 'Bring it on,' he said. 'I

will not be known as that wimp who came over for dinner and asked for it medium for the rest of my life!'

'OK,' Jem laughed, and fried the chicken in a wok with two mounds of dung-green paste until it released acrid smoke into the air. Then she added a can of coconut milk and a cup of water and let it all simmer for just long enough to give Blake his bedtime bottle and get him into his pyjamas.

Joel played with the girls while she dealt with the baby, and by the time Blake was in bed and the food was ready, the girls were installed in Scarlett's bedroom, the sun had fully set and Jem was pleasantly drunk. She turned off the overhead halogen lights and set the table.

'This all smells fantastic,' said Joel, eyeing the green curry, the tomato and coriander salad and the pile of fluffy white rice enthusiastically. 'Would it make me sound really quite pathetically tragic if I said that this was the first meal that has been cooked for me in about three years.'

'What, not even your mum?'

'No, not even my mum. She bought herself a microwave in 1990 and never used her cooker again. So this is a real, real treat. Thank you so much.'

'It's a pleasure. It's nice to cook again. I haven't really cooked a proper meal since I was pregnant.'

'So Ralph doesn't get this treatment then?'

Jem grimaced. 'Poor bugger,' she said. 'No. I do try but I just got out of the habit of it because it was too painful for me to stand when I was heavily pregnant and then having a small baby demanding my attention put paid to it after he was born and then, I suppose I've just been lazy. But it's just – I don't know – I do so much already, I just resent having to add something else to my infinite to-do list. I suppose I would have to feel more warmly disposed towards him to want to make the effort and . . .' she stopped. Two Tiger beers and her mouth had found a way of operating without her permission. 'I'm sorry,' she said, 'I'm doing it again. You must think I invited you over here just so I could moan about Ralph, but I really didn't. Anyway. How's the curry, not too hot?'

He was chewing and fanning his mouth the side of his hand. 'Wooph,' he said, 'it is a bit hot. But no,' he swallowed and reached for his Tiger,' it's fine. It's delicious. Really. Not too hot at all.'

Jem looked at his red watering eyes and laughed out loud. 'Are you sure?' she said.

'Yeah!' he exhaled, breathlessly. 'I love it. Honestly.'

Jem smiled at him. She thought about the packet of red-hot Thai bird's-eye chillies in the vegetable drawer of the fridge. There were loads left. She thought about making a suggestion, about taking Joel on in a head-to-head chilli challenge, about recreating the madness and pandemonium of the night she and Ralph had first bonded together over spicy food but she couldn't bring herself to. As distant as she was feeling from her partner of eleven years, and as many unresolved issues as they still had to deal with, that would not be right. That would, in some strange way, be worse than physical adultery. Instead she opened the lid on her third Tiger beer and changed the subject. 'So, I hope you don't think I'm being incredibly nosy, and just say if you'd rather not talk about it but – Jessica's mum? What the deal with that?'

She looked up at him, to gauge his reaction.

'Ah,' he said, 'yes, well, that's some story.'

'I mean, you don't have to, if you don't want to . . .'

'No, it's fine. It's just, it's a bit messy, a bit depressing. If you're OK with messy and depressing?'

'I am,' she nodded.

'Well,' he put down his spoon for a moment and picked up his beer, 'Paulette and I, God, we were a car crash. I met her in 1996, so I suppose around the same time that you met your Ralph. She was working as a nanny when I met her, living in this nice little house in Dulwich so I had no external clues as to what she was really like. But, ha! Turns out she was a junkie, turns out she'd been on smack since she was thirteen years old and was down to methadone then, when she was nannying. I mean – a nanny! Who the hell employs some ex-user junkie from Bristol to look after their kids? By the time I found out, I was in love with her and, bleeding-heart arsehole that I am, I thought I could save her. You know, that's my work, saving youth from the folly of themselves. That's what I'm trained to do. Not that she was young – she was, you know, nearly thirty by the time I really knew the score. And once I knew she kind of let it all hang out, lost her job, quit the methadone, back on the smack and expected me to keep the whole act hanging together, and I was this close,' he measured a smudge of space between his thumb and his index finger, 'this close to ending it when she got pregnant. And I thought, yes! Yes, a baby, you know, that's exactly what she needs, exactly what we need, and she was brilliant. Cleaned herself up the minute she found out, did everything you're supposed to do when you're carrying a baby, didn't even have a drink or a can of Coke. I mean, you can see it in that photo, that's why I keep it; it's the only photo I've got of her when she looks like a real human being. Her hair, her skin, her figure. That's the person she would have been if it hadn't been for the smack. And then, well, Jessica came and we did the whole happy family thing for a few months, and then I knew, I just knew, she was back on it. And I would look at our girl, *that*,' he pointed at the ceiling, indicating the rooms above, 'that girl and I just could not understand how anyone with that in their lives could possibly want

175

anything else. Especially, something so, you know, *dirty*, something evil. Why? It didn't make any sense. Anyway. I kicked her out in the end. I didn't want that for our girl. I didn't want that for me. And now she's kind of cut herself off from us. She'll never forgive me for kicking her out and uses that as an excuse not to see her daughter.' He shook his head sadly. 'It's pathetic really. A grown woman. A woman who had everything. And she'd rather have that. She'll end up dead before she's forty.'

Jem gazed at him unblinkingly. 'That's terrible,' she said, somewhat inadequately, she felt.

'It's a nightmare,' he said, his jaw set tight with suppressed anger.

'And there's nothing anyone can do? Nothing to help her?'

'No,' he said, decisively. 'No. It's very simple. You either want to help yourself. Or you don't. Paulette doesn't. It's easier for her to live the way she does than to change. As hard as it is to imagine, she's taken the easy option.' He shrugged. Jem watched him with interest. The cool, soft façade had slipped a bit and she could see someone underneath that she wasn't entirely comfortable with. There was something there in the hardness of his jaw when he talked about his ex, something more than just anger or resentment, it was more like *hatred*. It unnerved her slightly and she cleared her throat.

'Sorry,' he smiled. 'Sorry. I told you. A bad story. Anyway, moving swiftly on . . .'

'No, it's not that, it's fine, it's just really, really sad.'

Joel's face had lost its cruel angles and he looked serene again, gentle and calm. 'Yes,' he smiled, 'really, really sad.'

'And there's been no one else?'

'Nope. Just me. And Jessie. Just us.'

'And you've done it all yourself, all the parenting?'

He nodded.

'Well,' she raised her beer bottle to his, 'in that case, a toast, to you, to Superdad.'

'Well, I don't know about that, but yes, to me, why not?' He grinned at her and they brought their bottles together and as they did so their knuckles whispered against each other, just a touch. Jem waited for her body to process the touch, to react in some way, but it didn't. Joel on the other hand flushed and glanced at her in surprise. And it was then that Jem knew, in that tiny, barely perceptible pinch of time, that she had him. And the moment she knew she had him, it was immediately clear to her that she didn't want him.

She did not want to stand naked in front of him. She did not want his hand against her cheek, her bare flesh. She did not want him to stare at her with longing in a shadowy room. She just wanted to have a nice evening with him. And then she just wanted to go to bed alone, with a clear conscience, and see Ralph tomorrow morning and maybe stand naked in front of him.

But it seemed as though the flimsy, lacy, silly narrative she'd written in the air with the dull ache of her loneliness and the giddiness of her confusion had developed its own momentum. This, she would think when she looked back at this moment as she would a thousand times over the next few months, was the moment at which her baby should have awoken, should have shredded the mounting tension with a plaintive cry through the winking monitor on the kitchen counter. This should have been the moment when the girls came careering helter-skelter into the kitchen all breathless anecdotes or complaining dissonance. This should have been the moment when the phone rang, when the doorbell went, when the roof blew off the house in a freak tornado, when in fact anything at all had happened that might have ended the silence and broken the spell and prevented Joel from opening his mouth and saying: 'And a toast to you too, for this amazing meal, and for making me feel special for the first time in a very, very long time. I'm really blown away by this,' he indicated his food, then he stopped and stared at Jem, meaningfully, 'and by you.'

Jem caught her breath. She smiled. 'Oh, honestly. It's nothing. It's just nice to have some company.'

Joel's face fell into serious lines. 'No, seriously. It's been a long time since I met someone like you, someone so genuine, someone so real. I was starting to get a bit cynical about, well, people in general, but women especially. But you – you're different.'

The smile on Jem's face had frozen. There it was. The declaration. She hadn't heard it for many years now: *You're not like other girls. You're different from anyone I've ever met before.* As a young woman this had been the pattern to Jem's relationships. She would meet a boy. She would like a boy. But the boy would very quickly like her more than she liked him and she would be too polite and too soft to pull out as quickly as she needed to, and then the boy would fall stupidly in love and become very clingy and very needy and she would stick it out until the last possible moment before ending it, usually in a scenario involving tears and, on two separate occasions, threats of suicide. Then she'd met Ralph and Ralph had said: 'You're not like other girls. You're different from anyone I've ever met before.' And Jem had breathed a sigh of relief and thought that it was the first time it had been said to her and not made her feel like she was sinking in emotional quicksand.

But something had happened over the years, and it was clear to Jem that Ralph felt cheated. She was no longer 'different from the other girls' she was just like them. 'You mums,' he would say disparagingly, lumping her into a pot of nagging, shouting, preoccupied women. 'What is it with you mums?'

So, Jem had been primed and ready for someone to see the girl she used to be. And now someone had, and, in a way, she felt pleased: *See, Ralph, it's you that's changed, not me, I am still delightful, I am still special, you just can't see it any more.* But in another way, she was unnerved. She felt transparent, she felt naked. She felt vulnerable and stupid. And more than that, she felt guilty.

She had brought this man into her life, through curiosity, through loneliness, through vanity and yes, through boredom. He was here because she had wanted him to come here and make her feel like the sort of woman that men painted pictures of again. She felt slightly ashamed of herself for using this man to discover what she had already known deep down inside: that there was no other man for her than Ralph. There never had been and there never would be. It was not destiny that had brought this man into her kitchen, it was her, Jem, plain and simple. And now she wanted him gone from it.

She rubbed her elbows with the palms of her lightly sweating hands and stretched the frozen smile a little further. 'Oh, hardly,' she managed. 'Just a mum, just like all the other mums.'

'No,' said Joel, his eyes never leaving hers. 'Not like all the other mums. Better than the other mums.'

Jem flushed and she let her gaze fall to the tabletop. No babies cried. No three-year-old girls appeared. The silence drew out. 'Well, that's very, very nice of you to say. Thank you.'

'No,' said Joel, 'thank you.'

This time Joel looked away first and the moment vaporised gently between them. The clatter of cutlery against crockery filled the air again, the creak of the cat flap, the claws of the cat, click-click-clicking against the wooden floors. Time resumed. Things returned to normal. They could carry on being two parents killing some time together.

It was over.

For now.

Chapter 15

Ralph appraised his front door in the early morning light. His street slept for it was a Saturday morning. Spring had come to his home while he'd been gone. Bead-like buds of pearly white and green adorned the tips of bushes and the trees were starting to show their new leaves. Glancing up he could see that the curtains in his bedroom were open wide. No lie-ins with small children. He imagined the kitchen, Jem in her vest and shorts, her black hair around her face. He imagined Scarlett, chocolate spread around her mouth, her feet in pink slippers. He imagined Blake, in his night-time babygro, bouncing in his chair on the kitchen counter. The TV would be on, they would be watching *milkshake!* Nine o'clock, what would it be, *Jane and the Dragon*? Maybe *Little Princess*? The sounds of a Saturday morning in his home.

He put his key to the lock and he turned it silently. He wanted his return to be a surprise. The air smelled of toast. And of something else, something much more subtle and indescribable, the nuanced and unique smell of home.

'Daddy!' Scarlett saw him first and threw herself around his legs and then into his arms. She wrapped her legs around his torso and her arms around the back of his neck and screamed 'Daddy!' again. Ralph carried her into the kitchen, triumphantly. Jem looked up from the kitchen table where she'd been reading the paper and smiled at him. 'Well, look at you,' she said.

'What?' he said, moving Scarlett on to his hip.

'You're so brown!'

'Am I?' he said, reaching to view himself in the mirror behind the table. 'I didn't think I'd picked up any colour.'

'God, you really have, you look amazing.'

Jem got to her feet and came towards him. She had Blake over her shoulder, where he gnawed pensively on the side of his balled-up fist. Ralph glanced at him tenderly and then at Jem. 'God, I missed you,' he said.

Jem reacted as he'd hoped she would to his words and came to embrace him. Scarlett pulled Jem towards them with her other arm and the four of them stood like that for a moment, smelling each other's forgotten smells, feeling each other's warm breath, absorbing their togetherness. Ralph kissed the top of Jem's head and Jem looked up at him and smiled. 'I missed you too,' she said.

'Did you miss me, Daddy?'

Ralph looked into the dark serious eyes of his daughter and said: 'Every minute of every day. And you,' he said, passing his daughter towards Jem and holding out his hands for his baby boy, 'I missed you too.' He plucked Blake from Jem's shoulder and turned him to face him. He looked different, his skin was less blotchy, his features were more defined and he felt heavier and more solid in his arms. Blake blinked at him in surprise. Ralph laughed and blinked back. 'Yes, indeed,' he said. 'Who is this strange man? Well, I am your daddy and I know you think you managed to get rid of me, but I'm afraid I'm back and you're going to have to share your mummy with me again.' Blake blinked again and then slowly his face collapsed into a grimace of sheer terror and he started to wail, but instead of taking this as yet another sign that his son was not really a part of him, that his son belonged to his mother, Ralph brought his baby towards his body and held him there, held him chest to chest, whispered soothing words into his ear, rocked him gently, whispered in his tiny ear, 'It's OK, little man, it's OK, little man. You don't need to cry, Daddy's here, Daddy's here.' He held the back of his head in the palm of his hand and he let the baby go floppy against his body. 'There,' he said, 'there.'

He looked at Jem. Jem looked at him. They didn't say a word but they both knew. This was a fresh start. This was a new beginning.

'It's great to be home,' said Ralph, his nose buried in the soft, warm scalp of his baby son. 'Really, really great.'

But what neither of them knew was that during their week apart both of them had opened doors into their souls, not very wide, just a crack, but while those doors had been open something had got in, something strong and determined that would eat away at the very foundations of their union until there was almost nothing left to see.

PART THREE

Chapter 1

Jem was very happy to have Ralph back. From the moment she saw him walk into the kitchen with Scarlett in his arms, his skin tanned to a delicate shade of chestnut, in his low-slung jeans and beaten-up leather jacket, looking so relaxed and so handsome and so like the man she'd been in love with for eleven years she knew that she wanted to keep him. She'd known it even before; she'd known it last night at the dining table with Joel. It was blindingly obvious that her attraction to Joel had been nothing more than a blip. It was as clear as light that she would never be able to share either her life or her body with any man other than Ralph. She'd lain in bed last night replaying the memories, the times they'd shared before the babies, the nights she'd lain awake, her nose above Ralph's sleeping head, breathing him in, whispering silently to him, *I love you I love you I love you*, aching for the love of him. She remembered walking down the street, their hands entwined, their arms entwined, always touching, never apart. She remembered – God, she remembered crying after sex. *Crying after sex*. Such a cliché. But still, how many times did a person cry after sex in a lifetime? It all meant something. She thought about how much they'd sacrificed to have their babies, the intimacy, the passion, the fun, more than anything, the fun. She realised that this, what they were going through right now, was nothing more than a page in a book. And then this morning, before Ralph had come home, she'd been gazing into the garden through the kitchen window and as her gaze retreated from the garden and back towards the window sill she'd noticed a small green bulb pushing through from the depths of a potted orchid. The orchid had been a gift from her sister for her birthday about two years ago. At first it had been lush and plump, five fat cream and pink flowers quivering gently from an arced stalk. Over a period of about four months each fat bloom had thinned and lightened and fallen in turn, tissue-light, on to the kitchen counter below. The leaves shrivelled and browned and they too fell away from the orchid until all that was left was a thin brown twig. The orchid was dead.

But now, here was new life. All those months when it had sat there pretending to be dead it was just gathering its strength, biding its time. Before long there would be more leaves, a new arc of plumptious flowers. And as Jem stared at the small green bulb pulsing from the arid remains of the orchid it occurred to her that maybe relationships were like orchids. Just because it looked dead it did not mean that there was not still life in it, it did not in fact mean that the relationship could not be once more spectacular. An orchid could die and grow, and die and grow and every time be transformed to its state of original splendour. So too could her love for Ralph, so too could their union.

Imagine, she'd thought, if she had been more organised, she would have thrown away the potted plant and never known that it still had life. The same of her relationship with Ralph. It had been perfect. It had been everything that Jem could ever have wanted from love and from a partnership. She had not come close in all her thirty-eight years to such perfection. She could not throw it away because it had lost its blooms.

And it was there, when she saw him for the first time, like the ripe green bulb in the plant pot, she knew it was still there. And then when she saw him holding Blake so close and so tenderly she'd felt it again, for the first time in months, in *years*, that dull ache of love for him in the pit of her belly.

She didn't tell him about her week, he barely told her about his. It didn't really seem to matter for now. And that night, of course, they went to bed together and they took off all their clothes and Jem didn't cry but definitely felt, on reflection, that it was a hundred times more fun than roller-blading.

Jem didn't see Joel for nine days after Ralph came back from California. It was almost as if, because she had stopped thinking about him, he had ceased to exist.

For nine days she and Ralph had been on Best Behaviour. They had spoken to each other in Pleasant Voices. They had Hugged in the Kitchen. They had Kissed in the Morning. There had been much Agreeable Conversation and Positive Mental Attitude.

Ralph, who acknowledged that he had the most ground to cover in making amends, had trimmed his working patterns to a more family-friendly shape. He now stayed behind after breakfast to clear the kitchen and spend some time chatting with Jem. He took Scarlett to nursery twice a week and at five o'clock he came down from his studio to have tea with the kids and, on occasion, to start preparing supper for himself and Jem. He went to the gym three times a week and he went to Tesco when it was required, and sometimes he just took Blake out for a walk in his pushchair for an hour so that Jem could get some work done or simply have a bath.

These were all such small things, things that required no physical labour or mental effort, that cut no more than an hour or two a day from his working schedule, but that made such a difference to the rhythm of Jem's days that she felt like a different person. This was what she'd always imagined having kids with Ralph would be like, that they would be a team, a unit, sharing the workload and making sure that they each got what they needed in terms of space and time.

Once, about two years earlier, pre-Blake, when things were better with Ralph, but not perfect, Jem had been walking down Oxford Street on her way to a meeting and had passed a young family. The parents were no more than thirty years old, both very attractive, both very trendy. Between them was a three-wheeler buggy in which sat a sleeping toddler in cool clothes. The couple held one handle of the buggy each, and had their spare arms slung over each other's shoulders rendering the entire family into one solitary, impenetrable slow-moving unit.

Jem had felt oddly depressed at the sight of them. They were breaking the rules! Having convinced herself that it was impossible to maintain that level of affection and intimacy once you had a child, having persuaded herself that nobody was able to stay in love post-babies, she had felt the crutch of self-deception being ripped away from her. There they were, the perfect family unit, flaunting themselves and their intact relationship on Oxford Street for all to see. Look, they were saying, aren't we just the most perfect thing you ever saw, we never say mean things to each other, we have sex every night and our child is being brought up in an environment of tender, intimate love.

Jem had wanted to beat them round their smooth, smug faces.

But now, tentatively, slowly, she was feeling the possibility of that reality for herself. She and Ralph were yet to walk out in public attached limpet-like to each other and their children, and possibly they never would, but the suggestion of that image, the suggestion of such familial harmony – it felt as if it were within her grasp.

Until one warm Monday afternoon, nine days after Ralph's return.

It was three thirty and Jem was at home, trying to word

Karl's biography to send to the ITV people. It was harder than she'd expected as so much of Karl's career was lightweight and meaningless, and trying to find words to give it form and substance was rather challenging. Ralph had taken Blake out to collect Scarlett from the nursery and was due back in ten minutes. The house was silent and empty. Jem decided to take a short break from the laptop and rounded the kitchen counter to fill the kettle for a cup of tea, but as she got there the doorbell rang. Assuming that Ralph had returned early and without his keys she tutted and made her way to the front door. There was a man-shaped movement just visible through the coloured glass and the sound of a small girl's voice. It wasn't quite Ralph, and it wasn't quite Scarlett but Jem opened the door anyway, assuming that her eyes and ears had been deceiving her. And there, on the doorstep, were Joel and Jessica.

Joel grinned at her. 'You live!' he said.

Jem smiled back at him quizzically.

'Hello,' she began, 'I, er . . .'

'Yes, sorry to butt in unexpectedly, just, well, we were passing and I thought, funny how I haven't seen you around lately . . .'

'I know,' said Jem. 'I thought that too. It's been a while.'

'Yes, and, I don't know, last time I saw you, well, anyway . . .' He seemed to have run out of reasons for his presence on her doorstep and looked slightly flustered. 'How are you?' he said eventually.

'I'm great,' she said, wanting him to see without words that she was not the same person she'd been two weeks ago, that things had changed. 'How are you?'

'Yeah,' he put his hand on Jessica's shoulder, 'we're all right. You know. Struggling on.'

Struggling on. Jem wondered at the choice of words. Struggling on. It sounded so . . . hard, so out of keeping with living a reasonably comfortable life in a modern country with all your basic needs provided for.

Sensing the awkwardness, Joel sighed deeply, almost a sigh of deep disappointment. 'Anyway,' he said, 'we were passing. Just wanted to check on you, make sure you're OK. Now that the *Artist's* back.' He ended on a little laugh and Jem found it vaguely offensive. She no longer wanted to share spiky in-jokes about Ralph with a stranger. That wasn't funny any more.

'I am,' she said, 'I'm OK. Everything is OK.'

Joel squinted at her briefly, as though scrutinising her. 'Good,' he said, after a brief pause. 'Well, anyway, nice to see you. Glad you're well, and we'll, er, see you around, no doubt.'

Jem turned up her smile. 'No doubt.'

He guided Jessica away from the door with his hand on her shoulder and Jem was preparing to close the door when he suddenly turned back. 'I saw him,' he said. 'Just now. I saw your artist. I knew it was him because I recognised your baby.'

'Oh,' said Jem, 'yes, right, on his way to collect Scarlett from nursery.'

'Ah, I see. Good,' he said. And then he went.

Jem closed the door behind him and let herself slump against it.

She closed her eyes and inhaled deeply.

Everything about that encounter had been wrong. She felt itchy and awkward. A moment later she heard voices outside the front door and stood up straight, her heart racing slightly. But the voices belonged to her family, to Ralph, to Scarlett. She breathed in deeply and opened the door. 'Boo!' she said.

Scarlett laughed and Ralph smiled. 'What are you doing hiding behind the door?' he said.

'Ah, I was just so desperate to see you all that I decided to sit by the door until you got back.' She kissed Scarlett on the mouth and ran her hands over her curly mop. 'Did you have a nice day?' she asked.

'No,' said Scarlett.

'Oh, why's that?'

Scarlett shrugged dismissively, and headed past her towards the kitchen. 'Can't remember,' she said. 'Can I have a fairy cake?'

Ralph and Jem smiled knowingly at each other. Everything with Scarlett was on a need-to-know basis. 'Who did we just see?' he called out after Scarlett's retreating figure.

'I don't know,' Scarlett called back.

'Just now?' called Ralph. 'About one minute ago. Who did we see?'

'Nobody!' called Scarlett.

Ralph raised his eyebrows in exasperation. 'A FRIEND of yours?'

'I CAN'T REMEMBER!' Scarlett cried out angrily.

Ralph shook his head and smiled, defeated. 'Did we see a girl called JESSICA?' he shouted.

'YES!' snapped Scarlett. 'But it doesn't MATTER!'

Ralph and Jem smiled again. 'Anyway,' he said quietly, 'yes. We just saw a friend of hers called Jessica. Jessica seemed very pleased to see Scarlett, and Scarlett seemed not quite so pleased to see Jessica.'

'That sounds about right,' said Jem, trying to keep her nerves from her voice.

'Who is she? Is she from nursery?'

'No,' said Jem, 'no, they play together at the playground sometimes.'

'Ah,' said Ralph. 'Anyway, her dad seemed a bit ... *strange.*'

Jem looked away. 'Oh, really?'

'Yeah, looked at me really weirdly. Like he thought I was stealing the kids, or something. Like he didn't trust me.'

Jem shrugged and began to unpop the buttons of Blake's sling. 'Probably just never seen you with them before. Probably just thought I was a single mother.' She winked at him so he would know she was only teasing.

'Yeah,' said Ralph, 'probably. Still, funny bloke. I mean, why would he even care?'

Jem didn't answer this question. It didn't appear to require a response and anyway, she had absolutely no idea what she would say.

Chapter 2

As he'd always half-suspected but refused to acknowledge, Ralph was just as productive in his new truncated
days as he had been when he'd allowed himself the luxury
of infinite flowing hours in his studio. He just didn't smoke
as many cigarettes or drink as many cups of tea or spend
as much time on his balcony staring mindlessly into the
distance. Neither did he spend the first two hours of his
working day on his laptop farting around on the internet
or a whole hour at lunchtime reading the *Guardian* online.
Now he started his mornings with a small moment of
meditation and prayer before turning himself towards his
latest canvas and starting to paint.

He was painting some Angel's Trumpets now, from
photos he'd taken in Santa Monica. They were extraordinary flowers, overlarge and unlikely, almost obscene, but
tumbling *en masse* over walls and doors and walkways,
juxtaposed against Californian shades of cobalt and white-
wash and faded prom-night peach, they were magnificent. As Ralph stared at the image on his wall now, in this
watery English light, he could almost smell the warm air
and feel the sticky pavement beneath his feet. But did he
want to be there? No, not now, because if there was one
thing he realised more than anything – and it sounded
corny, but it was true – the only place he really wanted
to be was where his family were, and right now that place
was here, in a small road of terraced houses in London
SE24, in a nice little Edwardian house with original art
nouveau features and a kitchen that needed an extension.

It wasn't glamorous and it wasn't aspirational, it was just a house in a road, but it was his house, his road, his postcode and his family, and until life changed direction and unforeseen moments collided and showed his family a new path to take, then this was where they would stay.

It was a warm morning. Jem was taking Scarlett to nursery. Ralph was going for a run. Running was an activity that Ralph had always viewed with some suspicion. There were three women who ran past Ralph and Jem's bedroom window every single morning at 6.45 a.m. exactly. In the winter months this would occur in pitch-blackness and be utterly unthinkable to Ralph. Why, he wondered, would anyone peel themselves from a warm bed, pull on a pair of leggings and pound the streets in the dark? Even during more civilised hours it struck Ralph as a slightly unnatural thing to do. If an alien were to land in Herne Hill, sit himself at a pavement table outside a café and look around himself at humanity, after a while he might think he had worked out what was going on, and then someone in neoprene would run past, pat-pat-pat, ears plugged with white wires, eyes staring blankly ahead and throw the alien completely off course.

But then spring had happened and the idea of cloistering himself away in the windowless, strip-lit obscurity of the gym had lost its appeal and Ralph had put his prejudices to the back of his mind, his trainers to the pavement and become a born-again runner.

He loved the feel of his feet against the pavement and the music in his ears. He loved the searing coldness of the air being dragged into his lungs and shot out again. And he especially loved the sense of being both part of humanity and yet removed from it by speed, by mission.

He left the house at 11 a.m. that morning, the precise point in every day when his post-breakfast energy levels began to sag, and he turned his face in amazement to the warmth of the sun. Finally the early outposts of summer were staking their ground and Ralph still had most of his Californian tan. He popped his earphones in and switched on his iPod and began to run. Ralph rarely took the same route twice; this part of London was too unknown to him, there was too much to explore. He had not wanted to live here at all when they'd begun house-hunting in earnest five years ago. Jem had dragged him here kicking and screaming and ranting about weird postcodes ('SE24! SE24! We might as well move to Denmark and be done with it!') and proximity to Brixton (You seriously want to raise a family in *Brixton*? Are you *serious*?') and lack of proximity to various friends and landmarks, which had never appeared to be as important to him as when he was threatened with imminent departure from the hallowed ground of Battersea. He'd hated every house she'd brought him to see on pure principle and had agreed only grudgingly to making an offer on the one where they now lived due to the fact of Jem being seven months pregnant and having already moved out of the flat in Lurline Gardens.

As far as Ralph was concerned Herne Hill consisted of a train station, a bus stop, a reasonable branch of Tesco, a playground and the rather uninspiring view from his studio balcony. Even on a fragrant summer's day he'd seen little in the area to move him from his original position that SE24 was the armpit of south London and that moving here had been a Great Mistake and All Jem's Fault.

But now as his feet traced their way randomly through the area he found something to charm him and interest him every single day. An oversized Buddha sitting in the back room of a Vietnamese restaurant, a seemingly disproportionate excess of nail bars, each one packed to the brim with black women of all ages, the clock tower in Brockwell Park that always showed the wrong time, the ornate tiles on the front of the old shops on Milkwood Road. And then today, on this tentative early summer morning, on a curve of the road partially masked by a blooming sugar-pink cherry tree, a small church. Not a church – a chapel. It was a simple building, a pitched roof, two plain glass windows on either side of an arched wooden door, a lintel above the door with the date 1887 engraved into it, a few posters and flyers arranged inside a glass-fronted box.

One of the small wooden doors was ajar and Ralph, even though he was only six minutes into his run, found himself entering the building. It was similar to the church that Rosey had taken him to, just outside Santa Monica, in its simplicity, in its calmness. But where that chapel had been warmed by the ocean breeze and the pounding Californian sun, this small building was chilled to its core by months of London winter.

Ralph pulled the plugs from his ears and switched off his iPod, and then he sat on the third pew from the front. He felt it again, as he had in California, a sense of gladness that he was here, a sense that he was welcome, that he'd been *expected*. He closed his eyes, as he had before, and he let the peace and stillness sit deep within him. But this time as his thoughts focused he knew that he was not here to ask for help. This time he was here to give thanks.

He brought his bunched fists to his mouth and he whispered words into them.

Thank you for Jem.
Thank you for Scarlett.
Thank you for my beautiful baby Blake.
Thank you for my talent.
Thank you for my home.
Thank you for keeping us all safe and healthy.

If someone had walked into the chapel now and asked him what he was doing, he would have been unable to explain. He was not praying. And although he was feeling thankful, he could not easily say that he was giving thanks because that would imply that he was giving thanks to somebody and he was not giving thanks to anybody because there was nobody there but him. Ralph did not believe in God. Ralph was not a man of faith. But Ralph would have to find some explanation for being here, for feeling the way he was feeling, for saying the things he was saying to the thin air of an empty church. What would he say?

He stopped for a moment to consider himself and decided that if someone were to ask him why he was here and what he was doing, he would say this: 'I am letting myself consider the possibility of something else.'

Before he left he lit a candle for his family and then he pushed his earphones back into his ears and resumed his run. He imagined what Jem would have to say about his burgeoning spirituality and realised overpoweringly that he would never be able to tell her. She would freak out. He pounded the streets of south London feeling oddly as if he was nursing a terrible secret.

Chapter 3

Jem brought her head up from the toilet bowl and took a deep breath. She had not been sick but she had thought very strongly that she might be. Her flesh was covered in goose bumps and her face was flushed. This was the third time she had run to the toilet since this morning and the third time she had failed to be sick and she simply did not have the time to be ill. She pulled her hair back from her face and appraised herself in the mirror above the sink. She looked clammy and grey. She shivered slightly, feeling the dread crawl of nausea across her skin.

It did occur to her as she made her way downstairs that she might be pregnant. Having been in a state of early pregnancy four times she was quite familiar with the signs and symptoms, but it didn't add up. First, she and Ralph had had sex only twice since he got back from America, secondly, her periods had still not resumed since giving birth to Blake, and thirdly, they had used a condom. Admittedly they had not utilised the condom until the last possible moment, but then Ralph and Jem had always used condoms like that and they had never, even when they were at it daily, got pregnant accidentally. Each time they had been pregnant it had been as a result of planning and meticulous timing and even then it had never taken less than three months, and in the case of Blake, a full nine months of concerted and scheduled effort. The chance of having conceived by accident, with a condom, while breastfeeding and at the age of thirty-eight was so slim as to be not worth considering.

But still.

She could not ignore the fact that her breasts, which had just settled down from the over-inflated early stages of breastfeeding into a more realistic shape and size, were suddenly tender and swollen again. And that she had a taste in her mouth that was reminiscent of biro ink.

No, she decided, making her way into the kitchen where Scarlett was patiently watching her baby brother, no, it was all too unlikely. And too, too awful possibly to contemplate.

'Did you be sick again, Mummy?' asked Scarlett

'No,' said Jem, 'no sick. Just feeling a bit yucky.'

Scarlett looked at her sympathetically. 'Maybe you'll be sick later?' she said encouragingly.

Jem smiled. 'Maybe,' she said.

Jem strapped Blake to her chest and the three of them made their way over to Lulu's house for tea. It was a mild afternoon and the sky was milky white. The nausea had dissipated and Jem liked the feeling of the soft air against her skin and her little girl's fingers held inside her hand. They walked slowly enough to stop and look at flowers and berry-stained bird poos and a bag of cement left on the side of the road. By the time they reached Lulu's road at five o'clock Jem was feeling a deep sag of contentment in the pit of her stomach and was in just the mood for a couple of hours in her sister's kitchen surrounded by exuberant children and mess.

And it was in this state of mind that she walked round the corner and came face to face with Joel.

'Hello!' she cried, rather too effusively.

'Oh.' He smiled wanly at her. 'Hello.'

She searched his being for Jessica. 'No Jessica?' she asked.

'No. Not today. She's with my son.'

'Oh, right.' Jem smiled brightly. She wanted to ask Joel what he was doing here. This was the second time that their paths had crossed here, outside Lulu's house, and the second time he had been here without his daughter.

'So,' he said, 'this is your sister's place, right?'

'Er, yeah,' Jem muttered, unsure whether it was wise to be furnishing this man with yet more personal information about herself. 'Off for tea!' she said.

'Right,' he said flatly. 'Well, I'd better get back. Don't want to be late for Jess. Good to see you again.'

'Yes, you too!' Jem beamed at him, aware of the fact that she was being rather over-fulsome with her responses.

Jem glanced down at his feet. She looked at his shoes. They were old loafers, slightly stretched out of shape, showing a slice of thin nylon sock. She would not want to see such shoes next to her bed in the morning and she could not imagine why she'd ever thought she would. He saw her look at his shoes, although it was just a heartbeat of a moment and then he looked at her with such a look of contempt that it nearly knocked the breath out of her lungs. He didn't say anything, but just turned and walked away, very slowly, with heavier footsteps than usual.

Jem gasped slightly. The meeting had been short, but as with the episode on the doorstep the other day, alarmingly intense. She took a moment to gather herself and then she knocked on Lulu's door.

Lulu greeted her wearing her wedding dress.

'What the hell are you doing?' Jem exclaimed, her thoughts distracted immediately from the oddness of her recent encounter.

'Well, funny you should ask.' She held the door open for them. 'I was going through some old stuff, getting ready for an eBay sale, saw this hanging there, wondered if I could still get into it, and yay! Look!' She twirled round, yards of antique silk dupion rustling as she did so. 'Look! Fits like a glove. I haven't taken it off since. In fact,' she said, following them through to the kitchen, 'I think I will keep it on until bedtime, see what Walter makes of it.' She winked. Jem smiled tightly. Although she and Ralph had broken their sexual drought, she could still think of at least half a dozen better ways of filling an evening.

Scarlett stared at Lulu in awe, as though she were a fairy princess.

'Mummy,' she said, 'why don't you never wear your lovely dress like that?'

Jem smiled. 'Because, my darling, I don't have a lovely dress like that.'

'Why not?'

'Because Daddy and I have never had a wedding.'

'Why?'

'Because,' she paused for a moment, 'because we've been too busy trying to make our family.'

'Yes, but Auntie Lulu has a family *and* she's got a lovely dress.'

Jem looked from her daughter to her sister and then back again. 'That,' she said, 'is a very good point. You'll need to ask Daddy about this because Daddy thinks that weddings are a waste of money.'

Scarlett's jaw dropped. She was unable at first to comprehend that her perfect Daddy could possibly hold an opinion that she found so repellent. But then she rallied herself and smiled. '*I'll* pay for it,' she said. 'Tell Daddy that I will pay for it. I've got about a hundred pence.'

Jem and Lulu smiled at each other. 'I will,' said Jem. 'I'll tell him tonight.'

'Tea?'

'Yes, please. Decaf if you've got it. But God, be careful with that dress. Don't spill any on it.'

'Oh, why, it's not as if I'm ever going to wear it again. Biscuits?'

'Definitely. I'm starving. You do look beautiful in that,'

she said. 'God, that was such an amazing weekend, wasn't it?' she sighed, thinking back to Lulu's fairytale wedding in Tuscany eleven years earlier, just after she and Ralph had got together, their first holiday as a couple, possibly the two most romantic days of Jem's life.

'And what's new with you?' She shook a packet of Morning Coffees on to a plate and slid it on to the counter in front of Jem.

Jem smiled tightly. There were no secrets at Lulu's house. 'Well,' she began. 'First of all I think I might be pregnant . . .'

'Whooppee!'

'No, not whoopee.'

'Yes, whoopee. If you think you might be pregnant then clearly you and Ralph have got back to business.'

'Well, yes, we have, but if I am pregnant then that means that *I am pregnant*. Which is not even slightly whoopee.'

'Oh, why not?'

'Er, because my existing baby is not even six months old? Because I am still feeding him on demand? Because I do not want three children? And because right now I really think that the most important thing is for me and Ralph to get back on an even keel, you know?'

'Yeah. All right. Fair enough. Though I, for one, would be delighted.'

'Well, yes, of course you would. It wouldn't be you getting stretched out of shape for nine months and then having to push it out of an unfeasibly small hole and then having to feed it every two hours.'

'No, it would just be me giving it kisses and cuddles and thinking how lucky I am to have so many lovely nieces and nephews. And wow, so lovely for Blake to have a brother or sister so close in age. No sibling rivalry.'

'Lulu! I do not want to be pregnant, OK? I do not want to have another baby! If you want another one, then feel free, but leave me out of it!'

Lulu tutted and raised her brow. 'So what'll you do then? If you are?'

Jem shrugged and picked up a biscuit. 'Not have it, I suppose.'

Lulu winced. 'Ooh, really, are you sure?'

'No, I'm not sure. But I am sure that there is no way I am ready for another pregnancy and another baby, so, well ... Anyway, I probably am not even pregnant. It's highly unlikely.'

'But seriously, would you really consider not going through with it, after what you've been through with losing babies in the past? It just seems a bit ...'

'Hard?'

'Well, yes.'

Jem shrugged. 'You know,' she said, 'maybe I have grown something hard in me. I don't know. I love the idea of having another Blake or another Scarlett but God, by the time me and Ralph make it to the Blake and Scarlett stage, I reckon we'll have imploded. Things are so fragile between us right now. I just don't think our relationship could take the stress. I really don't. And then, wow, that'd be nice, I'd be a single mother of *three*. Christ ...'

Lulu appraised her. 'Are things really that delicate?'

Jem considered the question. 'Yes,' she said, 'they are. It's like we're both practising, you know, practising being happy. And the idea is that if we keep practising for long enough it'll just feel natural. It's like, I know now that I love him enough to want to stay with him for ever and I know that I don't want to be with anyone else, but it's baby steps. Things had got pretty bad between us, you know, before he went away, bad enough for me to consider life without him. And now, well, I just really want to focus on life with him. Not life with another baby. People say that a new baby can bring two people back together but new babies seem to have had totally the opposite effect on me and Ralph. It would break us. Trust me on this.'

Lulu nodded her assent, but Jem could tell that she did not really understand. Then she changed the subject. 'And what was the other thing?'

'What other thing?' replied Jem.

'You said "first". What's "second"?'

Jem grimaced. 'Oh God, remember that guy I told you about?'

'The single dad?'

'Yes, the single dad. Well, while Ralph was away we spent a bit of time together . . .'

'You did?'

'Yes. I mean, nothing controversial, just a couple of play-dates. But I think by the time we had our second play-date I'd got myself a bit wound up, into some kind of daft romantic delusion and it's possible that he might have got the impression that I was sort of . . .'

'Interested?'

'Yes, interested. Not that I did anything even vaguely provocative, I really didn't, it was all very above board, just two people killing some time together. And then Ralph came back and I remembered why I liked him in the first place and he's been so brilliant with the kids and helping out around the house and I just stopped thinking about this guy completely, and then last week he turned up on our doorstep.'

Lulu clamped her hand to her mouth and widened her eyes. 'No!'

'Yes. Nothing happened but he was just a bit odd with me, a bit, I don't know, disapproving. I think it was pretty clear that whatever had been going on between us, which was as I say, virtually nothing, was over. And he just seemed a bit . . . *angry* about it. Anyway, he left and that was that but then I bumped into him again. Just now. Outside your house.'

Lulu's eyes widened further. 'What, out there?' She pointed towards the front door. 'Just now?'

'Yes. Literally. He was on his own and it wouldn't be so weird if it wasn't the second time it's happened.'

'You mean you've bumped into this man outside *my house* before?'

'Yes. A few weeks ago. Just after Ralph went away. I was on my way home. He was alone that time too.'

'How weird,' said Lulu, stirring the teapot with a big spoon. 'I mean, it's not as if there's anything on this road. It's a dead end, doesn't go anywhere, and he's hardly going to walk all the way up here for a kebab from the Golden Triangle. Unless . . .'

'Unless what?'

'Well, there's a place on the corner down there. A hall where they have meetings. AA. NA. All the As. You know. I wonder . . .'

'His daughter's mum is a junkie.'

'What!'

'Yes. He told me all about her. They live apart because of it. She doesn't even see her little girl.'

'My God, that's so sad.'

'I know. But now I'm wondering.'

'Yes. It does kind of make sense. Well, it makes more sense than him hanging around outside my house on the off-chance that you might be passing by.'

'Yes,' agreed Jem, 'I suppose it does.'

'You know,' said Lulu, narrowing her eyes at Jem in a way that normally signified that she was about to impart sound but potentially aggravating advice, 'I think you need to draw a line under the Single Dad thing.'

'I have!' cried Jem. 'Totally! It's not my fault he keeps showing up places.'

'Isn't it?'

Jem pinched at some fluff on her cardigan and didn't reply.

Lulu plucked Blake from Jem's lap then, her way of signifying that the conversation was over. She held Blake like a tiny dancing partner and twirled him around the room, her silk skirts scraping the wooden floors, picking up biscuits crumbs and cat hair, her dark shiny hair swirling around her shoulders like a cape. Lulu was the mother that Jem wished she could be – spontaneous, fun, worry-free. Blake stared into her eyes as they spun round, looking slightly alarmed.

'I wouldn't,' said Jem. 'He just had a full feed before we left. There's a high probability he might . . .'

But it was too late. Blake had just been sick all down the back of Lulu's vintage wedding dress.

Chapter 4

Ralph looked at Jem and gulped.

'Seriously?' he said.

'Yes. Seriously.'

'I mean,' he continued, 'you've done the test?'

'Yes,' said Jem, 'I've done the test. I've done the test three times. I am really, properly, officially pregnant.'

'Fuck.' Ralph pulled the palm of his hand down his face and sat on the bed. 'But I don't get it. We used a condom.'

'Yes, I know, but you and I both know that we don't use condoms properly, that we never have done. There has always been a chance of this happening.'

'But I thought, I thought you couldn't get pregnant when you were breastfeeding?'

'Yeah, so did I. But there you go. Clearly I was wrong. We were both wrong.'

Ralph looked up at Jem, who was standing in the doorway holding a towel-wrapped Blake across her belly. He looked so small, suddenly, so fresh and newly arrived. How was it possible that so soon after his appearance in their lives, there could be another on its way?

He took a deep breath and considered his position. He had only just got to grips with the concept of his new son. His new son was still very much His New Son. It had taken him five months to bond with him. He had only ever wanted one child to start with and now he was being told that a third was on its way. 'Right,' he said in a voice pitched at pragmatic, yet thoughtful. 'So, what are your thoughts?'

Jem sighed, then joined him on the bed. 'I have no idea,' she said. 'All I know is that I cried for half an hour non-stop after I took the test.'

'Oh, Jem,' he pulled her to him by her shoulder and buried his face in the crook of her neck, 'why didn't you tell me before?'

'Because I thought it was wrong,' she replied. 'Because I thought that if I took another test it would give me a different answer, one I actually wanted to see. But, ha, it didn't. So there you go. And no, I have no idea what to do about it. No idea whatsoever.' She looked up at him sadly. Ralph could see now that the rims of her eyes were red and swollen. 'What about you?' she asked. 'What do you think?'

Ralph sighed. 'I, er, I might need some time to digest this.'

Jem shrugged. 'That's fair enough,' she said. 'It took me a while. But, Christ, I have digested it now and I still don't have the first fucking clue how I actually feel about it. I mean, look,' she gestured at the baby on her lap, 'look at him. I mean, he is so utterly perfect and blissful and I should be jumping up and down with joy at the thought of another one. But –'

'No, I know,' interrupted Ralph. 'Timing.'

'More than that, though, it's more than that. It's about dynamic, it's about me. I just don't think I would be cut out for a big family. I just don't think I've got the guts and the gumption. You know. I'll never get my career going properly, the house would be a bombsite, I'd spend all day screaming at people, I would not be a very nice person, and I know it's another person to love – another little Scarlett, another little Blake – but quite frankly, right now, I don't want to love anyone else. Quite frankly my hands are full with people to love. And I know,' she continued, 'that it is so horribly ironic how hard I tried to hold on to the two babies we lost, how empty I felt when they'd gone, how destroyed I was, and now I am considering taking this baby away deliberately. I get that. It computes. But still, it doesn't really change anything. Because having a third baby, having a baby now, well, that just doesn't compute at all.'

Ralph sighed and nodded. He had thought it all his life: if you didn't want to have a baby, you didn't have it. It had always struck him as the essence of a civilised society, that the means were there to reverse a terrible mistake and to choose your own destiny. Everything that Jem was saying to him made perfect and utter sense. Everything she was expressing was utterly sound and level-headed. In a way Jem was taking a masculine approach to the situation, a practical, realistic approach, and he respected her for that. But still, he thought, there was something oddly indigestible about the scenario. He wasn't sure what it was, because he didn't particularly want another baby and he certainly didn't want Jem to be unhappy, but neither could he quite stomach the thought of slaughtering the new life in Jem's womb. It seemed barbaric.

'Look,' he sighed, 'let's just sleep on this, shall we? And God, you never know, things might just, you know . . .'

'Yes, you're right. We've got a fifty-fifty track record on keeping babies. It's very early days.'

'Yes. We could be fatalistic?' he suggested, happy with the non-committal nature of the concept.

'Yes. We could,' said Jem, getting to her feet and stroking Ralph's cheek gently, 'we could be fatalistic. But not for very long.'

Chapter 5

Ralph received an e-mail from Rosey the next morning. He had not expected to receive an e-mail from Rosey. He had not, as far as he could remember, even given Rosey his e-mail address. But there it was: Roseypowell74@ hotmail.com.

> Hi there Ralph! Seems like a long time since we said goodbye to you! Hope it was good to get back to dear old Blighty and that the weather's being kind to you. Just thought I'd send over some of these photos I took while you were over. Me and Smith have parted ways so it seemed a bit strange to have all these photos of you. Anyway, I really enjoyed hanging out with you in SM and hope all is well with you and your lovely family. Lots of love, Rosey xx

Ralph absorbed Rosey's words: 'Me and Smith have parted ways.' They didn't seem quite to make sense. Only a month ago they had been a fully fledged couple, not necessarily following quite the same path but clearly committed to each other. And now they were no more.

Ralph tried to ignore the little wave of excitement and pleasure that came over him. The remarkable Rosey was single. The remarkable Rosey was free. But the remarkable Rosey was also, he quickly reminded himself, over five thousand miles away and not the mother of his children. He opened the attachments. The first one was a shot of Ralph and Rosey that one of the guys from her

band had taken in the bar after their gig in the community hall. She had her arm around his shoulder and her
head was angled towards his. His body language was
more neutral. It was taken before Ralph got drunk so he
still looked relatively fresh-faced. But Rosey looked
incredible. The light from the street had caught the side
of her face and her smile was enigmatic, her full lips
furled up like petals. Ralph remembered her words, in
the street, outside her apartment: 'You could paint me
from memory.'

Now he could paint her from a photograph. He sent
the picture to his printer and listened to the sound of it
churning through it while he worded a reply.

Hi Rosey, thanks for the photos. I wonder what
happened to that tan?! Actually, I do still have most of
it and summer's on its way so should be able to start
topping it up soon. I was really sorry to hear about you
and Smith. And kind of surprised. You seemed like
such a solid couple. I hope you're both OK.

Being at home has been great. I'm not quite sure
how to put this without sounding weird, but spending
time with you really helped me sort some stuff out in
my head. You were a really good sounding board and
opened my eyes to a lot of stuff that I hadn't considered before. I have a new appreciation of everything
that is good about my life (which is pretty much everything really) and I owe a lot of that to you, so thank
you, I am in your debt ☺

He paused as he was about to sign off, because there was
something else he wanted to say but he was not quite
sure how appropriate it was to say it. But then he realised
that he had nobody else to share this with and he really
needed another point of view, so he went ahead.

Some unexpected developments on my return, however. Jem is pregnant again. We're both slightly shell-shocked by this development, as you can imagine, with our little one still so young and we've got a lot of talking and thinking to do. Some sleepless nights ahead, I suspect!

Anyway, thanks for getting in touch and if ever you find yourself in London, would love to meet up, possibly over a proper European beer!

All the best,

Ralph

He contemplated signing off with a kiss, as Rosey had done, but decided against it. A kiss was tiny, but still significant, especially in the light of what had happened on Rosey's doorstep in California. He read and reread his mail three times to check that it contained nothing that if Jem were to read it she would find upsetting or suspicious, and then he clicked on Send. But even as he did so he had an overwhelming sense of having pushed a tiny domino, flicked a tiny switch.

Then he wandered towards his printer and picked the photo from the tray. He stared at it for a moment before slotting it tenderly and with some purpose in between the pages of his sketchbook.

Chapter 6

Jem had not been to the local playground for nearly a month. She had walked half a mile out of her way and taken buses to get to alternative playgrounds. She had, in fact, taken painfully circuitous routes to get to all her usual haunts in her efforts to avoid a street meeting with the increasingly mysterious Joel. But today she had decided to take a chance.

She had just about managed to convince herself that there was no way he'd be there on this random afternoon, but he was. Of course he was. He sat on his usual bench, wrapped in his usual overcoat. His newspaper was folded on the bench next to him and he was peering at his daughter over the rim of a large paper coffee cup. He didn't see her at first and it occurred to Jem that she could sneak to the other side of the playground and hide behind the climbing frame. But Jessica, lovely, bouncy, over-excitable Jessica scuppered this fledgeling plan and came scooting across the playground towards them hollering Scarlett's name. Joel lifted his head and acknowledged Jem with a small smile and a slight nod.

Deciding that a stilted, rather awkward conversation was preferable to fuelling his simmering rage with her, she slapped on her best smile and headed towards him.

'Hi!' she began. 'Haven't seen you here for a while!'

'I was about to say the same to you,' he smiled drily.

'How are you?'

'Oh, fine, fine, you know. The usual.' He turned his paper coffee cup round and round between the palms of his hands. 'You?' he said after a short pause, as though it had been an effort to pull the word out of his mouth.

'Yeah, great. Nice to have got winter out the way.'

'Well, yes, although today is not exactly a precursor to balmy summer nights.'

'No, today is a bit rubbish, it has to be said.'

'How's the little one?' He gestured at the increasingly fat baby dangling from her chest.

'Er, not so little. Blowing up like a barrage balloon, in fact. Not sure I'll be able to carry him around in this thing for much longer.'

'Must put quite a strain on your back?'

'Yes. It does.'

She smiled tightly and perched herself on the arm of the bench. The conversation was going absolutely nowhere so she decided that she could either slink away now or get something out of it. 'So,' she began, 'funny to see you outside my sister's house again the other day. Do you have a friend in the area?'

'No,' he said bluntly. 'No. It's, er, it's more of a . . . it's a group thing I attend. For partners of people addicted to drugs. A support group thing.'

Jem nodded. It was a plausible and decent explanation that made perfect sense in the light of what Lulu had told her the other day, but still, there was something about his delivery that didn't quite ring true. Feeling a strange need to prod at Joel, she continued.

'That sounds great,' she said. 'Must be brilliant to be able to talk to other people who are going through the same thing as you?'

'Yes.' He dropped his head and stared into the lid of his coffee cup. 'It's really useful.'

They fell silent for a moment and watched their children playing together. 'Does Jessica know?' she said. 'Does she know about her mother?'

Joel shrugged. 'You know what?' he said, turning to look

at her for the first time since she'd sat down. 'I don't mean to be rude, but I'd prefer not to discuss my family life with you. I mean, it's clear to me that the time we spent together last month was just a little *blip* in your perfect world,' he made facetious quotes with his fingers around the words, 'just something to do because you were bored and your perfect *trendy* artist husband wasn't paying you enough attention. I get all that, and now I think we should just get on with our lives. Don't you?' His face was set hard with repressed emotion as he returned his gaze to his coffee cup.

Jem stared at him in amazement, unsure whether what had just happened was real or something vile offered up by her imagination. 'Right,' she said, 'OK.'

'Yeah,' he said, to his cup. 'OK.'

Jem wanted to remove herself from this unsavoury situation, but she also wanted to try to understand why it had happened.

'Listen,' she began, 'I'm not sure what I've done to make you angry –'

'I am not *angry*,' he muttered. 'I am just a quiet, ordinary man, wanting to get on with his life, without any of this shallow yummy-mummy *bullshit*.'

'Sorry? What?' She was almost amused.

'Yeah, you women with your stupid boots and your perfect little houses and your fee-paying nurseries and your *big cars* . . .'

'I haven't got a big car!'

'You think because you've moved to some "edgy" little corner of London that that makes you all kind of urban and cool. But it doesn't, you know. Cause all you do is make your edgy little corner into yet another chi-chi, gentrified little mini Hampstead.'

'Right,' said Jem again, feeling a chill anger slowly percolating through her. 'I think it's clear that you and I have had some kind of misunderstanding . . .'

'No, there's no misunderstanding,' he said slowly and coolly, 'none whatsoever. You know *exactly* what I'm talking about. See that?' He pointed at their two girls playing together. 'That's real, that is. That's two people, different backgrounds, different personalities, coming together, *killing time*. You know, for fun. You and me,' he turned his mouth down to demonstrate his disapproval, 'that was just a game, a little fantasy you were playing out inside your pretty little head full of fluff and kittens and organic bloody this and that. Do you think I'm stupid? Do you think I'm blind? I saw the way you looked at my shoes the other day.'

'What!'

'Please, don't patronise me by trying to deny it. I saw it, it was blatant. You looked at my shoes like they disgusted you, like *I* disgusted you. And that's fine. I don't really care either way. But do me a favour, eh, don't treat me like some special case, like, oh, I know this guy, his wife's a crack addict, yadayadayada. Like I say, I'm just a guy, living his life. I'm not here for your entertainment. I'm not here to give you something to talk about at dinner parties.'

Jem got to her feet. She was halfway between tears and fury. 'Look,' she started, 'you're entitled to your opinion.'

'*You're entitled to your opinion*,' he mimicked. 'How very Jeremy Kyle of you. That's exactly the sort of thing someone says when they don't give a shit about anyone else's opinion. Look, I'm not saying I don't think you're a nice person. You are a Very Nice Person. You're just not what I thought you were. That's all.'

Jem drew in her breath. She wanted to let it out and scream, 'What the fuck is your problem, you crazy son of a bitch?' After a moment she managed to say this: 'Well, I must say, neither are you.'

He shrugged at these words and then he sank his face

218

back into his coffee cup, looking, for all the world, like a sulky teenage boy.

Jem strode then to the other side of the playground, to hide behind the climbing frame. She sat there for a moment, determined that she would not be chased from her local playground by a psychotic man with a gigantic chip on his shoulder, but once the adrenalin had stopped pumping through her veins she realised she needed to cry and she did not want him to see her crying so she ignored Scarlett's squawks of protest and two minutes later they left the playground and headed for home.

Ralph came downstairs a moment after they returned home. Scarlett was still screaming and crying because of the unexpectedly abrupt end to her playground jaunt and Jem had had to drag her pretty much the whole way home by the wrist, looking, no doubt, to people passing by, like she was abducting her. Her shoulders were aching from the weight of the hefty infant Blake and she was hot, flustered and out of sorts. It was ironic that after all the times she had cursed Ralph for cloistering himself away from moments such as this when all she wanted was another human being to appear and say, 'God, looks like you're having a bad afternoon,' that now she wished he had stayed in his studio. She was not ready to see him. She was not ready to see anybody. The last fifteen minutes of her life had been so unsettling on so many levels that she needed just to sit down with a glass of wine and stare at a blank wall for half an hour.

'You're back early,' he commented.

'Yes,' she said, stepping over Scarlett's prone and writhing form on the kitchen floor. 'It was a bit chilly. And this one was getting cranky. That one,' she pointed at the hysterical Scarlett, 'as you can see, was not impressed.'

Ralph gathered Scarlett into his arms and she threw her arms around his neck with melodramatic relish. Ralph smiled at Jem over her small heaving shoulders. 'Oh, well,' he soothed, 'you can always go tomorrow. The playground will always be there.'

Jem smiled tightly. No, she thought to herself, no, the playground will not always be there. Some insane man had set up camp in the playground and now it was somewhere she would have to avoid for eternity.

'What are you going to have for your tea?' he continued, trying to distract Scarlett from her tantrum. 'What's for tea, Mummy?'

'Er,' she pulled open the fridge door and stared at the contents blindly. None of it made any sense. Her head was too full of Joel and his cold, hard face and his spiteful words. 'Pizza?' she offered, her eye suddenly caught by the royal blue of a Pizza Express box. *Pizza Express*. What would Joel make of that, she wondered. Would that be shallow and yummy-mummy? Would that make him hate her even more?

Scarlett shook her head glumly, but Jem knew that it was just her mood, that if Jem just ignored her and cooked the thing, Scarlett would eat it. She switched on the oven and appraised her surroundings. They still had the kitchen that had been here when they bought the house nearly four years ago. It was farmhouse style, distressed pine, wrought-iron fittings, and Jem had a strange fondness for it. She did tend to salivate a little when passing kitchen showrooms full of sleek lines and glittery extractor fans that looked like chandeliers, and shiny aubergine veneers, but in her heart she knew she wasn't that type of person. In her heart she knew that she and this rather modest, rather bashed-about kitchen were soul mates. In fact there was nothing in her entire house that could be seen in any way as aspirational or chi-chi, nothing to inspire the ire and contempt that she had just been subjected to. And so what if she'd looked at his shoes in a less than enthusiastic manner. The only reason she was looking at his shoes in the first place was to persuade herself that she should not have a potentially seismic extramarital affair with the man, not because she was some snotty, four-wheel-drive-owning, high-maintenance gym bunny. What did he mean, she wasn't what he'd thought she was? What had he thought she was? As these thoughts swarmed angrily around her head, she began to take out her feelings on inanimate objects. She slammed the oven door open and smashed the baking tray on to the draining board. She ripped the Pizza Express box apart and pulled violently at the Cellophane wrapping. Cubes of cheese fell from the top of the pizza on to the floor and she growled loudly.

Ralph watched her quietly. 'You all right?' he asked.

'What?' she snapped.

'I said, are you all right? You seem a bit tense?'

She brushed the mozzarella cubes from the palm of her hand and into the bin. 'No,' she said, 'I'm not tense. Well, no more tense than I always am. Apparently.'

Ralph looked at her, slightly alarmed, clearly biting back on words he wanted to say.

Jem sighed. She had broken the truce. For four weeks they had been pleasant to each other, bat bat bat, like a friendly game of tennis, and now she'd broken the rally. The ball had gone over the fence. Someone would have to go and collect it. And even though it was her fault that it had landed there, she was not in the mood for being conciliatory. She was too angry and she was too shaken. So she left it lying there and hoped that Ralph would pick it up. He did.

'Sorry,' he said. 'I wasn't trying to get at you. I was just checking you were OK. Here, I'll take the kids up to the studio, give you some time to yourself.'

'Fine,' she snapped gracelessly. 'But not for too long. Pizza will be ready in fifteen minutes. OK?'

Ralph shrugged. 'No problem. Did you hear that, Scar? Fifteen minutes in my studio, before tea. Yeah?'

'Yeah!' shouted Scarlett, who was rarely allowed inside Ralph's studio and viewed it as the Biggest Treat Imaginable. Ralph plucked Blake from the rug where Jem had left him and the three of them disappeared upstairs to the attic.

The silence was immediate and overwhelming. Jem slumped on to a dining chair and exhaled. She felt bad about snapping at Ralph. Ralph had been nothing but great since he'd returned from his trip to the States. She would apologise to him later, she would blame it on the pregnancy. And now that she had excised her anger and her humiliation she also felt bad about Joel. He'd obviously read even more than she'd imagined into their brief dalliance. And deep down she couldn't really blame him for being so angry with her. She'd led him on. She'd brought him into her life. She'd toyed with his affections. All in the name of idle experimentation. She was a stupid, vain and very hormonal woman.

And not only that but he'd seen through her flimsy façade. Just like Ralph had done – *you mums.* She had spent so long blaming Ralph for everything that it had never really occurred to her that maybe she'd been a disappointment too. Maybe Ralph was right, maybe she had turned into a dull and shallow mum. Maybe she was far from the woman he'd fallen in love with all those years ago. Maybe it was time for her to take a long hard look at herself and see what needed to be changed. But then she remembered she was pregnant. Change would have to wait.

She sighed again, and then she let herself cry for exactly twelve minutes before slowly getting to her feet, mopping her eyes and taking a slightly overcooked pizza from the oven.

Chapter 7

Ralph had decided. He wanted the baby. He didn't just want the baby but he really, desperately, *dearly* wanted the baby. It suddenly seemed so simple and so clear. It was something that Rosey had said in her e-mail reply to his.

'What is an unwanted child? An unwanted child is just an unknown child. You'll want it once it's here.'

He had argued back that actually it had taken him nearly five months to 'want' Blake, but she had come back with: 'So what? You want him now. Five months is not very long in the scheme of a lifetime of love. And anyway,' she'd continued, 'if you go through with it, there'll be a ghost in your house for the rest of your lives. You have to decide whether or not you can live with that.'

He'd decided there and then that he couldn't live with that. There were already two ghosts in their house: the baby that should have been born in May 2002, the baby that should have been born in July 2005. Ralph could be philosophical about those babies. They were not meant to be. They were genetic rejects of some sort, or maybe, if you followed some of Jem's crazy fate-focused thinking, they were just not the right babies for them. But this baby, this ghost, it would crawl the corridors of their consciences, wailing and clanging chains, crying, why me, why me? There could be no philosophical musings on the lost existence of this child. *Well, really, we just didn't have the room, the time or the inclination. It had to go, terribly sad, but really, anyone would have done the same in our position.*

No, thought Ralph, not anyone. The world was full of people who would not think twice about going through with the pregnancy, about bringing the baby into being, welcoming it into their family. Ralph was painfully aware that it was not him who would have to carry the child, bear the child, nurse the child, but he also knew this: he had been a so-so father to Scarlett and a worse than useless father to Blake. He had decided early on in the parenting game that because it was Jem who had forced the issue of having a family, that the children she so dearly craved would be hers. She would be the one to fill her brain with schedules and socks and term times and goodie bags and tooth-brushing and nappy-purchasing. She would be the one to carry her children around in her head all day like unwieldy bags of heavy shopping. She would be the one to work her own life and her own needs around those of her children. Ralph would continue to do what he'd always done: stand alone in a well-lit room and paint.

She could have it worse, he'd always reasoned with himself. It's not as if I go out every night and come home steaming drunk. It's not as if I'm out with clients or off on business trips. It's not as if, he'd even thought self-righteously to himself, it's not as if I hit her.

But that person had gone and now he wanted to experience fatherhood through this new, clean lens. He wanted to watch Jem growing daily with a sense of wonder and awe rather than the slightly nauseating dread he'd felt before. He wanted to look forward to the birth of this child, to feel that this was something that they were doing together rather than something that Jem was doing to him.

He and Jem had not really discussed the concept of termination since that first conversation three days earlier. In four days' time they would have that conversation and although Ralph knew in his heart that Jem had probably already made up her mind he felt sure that he could persuade her, that once she realised the extent of his commitment to her, to the baby, to their family she would feel more relaxed about the concept. But just now, in the kitchen, he'd seen something inside her, something sad and scared, and he'd been inspired. Suddenly he knew exactly how to fix this thing.

He pinned a piece of cartridge paper to the wall and gave Scarlett an old tin of watercolours and a jar of water. Then he propped Blake up between some cushions on the floor and gave him a ball of blue nylon string, which he gnawed at gratefully as though all his life he'd been waiting for someone to give him a ball of blue nylon string. Then Ralph flipped open his mobile phone and called Lulu.

'Hi,' he began, 'it's Ralph.'

'Oh, Ralph, hello, how are you?'

'I'm fine,' he said, 'I'm great, just, er, thinking about stuff and thinking that I really need to take Jem out for a night, you know, a nice dinner, somewhere local. It's been ages, and she's, er, well, a bit rundown . . .'

'A bit pregnant, you mean?'

'Oh,' said Ralph. Of course. Of course Jem had told her sister. And her sister probably already knew exactly what she planned to do about it. 'Yeah,' he continued, 'she is. And anyway, I was wondering, would you be able to baby-sit one night soon, just for a couple of hours, you know, not for a whole night . . . ?'

'Tonight?'

'You can do tonight?'

'Uh-huh. Walt's been working from home today so I could get away whenever you need me really. Just say when.'

'Oh, right, the thing is, I haven't actually spoken to Jem yet.'

'She'll love it. Just book something. Tell her it's a done deal.'

'Right, OK, I'll –'

'Actually, I'll leave now.'

Ralph glanced at the time. It was five o'clock. 'God, you don't have to . . .'

'No, I know I don't. But if I get there now I can help you with the kids while Jem has a bath and makes herself look gorgeous. I literally have one arm in my coat as we speak. I'll see you in ten minutes. Bye!'

Chapter 8

Jem yanked clothes across the narrow gap in her wardrobe disdainfully. She hated all of her clothes. All of them. Even her Vivienne Westwood Red Label jacket that she had been so overjoyed about winning in an eBay auction. Her body shape had changed so frequently over the past few years that she had kind of forgotten what shape she was, forgotten what suited her and she was always just pleasantly surprised to find something that fitted her.

And now, ha! she was bloody well pregnant again. More billowy tops, more elasticated jeans, more voluminous bras. She eyed her clothes angrily, blaming them in some way for her predicament, as if they had somehow colluded to bring her back to square one so abruptly.

Eventually she pulled a floral Jigsaw blouse and a pair of black jeans from her wardrobe. She took off her bulky nursing bra and replaced it with something less functional, slipping a pair of breast pads in first. She hung a string of blue stones around her neck and tweaked her curls. She looked pinched and miserable. She did not look like a person she would want to know. She looked like a shrew. She felt like a shrew. She felt dry and scratchy and spiky. She felt mean and miserly and cruel. Pregnancy did not suit her, it never had done, but at least with her previous pregnancies she'd had the lure of the ultimate goal: the baby in her arms, the extension of their happy family. This time all she could feel was panic and fear. Fear that this baby would be the final undoing of them. Fear that it would tear them apart.

She adjusted the paper pads inside her bra and she headed downstairs.

Ralph thought that Jem had rarely looked as beautiful as she did that night through the amber glow of a flickering candle in a glass jar. He had taken her to Olley's, a quirky pine-panelled fish restaurant around the corner, a place he'd passed a few times on his morning run and been surprised about, not like a London restaurant at all but more like the kind of friendly popular place you'd find in a chi-chi seaside town. Jem was sipping a sparkling water. It was her pregnancy alcohol substitute. If it had bubbles in it and it was cold she could convince herself it was beer or champagne or even a gin and tonic. The fact that she had ordered it was reassuring to Ralph. If she was not drinking then it meant that she had not yet decided. And if she had not yet decided then what he was about to do was more likely to be effective.

She smiled at him wanly across the table. 'Been a long time, eh?' she said.

'Yeah, when was the last time, exactly?'

'I don't know, but I seem to recall I was pregnant then too.' She smiled wryly. 'I have spent most of these past five years pregnant, as we know.' She smiled again, a tired, weary smile. A beautiful smile.

Her mobile phone sat on the side plate, blinking re-assuringly. She glanced at it, furtively, as she had done every thirty seconds since they had sat down. Blake had still been awake when they'd left and Jem would not be properly relaxed until she got the text confirmation from Lulu that he was sound asleep.

'I'm sorry I snapped at you earlier,' she said, tearing apart a piece of crusty bread.

He shrugged and smiled. 'It's OK,' he said, 'I can take it.'

She nodded and glanced down at her phone again.

'Yeah,' she said, looking up again, 'I know. But it still

wasn't really fair. I know you've been bending over backwards to be, you know, supportive and I really, really, really appreciate it, honestly I do. But I've still got, I don't know, some backed-up resentment issues I guess. And, yippee, now I've got Hormone Soup too! So, I'm just saying, I'm doing my best to be soft and kind but inside I'm still a bit hedgehoggy. You know.'

Ralph reached his hand across the table and took Jem's. 'I quite like hedgehogs,' he said.

Jem smiled.

'I mean, I know things haven't been great these last few months –'

'Years,' interrupted Jem.

'Well, yeah, years probably. And I know I've had to do some growing up and that I've left you with too much on your plate and that, well, you know the score, I take most of the blame, and I know we're not going to talk about the baby tonight . . .'

'Ha!' interjected Jem. 'Which one?'

'Yeah, you know which one. And we're not. But I just wanted to say something to you tonight, something I should have said years ago, something I can't believe I've never said to you before. You know, you are my life, you are everything to me. I am the luckiest man in the world to be with you, to have made babies with you and I don't know why you've put up with me these past years. I don't ever want to be apart from you and more than anything, I want to, well – I want to marry you.'

Jem, who had been staring accusingly at her sleeping mobile phone, looked up at him with wide eyes. She put a hand to the pale thin skin of her collarbone, where her fingertips rested against the iridescent blue beads of her necklace. 'I beg your pardon?' The words tripped off her tongue quickly without spaces. *Ibegyourpardon?*

'I said, I want to marry you. For us both to get married. To each other.'

'What, seriously?'

He nodded. 'Yeah, seriously.'

He drew in his breath. He and Jem had drifted so far apart over the past few years that he found it impossible to hazard a guess as to what might currently be taking place inside her head. Had she started thinking flouncy tulle skirts? Or was she already trying to find the right words to let him down gently? He stared at her beseechingly.

'Fucking hell, Ralph.'

'Yeah,' he smiled pathetically, 'I know.' They had discussed getting married before, in a conceptual, non-specific kind of way. They had agreed that it was not a priority, that there were more important things to focus on. They had agreed that having children together was the greatest commitment two people could make to one another. They had agreed that they might do it one day, maybe run away to Las Vegas, maybe do something small and informal in a registry office.

'Wow,' said Jem, 'I'm flabbergasted. But in a good way.' She put a reassuring hand against his arm. 'I just, er, well, I was going to say, I need to think about it, but that's a bit stupid really. Of course I don't need to think about it, obviously I'm going to say yes.'

'You are?'

'Yes! Of course I am! You're the love of my life. You're the father of my children. What would it say about any of that if I were to say no?'

'So you mean you're only saying yes because if you said no it would be far more damaging to the status quo?'

'No! No, I'm not saying that. I'm saying that getting married is the right thing to do. I'm saying that yes, I want to marry you! Maybe not for the same reasons I would have wanted to marry you five years ago, ten years ago, but for better reasons, probably, because it would make sense, practically. And because Scarlett would love it.

And because, I don't know, because in spite of everything, we still love each other.'

Ralph looked at her over the tips of his fingers and tried to smile. 'Ooh,' he said, 'romantic!'

Jem groaned. 'Oh, Ralph, come on, how can you expect me to be romantic?'

Ralph smiled sadly. 'No, of course, I don't expect you to be romantic; I just thought you might be, that's all.'

'Listen, Ralph. I'm really sorry. I'm tired. I've had a bad day. I've got a lot on my mind, but I want you to know this: I'm really glad you asked me to marry you. It's wonderful and I am delighted. Really I am.'

'Even if you don't seem it?'

'Even if I don't seem it. Honestly, inside me there is a giddy twenty-year-old doing a happy dance.'

'With the hedgehog?'

Jem smiled then, properly, with her whole face, for the first time that day. 'Yeah,' she laughed, 'she's dancing with the hedgehog.'

Chapter 9

Jem's head felt like it had been opened up, emptied of anything sensible, intellectual or useful, stuffed with horsehair and mud and closed up again. The world appeared to her like a thick gloop of disconnected events and appointments. Her life, which had once felt like a smooth machine of routines and schedules, now felt chaotic and strange. Everyday activities and situations had lost their soothing veneer of familiarity. Partly, of course, it was hormonal; baby-brain they called it, though she'd always thought that was a myth. But mostly it was because her territory had grown new humps and hillocks, valleys and ravines. Suddenly there were towering land-marks in her life that hadn't been there before: weddings to plan, babies to decide about, an angry-looking man pacing about outside her house.

Yes. Joel.

He was there right now.

She only knew he was there because she'd just popped out to empty the recycling bin. She'd been aware of a presence, on the other side of the street, a sense of being watched. She hadn't looked up, just slammed the lid down on the green box as fast as she could and returned inside. And then she'd darted into the front room to peer through the curtains. And there he was, leaning against the wall of the house opposite, a folded newspaper in the pocket of his jacket, staring, not towards Jem's house, but up into the sky, watching the swirls and pirouettes of a swallow overhead. Jem let the curtain fall and sucked in her breath. Her heart began to race. What on earth was he doing there? She had imagined after their last exchange that he would do his best to avoid her. She peered once more through the curtain and saw with alarm that he was moving towards the house, with a sense of urgency and something clasped behind his back. She gasped and ran to the front door, crouched herself beneath the stained-glass panels. She could hear his foot-steps crunching urgently up the front path. She heard him clear his throat. And then she heard something else; a scuffing noise against the doorstep. She held her breath, felt her heart hammering against her ribcage. The scuffing noise stopped and then, after a long painful moment, she heard him walking back up the footpath and towards the street.

She waited a full three minutes like that, crouched behind her front door, sweating and vaguely hyperventi-lating. Then she ran back to the front room, studied the road through the window and having finally reassured herself that he was gone, she opened the front door and glanced at the doorstep.

It was a bunch of flowers.

White flowers.

She wasn't sure what they were; they were somewhat undistinguished, saved from ugliness only by their stark whiteness. (Though of course, the moment the thought passed through her head she knew that it was exactly the sort of thing that Joel imagined she would think about a bunch of perfectly nice white flowers. 'Hmph,' she imag-ined him grunting, 'I suppose only the best lilies are good enough for you, or meadow flowers hand-picked that very morning by rosy-cheeked organic wenches in Somerset.')

Attached to the cheap flowers was a card in a pale blue envelope. She eyed the street, both ways, to make sure nobody was watching and then took the flowers and the card indoors. With slightly trembling fingers she pulled the card out and read it.

'Jem – I don't know what came over me. I am truly sorry. I hope you will forgive me and that we can still be friends. Yours, with respect, Joel.'

Jem read and reread the card three times before conceding a small smile. Her immediate reaction was relief that someone she'd feared disliked her had rethought their position. The idea, in fact, that someone disliked her had been so sickeningly overwhelming for the past few days that it had tainted her every waking moment. Jem had spent most of life ensuring that everyone she came into contact with found her pleasant, even charming. For someone to have taken against her so vigorously had been a big shock. So now that he had clearly changed his mind, she felt a warm sense of vindication. Of course she wasn't an awful person! Of course not! And for someone who barely knew her to suggest such a thing was clearly an aberration.

But still, the words could not be taken back completely. Whether or not he regretted saying them, he had meant them at the time. And whether or not his words held any truth (Jem had enough self-awareness to know that they probably did), the fact that he'd felt able to say them to her in such a vociferous and aggressive way pointed Jem very much towards the conclusion that he was a) unpleasant, b) an inverted snob and c) possibly mentally unstable.

Which led her back to the plain white flowers on her kitchen table. She did not want to be in receipt of any kind of flowers from a man like Joel. She had been led astray by flowers before. While sharing a flat with Ralph and Smith all those years earlier, she had convinced herself that Smith must be the man of her dreams, purely because he had come home one night bearing a bunch of nodding peonies – her favourite flowers. She had then wasted a few months of her life that she would never get back in Smith's bed, unaware of the fact that all the while Smith was using her to give him some kind of kudos in his silent pursuance of the woman on the top floor of their house. She still shuddered when she thought about it, all these years later, shuddered at her stupidity, her blind adherence to her self-imposed laws of romantic destiny.

But then it had been flowers again, that had saved her from herself. A whole room full of them. Not real flowers, but the painted flowers that Ralph had exhibited in a small room in Notting Hill. It was not just the most romantic thing that had ever happened to her, but the most romantic thing that had ever happened to anyone she knew. And to recall that moment, the mania of it, the youthful, lustful craziness of it, and then to look upon the sad handful of supermarket flowers left on her doorstep by a lonely, bitter man she barely knew – well, it was obvious what she had to do. She took the flowers and with some relish she dropped them, blooms down, into the slightly rancid, nappy-scented depths of her large, shiny and terribly middle-class Brabantia bin.

Jem could not sleep that night. There was nothing worse, as a mother of two small children who made it their lives' work to drag you out of bed and away from sleep once if not five times a night, than to be the architect of your own awakeness. It was painfully infuriating, and feeling infuriated was, of course, the very best way to ensure that you would remain awake.

So, the house slumbered, Ralph, for once, did not snore, the road outside was still and quiet, no cater-wauling foxes patrolled the gardens, the baby snuffled and Jem lay on her back, her hands clasped across her sore breasts, wondering and cogitating and worrying and thinking.

Tomorrow it would be a week since she had told Ralph that she was pregnant – and she was still pregnant. Tomorrow they would have a conversation that began with the words: 'Well, what have you decided?' And she could not just stand there, as she currently felt she would, humming and hawing, rolling her thumbs and muttering, 'I don't know. You decide.' She would have to have an answer and it would have to be an answer that she was prepared to stand by, otherwise this thing was going to drag on infinitely, painfully.

As she watched the clock turn from 2.59 to 3.00 and realised that she had now been awake for nearly an hour and a half, she gently peeled back the duvet, tiptoed quietly from the room and headed downstairs.

Smith the cat looked up as she entered the moon-bright kitchen. His face lit up at the sight of an unexpected visitor and he headed towards her sleepily, polishing her bare legs with his soft cream fur. 'Hello, old boy,' she said, scooping him up into her arms and carrying him to the old sofa by the garden door. Once upon a time Smith the cat had been her baby. Once upon a time she had worried about his eating habits, discussed his behaviour at great length with Ralph and other cat-owning friends, bought him toys, missed him deeply when they went on holiday. And then she'd brought Scarlett home from the hospital and barely given him a second thought since. Poor old Smith. He'd been affronted at first, but slowly settled into his new role as bottom fiddle and occasional plaything. It was rare for Jem to have a moment to herself with Smith the cat, and sitting curled up with him on the sofa in the dark, hearing his contented purring, the pull of his padded feet against her pyjama bottoms, she could almost imagine herself at a time before, when it was just her and Ralph in their beautiful big flat in Battersea, in the days when Ralph would cycle off to work every morning to his studio in Cable Street and Jem would jump on the number 38 at the top of their road and go to her job in Soho.

Those days were gone, Jem accepted that. And she didn't really want them back. To take them back would be to give her children back to the universe. Having children meant an irreversible march into the future. And actually, she didn't really want lie-ins and Sunday papers and long baths and spontaneous holidays and summer afternoons in Battersea Park with just a bottle of champagne and a blanket. She loved the padded upholstery that children gave to her existence. She loved fulfilling their needs and requirements, filling them with her love, giving herself to them in chunks of her own precious time. But there was one thing she would like back, one thing from the past. She would like some of the magic that she and Ralph had once shared.

She moved Smith the cat to one side and pulled some photo albums from the shelving next to the sofa. She and Scarlett looked through these albums regularly. Scarlett liked to see the pictures of herself as a baby, the pictures of Jem cradling a large naked pregnant belly, Ralph in green scrubs just before the Caesarean. She was less interested in the photos of life before she arrived, unable at only three years old to quite grasp the concept that she hadn't always been here.

Jem found the photos she was looking for: Lulu's wedding. She smiled at the photographs. Ralph in crumpled linen trousers and an old white shirt, his skin soft and tanned; Jem in a floral sundress, shirred across the bust with floaty chiffon sleeves and strappy silver sandals. They both looked so delighted with themselves. *Look at us,* said their gleeful expressions, *we have found each other!* There was nothing about the young woman in this photograph to predict bitterness or a preoccupation with organic produce or a latent desire to drive a large black vehicle or a tendency to use hapless single

238

fathers as conversational dinner-party fodder. That girl looked like a free-spirit, like someone who if she had children would let them run barefoot wherever they chose, pick dark berries from brambly bushes and stain their clothes with them, let the housework slide, chase her husband into the bedroom after the children were asleep and pin him to the bed, read important novels as she pushed a pram down the street, make friends with the local shopkeepers and invite her children's friends home after school to run riot in her home, throw home-made stew into rough-hewn bowls for them to eat off their knees and have enough left over for an impromptu drunken supper for some colourful local friends later that same night. She would flirt innocently with her husband's friends, who would all secretly adore her, she would make potato prints with her daughter on a Saturday morning and not even notice when the paint-muddy water got tipped on to the kitchen floor. That woman, the carefree woman in the photographs, would walk down the street with one arm around her husband and one arm pushing the buggy. Yes, she would.

But no, just like Jem's unborn babies, that mum had never existed and instead the flushed, exhilarated girl in Tuscany had become just another harried suburban mum, caught up in routines and timetables and the sheer utter bloody exhaustion of trying, and failing, to keep every-thing perfect. She had become the shallow yummy mummy that Joel had accused her of being, with no life outside her house, no sense of adventure or spontaneity, little to no libido and a deep-seated antipathy towards her husband for his part in letting her become this way.

She flicked faster and faster through the photo album. She flicked through Tuscany and Bruges and Port Isaac and Sydney and Bordeaux. She flicked through weddings and births and thirtieths and fortieths and the funeral of Ralph's old mum. And suddenly as her life swarmed in front of her eyes, month by month, year by year, event by event like a zoetrope, it was blindingly obvious what she needed to do.

She went upstairs then, to Ralph's studio. She rarely went into Ralph's studio. It was never quite warm up there, except on scorching summer days when it was pungently hot. There was nowhere comfortable to sit and Ralph was always distracted when he was working.

Ralph's studio was light. The moon was directly overhead and falling through the glass panels in the roof like milky sunshine. She walked gently across the knotty wooden floors, careful not to cause a squeak, and she studied Ralph's works in progress. He'd told her that he was painting flowers from his Californian trip for his next exhibition but she hadn't seen any of them yet. Strange, really, that she expected Ralph to take an interest in her career yet she showed very little in his. She'd stopped being interested in Ralph's art a long time ago. It was good, he was a very talented man, but once you'd seen thirty minutely detailed studies of sweet peas and ranunculus you had, Jem suspected, seen them all. They left the house like a factory production line, two, four, sometimes ten at a time. Every now and then there was an exhibition and a lorry would arrive and fifteen or twenty would be shuffled down the spiral staircase and out through the front door. They were bread and butter. They were, from Jem's point-of-view, no different to packets of biscuits or cars. If someone had told her twenty years ago that one day she would be living with an artist, a remarkably talented artist, a man who could paint anything he saw in breathtaking, lifelike detail, she'd have imagined that she would have been swathed from head to toe in chiffon all day, muse-like, swanning around parties full of interesting people, bursting with pride. But no, she was not impressed by Ralph. He would have to go a very long way these days to impress her, not just paint a flower but possibly grow a flower within his own body and allow it to blossom forth from his belly button. There was no mystique left about what Ralph did for a living. There was no mystique left about Ralph. But she was vaguely surprised as she eyed the two canvases at the far end of the studio, to note that there appeared to be a new mood in play.

Flowers, yes, but not reticent British flowers: long, slightly phallic flowers, tubular in shape, dangling pendulously across vividly coloured backdrops, hints of graffiti on sun-bleached walls, acid sunshine, the stencilled shade of a palm frond. She remembered Ralph saying something about trying a new style, but typically, she hadn't really been listening.

'What do you think?'

She jumped.

Ralph was in the doorway, naked apart from his boxers, his newly recovered abs gleaming in the moonlight. Jem felt oddly shy for a moment.

'Yeah,' she said, turning back to look at the paintings, 'they're great. I can see what you've been working on now. It's a real change.'

'Yeah,' he walked towards her, 'it's so good to finally have got out of that rut. Although, ha, knowing me I'll probably just end up spending another ten years painting Californian street flora.'

Jem smiled. 'Aren't you going to ask me what I'm doing up here?' she asked.

'Well, I'm going to suppose that you couldn't sleep.'

She shrugged and nodded.

He smiled and leaned against the wall next to her.

'Want to talk about it?' he said.

She looked at Ralph's paintings and then she looked at Ralph. He had changed. He was now the man she'd wanted so badly for him to be. He was fit and considerate and caring and involved. He pulled his weight, he acted without instruction, he treated her with respect and affection. But still her defences were up, still she resented his second-in-command role in their lives. He had changed but *she had not*. And now it was up to her to change too. And in order for her to change she needed to draw a line underneath this stage of their lives, the baby stage, the pregnancy stage. She needed to be able to look back upon it and say, yes, it was tough when the children were small, yes, I found pregnancy stressful and it all took its toll on our relationship, but now the kids are older, well, we've never been happier.

Having another baby now would put the whole family back to square one. Their sex life would suffer, her body would suffer, there would be more sleepless nights, more people to shout at and tidy up after and remember things about. She wanted to try to find that girl in the photograph downstairs, the girl who was going to be a fun mum and a great wife. She wanted to start going out on dates with Ralph again, to get drunk, Christ, maybe even get stoned (it had been a Very Long Time). She wanted this family to have at its core a fantastic mum and a fantastic dad who truly loved each other – and showed it. Her children never saw their parents hug. They rarely saw them laugh, except at them. Her children deserved to have two parents who were mad about each other. And if she had to spend another eighteen months pregnant, sober, tired, breastfeeding and stressed then that would never happen. No. She wanted to shut up shop, turn the sign around on the door, head inside and get on with her life.

She stared for a moment through the glass roof, into the grey blackness of the night sky at the distant stars, trying to find the right words for what she needed to say next. She turned and held his hands. 'I really, really don't want to have this baby. I'm so sorry, but I want to

242

have . . . I want to . . . I don't want to have it. And that is my final decision.'

Ralph looked down at her, the moon shining on to the scalp beneath his thinning hair. She saw heartache in his eyes. 'I thought you might say that,' he said.

'I'm really sorry,' she said again.

'No. I don't want you to be sorry. I don't want you to be sorry about anything. It's your body. It's your decision.'

'But, no, it isn't, is it? I mean, yes, ultimately I have to make the final call, but this would be your baby too, your daughter or your son, and I feel like I'm robbing you of that.'

Ralph shrugged and inhaled. 'Look,' he said, 'I can't pretend I'm not gutted. I do, I did want this baby. Very much. But I can't make you have it. I wouldn't dream of making you go through with it if you don't want to. I just really hope, though, that you made this decision for the right reasons.'

'What do you mean?' She could not tell Ralph her real reasons for not wanting to have the baby. She could not tell him that she was scared that he would turn his back on them all again, like he did after Blake was born. He would say it wasn't true, he would say it wouldn't happen again, he would say that he was marrying her, that he would never leave her. But babies had taken them so far away from each before, she had no faith in it not happening again.

'Well, no, not for the right reasons, but I hope you feel like you've had time to think things through properly, that you haven't rushed this decision . . .'

'Ralph! This is all I've thought about for the past ten days! Literally! I'm half insane with it!'

'No, no, I know, I just mean, you have a very busy life, you don't get much time just to sit and, you know, think. Would it help if you went away for a couple of days? I could look after the kids. Blake's almost off the breast now. You could go away and really, really think about what you want to do. Another couple of days won't hurt.'

Jem shook her head. 'No!' she said. 'I want this thing out of my head and out of me. I don't need to go away anywhere to know that.'

'But are you sure? Are you really sure you haven't just made this decision in a state of panic?'

'Of course I've made the decision in a state of panic!'

'Well, then . . .'

'Well, then, what?'

'Well, then give yourself some time to stop panicking. Give yourself another couple of days. Please. What I would hate more than anything, more than you getting rid of the baby, more than you having the baby, is that you would make the wrong decision. Do you see? That you would look back and think: if only I'd thought it through calmly and properly, I wouldn't have done that. I couldn't bear there to be any regrets.'

'There won't be any regrets, Ralph.' She wasn't one hundred per cent convinced that this was true, but she knew that any small regrets would be a price worth paying to avoid the potential devastation to their relationship of another baby.

'Ghosts,' he said suddenly.

Jem squinted at him. 'What?'

'Ghosts. We've already lost two babies. I know you still think about them. But this one, could you live with that? Could you live with that date, January 2009? It'll be there every year, every January we'll think: baby would have been one, baby would have been two, baby would have been starting school this year, baby would have . . .'

'Yes,' said Jem, 'I could. I could live with that.'

'Fine, then,' said Ralph, in that soft, controlled voice, holding her head against his chest. 'Whatever you want to do, whatever you want to do.'

They stood for a moment or two like that, the moonlight on their crowns, rocking gently back and forth. And then, hand-in-hand they went back to bed where Jem slept and Ralph lay wakefully until Blake's first murmurings at 5 a.m.

Chapter 10

Ralph flipped open the lid of his laptop at nine o'clock the following morning, clicked on his Outlook icon and waited impatiently for his in-box to load.

Nothing from Rosey. He sighed. He always felt curiously uplifted when he saw her name in his in-box. He clicked on her last e-mail to him and pressed reply. The words poured from his thoughts on to the keyboard.

Hi! Me and Jem talked last night. Late last night. She's decided to get rid of the baby. I mentioned everything that you said. I even offered to look after the kids for a couple of days so that she could get away and really think about stuff. But she's adamant. When she told me, I was really angry at first. I could feel all the old negativity coming back. I just wanted to shout and rant and have it all my own way. But then this weird thing happened – I felt something, like strength, but not inner strength, not like I was having to tell myself to feel a certain way or behave a certain way, but like something external. It was like I was taken over by something . . .

Anyway, I know you won't think I'm crazy for saying something like that, I know you understand. Jem's downstairs now, phoning the clinic. I can't watch her do it. I'm not happy with the situation, but I've accepted that there's nothing I can do about it, that Jem's happiness is paramount. I just really hope that this brings her the happiness she thinks it will. I really hope that it brings us ALL the happiness she thinks it will.

Sorry to load you up with all this shit, I just haven't got anyone else I can talk to about it, and I know you understand. Now I'm just praying (yeah – literally!) that she has a last-minute change of heart. And if she doesn't, well, then I will just have to try my hardest not to hold it against her and assume that this has all happened for a reason.

Hope you're OK. Lots of love, R x

He pressed Send and then pulled on his running shoes. As he sprinted through the house he heard Jem's voice, a thin ribbon of sound, somewhere out of sight, saying words he did not want to hear, and he felt a sense of blessed escape the moment his feet touched the street outside the house.

He pounded the streets that he had only just grown to love, thinking of the baby he had been looking forward to meeting. He tried to be philosophical. Maybe the baby would have been stupid, ugly, evil, hyperactive, a nightmare. Maybe they'd have looked at the child and sighed and thought, we should never have had it, should have stuck with the two we already had.

But Ralph knew that was drivel. Of course they would never think such things, even if the baby arrived two-headed and breathing fire. Well, possibly not, but really, a baby would have to go a very long way indeed not to be innately lovable.

He would go with Jem to the appointment, of course he would. He would tell her all the right things, hold her hand, tell her he loved her, tell her it was fine. But it wasn't fine. It was far from fine.

His feet hit the pavement, thud thud thud, his heart pressed against his ribcage, two lines of sweat formed on his temples and rolled towards his eyes. He found himself, as he did more and more often these days, at the small chapel on Underwood Street. He pushed open the doors and then pulled out his earpieces. The sun was angled through the small windows at the front, filling the room with chunks of rosy May sunshine. He sat on a pew and closed his eyes. Whatever it was he was finding when he sat in this place, he was needing it more and more every day, like a tincture. He found it here, he found it when he ran, he found it when he exchanged e-mails with Rosey. He'd alluded to God earlier when he was writing to Rosey and although he still wasn't sure that that's exactly what it was, with every day that passed it was seeming more and more likely.

He prayed as he sat there. He prayed a lot these days. He wasn't ashamed to call it that any more. There was nothing wrong with prayer, as long as it was private, and well-intentioned.

After a few moments, once he felt filled with the stuff of this place, he got to his feet, reinserted his earphones and then left, hoping that someone, somewhere had heard his plea for a second chance for their unborn baby.

His head was stuffed full with the business of his life and Elbow were on volume 22 in his ears so it took him a moment to realise that he was being watched. A man, across the street. He'd been there when Ralph arrived at the chapel and he was still there now. And yes, as Ralph gazed at the man he realised that he recognised him. It was him, that strange man he'd seen when he was out with the kids. The dad. The one that Jem knew. Ralph stopped for a moment, his hands on his hips. A car zipped along the road between them. Then a van. The man still stood and stared. It was possible, of course, that he was staring at some random point just behind Ralph, but no, Ralph could see the man's gaze following his, even from here. Ralph lifted his hand from his hip and held it up to the man, in a kind of neutral greeting. The man mirrored his movement. Ralph smiled, tentatively. The man did not. A small line of cars passed between them then, and by the time the road was clear again the man across the street had gone.

Ralph looked from left to right, grimaced and then headed towards Brockwell Park.

Chapter 11

Jem took the first available appointment.

'Is tomorrow morning, 8 a.m., too early?'

'No,' said Jem, 'no. That's perfect.'

She knew that meant that Ralph wouldn't be able to come. He'd have to stay at home to get the children up, to take Scarlett to nursery. She was sure if she'd asked she could have been given a later appointment, something that Ralph could have attended. But she didn't need him there. It would have been nice to have had him there, nice but not altogether necessary.

In her bag, Jem packed photos of her children, a banana and a book. At the last moment, just before she left the house in the early morning sun, she took the photograph of herself and Ralph at her sister's wedding from the album in the kitchen. She put it in her handbag, in case she lost her resolve and needed to remember why she was doing this.

Ralph saw her off at the door, Blake in his arms suckling on a bottle of formula. He looked tired and wan, but managed a smile and a lingering kiss. She brushed the kiss away. She did not want lingering kisses or any kind of intimacy at all until this was done. Jem, who spent most of her life feeling like pretty much everything could go either way at any time, who left most of her decisions until the last minute, who believed in fate and destiny and the theory of probability, had never felt so certain or in control before in her life. This was absolutely the right thing to be doing, she had not a shadow of a doubt.

'I love you,' said Ralph, 'I'll come and pick you up at eleven, OK?'

'I'll call you,' she said, 'once I know for sure.'

'OK,' he said, 'I'll keep my phone on loud.'

Jem smiled, pulled her hand from his.

'Say bye-bye, Mummy,' Ralph flapped Blake's hand from side to side, 'bye-bye, Mummy.'

Jem smiled at Blake and kissed his tiny hands. 'See you later, baby boy! And give your sister a big kiss from Mummy when she wakes up!'

Jem ignored the film of tears she'd seen over Ralph's blue eyes and the dull sadness in his voice. He's just tired, she told herself, just tired and full of sleep.

In the waiting room she read a copy of *Grazia* magazine and tried not to look at the two other women – not actually women, but girls; eighteen, twenty, possibly twenty-four. Here she was, nearly forty, the twilight of her fertile years, a nice house, a good man; would either of these conflicted, surprised, unprepared girls have had the slightest understanding of what she was doing? She didn't suppose so.

She pulled out the photo of Blake.

Her baby.

Now he would get to stay her baby, unusurped.

She pulled out a picture of Scarlett. Sweet, kind, shirty, opinionated Scarlett. Enough personality for all of them.

And then she took the Tuscan photo from her bag. She stared into the bright, shining eyes of the girl and the boy in the photograph. *I'm doing this for you*, she told them, *for you and for all your silly, wonderful, crazy dreams.*

'Jemima Catterick?'

'Yes.' She slid the photograph back into her bag and looked up. 'Is it time?'

Ralph dropped Scarlett at nursery fifteen minutes earlier than usual and found his way, as fast as possible, to the

Marie Stopes clinic in Streatham. He could not let her do this. It would destroy them. They would never be able to tell their children about it and there it would be: a secret, a lie, buried within the heart of their family. Ralph did not want secrets and lies inside his family. He wanted transparency and honesty. And how would he and Jem ever be able to talk about this to each other, let alone their children? It was a conversation that they would never be able to have. One or other of them would end up hurt. There wouldn't just be a ghost in their house, there would be a chasm.

He pulled the car up on a yellow line on Brixton Hill opposite the clinic – forty pounds was a small price to pay for stopping a cataclysm – and unclipped Blake from his car seat. He was about to leap, hero-like, up the front steps and into the building when it occurred to him suddenly that he would be carrying a small and very appealing baby into a room full of woman about to get rid of theirs. He stopped, halfway up the steps. He considered Blake, fat in his arms. He considered the front door. He peered through the window. He saw a woman behind a desk smiling beatifically at another woman carrying a set of notes. He saw a row of chairs and he saw Jem, upright, prim, reading – not flicking mindlessly, he noted – but *reading* a copy of *Grazia* magazine. My God, he thought to himself, she's studying seasonal trends, in an abortion clinic. He felt a rush of strangeness to his head then, of unreason. Surely this wasn't his Jem? His Jem would not abort a baby. And even if his Jem had good reason to abort a baby, she would do so with a grey face and wrung hands and an air of desperation. His Jem would not be sitting there so coldly composed.

As he watched, the kind-faced receptionist put down her phone and trained her kindly smile upon Jem, uttered some words which gave Jem cause to discard her fashion magazine and loop her bag across her shoulder and head to a door to the left where a less kindly-faced nurse was waiting to meet her. Peering from left to right Ralph could see that there was nobody else in the waiting room, that Jem appeared to be the only woman in south London at this particular moment with a taste for killing an unborn child. He rang the intercom and told the receptionist that his name was Ralph McLeary that he was here to collect Jemima Catterick. He held up the baby Blake as if to prove his credentials and then as the lock clicked, he pushed open the front door and stormed (yes, he felt that stormed was the correct term) through the waiting room and down the corridor where he could see Jem and the nurse slipping through a door. He ignored the over-excited shouts of the receptionist: 'Sir! Sir! You have to sign the register. Sir!' and pushed open the door and then he was there, face to face with Jem, and all he could say, in a voice quiet with fear was: *'Don't.'*

Jem looked at him blankly, as if trying to place his face. The consultant got to his feet as though he fancied himself as something of a hard man.

'What?' said Jem, quietly.

'Don't,' he repeated. 'Don't do this. Don't kill our baby. We'll never get over it. We'll never recover.'

Jem gazed at him in awe. 'But ... that's exactly why I'm doing it, because I honestly believe that if we have this baby we'll never recover ...'

'No!' cried Ralph. 'I mean, yes, I know what you mean, and it will be tough, of course it will, but not as tough as the repercussions of doing what you're about to do. I –'

'Erm,' came a third voice, the consultant, still on his feet, looking from one of them to the other, his hands outstretched in a conciliatory fashion, 'I'm sorry to interrupt but there's something you both need to know.'

They turned to look at him. Ralph bristled slightly.

'You're not pregnant,' the consultant said flatly.

'What?' said Jem.

'You're not pregnant,' the man repeated.

'But ... I took five tests. I mean, I even took a test yesterday, just to be sure, I ...'

'Yes, well, you might well have been pregnant yesterday but today, I can guarantee you that you are not. I promise you.'

A small silence filled the room while Jem and Ralph digested this announcement.

'So you mean,' he began, 'that we've lost the baby?'

The man nodded and sat down, very slowly. 'Yes,' he said, 'or so it seems. And now you have two options. You can either go home and wait for the baby to miscarry naturally, or we could go ahead with the D&C today, as planned.'

Ralph felt his brow gather tightly with confusion. Was this man offering to abort Jem's non-existent baby? It didn't make sense.

The consultant looked at Ralph and sighed. 'The advantage to having the D&C now is, of course, that there will be no waiting. You will not have to leave here knowing that you are carrying the foetus. You won't risk miscarrying somewhere where it is not convenient. You are also sparing yourself the possibility of a missed miscarriage. The advantages to not having the procedure are more personal, really – you may feel you'd rather leave it to nature to choose its moment, you may feel more comfortable with coming to terms with the loss, believing that it is true?'

Ralph and Jem looked at the doctor, looked at each other, looked again at the doctor.

'You can go outside and discuss it, if you'd like?' suggested the doctor.

'No,' Jem looked at Ralph, slightly desperately and shook her head. 'I'd like the procedure, now, today, please,' she said, in a small, soft voice, tinged with tears.

The doctor nodded, with the suggestion that he approved of her decision.

Ralph glanced at her. Her eyes were watery but her neat little chin was set with certainty. She wanted to finish what she'd come here to do, it was clear. She wanted herself empty. He made a shape with his face that was meant to convey understanding but probably more resembled weary capitulation. And then he took his baby boy to the waiting room where he sat in a state of warped shell shock for twenty-five minutes, mentally saying goodbye to a baby that had never stood a chance.

That night Blake slept through from 8.30 p.m. until 7.15 a.m. Jem blinked at her radio and then peered across the room into the cot. She racked her memory for the bit where she had pulled her sleep-heavy body from the warmth of her bed and put a warm baby to her breast and sat upon her bed with her eyes closed, half awake, half asleep, waiting to be released back to her dreams. But it wasn't there. Her heart began to beat wildly at the possibility, always there, that her baby had died in his sleep. She saw his arm twitch, heard a small puff of air leave his nose, felt her heart slow down. He lived. She smiled.

She turned then and looked at Ralph. He was starting to stir. She leaned down and whispered into his ear: 'Ralph. Blake slept through!'

Ralph opened his eyes and turned to face her. 'What?'

'Blake. He slept through. No wake-ups! We've cracked it!'

Ralph grunted and turned again on to his back. Of course, thought Jem, he is not the one who has had to get out of bed two, three, four times a night for the past six months, this is not such a huge marker of progress for him as it is for me. She smiled again but then stopped as she felt the damp between her legs, the bulky towel, the stark reminder of yesterday's events. She would bleed for another week or so, she would continue to feel sick, her breasts would remain sore and swollen. Her baby was gone but her body was playing catch-up.

She cupped her hand over her empty belly and felt a jolt of sadness pass through her. It was gone. Her baby was gone. But rather than feeling relief and liberation, Jem felt deflated. Once again her body her taken control of her destiny, once again her body had failed her. And she wished now for her baby back, just for one more day, just to be able to say goodbye, properly, before it was too late. The baby that had withered and perished inside her felt much more real to her than the one she'd been ready to terminate. She felt love and compassion for that poor blighted lost soul where she'd felt none for the big robust baby she'd imagined to be gestating inside her unwilling body.

She stopped the thought processes there. No, she thought, today is a new day, a new start. Today is the day on which I will begin to plan my wedding, to tell people my happy news, to book baby-sitting nights so that my man and I can spend nights out together drinking beer and rekindling our lost magic. Today is not the day to wonder what if.

She tiptoed quietly from the room and then did something she had not done for seven months because she always had her arms full of baby: she tiptoed into her daughter's room and snuck into her bed, nestling herself against Scarlett's warm, bony body and burying her nose into her wild, musty hair. She could trick a moment's affection out of Scarlett like this, before her consciousness was fully aroused. Scarlett wrapped a small leg round Jem's knees and the two of them lay like that for a few moments, still and warm, until suddenly Ralph appeared in the doorway, a beaming Blake in his arms.

'Look who finally woke up,' he said.

'I want him!' said Scarlett, suddenly sitting bolt upright. 'I want Blakey!'

Ralph put Blake on the bed, between Jem and Scarlett, who immediately threw her arms round his neck and rubbed her forehead against his. Jem watched them. Now that Blake was sitting up and eating real food Scarlett was taking more and more of an interest in him. Scarlett's face lit up at the sight of him in a way that it had never lit up at the sight of either of her parents (well, maybe Ralph, on occasion, but certainly not Jem) and he was now considered something of a treat, especially in his pram at the end of her day at nursery and even more so first thing in the morning. Ralph perched himself on the edge of the bed and smiled at Jem.

'You OK?' he said.

Jem smiled at him. 'Good,' she said, 'I'm good.' The sun was shining, her daughter was kissing her son's nose, her baby had slept through the night. Yesterday was yesterday and todays didn't get much better than this.

'Are you sure?' he asked again.

Jem nodded. She knew what he was asking her. He was asking her how she felt almost exactly twenty-four hours after the end of her pregnancy.

'Honestly,' she said, 'I really am. Fine.'

She smiled at her children again, children she'd spent months and years gestating, feeding, nourishing and teaching. These were her children. This was all she wanted. She didn't ask Ralph if he was OK. She didn't want to hear his answer.

Chapter 12

Ralph had a history of snooping. He found the limitations of questions and answers, the insufficiency of ordinary conversation utterly frustrating. One day, he was certain, some brilliant person would invent a computer that could transcribe a person's innermost thoughts into text on a screen. But until that day the only way to get any really useful insight into another person's inner workings was to snoop through their stuff. Eavesdropping was another way. It was not something that Ralph felt proud of, it was just part of his make-up. He'd fallen in love with Jem after snooping through her things before he'd even had a conversation with her. He'd read her diaries, five years worth of them, from cover to cover while she was out at work. He'd found out all about her ex-boyfriends and her PMT and what she really thought about her flatmates. He'd fingered her clothes and examined her shoes, become familiar with the golden retriever called Maisy, whom she kept a photo of by her bed. If it wasn't for his snooping habit, Ralph and Jem might never have got together. And in fact, in his defence, he had not been actively snooping at all when he found the text message from a strange man on Jem's phone that morning. He had merely been curious as to why someone would be sending Jem a text message at seven o'clock in the morning.

The fact that he was alone in the kitchen at the time and that Jem was upstairs having a shower was also a contributing factor to him picking up the phone and pressing the mail icon.

He had been expecting something dull, a message from Lulu saying, 'Don't forget to bring pizzas tomorrow,' or a message from the nursery saying 'Due to inclement weather the planned trip to London Zoo has been cancelled and children will NOT require a packed lunch today.'

He had not been expecting to read the words: 'Dear Jem, I am still waiting for you to forgive me. Did you get the flowers? I miss you. Please let me know that we are still cool. Love, Joel x'.

He dropped the phone to the kitchen counter and reeled slightly on the spot, as though an invisible man had just shoved him roughly in the chest.

After a moment he picked up the phone again and reread the message, trying to extract something from it that might offer a reasonable explanation for its presence on his partner's phone. But no, it was all there: flowers, apologies, kisses, the word 'love'. There was no reasonable explanation for it, none whatsoever.

He quickly restored the message to 'unread' status and switched off the phone.

He looked at his bowl of Bran Flakes and felt queasy. He heard footsteps overhead, Jem's, padding from the bathroom to the bedroom. He forced himself to swallow and listened to some buzzing in his ears for a moment. It was the sound of his thoughts arranging themselves.

What to do?

He had no idea.

He was not a fan of confrontation, especially not at seven in the morning.

He tried to step away from the situation by concentrating on making up a bowl of baby porridge for Blake, who was sitting in his Bumbo on the kitchen table looking at Ralph expectantly. He poured boiling water on to the translucent flakes and stirred in a spoonful of puréed raspberry. It looked like something that had been extruded from a lanced boil. He swallowed again and fished a plastic spoon out of the cutlery drawer, waving it in front of Blake's nose.

'Have *you* got any idea?' he whispered to Blake. 'Any idea? Who is Joel? Have you met him? God, I bet you have. I mean, Mummy never goes anywhere without you. Except . . .' He stopped mid-thought. That day, that day when she'd taken Blake over to Lulu's, when she'd been wearing those heels. Said she was going for a business meeting in town. He'd never really asked her about it, been too preoccupied first with wanting to get her into bed and then with feeling aggrieved that she wouldn't let him. Could that have been the first meeting? But then, what since? She hadn't been out in the evenings, there'd been no more business meetings, she was either here or she was out with the kids. How could she possibly have been conducting an affair with a man called Joel? She didn't (as she herself would probably have said) have the time.

He spooned the last of the porridge into Blake's eager mouth and scraped the mess from his face with the side of the spoon.

'Oh, thanks for doing that.' It was Jem, in the doorway, hair freshly washed, in jeans and a lavender cardigan. Scarlett was behind her in her pink tartan dressing gown, peering cheekily between her legs.

Ralph glanced at the well-fed baby, the empty cereal bowl, barely able to recall doing it. 'That's all right,' he said, putting it in the sink and rinsing it out.

'That's three nights now.'

'Three nights of what?' Ralph felt unplugged from reality. Now that Jem was in front of him, in the flesh, in her soft, almost childlike cardigan, it seemed even more unlikely to Ralph that there could be a mysterious, apologetic, flower-bearing man called Joel in her life.

'Blake,' she replied, helping Scarlett on to her chair and

pulling another cereal bowl from the cupboard. 'Three nights sleeping through. You know what that means?' she smiled at him, impishly.

'No,' he said in a voice that didn't sound like his own because it was so full of words he couldn't say. 'What does it mean?'

'It means,' she curled her arm around his waist, 'that we can go out and that I can get drunk and *go to bed late* and not worry about being woken up or giving him boozy milk. It means that you and I are *free*.' She kissed him on the cheek and Ralph thought that he could not remember the last time that Jem had voluntarily kissed him on the cheek. 'So,' she said, 'where shall we go? I was thinking ... maybe our old stomping ground. Maybe a night out in Soho, a few pints, a curry?'

Ralph nodded distractedly. 'Yeah,' he said, 'why not?'

'Cool,' Jem tipped Scarlett's Shreddies into the cereal bowl and opened the fridge door. 'I will call Lulu this morning, find out when she's free. And also, I was thinking I might ask her if she could take the kids for a couple of hours during the day this weekend, so you and I could go ring shopping?'

'Ring shopping?'

'Yes. A ring. For me.' She looked at him and laughed. 'You hadn't even thought about it, had you?'

Ralph shrugged. He couldn't really remember anything he'd thought about at any point in his life before reading a text message from a man called Joel.

'An engagement ring. Doesn't have to be anything flash.'

'Er, yeah. OK.'

'You all right?' asked Jem.

'Yeah,' Ralph pulled at the back of his neck with his right hand. 'I'm just, you know, morning-brain.'

Ralph took his morning-brain into lunchtime and through to the afternoon. He simply could not form a reasonable thought in his head. Everything he tried to contemplate just got ricocheted back into his conscious-ness as the word 'Joel'. When he heard Jem leaving the house that afternoon with a cheery 'Bye, Ralph!' (another new development, in the past she'd just go, leaving nothing but the sound of a slammed door in her wake) he immediately left his studio and started hunting for more clues.

Without her phone he didn't really know where to start. He looked for evidence of flowers in vases, on tabletops, in bins and on the patio but found none. He opened and shut all of Jem's drawers in the chest in their bedroom, wondering what evidence he thought he would possibly find therein – a hastily hidden condom, a stack of love letters tied with silk ribbon? He accessed her e-mail account and scrolled through her in-box, her deleted e-mails, her drafts and even her junk mail. He looked especially at e-mails sent and received around the time of her 'business meeting' in the high heels, but there was nothing there. He glanced at her recent documents and found nothing. The whole concept of her affair seemed to be evaporating. Suddenly the little missive he'd seen that morning seemed totally without context.

He wondered how he would get to Jem's mobile phone without being caught red-handed and then, at the very moment that he thought it, he heard a ringing noise coming from somewhere beyond the kitchen. He followed the noise to the hallway and located the source in Jem's parka. She'd left her phone behind! He plucked the phone from her pocket and saw that it was Lulu calling. He waited for the phone to go through to voicemail and then he opened up her messages. They were nearly all from Lulu. Lulu, Lulu, Lulu, Karl, Lulu, Mummy, Happy Days Nursery, Lulu, Lulu, Unknown. He clicked on unknown:

'Friday night sounds great. Let me have your address. Jx'
Let me have your address? Friday night?

With clammy fingers he flicked to the sent messages

262

folder, looking for one to correlate with this one. And there it was. Thursday 17 April, 13.08 p.m.

Hello! Thanks so much for yesterday. Scarlett had the best time EVER and won't stop talking about Jessica! It's my last night of single motherhood tomorrow, wondered if you wanted to help me celebrate with a curry and some beers at our place. Maybe 6ish, keep the girls up late? Let me know and I'll give you the details. J.

Ralph stopped and sucked in a big lungful of air. Jem had invited a man here, while he was away. In Santa Monica. Jem had invited that man. THAT MAN. Of course! The man with the little girl. Jessica, that was her name! The man who'd given him such a funny look that day just after he got back from the States. That man who'd been watching him coming out of the church the other day. That man called Joel.

But no, surely not? I mean, there was nothing untoward in either text message and if you took the fact that Joel was a man out of the equation and pretended that he was a woman called, say, Julie, it would all seem perfectly innocuous. But he wasn't a woman called Julie, he was a man. A not particularly good-looking man, it had to be said. So maybe there was nothing to it. He came for supper. They had a beer or two, probably Jem's way of sticking her finger up at Ralph, metaphorically speaking, the children played together, Joel went home. But then he'd obviously subsequently done something to upset Jem. There were flowers involved. He *missed her*. And now he was prowling about the place looking aggrieved. No, it was not innocuous. It was meaningful.

He switched off Jem's phone and slid it back into the pocket of her parka.

Then he scurried back upstairs to his studio, smoked a

263

cigarette on his balcony, smoked another cigarette on his balcony and then, with his heart pounding like a piston in his chest, he wrote an e-mail to the only person he felt he could talk to about this. He wrote to Rosey.

16 May 2008
Dear Ralph, I'm not quite sure what to say. First losing the baby and now this. I'm not sure that a confrontation is the way forward. As you say, you and Jem have a history when it comes to 'snooping' and as the messages are so ambiguous you might just end up stirring up a load of trouble for nothing. I have a friend in London. Her name is Sarah Betts. She runs a prayer group near you. If you needed to offload on someone completely neutral she might be just the person. Here's her e-mail address.
    Good luck.
    Love, Rosey x

Chapter 13

Sarah Betts was not what Ralph had been expecting. She had the voice of a sweet young Southern belle, but the look of a hard-nosed City lawyer. She was also older than he'd expected and dressed in what looked oddly like bondage gear – rather shiny black leggings (she had very good legs for a woman of her age), a black brocade waist-coat, high boots in oxblood leather and an oversized Barbour coat that skimmed her ankles.

'I am not a Christian,' she said. 'Not in the universally accepted definition of the word, at least.'

She swirled red wine around a large glass and beamed at him, revealing small, wine-stained teeth inside a slickly executed smile. They were sitting in a gastropub at midday. Ralph was sipping a Virgin Mary. He'd been taken aback by Sarah's request for a glass of wine, the clock hand not quite nudging twelve, but then, he mused, she had the look of a woman who subsisted largely on complex red wines.

'No,' she continued, probing an olive with a cocktail stick, 'I gave up on that old game a long time ago. The church is full of donkeys. Like everything in this life, there are newer better versions of faith out there and I found one I like. One that works for me. You know, like a new shampoo!' She leaned towards him as she said this and then laughed, a big pantomime belly laugh. Slowly she leaned back again, into her chair and then she let her smile dim a little and exhaled. 'So, Ralph, would you care to enlighten me. Your note was oblique, to put it mildly.'

'Yeah, sorry about that. My friend Rosey gave me your e-mail because she thought you might be able to . . .'

Sarah raised an eyebrow at him, encouragingly.

'Well, I've been feeling things. Strange things, for weeks, ever since I went to California, even before I went to California, really, and there just isn't anyone I can talk to about it. Jem, my partner, well, she's really strongly atheistic. She actually despises religion. And it's like there's this little door, inside my head, a little door I never knew was there and that somehow it got left open and now there's all this stuff getting in . . .'

'Stuff?'

'Yes, feelings, thoughts, spirituality. I've been sitting in this church, just around the corner, most days, just for five minutes and when I'm sitting there I feel moved and when I'm not there I kind of wish I was there. And even when I'm not there I'm full of all these ideas, all these emotions and I keep wanting to call it God, you know, but it's not God it's more like . . .'

'Love?'

Ralph paused and flicked his gaze towards Sarah. 'Yes,' he said, relief softening his voice, 'yes, like love. But not like a specific love, not like a love for a wife or for a child, just a general feeling of . . . compassion, I suppose, something bigger than me, something I can't quite control. And I'd got myself to this point of feeling right with the world. I'd faced up to myself, looked at things I didn't like about myself, changed them, started to treat my wife with more respect and then . . .' He stopped for a moment, not sure what words to use. 'Well, she got pregnant. We got pregnant. We've got a little baby, he's only a few months, so it certainly wasn't planned, you know, it was an accident. And I was a bit surprised but ultimately I thought, yeah, a baby, fantastic. I wanted a chance to appreciate it because I wasn't that over the moon about the other two. I was kind of in denial both times. I suppose, in a way, I felt

266

like this would be *my* baby. But Jem, well, she just totally wasn't up for it and then on Tuesday, she went to a clinic, and she got rid of it.'

Sarah's eyes widened slightly at this declaration. 'She aborted the baby?'

'Well, no, she didn't. Not in the end. Turns out she'd already lost it. But she had the procedure anyway, to, you know, get it out of her.'

'The dead foetus?'

'Yes,' said Ralph, running a fingertip round and round the rim of his glass. 'But I know she would have gone through with it. I saw her in the waiting room, through the window, before she knew the baby was already dead and she was reading a fashion magazine. Literally, just reading it.'

'So you'd both agreed, had you, to having this abortion?'

Ralph shrugged. 'Well, yeah. Up to a point. I let her take control. I let her choose, because it's her body and her life and because I love her so much. So I let her do it. She knew I didn't want her to do it. But I let her do it. And after she left that morning, for the clinic, I sat there, sat there with our baby just hoping and praying that she'd walk through the door and say she'd changed her mind, that she couldn't go through with it. I really thought she would, because she's soft like that. She's a soft person and I thought that once she was there, once she was right up against what it was she was about to do, she'd buckle, you know? But she didn't, so I put the baby in the car and I went to the clinic.'

'To stop her?'

'Yes. That's right. To stop her. And I kept looking at my baby in the back of the car, in the rear-view mirror, and just feeling overwhelmed by the baby, by his innocence and his potential, and that he was completely oblivious to the fact that his mother was about to kill his sibling. I just thought, wow, in years to come people will say to you, so, have you got any brothers and sisters, and he'll say yeah, just the one, an older sister, and he'll never know that he should have had another, a little brother, a little sister, another piece of . . . family. And you know, it was one of the most shocking things I've ever seen. I can't get it out of my head – I looked through the window and she was sitting there reading a magazine, as though she were about to have her legs waxed, you know? And now Jem's just bouncing around like nothing ever happened, plan-ning our wedding, the wedding I suggested because I thought it would make her feel more secure about having a third baby, and now that there is no baby I'm just not sure I've got the heart to go through with it any more – not that I don't want to be married to her but that I just can't feel enthusiastic about it. It was for the baby. And now the baby's gone. And Jem's just carrying on as if everything is absolutely fine. But everything's *not* fine. It's not fine at all, and the longer it goes on with me pretending that I'm OK, the more knotted up I'm getting inside and the harder I'm finding it to be . . . to feel the way I'm supposed to feel, that way I want to feel.'

'You mean you're resentful?'

Ralph nodded. 'Yes. I am. And it's bad. It's negative. So much of what was wrong between me and Jem for so long was about resentment, hers against me, and I've worked so hard to turn that round and now it's all starting up again and I don't know how to stop it.'

'Right.' Sarah drew herself up and spread her fingers out along the edge of the table. 'There are a few issues there. You seem to be having trouble defining your spir-itual path right now. You are battling to keep your marriage afloat. And you are mourning the loss of your baby. Added to which you are now feeling negative emotions at a time when you are desperate to stay positive.'

'Yes,' Ralph nodded, fervently, 'that's it. Exactly.'

'I see,' she said, lowering herself back into her chair. 'I mean,' she continued, 'you know I'm not a counsellor? I can't offer you the world, but I can offer you people.'

'People?'

'Yeah, look, there's a meeting, tomorrow evening. I'll be there, and lots and lots of other people will be there. And if you like those other people, if you feel those other people have anything to offer you, then you can come again.'

'Right,' said Ralph, his internal antennae sending him worrying culty secty Reverend Moon warning signs. The lightly couched invitation sounded a bit evangelical to him. How could he reconcile the idea of joining a church with living with Jem? Jem had once said to him: 'I would rather you had an affair than found Jesus. Nothing scares me more than organised religion.' He'd laughed at the time and said, cool, I get to have an affair! But it didn't seem particularly funny now. 'So this is your, er, church you're talking about?' he asked, nervously.

'No,' she shook her head, still smiling at him fondly, 'no. It's not a church. As I say, I am not a Christian. None of us are Christians. Neither are we Jews, Mormons, Muslims or Scientologists. We are part of a group of people who have read the Bible and rejected it, who have tried many other forms of faith and found them to be lacking, trying or simply barking. But we want to feel something, that togetherness that comes from group worship, that love that comes from congregational prayer. We are a group. That is all.'

'So you don't worship anything?'

'No, we don't worship any*one*. We find our inspiration in the world around us, in what you can see, smell and touch. And not just that, but in the internal spirit, in the

269

beauty of mankind. It's a cult, if you like, but a cult of humanity, of love. It's a cult for the right-minded, the intellectual, the successful, the creative. We have quite a few celebrity members.'

'You do?'

'Yes, you may have seen them; they get papped occasionally leaving our centre in Notting Hill. It's deliberate, a PR operation, which of course is my area of responsibility. They can choose to leave by the back door but they leave by the front, for us, for the group, to show the world what we're doing.'

'Is it, is it like that Madonna thing?'

Sarah laughed her big, hooting laugh. 'No! It is NOT like that Madonna thing, that watered-down Judaism for numbskulls! All that blessed water for a thousand bucks a pop and bits of string that have touched some dead person's ass or whatever.' She tutted and frowned, but her face soon sprung back into its smile-shaped form. 'No, what we do is much more personal. We do not impose any form of structure or ritual and we most certainly do not ask for any money.'

'So, how are you financed?'

She shrugged. 'People give. They don't need to be sold bits of string. They just give. And if they don't give in financial form, they give in other ways. Their time, their expertise. Like me, with my role as PR director. I don't have any money but this is something I can do. But anyway, anyway, I'm not here to recruit you. We don't need to actively recruit. I'm just here because you wanted to see me and I'm telling you all this because you asked. And the bottom line is this: if your life is hurting you right now, and clearly it is, then I know a place where you will find strength and love, and if that sounds like a place you'd like to be, then you are so welcome to be there. Tomorrow night. Six thirty. Here.' She scribbled an address on to a piece of paper torn from a notepad in her handbag and passed it to him across the table. 'I think you should come,' she said, smiling her beatific smile. 'I think you're just our kind of person.'

Chapter 14

Ralph felt curiously let down. He was sitting on a blue plastic chair in the Maygrove Centre at the bottom of Lulu's road in a room with thirty other people. A guy in a lilac jumper had spoken very briefly about the importance of human interaction to a room full of ordinary-looking people, and then everyone had stood up and started drinking tea. It was neither inspiring nor moving, and not even vaguely controversial. Ralph was at a social meeting of Sarah's prayer group. He had not told Jem he was going to a prayer group meeting. He had told her he was going for a run. He was even wearing his running gear.

As the group splintered apart and started to mingle, Ralph felt both relieved that he would not be joining a prayer group and disappointed that his life appeared not to be about to change path.

'So,' said Sarah, guiding him away from his seat and towards the group of people, 'what did you think?'

He shrugged. He wanted to say: 'Was that it?' But it didn't seem polite.

'Is there anyone here you'd like me to introduce you to?' she continued.

Ralph glanced around. Really he just wanted to go home now. He had no idea why he'd come in the first place. He'd thought . . . well, he wasn't sure what he'd thought. He was about to say, 'Well, no actually, thank you, Sarah, but I think I'll be on my way,' when a tall man approached him, a tall thin man with white hair and a long, weathered face. His eyes were china blue and his smile was warm and welcoming. 'A new face,' he said, in a baritone Scots accent. 'Glad you could make it.'

'This is Ralph,' said Sarah.

'Good to meet you, Ralph. My name's Gil. Where are you from?'

'Croydon,' he replied. 'What about you?'

'The Southern Isles,' said Gil, 'the Hebrides. The oldest of twelve, the tallest and the strongest. My family worked me into the ground. Escaped on the first boat out of there the moment I turned sixteen. Been on my own ever since. You have any family?'

Ralph blinked, surprised by the frantic pace of Gil's conversation. 'Yes,' he replied, 'a partner, two small children.'

'Lucky man. I never managed to keep anyone. I lost everyone I ever loved, either by accident or by my own actions. Or inactions, on the whole. Are you happy, you and your family?'

Ralph shrugged. Clearly this was a man who appreciated candour. 'Things have been better.'

'Rocky times?' Gil appraised him through slanted eyes.

'Well, yeah.'

'Figures,' said Gil, 'otherwise you wouldnae be here. What mountains are you climbing?'

Ralph scratched his chin. 'You really want to know?' he replied.

Gil peered at him with dry amusement. 'Sonny,' he said, 'you cannot know yourself if you do not know others. You cannot belong to this world if you do not let it touch you. Did you come here for nothing, or did you come here for something?'

Ralph blew out his cheeks. 'Well, yeah, for something.'

'Well then, talk to me, man. And when you've done talking, listen. You hear?'

'Right,' started Ralph, 'well, the last few months, since our second child was born, they've been a bit of a roller-coaster.'

He told Gil about his lack of paternal feelings towards his son, about the state of their sex life, about running way to America and falling in love with his best friend's girlfriend. He told him about finding peace in the little clapboard church, about finding peace within himself, his homecoming and the subsequent pregnancy, miscarriage and uncovering of possible infidelity and worse, and that he was now feeling more lost than ever.

All the while, Gil kept his blue eyes on Ralph, licking his large dry lips occasionally, nodding slowly.

'That's a big tangle, boy,' he said. 'You're clawing your way out of a bramble bush there. Have you spoken to your woman?'

'To Jem?'

'Yes, have you told her about your suspicions, about this odd man with his flowers and all?'

Ralph shook his head.

'Why not?'

Ralph blinked at him. It was an entirely reasonable question. 'I'm not sure,' he said. 'I suppose that if I ask her and it's something, then we'll have to split up and if I ask her and it's nothing then she'll know I've been snooping around and thinking bad things about her and then we'll have to split up. I just don't want to put her on the spot, I don't want to watch her lying or squirming or getting cross with me for doubting her.'

'You don't want a confrontation?'

'I don't want a confrontation.'

'Well, boy, you're going to have to have one. No point

standing here talking to me. No point at all. Sounds to me like your little woman is in as much of a mess as you are. Take her out. Give her a beer. Talk to her, man, *talk to her.*'

Chapter 15

Ralph and Jem went out the following night. They got a cab to Battersea Park Road and sat in the Latchmere for two hours. Jem was wearing something chiffony and flouncy that she'd bought from an on-line vintage boutique, which had arrived in the post that very morning. Before they'd even left the house Jem had had two Bacardi and Cokes, which she'd drunk at the kitchen table with Lulu. Not that she felt she needed to be drunk to go out on a date with Ralph, but alcohol, she had decided, had been at the core of their *good times*. They hadn't thought of it as a crutch back then. They hadn't thought: how come every time we go out together we end up in a pub? It had just been a part of their lifestyle: beer, spliff, another beer, wine with dinner, the occasional cocktail or glass of champagne.

Scarlett had seemed pleased to see them leaving the house together that night, thrilled, almost, that her mum and dad had nice clothes on and were going somewhere on their own to have a nice time. Jem was excited too. Not only was she keen to recreate the sort of nights that she and Ralph had enjoyed in their early years, but she hadn't been out since she'd lost the baby and she needed desperately to let her hair down and forget for a night at least about the last few unsettling weeks.

Jem looked around the old pub, the place they'd been to once or twice a week when they'd had their flat on Lurline Gardens. It hadn't changed at all. Except – well, it did seem that everyone in here was very young. She was sure that hadn't been the case five years ago. She was sure that back then everyone had been about thirty, thirty-five and now they all looked, what, about twenty-six, possibly younger. But still, it was nice to feel plugged back into a world that she'd previously inhabited so carelessly.

When she looked back at her life before children she wanted to leave a little metaphorical Post-it note for her unknowing self. And that note would say: 'GO OUT MORE!' She thought back to the nights in, because they were (yawn) too tired to go out. *Too tired to go out?* At thirty-four years old? With nothing but a cushy job in an office and a cute commute on a Routemaster to drain her energy resources? What had she been thinking? She should have been out every night. She should have never seen the four walls of her home. She and Ralph should have met up every night after work, in Soho, in Clerkenwell, in Marylebone. Every night should have been a pub crawl, every weekend should have been lost. Why had they spent so much time in garden centres and Wickes when they should have been daytime drinking? Why had they decided not to go on holiday one year 'because we haven't got enough money'? She looked around her again at the young and the child-free and knew that for the majority of them it was only a matter of time, a year, maybe five, maybe ten to fifteen, but most of them eventually would end up in a little house with a kid or two, tied to baby-sitters and feeling old. All that divided Jem from them was time.

'Funny, getting old, isn't it?' said Jem.

Ralph smiled. 'Well, we're not quite there yet.'

'No, I know, and I know that forty these days is nothing like forty thirty years ago and that we're all much younger than we used to be, but still, let's face it, we're the oldest people in here.'

Ralph looked around and shrugged. There was something eternally youthful about Ralph. While Jem had kept her figure and her looks, she had said goodbye to a fresh face. She looked mature. Ralph did not look mature. His style of dressing, his slightly gormless teenage demeanour, his slouchy walk, his air of injured vulnerability, the way his jeans hung low around his hips because he didn't have much of a bum; he could have passed for a thirty-year-old with laughter lines. He was not much interested in the process of ageing; he didn't care much about his hair loss or the diminishing elasticity of his skin. Ralph, Jem suspected, was one of those people who would remain forever youthful just because it had never occurred to him that he could get old.

Ralph shrugged. 'Not really,' he said, 'look at them.' He pointed at a group of people in their early to mid-thirties, perfectly proving Jem's theory.

Jem laughed. 'Ralph,' she said, 'they're not even thirty-five! God, I can't believe I'm going to be forty soon,' she continued. 'Forty. I mean, I remember my mum's fortieth birthday party. I was fifteen! And I thought she was ancient. Her and all her really old friends. And here I am with a baby, feeling like I've only just started out in life.' She shook her head slowly.

Ralph smiled tightly and drummed his fingers against the tabletop. He seemed preoccupied.

'Are you OK?' said Jem.

'Yeah. Yeah, I'm fine.'

He didn't look fine, but Jem didn't push him. This was supposedly the night that they would begin to rediscover each other and she hoped that rather than drawing them into a tedious discussion about whether Ralph actually was 'fine' or not, she could lead by example and keep the evening buoyant. So she chatted and she nattered and she yakked and she blathered, and all the while she poured cold lager down her throat and felt some kind of happiness descend upon her thickly and obscurely.

By the time they left the pub at nine thirty, Jem was too

full of beer to contemplate curry, so she went into a mini-mart a few doors down and bought herself a packet of Hula Hoops and an envelope of Rizlas.

'A packet of green Rizlas, please.'

She could barely remember the last time she'd uttered those words.

'Let's walk across the bridge,' she said, grabbing Ralph's hand outside. 'I've got a surprise for you!'

Jem missed Battersea Bridge. For so long the traversing of the bridge, north to south, south to north, had been a constant marker of her days. For so long she had seen the river, her river, twice, sometimes four times a day, through changing seasons and changing times. She'd see it glimmering like crystal on spring mornings and black as tar at midnight. Battersea Bridge was her youth. And now she wanted to walk across it, late at night, hand in hand with Ralph, like they'd done a hundred times before.

Jem felt a kind of magic in the air as they headed east down Battersea Park Road. In her coat pocket she had a little plastic bag. Lulu had got it for her. Lulu, for some reason, still knew people who could procure drugs for her. It was yet another mystery about the endlessly mysterious Lulu. At the edge of the river, Jem pulled the bag from her pocket and showed it to Ralph.

'Where the hell did you get that from?' he asked, his eyebrows raised in surprise.

Jem shrugged. 'Just some guy in an alley,' she teased.

'What!' Ralph threw her a look of alarm.

'Joking,' she reassured. 'Lulu. Of course.'

She took a cigarette from Ralph's back pocket and then, crouching in the shadows of the bridge, she went through the ritual, the tearing off of a strip of cigarette, the licking and the piecing together of the flimsy Rizlas, the separating of the tobacco and the sprinkling of the pungent green herb, then the rolling and the licking and the twisting of the tip and the curling up of card and the inserting of the roach and there it was, perfect and ready to smoke, like it hadn't really been five years since she'd last made herself a spliff.

'Like riding a bike,' she smiled.

'Are you serious about smoking that?' said Ralph.

'Yeah,' she said, 'of course. Why not?'

He gestured towards the bridge. 'But what if we get caught?'

'We will not get caught,' she laughed.

'How do you know?' he said.

She laughed again. 'Because we won't.'

He frowned at her. 'Christ, Jem, just think about it. Just think if we got stopped. They could take us into a station. They could keep us there for hours. And how the fuck would we explain that to the baby-sitter?'

'Well, given that the baby-sitter sold this stuff to me I don't suppose she'd have much to say at all. Oh, come on, look at us – do you honestly think that the police force of south London have nothing better to do with their time than pull in thirtysomething parents off the streets of Battersea for having a little smoke?'

She lit the spliff and she inhaled. Ralph looked at her forlornly. She looked at him wantonly. The smoke hit the soft lining of her lungs and burned. She coughed and laughed. 'Jesus,' she said, 'I've lost the knack. My poor lungs!' She passed the spliff to Ralph, who eyed it, eyed Jem and then took it from her reluctantly. 'Why are you doing this?' he said, inhaling.

Jem didn't say: 'Because this is what we used to do when we were in love with each other and I want us to be in love with each other again.' Instead she grabbed his hand and said: 'Come on, let's hop on a bus, let's go into Soho. It's not even ten!'

Ralph glanced down at the spliff in his hand and then up at his partner and Jem knew immediately that he did not want to hop on a bus and go into Soho with her.

Jem sighed. 'Is that a stupid idea?' she asked.

Ralph shrugged. 'Come on,' he said, holding out his hand for her, 'it's late. Let's go home.'

Jem let her shoulders fall and acquiesced. Halfway back across the bridge, she flicked the burning spliff into the river below and watched it float away, a small white speck of nothing.

Jem pushed the door to her son's bedroom open a crack and peered through it. The room was dark, lit only by a small nightlight plugged into a socket above the skirting and the light from the hallway behind her. Blake was zipped into a pink sleeping bag (at £30 a pop Jem had felt no need to invest in new one after producing a boy child – he would never know). He had somehow managed to wedge himself into a corner of his cot against the (pink) cot bumpers and Jem swayed a little drunkenly into his room and pulled him back to the bottom of the cot. He stirred very slightly and rubbed at his cheek with a balled-up fist before settling back into a deep sleep. Jem stood straight and stared into his cot. Sober, she would have been out of here in a nanosecond, neurotic about the possibility of awaking him, but drunk and vaguely stoned she was quietly hoping that he would stir, that she would have cause to pick him up and hold him to her and soothe him home to sleep again. But he did not stir, he slumbered, and Jem stood above him and smiled and felt an ache inside her where a few days ago there had been another one, not slumbering and stirring but slowly, perfectly fading away.

She looked at her son and then she looked at her flat belly and then she looked at her son again. It hadn't been that bad, had it? Her time being pregnant with Blake? It hadn't been so awful nursing him in the night; it had been quite beautiful, in fact – the silence, the softness of it. And really, now, in retrospect, it hadn't taken so long to get to this point, to get to the point where she and Ralph could find time for each other again. So why had she been in such a desperate panic to stop her pregnancy? If anything she felt less close to Ralph since the baby had gone than she had beforehand. She felt tears rise upwards towards her eyes, but she pulled them back. She did not want to have to explain tears to Ralph. She could not tell him that she might have been wrong. Instead she sucked it all in, the emotion, the rawness, the sadness, sucked it all back inside herself and headed for her bed.

Ralph was lying down. He was on his side, his back facing her side of the bed. He turned when he heard her come in and glanced at her.

'Where've you been?'

'Looking at Blake,' she smiled.

'Is he OK?'

She nodded. 'He's gorgeous,' she said. And then she took off her clothes and didn't put on her pyjamas. Instead she climbed naked into bed alongside her partner and spooned her naked body up against his semi-naked body. They may not have had a laugh and got stoned and hopped on to a bus into Soho, but they could still salvage something valuable from their date. She rubbed the tip of her nose against the bare skin of his back and she smelled him and he smelled good. She touched her lips to his skin and she felt herself, for the first time in a long time, properly aroused, not just pleasing her man, not just maintaining the status quo, not even just enjoying herself, but wanting him, wanting it, insanely.

She ran her lips up and down his back and into the crook of his neck, until finally, he turned towards her, on to his back and he put his hand into her hair and stared into her eyes and Jem leaned down to kiss him and suddenly his other hand was against her breastbone, pushing her away. And he whispered, into the soft darkness of their marital bed, 'No, Jem, no. I can't.'

She raised herself to her knees and looked down at him. 'What?' she gasped.

'I can't. I . . . just. It doesn't feel right.'

She sank to a kneeling position and felt the sweet new rose of her passion shrivelling up.

'Sorry,' she said, 'I don't get it. What doesn't feel right?'

'This,' said Ralph, gesturing at their nakedness. 'I feel, wrong. I feel . . .'

Jem watched him, desperately hoping that he would somehow find the words from somewhere to explain his rejection of her advances. But words had never been Ralph's strong point. 'I don't know,' he said, finally. 'I don't know. I'm just tired. That's all.'

Jem stared at him for a moment longer, wishing there was something she could say or do that would reverse the last two minutes of her life. Her skin crawled with humiliation. Her heart raced with embarrassment. It was not only the first time that Ralph had rejected her sexual advances; it was the first time that any man, full stop, had rejected her sexual advances. She felt raw and exposed.

'Fine,' she said, climbing from the bed and towards her pyjamas on a chair in the window. 'Fine.' She pulled on her vest and her bottoms and she slipped back into the bed. 'All those bloody months . . .' she wanted to say, 'all those bloody months you put me on a guilt trip because I wouldn't have sex with you,' but then she stopped herself. He was punishing her, she surmised. This was his way of saying, you made me suffer, now don't expect me just to roll over and let you call the shots.

She pulled the duvet up around her shoulders and she turned away from him. She couldn't look at him. She couldn't talk to him. He had broken her in half, this new barely formed person she'd been trying to become. Tonight was the night that she was going to make sense of everything:

of Joel, of the baby, of the trip to California, of getting married. It had all hinged on tonight. And now there was nothing left to see. The girl in the chiffon dress in the photograph faded from sight. The evening, the rebirth, the imagined night of spontaneity, sex and fun – it had imploded. Suddenly she was hard and full of resentment again.

She let hot wet tears take her painfully into sleep.

Chapter 16

It was a warm May afternoon. Ralph had finished another painting and decided to celebrate by taking a walk and smoking three cigarettes, back to back. These days Ralph tried to limit his smoking very strictly to ten a day. One after breakfast, with a coffee. One ten minutes later to get his bowels moving. Two between breakfast and lunch, then one right after lunch. Then he was allowed two between lunch and teatime, one after tea and two between teatime and bedtime. There was never an opportunity to smoke three in a row. Three in a row was like a glass of Dom Perignon, a heavy-bottomed tumbler full of finest ten-year-old malt whisky. Standing on his balcony puffing away would have felt a bit hollow, but walking through the streets of south London, the sun on his back, the world on the pavement, he felt like the king of the world.

It was just as he'd put his second cigarette to the tip of his third cigarette and drawn in the warm leafy smoke that he saw them.

Jem and Joel.

They were standing outside the playground. Joel had a pink scooter in one hand and with the other he was stroking Jem's arm. Jem had one hand on the handle of Blake's buggy and the two girls were involved in some kind of skipping activity behind them.

Ralph caught his breath and coughed slightly as the smoke went down the wrong way. He stamped the finished butt to the ground with his booted foot and moved behind a parked van, his hand over his mouth to mask his coughing. Peering from behind the van he could see that Jem and Joel were involved in some kind of rather intense conversation. Jem, it was clear, was engrossed in what Joel was saying and at one point she covered his hand on her arm with hers. They both stopped talking then for a moment and looked at the ground, then they looked up at each other and Joel said something and suddenly he was falling against Jem and Jem put her arms out to hold him and the two of them stood like that for a good ten seconds, Ralph estimated, before finally pulling apart. Then the man called Joel put one hand out and stroked Jem's hair with it and Jem's body language, which should at this point have recoiled in horror, seemed to curl towards him, her eyes lowered coquettishly. Then they smiled at each other and rather than saying goodbye and going their separate ways, they strolled together in the direction of Ask pizza restaurant where Joel held open the door for Jem and the buggy and followed in behind her.

Ralph scuttled from behind the van and took a position opposite Ask, this time partially obscured by a phone box. They'd taken a seat in the window. Jem was hoisting Blake into a high chair, a girl with a dark ponytail was handing out a fan of oversized menus. Everyone was smiling at everyone. If you didn't know better, Ralph thought, if you were just a stranger walking past you'd be thinking: how nice, a family out for a teatime treat. (You might also think: what is that hot woman doing with that dweeb, but that was not really the point.) Ralph stood behind the phone booth for exactly twenty-eight minutes. He smoked ten cigarettes, back to back and he didn't enjoy one of them. He was going to wait until they left before moving along, returning home, but all the smoking and all the adrenalin had loosened him up inside. His bowels were wriggling with discomfort and fear, and he walked home at high speed.

* * *

'Nice afternoon?' he asked when Jem got home half an hour later.

'Yeah, lovely.'

'Good, what did you do?'

'Oh, the usual. Playground. Pizza.'

Ralph waited a beat, waited to see if Jem would offer the information, give him something innocent to grab hold of before he reached the worst possible conclusion.

'Just you lot?' he said.

He saw Jem pause for just a second before glancing down at Scarlett. She would not be able to lie in front of Scarlett, but he could tell she wanted to. 'No, actually we bumped into Jessica in the playground, didn't we, Scarlett?'

'Yes. And we all went and had a pizza together and Jessica's dad let me eat his ice cream from his cake because he says he doesn't like vanilla.'

Ralph nodded and smiled at her. 'Is Jessica's daddy nice, Scarlett?'

She shrugged. Scarlett was always the litmus test for the substance of people. She only liked about five people in the world, three of whom were her direct family. If Scarlett liked someone it meant something. 'Yes,' she said eventually, pulling at a black spiral of hair. 'I think he is. He's got a nice voice.'

'A nice voice.'

'Yes, he sounds like Daddy Pig. Except . . . not so fat.'

Ralph forced a smile. 'So, you've made a new friend, have you?' he asked Jem in as pleasant a voice as he could muster.

Jem threw him a strange look. 'Well,' she said, 'it wasn't really like that. He kind of, er, forced himself on us. I stupidly mentioned that we had to go because Scarlett had been promised her favourite pizza, and I thought that would be the end of it, but he just kind of invited himself along. I felt a bit sorry for him because he'd just told me all about having a really terrible time with his ex-wife . . .'

'He's not married?'

'Well, no, not any more. But the wife's trying to get custody of Jessica and he was so upset about it, it was a bit embarrassing really. I mean, I hardly know him, but it seemed a bit rude then to say no when he wanted to join us for tea. Just after he'd been so upset. You know.'

Ralph folded his arms across his chest. 'But it was all right, was it?' he asked, thinking of the picture of familial harmony he had witnessed for twenty-eight long and unpleasant minutes outside the pizza restaurant.

Jem shrugged and pulled Blake out of his buggy. 'It was fine. He's just not someone I really want to be friends with, that's all.'

There were a dozen things that Ralph could have said in reply to this last statement, any number of things that might have taken the conversation to a place where misunderstandings might have been ironed out and presumptions not given a chance to propagate and take root. But he didn't. Instead he just smiled at Jem knowingly and left the room.

Chapter 17

The following day was forecast to be the Hottest Day of the Year So Far with temperatures reaching twenty-five degrees so Jem decided to collect Scarlett from nursery early and meet Lulu and her two youngest boys on the South Bank for lunch and skateboarding. It was the last day of the half-term and London was awash with families. By the time Jem, Scarlett and Blake had dismounted the number 68 bus outside Waterloo station it was one o'clock, the sun was at its peak and Jem was sweating lightly. Blake had spent the last fifteen minutes of the bus journey screaming plaintively from his buggy and Scarlett had taken it upon herself to be responsible for soothing him, jumping up from her seat at regular intervals to squash his angry cheeks between the palms of her hands and pet him slightly too hard on the top of his head and attempt to distract him with a very noisy squeaky toy that hung from the straps of his pram. This meant that Jem had spent the last fifteen minutes saying: Sit down, Scarlett. Leave him alone, Scarlett. You're making him worse, Scarlett. SIT DOWN, SCARLETT until the very sound of her own voice combined with the incessant whine of her baby and clucky squealing of her daughter made her want to shoot herself in the head with a gun, so she had no idea what the other passengers on the mostly full bus must have been making of it. She was sure that the whole bus must have breathed out in relief as one as she and her noisy clan finally got off the bus and the hydraulic doors shhhed closed behind them.

She found her sister sitting on the pavement reading a book while her sons threw themselves nerve-rackingly around the skateboarding pit under the Festival Hall. Behind her a small steel band was belting out something cool and summery, which lent the entire area the feel of a Caribbean beach resort. Further along a sinewy man in cut-off leggings and nothing else was performing somersaults whilst simultaneously juggling three teapots. It was remarkable to Jem that every day while she walked the same triangular lines of her life: home – nursery – shops – home – nursery, etc., there was a man here on the South Bank, not three miles away, juggling teapots. She felt a small familiar pull of regret that she was not living her life to the full. She'd closed off entire sections of the world to herself because she couldn't face the logistics of taking children out of her comfort zone, because it just seemed easier to stay at home or close to it.

'God,' said Lulu, hugging her warmly, 'isn't it lovely?'

'Beautiful,' agreed Jem, 'though buses plus heatwaves plus children is a bit of a nightmare combination.'

'We walked!' said Lulu, her voice tinged with pride.

'What, all the way?'

'Yes, all the way. Though I wouldn't have got those two to do it if they hadn't had their boards with them.' She pulled Scarlett towards her and attempted to embrace her. Scarlett pulled away and looked vaguely affronted. A very Victorian child, Scarlett, when it came to public displays of affection. Lulu smiled.

'So,' she said, 'how are you?'

Jem smiled. 'Good,' she said, 'I think.'

'You think?'

'Yes,' she said, clicking on the brakes on Blake's buggy and lowering herself to join her sister on the pavement. Scarlett clambered on to her lap and she encircled her with her arms. 'Weird week.'

Her sister's eyes widened. 'How come?'

'That guy again,' she said, wondering how much Scarlett would be able to absorb and digest of what she was about to say.

'Single dad?'

'Yes,' said Jem, 'that one. A funny thing happened yesterday.'

'Right . . .' Her sister pulled her sunglasses on to her head.

'Yes, he was at the playground and it's the first time I've seen him since the other, er, incident.'

'The yummy mummy incident?'

'Yes, that one. And he was just bizarrely friendly.'

Her sister raised an eyebrow in surprise. 'Bloody cheek,' she said. 'Did he ask you what you did with the flowers?'

'Yes.'

'God, what did you say?'

'I told him I'd put them in the bin.'

'You didn't!'

'Well, yeah, I did. I mean if his whole thing with me was that he thought I was some incredible amazing person who wasn't like anyone else then really he'd have been disappointed in me if I'd lied. That's what he'd have expected me to do, to be all polite and tra-la-la with him. So I just told him bluntly and he laughed. He thought it was really funny.'

'Blimey,' said Lulu.

'I know! He said, well, I'm not really sure what to make of it, but he said he'd been in a strange mood that day because of the, you know,' she cast her eyes towards the crown of her daughter's head, explaining her obtuseness, 'the mother. She's off the drugs, apparently, got a new boyfriend and now she wants custody of their daughter. He'd just finished talking to her when I bumped into him in the park. That's why he was so stressed, that's why he was so, you know, *mean*.'

'But still,' said Lulu, 'everyone has bad days, everyone takes their shit out on people from time to time, but what he said to you, it was unforgivable.'

Jem shrugged. 'I know,' she said, 'but actually, the more I think about it, the more some of what he was saying was true. I *did* give him the wrong impression. I was playing games with him. And I did even look at his shoes and hate them. Plus what he said really made me think. I have turned into this tedious urban mum, all caught up in doing everything properly, in getting an early night, in timings and schedules and, I don't know, moaning about my husband and keeping myself to myself, and what he said, it touched a nerve. I knew what he was trying to say. He wasn't saying I was a bad person. He was just saying that I wasn't the person I thought I was. And he was right.'

'And you told him this, did you?'

'Yeah.'

Her sister raised her eyebrows and tutted.

'No, honestly. It's good.'

'It is not *good*. Some bloody lunatic man has been stalking you, insulting you and sending you tacky flowers and you tell him that actually, you really appreciate it?'

'Yes,' laughed Jem. And it was true. She'd lost sight of the big picture and Joel had seen it. He'd seen the real Jem buried away underneath her piles of baggage and then she'd snatched it back and he'd been hurt and surprised.

'Don't tell me,' said Lulu, 'don't tell me you like him again, now?'

Jem shook her head. 'No, categorically not. And there was this rather bizarre moment when we were leaving the playground and I thought we were about to go our separate ways, so I was saying goodbye to him and he looked at me and he said: it means so much to me that you've forgiven me, you really are a great person. I'm really sorry if I ever made you feel bad about yourself, and then he hugged me!'

Scarlett looked up at them then and smiled. 'He did,' she agreed. 'He did hug her. He did hug her really hard. And he did like this.' She passed her sticky hand across Jem's cheek. 'And he was *crying*.'

Jem and Lulu looked at Scarlett and then at each other.

'Crying?' said Lulu.

'Well, no, not crying exactly.'

'Yes! He was! His cheeks was all wet!' cried Scarlett indignantly.

'Yes,' agreed Jem, 'his cheeks was all wet and it was all a bit, well, odd, I suppose. But, you know, clearly the man had had a bad day and then when he asked where we were going I told him we were off for a pizza, thinking, well, he won't want to come because he won't be able to afford it but he did come.'

'And he let me eat his vanilla ice cream because he doesn't like it.'

'Yes,' smiled Jem, 'Scarlett was *very* impressed with the ice-cream incident. Has been talking about it rather *a lot*.'

'You mean all these years of trying to win Scarlett's affections and all I had to do was palm off some unwanted vanilla ice cream on her?'

'Apparently so. Oooh, OW!' Jem move Scarlett to one side and got to her feet. Theo had just fallen off his skateboard and landed on his chin. He scrambled to his feet and looked around desperately for his mother, suddenly a small boy again and not the prematurely teenaged skateboard supremo. Lulu pulled him into her arms and examined the grazed chin. 'Ouch,' she said, 'that looks sore,' She pulled a tissue from her shoulder bag and wiped away the gravel. 'Oh, it's fine,' she said, examining it again, 'just a scratch. Come on,' she continued, 'let's go to Giraffe.'

She gathered her elder son and her younger son and

the six of them made their way across the crowded walkway towards the restaurant.

Now that Scarlett was out of earshot, Lulu asked her: 'So, what is going on? Are you going to have an affair with this man?'

Jem threw her a look of astonishment. 'No!' she said, 'of course I'm not. I don't even like him. I told you, he's *odd*. And clearly his life is a mess. Why on earth would I want to get involved with a man like that?'

'Because you're looking for something?'

Jem threw Lulu a look. 'What do you mean?'

Lulu paused and licked her lips. 'I don't know,' she replied circumspectly. 'You've just got this aura about you.'

'Aura?'

'Yes, you know, that thing that people get sometimes when they're . . . up for it?'

'You mean I'm like a bitch in heat?'

'No! Just that you seem . . . *available*.'

Jem looked at her sister, aghast.

'No, no, that's not what I meant. I can't explain it. But if I didn't know you, I'd say you were single.'

Jem let out a shot of ironic laughter. 'Ha,' she said, 'when, in fact, I'm thirty-eight, I've got two kids and I'm about to get married.'

'Yeah,' said Lulu, 'I know.'

They walked to the restaurant forecourt and joined a lengthy queue for tables. Scarlett wandered off to look through the windows and Jem turned to Lulu. 'Ralph said no to sex,' she whispered.

Lulu widened her eyes at her in reply.

'Yes, last night. I instigated it. He said no.'

'But why?'

'I have no idea. He was all mumbly and incoherent. Just said he couldn't, he was too tired.'

Lulu nodded and grimaced. 'You don't think he's a bit

freaked out by the, you know, losing the baby, do you?' She whispered the last word.

Jem threw her a look. 'God, no, I don't think so. I think he's fine about that. Well, at least I assume he is. I mean, he *said* he wanted the baby, and he did turn up at the clinic to try to stop me but I think he was doing that for me, you know. I think he thought that I'd regret it if I went through with it. I don't *really* think he wanted a third child, not really, not deep down, and he was probably as relieved as me when it didn't happen. Anyway, no, I've been thinking about it and my theory is that he's just trying to pay me back, for all those times I turned him down.'

'But why? Why would he be so petty? I thought you two were getting on really well at the moment?'

'Well, yes, we are, but, I don't know, Ralph's been a bit strange the past couple of days, even before the no sex thing. A bit distant.'

'Yes, well, Ralph's always been a bit distant.'

'No, but more than that. I don't know. It feels,' Jem began, 'it feels like he's drifting away. Which is ironic, given that he's never spent more time with us as a family and he's physically so present, but emotionally . . .'

'You're not going to split up, you two, are you?' Lulu bit the corner of her lip.

'God, no, of course we're not. We're getting married! Of course we're not going to split up. Why did you even say that?'

'I don't know,' said Lulu. 'It just seems like the pair of you keep taking two steps forward and one step back.'

'Yeah, but two steps forward, one step back. You get there in the end. Don't you?'

She turned her head away. It suddenly occurred to her that she might cry and she did not want to cry, not here, not now. Something bad was happening to Jem and Ralph. Something worse than resentment about the division of labour, something worse than resentment about lack of sex, something worse even than complacency. It felt like they'd reached some invisible fork in the road and Ralph was striding away from her without a backward glance.

They reached the head of the queue and a waitress showed them to a table. The conversation got squashed by the perusal of menus and the placating of children and the distribution of crayons and colouring kits. Jem ordered herself a cocktail and ignored Lulu's look of surprise. It was summer. There were men outside playing steel drums. She'd had a stressful journey getting here. She wanted a cocktail, with fruit in it, and rum. She wanted something to alleviate the discomfort in the pit of her stomach.

She had two cocktails that day, but no lunch.

She didn't quite have an appetite for it.

Five nights later Jem went out with her sister and some of her friends from the local area. Lulu had had children at school for six years and had built up quite a gang of mothers in her neighbourhood who liked to go out drinking. Jem had never been out with them before. Jem and Lulu were close but their social circles rarely bled into each other. Jem knew these women by name and had met them on occasion if one of them had had a child over at Lulu's house for a play-date, but beyond that they were not a part of her life. But Lulu had persuaded her that it was time to get involved.

'You'll really like them,' she'd said that afternoon on the South Bank. 'Some of them are a bit painful, but *en masse*, you know, it's fine. And we always have such a laugh.'

Ralph had been strange when she'd mentioned it to him.

'Sorry, you're going out with who?'

'Friends. Of Lulu's. Just some local women.'

'OK,' he'd said, 'and why?'

'Because Lulu invited me.'

'Right. And where are you going, you and Lulu and her mates?'

Jem had shrugged. 'Don't know yet. Probably somewhere local. Or one of them's a member of Soho House, we might go there.'

He'd raised his eyebrows at her.

'What?' she'd demanded.

'Nothing,' he'd said. 'Just, I can just imagine the type of woman who lives round here, who has a child at Theo and Jared's school and is a member of Soho House.'

'Well, yeah, so can I, and Lulu did say that some of the group are a bit painful, but I don't really care. I just want to go out. I just want to have some fun.'

Ralph had sneered slightly and sighed. 'Good,' he'd said, 'that's good. I hope you have it.'

He'd been offish with her for the rest of that day. It was very unlike Ralph. Sulking and brooding were not his traits and he'd always been happy to see Jem going out to enjoy herself in years gone by, particularly since they'd had children. Jem couldn't quite see why the prospect of her going out after dark with a few local mums should have unsettled him so much, but she ignored his mood and waited for it to pass. She had not been out drinking since before she was pregnant with Blake. If Ralph wanted back the girl he'd fallen in love with all those years ago, and she suspected that he did, then he would have to accept that her independence was all a part of it.

On Wednesday night she wore her vintage chiffon blouse again, with skinny jeans and high heels. She wore her hair down, with a diamanté clip holding it out of her eyes and she wore more make-up than she normally wore, including a smudge of something from Benefit that turned her lips post-coital red. And then, with a flourish of liberation, she removed the obligatory packet of wipes and spare nappy from her handbag and dropped them on the bed.

Ralph was downstairs on the sofa with Blake on his lap and Scarlett curled into him in her nightie and a dressing gown. Scarlett let her thumb fall from her mouth when she saw Jem walk into the room.

'Mummy,' she said, 'you look very beautiful.'

Jem smiled and hugged her. Ralph looked at her with a tersely raised eyebrow. 'Very pretty,' he said, and lowered his gaze back to the TV. Jem kissed her daughter and her son and then she kissed the dry cold side of Ralph's face that he presented her with when she attempted to kiss him on the lips.

Chapter 18

Jem felt a warm buzz of vitality that evening as she criss-crossed the damp streets of Soho to find the small door in the wall of Greek Street, which was the only outward sign of the exclusive club within. She had not walked alone through Soho at night for many a year. She took the long route, although it was cool and wet. She retraced the journeys that she and Ralph used to make, the Chinese restaurant on Lisle Street where they used to share a crispy duck, the sex shop on Brewer Street where they'd stared at all the customers in awe one night when they were stoned, and an anonymous door on a street corner in Chinatown they'd once passed through to get to the flat of a guy called Pete from Manchester who'd invited them in for a beer and a smoke about a thousand years ago.

Lulu's friend Sam was the member at Soho House and had put their names on a list at the door. Jem made her way up the narrow staircase to a room on the second floor and saw her sister sitting on a sofa with three other women. There was a bottle of champagne already open and chilled by the side of the table and Sam – terribly tall with the sort of geometric and sculpted hair usually seen in the windows of unfashionable hair salons – rustled up an extra glass and poured one for Jem. Jem drank the champagne so fast that she barely had a chance to register the fact that she was drinking champagne, an activity she often daydreamed about during long, mundane afternoons alone with her children. Another bottle appeared and very quickly Jem had finished three glasses and was feeling thoroughly comfortable in her environment and with these three new and slightly forbidding women. Ingrid – who looked like her name – had four children, including a baby the same age as Blake, and hadn't worked since she was twenty-five. Diana – small and busty with thick yellow hair – was divorced with a nine-year-old daughter called Tansy and sold organic babywear from her own website. Sam had twin boys in Jared's year and a daughter in Theo's year, and was the marketing and publicity director for a women's celebrity gossip magazine.

'Have you got children, Jem?' asked Sam, who was the only one of the three mothers that Jem had not met before at Lulu's house.

'Yes,' she nodded, 'a girl of three and a half and a little boy of six months.'

'Ah, so you haven't hit the school years yet, then?'

'No,' she agreed, 'I've got all that to come.'

'And what do you do?' asked Sam. 'Do you work?'

Jem nodded, shook her head, nodded again. 'Kind of,' she said, and explained about the celebrity arm of the theatrical agency she'd been given to develop as an alternative to maternity leave by her much-loved boss. 'I've only got the two clients,' she continued. The women looked at her curiously, greedy, it seemed, for some juicy celebrity names to get their teeth into. 'Karl Kasparov,' she offered apologetically. The women nodded, encouragingly, as if to say, better luck with the next one. 'And Philip Samuel.'

'Ah,' Sam nodded, 'the little guy from, what's that soap called?'

'*Jubilee Road?*'

'Yeah, that one. He's cute.'

'Yes, he's been with the agency since he was fourteen. He was in *Oliver!*, and then he transferred to the TV and now, well, he wants me to make him famous. But not until his contract's up for the current run of this show. So, yes, in the meantime, I haven't really got much work to do. I guess when the baby's a little older and when my daughter's at full-time nursery . . .'

'Well, look, when you're ready and when little Philip's ready, you should come and have lunch with me,' said Sam, 'I know all sorts of people in the industry. I could definitely get you talking to some very helpful people.'

Jem smiled at her words. She was grateful for the offer of lunch. It was nice to have someone take her job seriously. And it was thrilling to think that in a couple of months' time she would be back inside this world, this glossy, frivolous, exhilarating and gilded world of work, properly.

'And you're married?'

'Not yet.'

'Jem's getting married next month,' said Lulu, proudly. The women all looked at Jem happily.

'And this is to the father of your . . .'

'. . . children, yes,' said Jem. 'Finally, after eleven years together.'

'Oh, congratulations,' said Ingrid, holding aloft her champagne glass. 'That's wonderful news. Cheers!'

The five women clinked their glasses together and Jem smiled happily. The sun was going down in Soho and the pretty room was bathed, briefly, in a wash of pomegranate light. The lead singer of Kasabian was sitting behind them and over there in the corner was Fearne Cotton, deep in conversation with someone else who looked familiar but Jem couldn't quite put a name to her. This room, four walls, a few chesterfield sofas, powered-down lighting, low tables bearing snacks and drinks and discarded newspapers, it could have been a room anywhere, but it wasn't, it was a room in Soho House, a room that only a select few would occupy, a room with its own potent energy. This place was alive. Pretentious – slightly, yes. Swollen with a disproportionate sense of its own importance –

definitely. But a place she'd like to be a member of? Well, it didn't matter much to Jem what any dead comedian might have to say on the matter, yes, she would like to be a member. She would like to belong here. She would like to sail through the reception area and have that pretty girl behind the desk say, hello, Miss Catterick, how are you this evening, Miss Catterick?

Jem ordered herself a cocktail and when it arrived she drank it very quickly, urgently needing to feel some kind of oblivion descend upon her. She went to the toilet then and engaged someone much younger and more sober than herself in a conversation about the hand soap. She smiled as she sat on the bowl in the cubicle. She felt like a grown-up. She wanted to get back to work, she wanted to plug herself back into the world. She wanted to make a success of herself. She smiled at her reflection over the sink as she washed her hands. She looked fine for an old lady of thirty-eight who'd had one too many to drink. She'd always sworn she wouldn't get drunk over the age of thirty, remembering her parents' friends at their vaguely sordid dinner parties, swaying and hooting, stained teeth and florid open-pored cheeks, usually with their arms around someone else's husband or wife. Drunkenness, like most enjoyable things, was best left to the young. But in the muted light of the toilets at Soho House, Jem concluded that she looked fine. In fact, more than fine. She looked good. She was going back to work. She was getting married. She and Ralph would find a way forwards, of course they would. She fixed a smile to her face, straightened the placket on her chiffon blouse and headed back to the bar.

Jem remembered very little about the rest of the night when she awoke the next morning at six o'clock to the sound of Blake bleating pathetically from his bedroom across the hallway. She turned over heavily on to her side to alert Ralph to the fact that their baby needed attention but found a cool empty mattress where her partner should have been. The monitor next to the bed was flashing frantic red and green as Blake's bleating escalated to anxious screaming. Ralph must be somewhere in the house, Jem concluded, and therefore she could just turn off the monitor, stick a pillow over her head and attempt to get another hour's rest. After a further three minutes the bedroom door opened and an exhausted-looking Scarlett stood in the doorway with quite magnificent bed hair.

'Mummy,' she said, 'Blake's crying.'

Jem resisted the urge to respond using base sarcasm and forced a smile. 'I know,' she said, 'and in a minute Daddy's going to go in and pick him up.'

Scarlett scanned the room. 'Where is Daddy?'

'I don't know,' croaked Jem, 'I suppose he's downstairs. Why don't you go and see if you can find him?'

Scarlett nodded and Jem sighed with relief. Until, 'Come with me, Mummy?' and a small hand proffered across the rumpled bedcovers. Jem groaned and pulled her body from the warm cocoon of her bed. Together they rescued the plaintive Blake from his cot and Jem held his small juddering body against her own small juddering body, and she and Scarlett padded down the stairs to find out where the hell Ralph was and what on earth he was doing. But a short exploration of the lower floor of the house revealed pretty quickly that Ralph was not in the house and that neither were his running shoes nor his iPod.

Jem felt her way around the kitchen, pulled the corner off a small carton of SMA, splashed it into a bottle, slammed the bottle into the microwave, located a plastic bowl with a picture of Peppa Pig at its centre, filled it with Shreddies, almost topped it with tap water, stopped herself just in time, topped it with full-fat milk, threw in a teaspoon and banged it on the table. She wedged Blake into his high chair, scattered a handful of dry cornflakes and the bottle of warm milk on to the tray in front of him and then finally busied herself with the work of preparing herself a very large cup of tea and, thank God, a stale croissant, resuscitated briefly in the microwave and smeared generously with butter. There was silence then for a moment, silence enough for Jem to wonder, a) how she had got home the night before, and b) what on earth Ralph was doing leaving the house before 6 a.m. for a run.

She remembered ordering snacks. She'd had a goat's cheese salad and a bowl of olives. She remember three more cocktails, she'd remembered the conversation turning to fun topics such as Isn't Sex Crap? and Men, What Are They Actually For? They'd also discussed schools (Jem now knew exactly what she had to do to get her children into the right schools in her catchment area) and post-baby bodies (Sam had shown them her over-hang, the result of bearing twins who'd been born weighing in at almost eight pounds each). And then, amidst wide eyes and hanging jaws, they'd discussed Diana's affair with the father of one of her daughter's best friends.

After that Jem had a vague recollection of some men. She could not remember their names or their faces, but there had been one that she had thought was flirting with her but she'd been unimpressed with him, and then she remembered Ingrid and Diana leaving and then Sam had disappeared and Lulu had suggested that she might have gone to a hotel with one of the men and Jem had been very, very adamant that that could not possibly be the case because Sam was married with three children, and then Lulu had looked at her, fondly, sadly, as if to say, really, you really think that things like this don't happen, and Jem had felt that she was somehow on the periphery of real life, this place where people had sex with their daughters' friends' parents and went off to hotels with strange men while their husbands and children slumbered obliviously at home, and that inviting a single dad over for a curry was really not such a big deal after all, and then after that? Nothing. Did they get a cab home? Did they get a night bus? They might have been transported home upon a magic carpet and funnelled unceremoniously into their homes through their chimneypots, for all she knew. The entire episode was a jet-black blank. Jem could vaguely remember the terrible hour of 3.45 a.m. flashing cruelly at her from the microwave in the kitchen when she stumbled towards the sink and a large glass of water. But beyond that, well, the only two people who could shed any light on the missing hours were her sister and her boyfriend, one of whom would undoubtedly still be asleep at this ungodly hour (oh, for the luxury of children who could pour their own cereal in the mornings) and the latter of whom was out. Running. While the morning dew was still gilding the streets of Herne Hill.

She noticed her mobile phone. It was sitting on the counter, plugged in to the charger. She blinked. The phone blinked back at her. Had she really had the foresight to charge her phone at three forty-five in the morning? She switched it on, wondering idly if her phone held any clues to the last two hours of her evening. And there it was: a message from Joel.

'Glad you got home OK. I'll sleep soundly now. X'

Joel?

Joel?

She looked at her sent folder and saw a message she'd sent to him at 3.48 a.m.: 'I'm in. Unmurdered. Sleep tight!'

Oh, yes, Joel.

She remembered now. He'd been there. Where? Somewhere. Last night. With a tall beautiful man, a young man of mixed race, with a shorn head and green eyes. His son. A unsettling thought came to her at that moment. Something had happened. *Something had happened*. But she could not for the life of her remember what it was.

Chapter 19

Ralph came to a halt opposite the clock tower in Brockwell Park and let his torso collapse against his thighs. His breathing came hard and tight, and sweat trickled from his temples and into his eyes. He had been pounding the streets of SE24 for nearly two hours and it was only now, as the deserted park slowly began to fill with people on their way to work and the sun sat high enough in the sky to light more than just the tops of the trees, that he felt like he could stop. He crouched down and let his chin hang against his heaving chest. He winced with discomfort and felt a tight stitch began to release its grip on his abdomen. Then he staggered towards an empty bench and sat down upon it heavily. He sighed and let his body relax. It had been a strange and stressful morning.

Jem had climbed into bed at nearly 4 a.m. the previous night. The sky was turning dusty blue and a small bird outside their bedroom window was warming up for the dawn chorus. But it didn't matter because Ralph had been awake since midnight, anyway, after receiving a text from Jem telling him that she was 'just leaving' and would be home 'within the hour'. As 1 a.m. had come and gone Ralph had become increasingly anxious. He'd called her phone but there'd been no reply and then a moment later his phone had rung and it was her and he'd answered it and realised very quickly that it was just a pocket call. Or, in this case, he imagined, a handbag call. For ten minutes Ralph had sat with his phone to his ear, listening to Jem's night out.

He heard male voices and female laughter. He heard a tray of drinks being delivered to a table, someone insisting that it was their round and then another male voice saying, 'I can't believe you've got two kids,' and then Jem saying, 'Why, what should someone with two kids look like?' And the male voice saying, 'Well, I don't know, just not like that. You're gorgeous.' And then Jem saying, 'Thank you, you're very kind,' and then the conversation being interrupted again by raucous female laughter and some men jousting about and then finally the call cut off and Ralph was left sitting in his bed, silence ringing in his ears, feeling very slightly nauseous.

Reassured at least that he would not to have to call the police as Jem was clearly not under the wheels of a car somewhere or being molested in a dark alley by a stranger, he had turned off the light and attempted to find himself some sleep, but none came. When Jem finally crawled into bed smelling of sour wine and old perfume, he feigned sleep and then he lay awake, watching the early morning sun staining his curtains, listening to the birds singing their songs and his partner snoring the snore of the comatose until 5.30 a.m., when he finally admitted defeat and got up for a run.

He was mildly annoyed. He was oddly anxious. He was cross, but not sure yet if he was cross enough to have a confrontation with Jem when she woke up. Until he decided on a whim to have a look at her mobile phone, sitting on the kitchen counter, plugged into the wall, flashing suggestively at him. He switched it on, immediately saw that she had mail, clicked the mail icon and there it was, a message, from Joel: 'Glad you got home OK. I'll sleep soundly now. X'.

He'd marked the message as 'unread' switched off the phone and fled, his feet murdering the pavement, slowly, with every ponderous step.

*   *   *

308

It was still, he could concede two angst-ridden hours later, inconclusive. Just because Joel had sent Jem a text message in the middle of the night telling her that he was glad she was home safely did not mean that they had had sex with each other. It just meant . . . well, it was unclear at this stage what other explanations there might be for the message, but Ralph was ready now to return home to find out.

Jem was lying on the sofa in her pyjamas when he walked into the kitchen. Blake was on the floor surrounded by toys and Scarlett was sitting two inches away from the TV screen eating a KitKat.

'I know,' said Jem, before Ralph could say a word. 'I know. It's disgusting. But it was all I could manage.'

Ralph pulled off his running shoes and began to clear away the breakfast table and the high chair. He scooped cornflakes into the palm of his hand and dropped them into the bin, then he rinsed out Scarlett's cereal bowl and Jem's oily croissant plate and put them in the dishwasher.

'I haven't changed Blake yet,' Jem croaked, 'I just really couldn't face it.'

Ralph strode into the hallway and pulled a nappy and some wipes out of the cubbyhole where they kept them and came back into the kitchen.

'I'm really sorry,' said Jem, 'I just assumed you'd be here to deal with everything. If I'd known you'd be out all morning, I might have tried to get a bit more sleep and drink a few less cocktails.'

Ralph gently lowered Blake on to his back and unpopped the buttons on his babygro. He pulled away the bulging wet nappy and replaced it deftly with a thin dry one. He'd gone from not knowing what to say, to not wanting to say anything. The sight of Jem prone on the sofa, the pathetic collapse of her body and the strained sighs emitting from her were driving him crazy.

His actions became more and more forced and aggressive with every moment that passed until: 'Ralph, are you pissed off with me?'

'Later,' he hissed.

'What?'

'Let's. Talk. About this. Later,' he hissed again.

'Oh God,' she said, suddenly upright on the sofa, 'you are, aren't you? You're pissed off with me? God, what did I do? Did I wake you up?'

'No,' he began tersely. 'You did not wake me up. Because I had not been to sleep. Because you sent me a text message at midnight saying that you'd be home at 1 a.m.'

Jem clasped her hands over her mouth. 'Oh God,' she said, 'I didn't, did I?'

'Yes, you did. And then, when you weren't home by 1.30 a.m. I called you, but you did not answer your phone. And then two minutes later you pocket-called me and I got to listen to you and your mates being chatted up by some braying tossers, and then you finally crawled in at 4 a.m. and started snoring within about two and a half seconds of closing your eyes and then, once I'd given up on the concept of sleep for the night, I decided to go for a run.'

Her hands were still clasped over her mouth and her eyes were wide with horror. 'Oh God,' she said, 'I'm so sorry. So, so sorry. Oh God, I feel awful. I just, God, I really don't remember much. I mean, the guy you heard me talking to, honestly, just some little shrimp. And I honestly have no idea what happened to the bit between then and getting into bed . . .'

'Well, I'll tell you someone who might know.'

Jem threw him a questioning look.

'Your buddy, you know, the single dad. He sent you a text message.'

'Yeah, I know,' she said, 'I saw it. I think we shared a

cab home. Me and Lulu, and him and his son. I can't remember why though, because they weren't with us before that. I'm guessing we must have bumped into them, somewhere along the way. I'm hoping Lulu might remember . . .' She rubbed her head and then stopped as her phone began to vibrate on the counter. Ralph looked at the display, unplugged it and threw it towards Jem on the sofa. 'Talk of the devil,' he said, before picking up his cigarettes and a cold coffee from earlier and heading into the garden.

He was shaking slightly, both from lack of sleep and from pure fury. He used three matches to light the end of his cigarette and then finally he drew the smoke into his lungs deeply and with relief. He had never felt this way about Jem before. She had been out before, she had got drunk before, she had got home late before, but he had always taken it in his stride. He'd always known what Jem was like, she was independent, a free-spirit, and before he'd even got to know her he'd seen from the words in her diaries that if there was one thing that was likely to make Jem run a mile in the wrong direction it was a man who would try to clip her wings.

But something had happened to the way he saw Jem these days. He no longer saw her as 'his girl'. For a long time now she had belonged to their children and then she'd shown Ralph another side of herself, a side that was hard and uncompromising, that could take an unborn baby into a clinic and ask someone to kill it for her. Purely, it now seemed, so that she could buy herself some pretty clothes, squeeze herself into tight jeans and go out and drink herself sick. The explanation for the text from Joel seemed reasonable enough. All her explanations regarding Joel seemed reasonable enough. And as he'd previously theorised, if 'local single dad Joel' was 'local single mum Julie' he wouldn't be giving any of this a second thought. Literally. The whole concept of 'Julie' would not occupy his thought process for a single moment. But then, Joel was a man and Jem was an attractive woman and Joel had sent Jem flowers. *Flowers that Ralph could never question Jem about because he should not know about them.*

He hurled the flowers from his thoughts.

He took a deep breath.

He needed to control this. He needed to control himself. He was going backwards, backwards into resentment and negativity. He closed his eyes. He should not be focusing on the past, on flowers, on strange men in the night. He had other priorities. To make Jem happy. To get married. To make this family strong.

He flattened the last inch of his cigarette under a flowerpot and hurled it into the flower beds. And then he went back inside. Right now he needed to find some peace.

Jem was just hanging up the phone when Ralph walked in. Blake was on her lap, pulling at the links of her silver bracelet and Scarlett sat, as she had been for the entire morning, no doubt, with her nose pressed against the TV screen watching CBeebies.

'Right,' he said striding through the room and reaching for the remote control, 'telly off.'

Scarlett spun round and looked at him in horror. 'Noooo!' she wailed.

'Yes, we're going out. Mummy's not feeling well.'

Scarlett's face collapsed into tears. 'No, Daddy!' she wailed again, as though he had just threatened to leave her at the workhouse.

'Sorry, baby, but look, it's a lovely day and there's no reason why you should suffer just because Mummy decided to stay out all night and drink too much beer.'

Scarlett screamed then and collapsed on to the floor, where she began to roll round and round with the sheer utter agony of not being able to watch any more telly.

'You didn't give her her two-minute warning,' said Jem.

Ralph resisted the temptation to spit something knowing and smug at her and instead concentrated on getting the writhing and livid Scarlett out of the kitchen and upstairs to her bedroom to dress her. 'You should have brought the clothes downstairs first,' called Jem, and Ralph thought, one more word, one more word, Jem, and I swear . . .

Finally he had both children in clothes that were suitable for outdoors, and Blake in the pushchair and himself out of sweaty running clothes and straight, unshowered, into yesterday's jeans and T-shirt and checked his wallet for cash and his pockets for door keys and there was a, 'Where are you going, when will you be back?' from Jem, which he replied to with a grunt and a 'No idea,' and then, bang, the front door slammed behind him and he was walking away from the house, far too fast, Scarlett clutching his hand for dear life as she was half pulled along the pavement and towards a place, the only place where he knew he'd find some peace. He took his children to church.

'What is this place?' said Scarlett.

'It's a good place,' said Ralph, stroking the tangled crown of her head. 'It's a very good place indeed. It's a place where people come who are feeling cross or sad or unhappy, so that they can feel better.'

'Like a hospital?' said Scarlett.

'Yes, like a hospital. But without medicine and needles and knives. Do you like it?' he asked.

Scarlett considered the question for a moment. 'No,' she said eventually, 'I don't. It's scary. And it's cold.'

Ralph smiled and rubbed her head again and then together they lit a candle for Nanny Joan, Ralph's mum, and for the cat they'd seen get run over on Brixton Hill over a year ago that Scarlett still talked about to this day. By the time they left the little church a few minutes later, Ralph was calm again, strong and ready to enjoy a morning out with his children.

Chapter 20

According to Lulu, this is what had happened the night before.

They had left Soho House at 2 a.m., apparently the last people left as the management frantically tried to close the place up for the night. The group of fruity young men who had been pestering them all night had gone in one direction, living as they all did in north and east London, and Jem and Lulu went in the other direction. They walked for an hour, trying and failing to locate a cab. They walked, in fact, all the way to Vauxhall Bridge, where they stood for a while on the side of the bridge admiring the lights on the thick black water of the Thames below and sharing a spliff that one of the fruity young men had given them as a parting gift.

On the other side of Vauxhall Bridge, two men had approached them. One was Joel, the other was (despite Jem drunkenly insinuating that he was actually a rent boy that Joel had picked up from under the arches at Charing Cross) Joel's son, Lucas. 'The most beautiful man I have ever seen in my life,' said Lulu. 'Crazy beautiful. Brown skin. Green eyes. Dark hair. Made me want to *weep*.' The two men were on their way back from a gig in Camden and had been dropped by a friend on the north side of the bridge to make the rest of their way home together.

'Isn't this just, like, the biggest coincidence ever?' Jem had demanded. 'No, I mean, really, what are the chances, what are the chances?' Not just once apparently, but over and over again. 'I am very drunk,' she had then declared. 'And also a bit stoned.'

They'd walked towards Camberwell New Road, the four of them and Jem had – oh yes, she had – *linked arms* with Joel. Like he was her best friend. Or her boyfriend.

'Honestly, Jem,' Lulu said when Jem began to wail down the phone at her over this revelation, 'it was nothing. You were just being silly. He knew that. It's not as if you went to a hotel with him or anything.'

'No, but, God, the last thing I want to do is give him the wrong impression. *Again*.'

'It wasn't like that. It really wasn't. I'd have told you if it was.'

They'd finally flagged down a cab and Lulu could remember very little about what they'd talked about. Except this: 'So, your partner,' Joel had said, 'not the sort of bloke I'd have expected to be a churchgoer.'

'A what?' Jem had exclaimed.

'Church,' Joel had repeated. 'I've seen him a couple of times, visiting that little chapel on Underwood Street. Are you a believer too?'

'Er, no, sorrysorrysorry,' Jem had interjected with her hands in front of her body, 'I think you might be talking about the wrong person.'

'No, definitely not. Definitely your partner. He runs, yeah?'

'Er, yes.'

'Well, then, it's him, definitely, halfway through a run, both times I've seen him, stops at the chapel, stays about five minutes, then he comes out.'

'Whoa,' Jem had said, waving her hands again, almost trying to shoo the weirdness away from herself. 'This is freaking me out. You are telling me that you have seen my boyfriend going into a church?'

'Er, yeah,' Joel had said, 'and I must say I had no idea it would cause such a stir. I mean, I assumed that you

316

must know. Generally that's the sort of thing that a person knows about the person they live with.'

Jem shook her head, very slowly. 'No,' she'd said, 'no. I had no idea at all. I suppose . . .' but then she'd trailed off. Lulu didn't know what she'd been about to say and Jem certainly had no recollection of her thought processes at the time. But the conversation had quickly descended into a battle of wit as each of them tried to outdo the other with amusing takes on the situation; the possibility that the chapel was a cover for a whorehouse, that he was peeing in the font, drinking the holy water or raiding the poor box.

The one possibility that nobody put forward was that he'd gone in there to pray.

Churches disturbed Jem. They were fine for weddings and funerals and christenings, but beyond that she could not find a reason for them. If someone wanted a place to think or to evaluate or just to be, what was wrong with a park bench or a library or a seat on the top deck of a bus? The Church, as far as Jem was concerned, in all its many forms, was an anachronism. And the sort of people who felt the need to be in a church, or worse still, to be a *part* of a Church, struck her as weak and unimaginative. And if she was wrong and there was, in fact, one divine being who sat and oversaw the whole massive, dirty sprawl of humanity, would he really want to watch them sitting in expensive-to-maintain old buildings, singing dreary songs and reading and rereading and rereading again the same dry old stories from the same dry old book, over and over and over? Would he not, in fact, just want to see them getting on with their lives, loving each other, having a laugh, raising their families, building things, inventing things, *evolving*? No, Jem was not a fan of God, or of organised religion, or of churches or of handing over your destiny to the promise of something impossible to comprehend. Jem was a fan of people and of real life. She was a fan of the inexplicable and the magical and the romantic. She was a fan of chaos and coincidence and random possibility. She didn't want answers and she didn't want salvation. She just wanted to live her life, in the order in which it came, and then to die, knowing that her time here had been well spent. No more than that. Why, she'd always wondered, did people feel a need for anything else? Wasn't life enough? And now it wasn't just nameless, faceless 'people' she was questioning, it was Ralph. Her Ralph. Ralph whom she'd known for eleven years. Ralph who'd always had the spirituality of a fork-lift truck. Ralph who drank and smoked and slept with unsuitable women and railed against family life and referred to people of faith as 'God-botherers'. *That* Ralph.

As she lay there, feeling last night's booze fizzing through her veins and the itch and crawl of a thousand tiny moments of remorse (she felt, in retrospect, that she had behaved quite badly), Jem hoped for an easy answer.

Please, she thought, let Ralph have been pissing in the font.

Chapter 21

Ralph had a vivid and awful dream that night. It woke him at 3 a.m., cold and clammy, entirely unsettled. He'd dreamed he was in his studio, dark and foreboding, the walls daubed with obscene flowers, himself curled in the corner, pale and gaunt, Jem, looming above him, too thin, too loud, vacuous, over-bright. Where are the babies? *I gave them away.* Who to? *I don't know. Here, have a toke on this . . .* a spliff the size of a salami, its tip burning ugly red. And then getting to his feet, the floors made of sponge, running to his balcony, the metal cage falling away as he jumped on to it, coming away from the walls and falling, falling, slowly but too fast towards the patio below, and then he felt a song, it sounded like birdsong, simple repetitive, three notes, la, laaa, lo. He let the song out and he squeezed hard on to the rail of the unfettered balcony as if it might keep him from falling, la laaa lo, la laaa lo. And as the melancholic song came from him he felt the picture change. He saw himself leap to his feet on the patio, light and nimble and then run across the tiny garden, vault across the garden wall and there, on the other side, instead of more grey houses and the backs of the shops, was space. Green, verdant rolling meadows; llamas, deer, birds of paradise, people in white smocks, sitting in circles, holding hands; heaven, nirvana. He looked behind him for Jem, but she wasn't there. Neither was the garden wall, neither was the house. But then, across the meadow, he could see two small figures, dark-haired and dressed in white. His children! They smiled when they saw him and they ran towards him and Ralph's song came faster now, joyful, tuneful and pure. He watched himself capture his children in his arms and hold them to him and then, suddenly, he opened his eyes and he was back in his bed, clutching the edge of the duvet with his fingertips and the children were gone and the meadow was gone and so was his song.

'Not every issue is a problem,' Gil began. 'Not every worry is a concern. Not every closed door is a rejection and not every thwarted plan is a disaster. The most important thing is to separate the real from the perceived problem. The important thing is to waste not a second of your precious given life contemplating the things that you cannot change and that do not need to be changed. Choose your battles, choose your worries, and think now. Think now about your deepest fear, your realest worry. Feel it fill your heart until you fear for the lasting damage.'

Ralph looked around him at the other members of the prayer group and did as he was told. He sucked the thought of Jem's mysterious flowers, the lost baby, the magazine in the waiting room, his inability to contemplate having sex with her, his growing hatred of his Californian flower paintings, the fact of the sense of impending doom that seemed to accompany his every movement of late and let it sit there for a moment. And it felt like a train crash in his soul.

'Hold it there!' he heard Gil implore from the podium at the front of the room, 'Hold it there until it almost kills you!'

He let the feeling of fear and despondency grow and grow inside him, this awful feeling that he'd been trying so hard to avoid for days now, this terrible lurch in the pit of his belly, and he let it almost subsume him until he felt like he wanted to peel off his own skin and throw himself bodily through the window.

'There!' shouted Gil. 'There it is. Now tell yourself this: God loves me. I have nothing to fear. God loves me. I have nothing to fear. Say it out loud. Say it again. Say it LOUD!'

And Ralph did say it. He said it quietly at first, not entirely sure even if he believed the words he was saying. But each time he said it he felt belief suffuse him. Yes, God DID love him and no, he had nothing to fear. He and Jem would be fine! Love would pull them through. God would pull them through. In a few weeks he and Jem would be married. His exhibition of California flowers would be over. If he could just hold on to this feeling, this strength, then everything would be all right. He felt the faith of the dozen other people in the room pulsing through him and he felt the sick dread in his belly start to abate. Sarah, who was standing next to him, placed a cool hand against his and glanced at him, reassuringly. He smiled at her. And then he shouted again: God loves me! I have nothing to fear!

'How was that, boy?' Gil boomed into his ear as the group dispersed half an hour later.

'Yeah,' said Ralph, 'it was good.' He was still feeling slightly shaken after what he fully believed to be his first real religious experience.

'Not too frightening then, eh?'

'No,' said Ralph, 'I was scared, and then I was . . . safe.'

'Good,' nodded Gil, 'that's good. And here, now, Sarah tells me that you are an artist?'

Ralph nodded.

'Much like myself then. Though I would classify myself as more of a painter, than an artist. What interests you then, man? What do you paint about?'

Ralph wondered at his choice of words: 'paint about'. He'd never heard it put like that before but the phraseology interested him. Because he didn't paint 'about' anything. He just painted.

'Still life,' he said, 'flora, mainly. But I'm drawing to the end of that phase. I don't want it to be just a job any more. I want it to mean something again.'

Gil looked at him and nodded his head slowly up and down. 'It's got to mean something,' he agreed. 'Everything's got to mean something. Here, you should come to my place. I paint in my shed. It's a magic shed,' he winked, but didn't smile. 'Bring a canvas. We can paint together. See if we can't find a meaning for you, boy.'

'Where do you live?'

'Ah,' he said, almost sadly, 'just there, just behind this hall.'

'On that estate?'

'Yes, on that estate. Been there forty years, since those buildings were fresh out of the box. I have a little house, a little garden. I have a little shed. I like my neighbours. It'll do. Anyway, what do you say? Come over. We'll paint together, man. Eh? What do you say?'

Ralph looked at the strong, handsome old man and smiled. 'Yes,' he said, 'yes. Definitely. That would be amazing.'

Chapter 22

It was hot enough for outdoor swimming the following day, and after collecting Scarlett from nursery Jem took the children to the lido in Brockwell Park. She was wearing a yellow sundress with a shirred bodice and shoestring straps and apple-green Havaianas flip-flops and her hair was tied up messily on top of head. Underneath her sundress she wore a bikini. It was a bikini she had not worn for almost five years and, at some points during the weeks following the births of both her children, had thought she would never wear again. Her stomach was not what it was, but this was Brockwell Lido, not the pool at the Mondrian, and she knew that there would be others in a far worse state than her.

Her footsteps were heavy as she pushed the buggy up the hill towards the park. She'd cooked Ralph a nice meal the night before and made sure to sit and eat it with him, although she hadn't felt hungry. He'd returned from an early evening run looking bright and almost freakishly happy. He'd kissed her on the crown of her head and hummed a tune under his breath. She'd tried to engage him in a conversation about their wedding plans. They'd barely discussed the wedding in recent weeks. Jem had bought dresses for herself and Scarlett, both eBay bargains, and they'd posted their banns and booked the registry office, but they hadn't discussed the logistics: how would they get there, where would they spend the night before, the night after, where would they eat, how much would they spend, who would take the children?

She'd drawn up a list, a checklist, and presented it to Ralph. He cast his eye fleetingly over it and said, 'I thought we'd decided all this?'

'No,' Jem had said, 'not the detail. Not yet.' Jem poured herself a glass of wine and let half of it splash into the depths of her empty stomach before picking up her cutlery and starting to eat.

'So,' she'd said eventually, 'what do you think?'

'I think it all sounds fine.'

'But what do you think about having the reception at the Soho Hotel? I thought it would be nice, you know, a reference to our history, the old days.'

'Brilliant,' he'd said brightly, his gaze shifting from the wedding plans to the newspaper.

'And you're all right to go into Hatton Garden next Saturday, to get our wedding bands.'

'What are wedding bands?'

She rolled her eyes. 'You know,' she said, 'wedding rings.'

'Yeah. Cool. Sounds great.' He smiled at her again. It was a full smile that showed all his teeth yet it seemed strangely hollow.

Eventually she'd said: 'Ralph, do you actually have any interest in this wedding, at all?'

He'd looked up then and squinted at her. 'Of course,' he'd said, surprisingly softly. 'Absolutely. How about you?'

Jem threw him a look of bemusement. 'Well, I'd hardly be sitting here with a bullet-pointed to-do list if I wasn't interested in our wedding, would I?'

'No, I don't mean the wedding. I mean, getting married. Do you still want to go through with it?'

A small moment of silence passed while Jem digested the question.

'Go through with it?' she said eventually. 'What do you mean?'

'I mean, do you still want to marry me?'

'Of course I do! Why on earth would you ask a question like that?'

Ralph had shrugged. 'I don't know really,' he said, 'I suppose I was just checking. It's getting close now but not so close that you can't change your mind.'

'God, Ralph, I'm not going to change my mind! Why on earth would I change my mind? I mean, we're getting married, you and I, parents of our children, long-term partners, soul mates, etc. What's there to change my mind about?'

'But are we?' he asked, circling his fingertip around a mark on the tabletop. 'Are we still soul mates?'

Jem had sighed and leaned back in her chair. 'Ralph, what's the matter with you?'

'Nothing's the matter with me. I'm feeling fine. I'm just giving you an opportunity, that's all, an opportunity to change your mind.'

'Well, thank you very much,' Jem had laughed nervously, 'but I don't particularly want an opportunity to change my mind. I want to get married. Plain and simple. The end.'

'Cool, then,' he'd said, 'that's cool. Because I want to get married too. I really do, and I'd hate it if you were going through with it just out of a, out of a . . . sense of duty, you know.'

Then he'd got to his feet and loaded his empty plate into the dishwasher. 'Thank you for dinner,' he'd said, politely. 'It was really delicious. I'm going back to my studio. I'll see you later.' He'd dropped a kiss on to her cheek then, just to prove that there were no hard feelings. But Jem had felt it, in his kiss, the cool detachment. And it had chilled her to the bone.

The lido was, unsurprisingly for such a perfect day, heaving. She laid towels out in the shade of the small angular Deco buildings that formed the perimeter of the pool and then she started the arduous process of readying the spot for the use of a baby and a toddler. She emptied a small bag of toys on to the towel and then she took Blake from the pushchair and stripped him and covered his small fat body in thick cream. She then forced his fat legs awkwardly into a very snug-fitting swimming nappy and then into a pair of trunks she'd bought from Gap just after she'd found out she was having a boy (miniature Hawaiian print trunks being one of the few things she could think of that was cute about boy's clothes). She topped him off with a hat and then repeated the same process with her daughter, this time helping her into a swimsuit she'd insisted on being bought in Woolworth's half an hour ago that was a very slimy nylon affair with a picture of Ariel, the Disney mermaid, on the front. She puffed into a pair of *Finding Nemo* armbands and slid them up Scarlett's skinny arms and then she topped her off too with a hat and an extra blob of sun cream on the end of her nose, which had burned last summer and which Jem still felt deep guilt about.

Then she set about removing her own clothes, keeping her gaze very much in short range, not wanting to discover that she was in fact surrounded by nubile Danish au pair girls and the *crème de la crème* of the local yummy mummy brigade. She rolled her elasticated dress quickly down her stomach and let it fall to the floor, where she stepped out of it and was about to squirt some sun cream on to her stomach when she heard a familiar squeal.

'Scaaaar-lett!' And there was Jessica, in a sensible navy swimsuit, the type that girls had always worn when Jem was a child, and a pair of goggles hanging around her neck. 'Scaaaar-lett!'

Scarlett eyed her up and down, circumspectly.

'Hello, Jessica!' said Jem, greeting her extra fulsomely, to compensate for Scarlett's reticence. 'Scarlett, say hello to Jessica!'

Scarlett mumbled something under her breath and Jessica skipped happily from foot to foot, oblivious to Scarlett's lack of effusiveness.

'Scarlett, come swimming with me! It's so cold! But it's so fun! Come now! Come now!'

Jem slid her sunglasses on to her head. 'Where's your dad?' she asked, as breezily as she could.

'He's at home! He's working!'

'Oh,' said Jem, feeling relieved. 'You with your mum?'

'No,' said Jessica. 'No. I'm not with my mum. I'm with my brother. Look!' She pointed behind her to a spot on the other side of the pool. 'He's called Lucas! He's my big brother! Come on Scarlett, let's SWIM!' She grabbed Scarlett's hand and dragged her towards the shallow end of the pool.

Jem put her hands to her hips and glanced across the water. Lucas smiled lazily at her and raised his hand to his head in a gentle salute. Jem put up a hand too and felt the colour drain from her face.

He was dressed in oversized swimming shorts in a sludgy green colour that set off the caramel tones of his skin. His hair was shorn and he had sunglasses on his crown and even sitting with his arms wrapped around his bent knees, his hairless stomach was smooth and flat.

Jem felt mortification on two distinct levels. First was born of the fact that the last time she had seen this man she had been the most drunk she had been in over four years, had probably stunk of booze and stale tobacco and had been linking arms with his dad. The second was that looking at him made her feel old. His gloss and vigour, his direct gaze, his sheer unapologetic youth – she knew that to his eye she was pointless. To Lucas she was just that nutty woman who got into a cab with him and his dad two weeks ago. She was not a girl. Jem's father referred to any woman of his age or younger as a 'girl'. A girl, basically, was any woman that a man would have an interest in sleeping with, either real or theoretical. A 'girl' was therefore entirely objective.

She sat down and busied herself with Blake, who had started to whimper ominously in a manner that suggested that he had just discovered that he DID NOT LIKE THE LIDO (taking small children to new places was always a bit like Russian roulette).

'He's hot,' said a male voice, by her right ear. 'I'll take him in the pool for you, if you like, cool him down?' Lucas beamed at her and yes, his teeth were white as ivory and very straight. Jem and Blake both gazed at him for a second. 'Would you like that, little guy?' he said, tickling the soft pink soles of Blake's feet. Blake gazed at him for a moment longer and then he smiled. 'I'll take that as a yes then.' Lucas smiled at Blake and then smiled at Jem. 'If that's all right with your mummy, of course?'

Jem stared at him, agog. She had no idea what to say. Lucas spoke with a soft Northern accent and when he smiled, which he did a lot, his green eyes literally twinkled. There was something about him, Jem suddenly realised, that reminded her of Ralph. When he was younger. When she'd first met him. The beauty of him, the leanness of him, the sweet simplicity of him.

She found her tongue and she said, 'Er, yeah, OK, sure. If it's OK with you?'

He directed his smile at Blake and said, 'Come on then, buddy, fancy a dip?'

Blake didn't protest at all as Lucas bore him towards the water. Jem watched anxiously from the side. She had only ever taken Blake swimming at the indoor pool before, where the water was tepid. She waited for Blake to yelp with horror as his naked feet hit the cold water, but his face registered nothing but pure delight as Lucas splashed him inch by inch into the shallow end.

It occurred to Jem that she should be worried. She may well have spent forty minutes in the company of this man two weeks ago but she had no recollection of it and now she'd allowed him to carry her one and only son off into a swimming pool. A picture zipped through her mind: Lucas smiling malevolently at Blake as he slowly forced his head under the water and held him there wriggling until . . . Jem shook it from her head. Jem had spent her whole life trusting first and asking questions later, and her instincts (with a few dishonourable exceptions) had always proved to be spot on. And her instincts about this young man were good. He was good. And Blake was loving him.

Lucas spent a full fifteen minutes in the pool with Blake before finally bringing him back to Jem. Jem was so busy staring at her darling son, at his bonny face and his swirls of wet dark hair and the mound of his fat, shiny belly over the drawstring of his colourful shorts that she didn't really register the fact of Lucas's own wet, shiny skin, gleaming like French-polished walnut in the lunchtime sun. And when she did she caught her breath.

She put her arms out for her cold baby and wrapped him swiftly in the thickest of the three towels she had brought. She bundled him on to her lap and cuddled him to her, letting the sun and her body heat bring him back to room temperature.

'Thank you,' she said to Lucas, who was squatting by her side.

'No worries,' he said, 'we had a gas, didn't we, little man?' He rubbed the top of Blake's head and smiled his strip-light smile again.

This was the point at which Lucas would head back to his spot on the other side of the pool, if he intended to, but a moment passed and he didn't. 'So,' he said, falling from his haunches and on to his butt. 'You get home all right the other night?'

Jem flinched and blanched. 'Oh, Jesus,' she began. 'You

know,' she said, feeling total honesty would be the best approach, 'I do not remember you at all.'

'And you just let me take your son and heir for a swim?' said Lucas, one of his eyebrows arching suspiciously, before he laughed to let her know he was teasing.

'No, really,' continued Jem, 'the only reason why I know I've ever met you before is because my sister told me about it the next day. Seriously, otherwise I would have been at a loss.'

'But would you have still let me take your baby in the pool?' he teased again.

'Yes, probably,' smiled Jem, 'I'm kind of a trusting person. And I knew you were Jessica's brother and Joel's son. So you came recommended.'

'Yeah,' he turned and squinted into the sun. 'I love kids. Can't wait to have a few of my own.'

Jem frowned. 'Oh, but not yet,' she said.

'Yeah,' he said, 'why not? If the right woman came along. I'm coming up twenty-five. I'm not a kid any more, but I wouldn't mind being a young dad.'

'Like your dad, you mean?'

'Yeah.' Lucas drew his arms around his knees and surveyed the pool, his eyes looking for Jessica, then finding her and turning back to Jem. 'Yeah. Not that he was a dad in that way. I mean, he wasn't there. But he's my dad now and it's cool, it's good that he's young. So what about you, you must have started out young?'

Jem looked at Lucas, looked at her baby, looked at Scarlett, looked at Lucas again. She could not judge his comment. Was he teasing her again? Was he visually impaired? Or was he, heaven forfend, flirting with her? She decided to play it straight, hopefully to extinguish anything playful between the pair of them. 'Bless you,' she said, 'but no. I was a very old lady when I became a mother.'

'Well, then, what? You can't be more than thirty, tops? That's not old.'

'I'm going to be thirty-nine in October,' she said.

Lucas let his jaw drop and stared at her agog. 'No way,' he said.

'Yes way, sadly,' said Jem.

'Well,' he held up the palm of his hand for a high-five, 'in which case you must have one of those paintings in your attic. Because you do not look that old. No way.'

Jem smiled and said thank you and made a fuss of taking Blake out of his wet trunks. This was uncanny. This was silly. This was not what she had expected when she'd left the house this morning. She unpopped a carton of raisins and tipped them on to the towel in front of Blake, who started plucking them one by one like a human skill crane and popping them robotically into his mouth.

'So,' continued Lucas, his voice sounding a change of tone. 'You and my dad. What's the story there?'

'Oh. God,' Jem began, glad in a way that he'd brought up the subject to take them away from small talk. 'Honestly, I have no idea. I was – clearly – somewhat the worse for wear that night, but me and your dad, honestly, nothing, a strange thing, a strange relationship.'

'Oh, yeah, in what way?' He ran his fingers across his naked scalp, dislodging a few lingering dewdrops of pool water.

'Oh, I don't know. We knew each other by sight, I was fascinated by him, fascinated I think by this man who looked after his child alone, without a woman, probably because at the time my own partner was leaving me to do everything and I suppose I found him, you know . . .'

'Impressive?'

'Yeah, I guess. And my partner went away for a week and I sort of tried to get to know your dad a bit better and, well, I possibly pushed it a bit far.'

'Yeah, you had him over for dinner, right?'

'Oh. He told you?'

'Yeah. Not in detail, particularly, just that he was getting mixed messages off you.'

Jem nodded and picked at a loose thread on her towel. 'It was a bit like that, yes, and then I saw him a few weeks later and, well, he basically verbally abused me.' She turned to look at Lucas, to watch his reaction, but there wasn't one, just an imperceptible nod of his head.

'Hmm,' he said.

'Hmm what?' asked Jem.

'Well, yeah, my dad's got his issues. You know.'

'You mean his ex?'

'Well, yeah, his ex is one of them. But, well, he's got his demons too.'

Jem looked at him enquiringly.

'Drugs. You know?'

'Your dad takes drugs?'

'No, he used to. Not any more, of course. He hasn't touched them since Jessica was born.'

'What sort of drugs?'

'Well, the hard stuff. Smack.'

Jem blinked and held her breath for a second. She was blind-sided by the revelation. 'Your dad was a junkie?'

'Yeah.' Lucas nodded. 'It was bad. I didn't see him for years. My mum wouldn't let me and besides, he wasn't really that interested, you know; he was only interested in the stuff. But then Paulette got pregnant and he totally turned himself around. Methadone at first and then he was one hundred per cent clean by the time Jessie was born. But every day's a struggle, he still goes to meetings.'

'Ah, right, at that community centre on Maygrove Road?'

'Yeah, that's right. How did you know?'

"'Cause my sister lives at the top of that road, you know, in that old pub.'

'Yeah, I don't know the road. I've never been there.

Just know that that's where he goes for his meetings. Three times a week, every week. But he was a user for five years, and, well, he's still not really the same as he was before. He's got this *dark* side now. He's very cynical and untrusting. And I think that you were the first person in a long time he let into his life. I think . . .' he rolled a piece of gravel around beneath his fingertips, 'and don't quote me on this, but I think he thought you were like him, you know, I think he thought you were lonely. And then it turned out that you weren't. You were just . . . bored.'

Jem nodded, not sure how to respond. She felt horrible. Even more guilty than before, now she knew a bit more about Joel's past. She wondered if Lucas judged her for her behaviour. 'Yeah,' she said, 'I didn't handle the whole situation very well. I was in a strange place at the time. I was a bit lost. A bit confused. And I was definitely partly to blame. Well, more than partly . . .'

'But still, that's not an excuse for him to lay into you the way you say he did. But yeah, my dad, he's a really good bloke, a really amazing dad, but just a bit screwed up about the rest of humanity.'

'It feels like,' Jem began cautiously, 'it feels like he's got a bit of a chip on his shoulder?'

Lucas smiled sadly. 'Yeah,' he agreed, 'that about sums it up. But don't let that put you off him. As long as you're straight up with him, he'll be a good person to know. But if you send him mixed messages, like you did? Well, you've seen what can happen.'

They both turned then to watch the two girls in the shallow end of the pool. 'So, you're baby-sitting today, are you?'

'Yeah, all week actually. My dad's got a freelance contract, deadline's next Wednesday. I've got a bit of time off from college so I said I'd take Jessica for a few hours a day. Not that it's a hardship. She's a really easy little girl. And with the weather like this . . .' he spread his hands, 'well, it's like a little mini-holiday.'

Jem kept waiting for Lucas to go back to the other side of the pool, to find some reason not to sit with her any more. But he didn't, and as lunchtime turned into teatime they sat and chatted and they shared their picnics with each other and the girls. Jem batted away every attempt Lucas made to flirt with her. He was that kind of man, she could tell, a man who loved women, a man who could not resist the temptation to flirt. She didn't take it person-ally. Some men were just programmed that way. But she enjoyed his company none the less. He was light-hearted and easy to talk to. He was refreshing.

They met up again the following week. It wasn't sched-uled or premeditated, it just so happened that London was hot and they both had children to entertain, and where better to entertain children in hot London than in an outdoor pool? Jem arrived every day at twelve thirty with her children and a picnic and a bikini under her sundress. Lucas was already there, in his sludge-green shorts, his silky toast-coloured skin growing browner by the day and he would, invariably, the moment he saw Jem arrive, pick up his towel and his bag and join her in the shade. They talked about life and love and children and families and London and books and dogs and the North. They discussed his degree (he was studying for a Masters in Applied Science) and her career (he'd never heard of Karl Kasparov) and they talked about the upcoming wedding (that's so cool, he'd said, that's exactly the way I'd like to get married, quick and cheap, and then blow the rest on a honeymoon). It was remarkable to Jem that she had found so much to talk about with a man who was so much younger than she, and she found herself looking forward to the daily trek to the park in the midday heat, Blake's buggy loaded down with towels and toys and snacks, Lucas's warm welcoming smile as she appeared from around the corner, more than she cared to admit.

And then suddenly it was Thursday and the skies filled with black and the rain came and the lido was just a distant memory, and anyway, Jessica was back with her dad and Lucas was back at college and this tiny, magical little window in Jem's long London summer was slammed shut in front of her very eyes, with nothing to remind her of it but the pale outline of her bikini marked out in triangular white across her breasts.

Destiny. Jem believed in destiny. But she questioned it more and more these days. She'd read too much into the coincidences that had led to her bumping again and again into Joel back in the cooler days of spring. She'd believed that it meant something. But now, in retrospect, it was clear that it had meant nothing. Just two people in the same locale with children of the same age. Destined, maybe, just to be slightly unconventional friends. That was all. And now there was Lucas. What a strange and twisted journey he had taken towards this point in her life. Born twenty-four years ago in another part of the country, chanced upon meandering home through south London at three in the morning with his father, and then placed right opposite her in the lido during four of the only hot days that June would have to offer this year. How much attention should Jem pay to encounters of this kind? What did it all mean? She was getting married next month. On paper and in essence, everything at home was fine. Ralph worked, he ran, he helped with the kids' tea, he cleared away after breakfast, he emptied the dishwasher, he picked up abandoned shoes and water beakers, he took responsibility for his children and the upkeep of his home and he was, in many ways, utterly beyond reproach. He was everything that Jem had wanted him to be for the past four years. But something had changed.

335

Something wasn't right. Jem wasn't entirely sure what it was. It was something about Ralph, about his smile, his demeanour. He seemed, well, fake was the only way she could think of to describe it, as though he were pretending to like her. He was clearly very happy with his home life and his children, and seemed to be enjoying his work, but whenever he looked at Jem, it was as if he wasn't seeing her any more.

Fate had thrown a man called Joel at her and all it had proved was that she wanted to be with Ralph. And now fate had thrown this man at her. A completely different man. Lucas. And what would his role turn out to be? Would she ever see him again? Did she *want* to see him again? Was he another ego-boost or was he something more significant than that? Was Lucas, in fact, the answer to the question she'd asked herself all those months ago: *what happens next?*

Chapter 23

On Saturday Jem, Ralph and the children went for lunch at the Prince Regent, a pub that Ralph had a few years earlier declared to be the 'only decent thing about this fucking shithole'. It was a big Victorian pub, set on an unprepossessing corner on Herne Hill and it was the very essence of a gastropub, full of chesterfields and newspapers and children.

Ralph came back from the bar with a pint of Kronenbourg for himself, a large glass of white wine for Jem and a cranberry juice with a lime-green straw in it for Scarlett.

'I want a pink straw!' she complained, immediately.

'They only have lime-green straws,' Ralph replied patiently.

'But I don't like green.'

He sighed. 'You used to like green.'

'Yes, but I don't any more! I only like pink!'

'Well then, you are welcome to walk down the road and see if you can find another pub that does supply pink straws.' He pointed his thumb at the pub door.

Scarlett flumped backwards into her chair and pushed the offending glass away, disdainfully.

Jem looked at her diva daughter and raised her eyebrows. Blake started wriggling then in his high chair and making the squawking sounds that were the precursor, they had both come to learn, of a full-blown scream.

Jem quickly plucked him from his high chair and placed him on her lap.

Ralph frowned at her. 'See,' he said, 'it's a short hop from that,' he pointed at Blake, 'to that.' He pointed at the sulking Scarlett, still eyeing her lime straw furiously.

'I'm not going to leave him in his high chair screaming,' Jem replied. 'It's not fair on everyone else in here.'

'But he wasn't screaming, he was just moaning. We could have tried to distract him.'

Jem grimaced at him. In the past she'd have been able to silence him with squinted eyes and words to the effect that he had no right to criticise her parenting techniques as he was not responsible in any practical or logistical way for the parenting of his children. But that was no longer the case and for the sake of a harmonious meal she smiled tightly and said nothing.

She stared at the top of Ralph's head as he perused the menu. From this angle there was little to differentiate him from Lucas. From this angle they were very similar with their neat clipped heads of dark hair. But when he looked up the difference was startling. Instead of Lucas's soft uncomplicated gaze, there was Ralph's blank smile. Instead of a ready joke and some simple banter there were barbed comments and objections coiled up like snakes.

And that was when it hit Jem. All these weeks, ever since that sleepless night when she'd roamed around her house in the dark, looking for answers to awful questions, she'd been trying to recapture the soft, flighty girl in the photograph taken almost exactly eleven years ago to the day, but she hadn't realised until now that Ralph had been most of the reason for her feeling that way. It was all about him and the way he looked at her. It was about the way he made her feel like a queen and a princess and a mate and a mucker, and the best and most incredible girl in all the world. That was why she'd looked like that, because of *him*. And where was he? Where was that attentive, doe-eyed boy who blushed at the merest glimpse of her? He said he wanted to marry her, but he didn't act as if he wanted to marry her. He acted as if he were simply letting life take him to its inevitable conclusion.

I don't know you any more, she thought to herself, and as soon as the thought was in her head she'd shaken it loose again. It didn't bear contemplating. She was marrying this man in a fortnight.

She drank her chilled wine faster than she'd intended and was drunk immediately as her stomach was, as ever, empty.

She went to the bar to place their food order and to replenish her wine glass and when she came back Ralph said: 'What did you order?'

'Soup,' she said.

'And what else?'

'Nothing,' she said.

He gave her one of his new pious smiles.

'What?' she said.

'You're not eating enough,' he said. 'You're too thin.'

'I am not too thin!' she exclaimed.

'Yes,' he said, 'you are. And it's not good for you to drink on an empty stomach. At least have some bread.'

'I don't want any bread.'

Ralph tutted. 'It's not good for you,' he said again, and Jem wanted to huff and say: what are you, my *father*? But instead she just ignored him and took another swig of wine. Very soon the day lost its hard edges and Jem lost her residual annoyance and life took on the honey-hued tones of another life and another time. Wine could do that, Jem had found. Especially on an empty stomach. Before long they were relaxed again and Scarlett was happily sipping her pink cranberry through her lime straw and Blake was chewing ciabatta and Ralph and Jem were conversing nicely about wedding plans and it seemed to Jem that if a stranger were to walk in now and look at the family on the right they would think, oh, how lovely, two cute children, trendy dad, happy mum, how very

339

civilised. But even as they sat there Jem knew it was all a mirage, fleeting and wine-fuelled.

She spooned the last of her butternut squash soup into her mouth and wondered what Lucas was doing.

Lucas had mentioned a festival in Brockwell Park. She hadn't really thought much of it at the time. She was not the festival type. But they'd had flyers on the bar in the Prince Regent and she'd slipped one into her pocket. It was this weekend, today and tomorrow. It meant something.

She called Lulu that afternoon. 'What are you doing tomorrow?' she said.

'Going to the festival at Brockwell Park,' Lulu said. 'Why don't you come with us?'

It meant something.

Ralph didn't come. Jem hadn't expected him to. He was not the festival type either.

It was not hot the next day, it was pale and cool, and Jem chose her clothes carefully, cropped skinny jeans, a fuchsia cotton camisole and fitted leopard-print cardigan, with silver pumps. She wore large hoop earrings and prayed that she didn't look like a middle-aged fortune-teller.

She felt a little shiver of nervous anticipation as she set off from the house at lunchtime with the children, and the sense of anticipation increased as they approached the perimeter of the park. She didn't expect to bump into Lucas today, the fair was sprawling, the chances were slim. But if she did, well, it was potentially seismic. What if she discovered that she had feelings for him? A week before her wedding?

She found Lulu, Walter and all five kids spread out in a patch of unconvincing sunshine over the surface area of four large blankets. Jem added her blanket to the patch-work and unloaded her children and her picnic and hoped

340

that Scarlett would fail to spot the fairground in the distance. Fairgrounds tended to make Scarlett somewhat emotional, and not in a good way.

She greeted Walt and Lulu with kisses and hugs and then she set about, very quickly, opening a bottle of rosé she'd brought chilling in a frozen thermal sleeve and decanting it into plastic tumblers.

'You fantastic person!' said Lulu, taking a glass from Jem's hand. 'I hadn't thought to bring anything.'

Jem downed the icy rosé, feeling it hit the pit of her stomach. A moment later the day blurred and happiness settled upon her. She handed Marmite sandwiches and small boxes of raisins to her children, and she chatted with Lulu and Walt. Lulu offered her a tub of hummus and a packet of carrot sticks. Jem took a handful of carrot sticks and passed on the hummus.

She had another glass of rosé and she thought about going for a wander, possibly in the opposite direction to the funfair. There was a small animals' enclosure, apparently. Small animals seemed a nice way to pass the time and less likely to end in a bloodbath of tears and hysteria than a psychedelic swirl of bright lights, loud pop music and rides that Scarlett would want desperately to go on until two seconds after they started moving, at which point she would want desperately to be taken off again.

She was considering her options when she looked up and saw him.

Lucas.

He was gurning at Blake, who was giggling at him, and before he'd even said a word to Jem, he leaned down to pluck him from the blanket and was holding him aloft.

'Hello, little dude,' he said. 'How've you been doing? I missed you!'

Blake beamed at him and then Lucas leaned down and looked at Jem.

341

'Hardly recognised you with your clothes on,' he started.

Walter and Lulu threw Jem wide eyes. Jem laughed.

'Very funny,' she said. 'Lulu – do you remember Lucas?'

'Vaguely,' laughed Lulu. 'But we definitely all had our clothes on.' She turned back to Jem. 'Didn't we?'

Jem laughed again and so did Lucas. 'We were hanging out at the lido,' he explained, 'last week. When it was hot. So I've seen rather a lot of your sister in a bikini.'

Lulu threw Jem a look of alarm and Jem grimaced. Her brief harmless little four-day flirtation seemed suddenly tawdry laid out like this in front of her sister and her husband. She wished that Lucas would leave.

But instead he did what he always seemed to do and made himself right at home. He sat down next to Jem, with Blake on his lap. 'How've you been?'

'I'm good,' said Jem. 'How about you?'

'Yeah, not bad. I'm here with some mates, just on my way to the beer shop to pick up some more wine. Spotted a familiar face, thought I'd come and say hello.' He jiggled Blake up and down on his lap and tickled him under the arms.

Jem could tell he was feeling slightly awkward, he wasn't as natural as he had been when they'd chatted at the lido.

'This is Walter, by the way,' said Jem, 'Walter is Lulu's husband.' They shook hands and Lucas looked around from side to side. 'And your husband?' he said.

'Not here. Working,' she replied cursorily. She didn't want to talk about Ralph. Not now. 'So, did your dad make his deadline?' she asked, feeling that although she didn't want to talk to him, now that he'd made himself comfortable it would be rude not to.

'Yeah, as far as I know. He's taken Jessie away for a few days.'

'Oh, yes? Somewhere nice?'

He shrugged. 'Don't know,' he said. 'He wouldn't tell

342

me where they were going. He's, er . . . well, he's trying to lie low while the ex is sniffing around with all her taking Jessica talk, you know.'

'Oh God,' Jem cried, 'is she still talking about getting custody?'

'Seems that way, yeah. So my dad's gone off the radar. And I don't blame him. That woman is a nutter. And what about you? What've you been up to since Wednesday?'

'Nothing much,' said Jem, 'just, you know, being a mum. Being a housewife. The usual boring old stuff.'

'Oh, now,' he exclaimed, 'don't say that! How can that be boring! Best job in the world, isn't it?'

Lulu and Jem looked at each other and laughed.

'Well, yes, maybe compared to stuffing chickens, cleaning toilets, painting bridges, you know.'

He laughed. 'But you've got your PR job, your little business going?' he asked Jem. 'It's not all just nappies and stuff. And besides,' he said, 'I reckon you could make anything interesting, anything you did. You've just got that sparkle about you, you know.'

Jem turned to look at him, to see what his face had looked like when he said these words, but he didn't look embarrassed or self-conscious. He looked cool and circumspect. She said nothing, unsure how to respond.

Lucas handed Blake back to Jem. 'Anyway,' he said, 'I'd better shoot off. But I'll be here all day, yeah? I'll look out for you. We could have a little drink together. Or maybe even a little dance. Are you a good dancer?' He eyed her up and down and smiled. 'Yeah,' he said, 'yeah. I bet you are a good dancer. Come and find me. Or I'll find you. But come and find me before you go. OK?'

Jem nodded mutely.

'Hey, look,' he said, 'are you on Facebook?'

Jem blinked. Then she nodded.

'What's your surname?'

'Catterick,' she said, 'Jemima Catterick.'

'I'll friend you,' he said, 'when I get home. Don't go without saying goodbye. Whatever you do.'

He got to his feet and he waved at Blake and he waved at Scarlett. He said nice to meet you to Walt, he said see you again soon to Lulu, and then he left.

Lulu stared at his receding back and she turned to stare at her sister. 'What,' she said, 'was that all that about?'

'What?' said Jem, disingenuously.

'God, that man. He was all over you!'

'What!' she said, a little less disingenuously this time.

'Totally,' said Lulu. 'I can't believe you didn't tell me you'd been hanging out with that boy at the lido!'

'Well, I haven't seen you. It was only a couple of days, nothing major.'

'Yes, but, God, he's got a crush on you!'

'No, he has *not*.'

'Yes. He has. *Are you on Facebook*? Ha!'

'You're being ridiculous,' said Jem.

'Er, Walt,' she turned to consult her husband, 'does that young man or does that young man *not*, have a crush on my sister?'

Walter shrugged his huge shoulders and smiled apologetically.

'No,' said Jem defensively, 'you're wrong. Honestly. He's just a naturally flirtatious person. I bet he's like that with everyone. I mean, come on! He's twenty-four years old. And he's seen me in a bikini. I could maybe get to grips with the notion of him fancying me if he'd only seen me in my clothes. But he has seen my wrinkly, droopy thirty-eight-year-old body, in a bikini, without a tan. There is no way he fancies me. And anyway I'm getting married in two weeks and I'm not interested. Thank you!'

She turned and hid the flush in her cheeks from her sister, from her nephews, from her children.

It was entirely inappropriate.

*   *   *

She did see Lucas again that day.

She saw the back of his head bobbing through the crowd. She saw his arm around a girl with short blonde hair. She saw him smiling and laughing with a friend. His friends were young. He was young. He reminded her so painfully of Ralph, when he was young, when he was in love with her.

She didn't catch him up to say goodbye. She turned the other way and moved in the opposite direction as quickly as she possibly could.

Chapter 24

On Monday the last of Ralph's Californian paintings was loaded into back of a specialist courier's van, the back door was unceremoniously banged shut and the van disappeared up the road towards Notting Hill. Ralph himself would head for Notting Hill tomorrow morning to help hang the paintings, but for now he had a whole day to himself and he knew exactly what he was going to do with it.

The day was blowy and the light was poor, but Ralph enjoyed the walk through the backstreets towards Gil's estate.

He kept his head turned to the side as he passed by Walt and Lulu's massive house on the corner of Maygrove Road, just in case she was looking from one of the front windows, just in case she came haring across the road to greet him and then would talk far too much and make him feel embarrassed (Lulu always made him feel a bit embarrassed, there was something very rude about her, she always seemed to be thinking about sex), and then she would want to know where he was going and he would have to say, oh, just off to an old man's shed to do painting. Not that there was anything intrinsically wrong with painting in an old man's shed, just that he couldn't be bothered to have to explain it, as he would have to because Lulu would definitely want to know.

Gil's house was neat and compact, one of a terrace of ten or so identical houses. The door was council blue and

Ralph banged the letterbox because the doorbell appeared to have been disconnected.

Gil greeted him at the door in blue checked shorts and a billowing blue T-shirt, his sunglasses as ever around his neck, his mottled kneecaps swollen with age, a cup of tea in one hand.

'Come in, Ralph,' he intoned, 'come in. I'll be offering you something to drink in a minute, but you'll have to wait. Nadal is *slaughtering* our boy Murray.' He followed Gil into the small living room, twelve by twelve, an antique Knowle sofa in tartan, a recliner seat, and a small television housed in an alcove. All other space was given over to books and paintings. It was cosy, clean and snug. On the table in front of Gil was a punnet of grapes and an unwrapped peppermint Aero. 'Sit down, sit down.'

Ralph took a seat on the Knowle sofa and, uninterested as he was in the men's quarter finals at Wimbledon, glanced around instead at Gil's paintings. As he'd suspected, they were simplistic, raw and unfashionable. Scrapings on boards and canvases in earthy tonal shades, of landscapes and seascapes and rocky outcrops. Nothing original but all of them possessed some kind of energy, the mark of the painter rather than his skill.

They sat in silence for a further twenty minutes while Gil winced and oohed and aahed and cursed at the television until finally it was all over and Murray was out of the tournament, and Gil took Ralph through to his kitchen, a small galley behind the staircase.

He brewed him a cup of thick, sturdy tea and handed it to him and then he took him across a small patch of ragged grass and into a grey-painted garden house in the corner.

The shed took up almost three-quarters of the available space in his garden. Inside the air was hot and woody, full of spores of dust.

'It's a wee bit squashed in, as you can see, but it's a

fortunate spot, this. Gets the light all day long. And a wee bit of something else too, if you see what I mean.' He winked at Ralph. 'Here, let me get you an easel.'

He pulled some paintings away from the wall to release another easel and set it up next to his. Ralph rested his canvas against it and then unclipped the locks on his paint box. He felt exposed. He had not painted in front of another human being since he was at the Royal College.

'We'll start with a prayer then, shall we?' said Gil, a statement, not a suggestion.

'Yes,' said Ralph, 'yes. Sure.'

'I think, though, a private prayer.'

Ralph nodded and let his head fall to his chest. He closed his eyes and he let the prayers come to him as they did more and more easily these days. He prayed for his exhibition, that it be a success, that he sell a lot of paintings, that he make a lot of money and he prayed for Jem, that she would find whatever it was she was looking for and that when she did it would not be too far away from him. And then he prayed, as he always prayed, for his children, his angels – he prayed that he would keep them safe and that the four of them would live in harmony and joy for evermore.

He could feel Gil's aura as he prayed, the purity of him and the strength of him and he prayed that one day he too would know the spiritual peace that this towering gnarled oak of a man had found in his life, here in this dusty room in the cramped corner of a tiny garden in the back end of an estate in a dead-end Brixton road. If he could find peace here then surely Ralph could find peace in his pretty Edwardian terrace with his beautiful wife and his beautiful children and his large studio attic room with its view of the streets.

Ralph felt so small compared to Gil; he felt ratty and half formed, an insubstantial creature of small mind and limited vision. His mind was shrunken and desiccated. He'd been bursting over with creative energy when he left the Royal College, the star of his year. And then just before he'd got together with Jem, when he'd been crazy in love with her but not allowed to have her, he'd found it again, found the essence of himself. But he was lazy and he was fearful by nature, and he'd let it go again.

Maybe this was his third chance, right here, right now, in this place.

He faced his canvas and he let go of everything, everything that had held him back for the past ten years and he opened his mind, as wide as it would go. He was not painting from life or from a photograph, he was painting from deep down inside him and he waited a beat to see what he would find, and he was about to pick out a colour when Gil began to sing. It was loud and it was alarming. He sang without words and without tune. Ralph threw him a quick look.

'You can sing too, if you like,' said Gil, pulling open his own paint box. 'Sing a song of your soul. Sing as loud as you like, boy, there's nobody here but me.' Gil smiled at him, his ice-blue eyes bright and open. 'Go on, boy, sing!'

So Ralph did. He felt the sounds rise up through him, from deep down in his heels, from the very bowels of himself, and he let them out and there it was, there was his song, light and rosy and sweet as raspberries. As he sang his hand unconsciously found the deepest, berry-est red in his palette and he squeezed it on to his paint-board and thrust a wide brush into it and he let the brush make marks on his canvas and the feeling as his soft wet brush hit the tense fabric was like nothing he'd ever experienced before. It felt like a sheer bloody miracle.

He sang and he painted and over the next hour his canvas took form and life.

And when an hour and a half later he felt he'd finished, he put down his brushes and he cried tears of utter joy.

Ralph brought his painting home from Gil's the following morning. He'd timed it so that he would return while Jem was dropping Scarlett at nursery, but when he got home at just after nine o'clock, Scarlett was sitting on the bottom step looking puce and tearful, Blake was strapped into his buggy looking confused and Jem was sitting at the kitchen table, drinking a cup of tea.

'What's going on?' said Ralph.

'Oh, indeed,' said Jem, getting to her feet. 'We are currently experiencing a marathon naughty step protest. It has been, ooh, nearly twenty-five minutes since Scarlett was put there and she is still refusing to say sorry.'

'What did you do, Scarlett?' asked Ralph.

'Nothing!' she snapped.

Jem raised her eyebrows and tutted. 'She threw her cereal bowl. On the floor. On purpose.'

'I did not!'

Jem sighed again. 'I then asked her to help me clean it up, at which point she smooshed it in with her shoe. So on to the naughty step and still no apology and now we are late for nursery.'

Scarlett stared at Ralph beseechingly as if she thought he might somehow be able to save her from the cruelty of her mother. 'Sorry, buddy,' he said, 'you're on your own with this one. You need to apologise to Mummy or else you will be spending the rest of the day on that uncomfortable stair. When you could be at nursery playing with your friends.'

'I don't like nursery,' she snapped, and then turned to face the wall. Ralph and Jem exchanged a glance and Jem rolled her eyes. This was the great flaw of the naughty step. It was no good at times when getting out of the house in a timely fashion was required.

350

'What's that?' said Jem, glancing at the cloth-covered canvas by the stairs.

'A painting,' he said.

'Oh, right. Where from?'

'Oh, nowhere, just one I've been working on.'

'Out of the studio?'

'Yeah.'

'Can I see it?'

'Erm, no,' said Ralph.

'What, seriously?'

'Yes,' said Ralph, tersely, 'seriously. It's not finished.'

'OK, but can I see it when it is finished?'

'Yeah, sure. And listen, Scarlett, if you say sorry to your mummy and help her clean up the cereal, I might just think about taking you to nursery this morning.'

She turned from the wall and stared at him. 'Just us?' she asked. 'Not Blake?'

He got visual confirmation from Jem that this would be acceptable and turned back to her. 'Yeah,' he said, 'just us. But first you have to say sorry to Mummy and then you have to go into the kitchen and help her clean up your mess. OK?'

'OK!' She leaped to her feet and threw her arms breezily around Jem. 'Sorry, Mummy,' she said, 'I'll never do it again!' Then she hurtled into the kitchen and pulled a length of kitchen paper from the roll on the table and started mopping away at the spilled milk and Shreddies on the floor.

'You jammy bastard!' Jem mouthed at Ralph.

'What can I say?' he shrugged at her nonchalantly and smiled smugly. 'I've got the magic touch.'

'Ha! Well, for that,' she cried triumphantly, 'I am going to look at your mysterious painting'

The smile fell from Ralph's lips, but Jem didn't notice. 'No!' he shouted, as her hand reached for the cloth that covered it.

'Yes!' she retorted, playful still. 'I want to see it!'

'No,' he said, harder this time and holding one of her small wrists in his hand, slightly too hard.

'Yes,' said Jem, cross that he was using physical force to stop her fun and more determined than before to see what was on the canvas. She pulled her hand from Ralph's tight grip and then she pulled the fabric from the canvas and then she stopped and stared for just a moment, unsure what to say.

From the kitchen came Scarlett's small, cross voice: 'Mummy! You said you'd help me! I can't do it by myself!'

'I'll be in in a minute,' she said, her eyes still glued to the image in front of her.

It was . . . well, it was *rubbish*. It was the sort of thing that an eighteen-year-old boy who'd just had his heart broken might have painted after smoking a big spliff. It was ugly, full of crass symbolism, smears of red paint, shapes that looked like they might be hearts, children, flowers, houses, black spots, ugly faces, but you couldn't quite be sure, just a huge, psychotic, meaningless mess.

'Jesus, Ralph,' she said, eventually, 'what the hell did you put in your tea this morning?'

Ralph's face fell and he pulled the fabric back over the painting. 'Nothing,' he snapped, 'I put nothing in my tea. It's just inspired by nature. You know. Real life. Purity. Spirituality. Things I wouldn't expect you to know anything about!'

Jem's jaw dropped at these words and she stared at Ralph in horror. 'I. Beg. Your. Pardon?' she intoned.

'Nothing,' mumbled Ralph, carrying the painting up towards the top floor, 'nothing. I just didn't expect you to understand. And you don't. That's all.'

Blake had started crying now and Jem lifted him from the buggy and held him to her, feeling her heart racing between them. Adrenalin coursed through her veins. Ralph had never talked to her like that before. He had never been physical with her before. And that painting? It was so ugly. Jem had seen his degree show work, published in a book that he'd kept since he graduated. It was dark and oppressive and dramatic, nothing like the exquisite flowers he'd been painting since, but it had meaning and form and impact. That painting had nothing. It was a mess. And what did he mean; real and pure, nothing like her?

She closed her eyes against tears and the rage and took Blake into the kitchen where she sat him on the floor and helped her daughter to scrape mushy Shreddies from the gaps between the battered old floorboards.

Chapter 25

Ralph's show was called Taco Belle:

'McLeary's ninth show at the gallery of Philippe Dauvignon marries together a new sensibility and an old obsession with form, texture and light. Inspired by his travels around the Californian seaside resort of Santa Monica, Taco Belle aims to showcase the 'soft' side of Americana. The street life depicted here is given new focus juxtaposed against the elegance and shapeliness of Californian flora and foliage. The light is electric and the mood is playful. This is Ralph McLeary's most energetic work yet.'

Ralph folded his arms across his chest and surveyed the room. It was fine. The light in the gallery was perfect for this work, especially here in the middle of summer. His work looked fine, perfectly acceptable. Philippe was over-seeing a minion unloading bottles of cheap white wine on to a table and another minion emptying bags of Japanese rice crackers into large white bowls. Ralph was in jeans and a white shirt with pointy-toed shoes. He looked slim and tanned and fit.

'You are looking very good, Ralph,' said Philippe, eyeing him up and down. 'Last time I saw you, you were a little bit . . .' he patted his own slab-flat stomach, 'but now, you are fit, no?'

'I've been running,' Ralph said listlessly, 'running every day.'

'Well, you should keep it up. It suits you, you look marvellous!'

Ralph smiled, but he was in no mood for Philippe and his incessant Gallic charms. He patted his jeans pockets to ensure that his cigarettes were there and then he went outside and stood on the street to smoke one.

Eleven years ago, he thought, eleven years ago I stood outside this gallery in a £600 Dolce & Gabbana suit smoking this same brand of cigarettes. Eleven years ago I'd pumped £500 of my own money into the evening so that my friends could drink champagne and eat canapés and be surrounded by plush arrangements of fresh peonies. Eleven years ago I was pale and thin and sick with nerves waiting for a woman to arrive.

Not Jem, but a girl called Cheri – Cheri, the love of Smith's life. He'd invited her to the private viewing of his exhibition deliberately so that she could sabotage Smith's stupid affair with Jem, so that Jem would see Smith for the idiot that he really was, so that Jem would be free, free to love him. And it had worked. Smith had got himself disgustingly drunk (so drunk in fact that he hadn't touched alcohol again for nearly three years afterwards) and asked Cheri to marry him. In front of Jem. Jem had taken one look at Ralph's lovingly rendered paintings, another look at Smith in a pool of his own vomit in the gallery toilets and fallen swooningly into Ralph's arms. And they all lived happily ever after. Except they hadn't.

They had seven years of fun and loving and then they bought a house and had a baby and slowly they became different people. And then they had another baby and began to drift even further apart. Then Ralph had kissed a stranger in California and Jem had got flowers from a stranger in London and Ralph had found prayer and Jem had lost a baby and somewhere in the middle of all this they'd decided to get married. Ralph still thought that getting married was the right thing to do – it was right

for the children and right for the future of the relationship – but he wasn't so sure about Jem. She seemed to be
going through some kind of mid-life crisis. She was
drinking too much, not eating enough, trying, it seemed
to him, to be something she wasn't. Or maybe just trying
to be something she used to be. Except she could never
be that girl again and they could never be that couple
again. Ralph had accepted that and he just had to hope
that Jem would accept it, too.

There were, he supposed, many different kinds of happy
ever after.

There would be no drama here tonight, just a slow trickle
of the critical and the curious and the local and those with
nothing better to do. His father would come up from
Croydon and arrive looking old and proud, as he did
every single time. He would eat some crisps, sip half a
glass of wine, tell Ralph which one was his favourite and
then he would leave again saying, 'Another great show,
Ralph. Your mother would be proud.' Jem would come,
but for her, he suspected it was just another opportunity
to put on something pretty and drink too much wine.
There may be a critic or two, a blogger or two, there may
be a buyer or a collector. He might, if he was lucky, even
make a sale. But there would be no punch-ups, no decla-
rations of love, thwarted or otherwise. It was just another
night in just another gallery in W11.

He trod his spent cigarette under the heel of his expensive designer shoe and then he went back inside, trying
to rustle up enthusiasm for something that, unlike the
work he'd displayed on these walls eleven years earlier,
he felt had nothing to do with him at all.

Chapter 26

The following evening Ralph emerged from his studio at six o'clock and told Jem that he was going for a run.

Ralph usually ran during the day. Since he'd got back from Santa Monica all shiny and transformed, his evenings had been devoted to his family, to group meals and bath times and the clearing away of toys. This was the second Thursday in a row that he had left at six to go for a run. Jem was about to call something out after him, a question of some description, but as she opened her mouth to speak she heard the front door go. She let her mouth close again and went back to stacking the dishwasher.

She was still a little hungover from the night before. She'd drunk too much nasty wine at Ralph's preview show. And then forgotten to eat. She'd got in the habit of taking a pair of Nurofen with half a pint of water before she got into bed every night these days, just to pre-empt the ill effects of half a bottle, sometimes more, of Chablis. But she'd forgotten last night, sort of landed in bed with very little recollection of how or when, in pyjamas and full makeup, slept like a corpse until eight o'clock when she'd awoken to the sight of all three members of her family sitting on the end of the bed, staring at her.

Ralph had been kind to her. He'd taken Scarlett to nursery with Blake in the buggy. She'd been able to come round slowly and gently, enjoy a long shower, eat a peaceful breakfast, make herself a proper coffee. He'd put Blake down for his morning nap when he returned about an hour later, checked that Jem was feeling OK and then tiptoed to his studio, from where he had not emerged until just now.

Jem's hangover had abated. She'd had a poached egg on toast for lunch and four cans of Diet Coke. But she could not shake a terrible overweening sense of sadness that had cloaked her since her eyes opened this morning.

She always found Ralph's previews slightly anti-climactic these days. It was inevitable. How could any preview show ever compare to that first one? But last night had been different. She'd felt their lost connection echoing and jarring around the gallery. Everywhere she looked she saw the way they used to be. The wine had tasted sour in her mouth, but she'd drunk glasses of the stuff, just to keep herself in the game. And then they'd sat, side by side, in the cab on the way home, and the air through the open window had been warm and full of London, and Jem had talked too much about the show and the paintings and how great they were and how he was sure to sell loads because they were so beautiful and Ralph had stared from the window and said nothing. Then she'd laid her hand upon Ralph's thigh and waited for Ralph to cover her hand with his own.

But he hadn't.

Instead he'd patted it, gently, condescendingly, as if it was the crown of a well-behaved dog, smiled at her cheesily, and then put his hand back on the seat.

After a moment she'd taken her hand back and placed it sadly in her lap.

Jem put her children to bed that night feeling glad of them in a way that she maybe never had before. 'Thank God for you,' she whispered into their damp hair. 'Thank God for you both. What would I do without you, my angels? Where would I be?'

After their doors were closed and the house was quiet she poured herself a glass of wine and she sat at her computer.

She opened up her e-mail account and felt her heart jump a little when she saw the words:

FACEBOOK
Lucas Warbush has added you as a friend.

The request came with a note: 'Hello there stranger! Sorry not to see you again at the festival. I looked out for you. Just hope this is the right Jemima Catterick – why haven't you got a profile photograph?!'

She clicked the link and accepted Lucas's friend request and then found herself very quickly immersed in Lucas-world. He was obviously a keen maintainer of his Facebook page. He had thirty-eight photo albums and a wall chock full of jaunty messages from some of his two hundred and ninety-three friends. His profile photograph, though, was enigmatic: the top of his head bearing his sunglasses, his perfect ears on either side, no facial features.

He looked so like Ralph. It startled her every time she noticed the similarity and sent her back in time.

His status update read: 'Lucas Warbush is going home to see his mummy.'

Jem smiled.

She thought about her own son, curled up in his pink sleepsuit across the landing, and wondered if one day he would have the sheer guts and confidence to tell his peers that he was going home to see his mummy without even a hint of irony. As she thought this thought she heard a banging at the window pane and jumped slightly before realising that it was just the rain, a tempestuous rainstorm breaking over the warm pavements, pelting the hot roof tiles with fat droplets. The sky lit up for a moment, she counted up to eight, then bang, distant thunder. She thought of Ralph. Poor Ralph. Running through the angry rain. Getting soaked to the bone.

Dodging the forked lightning. She pulled open the bedroom window and smelled the air, the distinctive musty smell of hot, wet, London paving stones. She glanced both ways up the street to see if she could see Ralph returning, but the street was empty. She closed the window and sat down again.

She looked through Lucas's photo albums and read his friends' comments. She saw pictures of Jessica and Joel, and of Lucas with his arm around a pretty black woman with short relaxed hair slicked back off her face, whom Jem assumed was Lucas's mother. He saw an older black woman with crimped silver hair sitting with a pair of cats with orange mottled fur. And then there were his friends, dozens of friends, all young and happy, in bars, on holidays, in halls of residence, in scruffy flats. Students. She recognised the blonde girl she'd seen him with at the festival. Her name was Malaika Fitzjohn. A very interesting name for a very interesting-looking woman. All his friends looked interesting, in fact, and all the messages and comments left by them on his page were warm and well spelled. And it struck Jem at that moment that it was very sad that she and Ralph had reached the end of their eleventh year together and had no circle of friends. Ralph's family consisted solely of his sad old dad, a man of eighty-two, who hadn't exactly been a livewire in his younger days and had lost his spark entirely since his wife had died three years earlier. Ralph's only real friend lived in California and all the friends he'd hung around with during his flat-sharing days in Battersea, who were mainly hoity-toity PR girls using him to attain some credibility, had gone by the wayside. They'd had two friends, local friends, Alex and Maria. They'd had a daughter the same age as Scarlett and they'd go for lunch together at the Prince Regent and have summer lunches in each other's gardens, and then Alex and Maria had sold their house around the corner and moved to Hastings. Since then the

Catterick/McLeary family had been a somewhat insular little unit, punctured only by the presence of the slightly nutty Lulu and her husband. Ralph was terrified of Lulu and found Walter, at six foot three and twelve years his senior, slightly imposing. Jem had been waiting, subconsciously, for Scarlett to start school. That seemed to her the time that local friendships began to be formed. But as she looked at Lucas's friends and felt the warmth and extent of their bond, she felt sad for her own small little world and suddenly wanted more.

She sighed and emptied her glass of wine, and was on her way down the stairs to refill it when she heard the door go and Ralph was standing in the hallway in his running gear, looking po-faced.

'Hi!' she trilled.

He glanced at her wine glass and said hello.

She looked him up and down. His T-shirt was dry and fresh. His shorts were still as crisp as they'd been when he'd pulled them out of his wardrobe two hours earlier. 'You're dry!' she said.

'Yeah,' he replied.

'But the rain,' she continued.

'What about the rain?'

'Well, I thought you'd get soaked. It was torrential.'

He shrugged. 'Must have missed it,' he said.

'But . . . how?'

'Localised?' he suggested, unconvincingly.

She nodded her agreement that yes, it must have been localised, and headed past him to get another glass of wine.

'Oh God, Lulu, you should have seen it, it was appalling.'

'What, like badly executed?'

'Worse than that,' Jem rubbed sun cream into her bare ankles, 'it was ugly. It was *unpleasant*. And if he'd just said something like, oh, well, you know, it was just a warming-up exercise, or, you know, it was just a bit of fun, I'd have thought, well, that's OK then. But he didn't. He just stormed off upstairs with it as if it was his pride and joy and didn't talk to me for the rest of the day.'

Lulu sneered delicately. She could not bear the concepts of bickering and sulking. 'Where is he now?' she said, her nose wrinkling mischievously.

'He's at the gallery, with Philippe, being interviewed for the local rag.'

'When's he back?'

Jem shrugged. 'I don't know, four-ish, I guess.'

'Come on then.'

'Come on what?'

'Let's go and have a look.' She pointed her beer bottle upwards towards the top floor of the house.

'What. In his studio?'

'Yeah, why not? Let me see this painting. Come on!'

Jem looked at Blake, who had fallen asleep in his bouncy chair, and Scarlett, who was playing happily in the sand box, and thought, yes, why not? 'Scarlett,' she said, 'we're just popping inside for a minute. We'll be back soon.'

Scarlett looked at them listlessly and carried on with her game.

'Have you asked him?' said Lulu as they curled up the spiral staircase towards his studio. 'About the church thing?'

'You mean about what Joel said in the taxi?'

Lulu nodded.

'No,' she replied.

'Why not?'

'I don't know,' she said. 'I suppose because I don't want to have a conversation that involves mentioning Joel.'

'Why not? Nothing happened with Joel.'

'I know, but it sort of did in my head and I'd rather not mention him, that's all. It makes me feel uncomfortable.'

'God, yes, but don't you just want to know? Don't you want to know why he's hanging out in churches?'

Jem shrugged. 'He took the kids there the other day,' she said, 'Scarlett told me. They lit some candles for his mum. Must just be that. Must just be a way of dealing with his loss.'

Jem had not been inside Ralph's studio since that night weeks ago when she'd told him she didn't want to have the baby. Then it had been full of his lovely, vibrant Californian flowers. Now it was empty again, just two canvases on display. The first was the one she'd seen the other day, the awful red and black affair.

Lulu gasped when she saw it. 'Oh God,' she said, 'is that the one?'

Jem nodded. ''Fraid so.'

'Oh, I mean,' Lulu circled it for a moment, 'I mean, it's not even a painting, really, is it? I mean, it's just marks. Just mess. And, oh my God, what is *that*?' She spun round as the other painting caught her eye. This one was a work in progress, still mounted on Ralph's easel, unfinished. And again, it was a visual affront. Jem stared at the latest creation in horror. Ralph had been so excited about starting off in a new direction. He'd been so looking forward to it, and so too had Jem. And this, it seemed, was it. Mindless, artless, charmless.

And then, just as she was absorbing the awful reality of Ralph's new direction, she saw something else, something that shocked her to her core. A photograph propped up on a bookshelf, a photograph of himself and a very beautiful blonde girl with thick hair the colour of butter and feline features and a small crucifix in the dip of her neck. Their heads were touching and they both wore smiles as joyful as Christmas.

She was about to say something to Lulu, when she noticed a look of horror on her face and followed her gaze to a dark corner of the studio where a small canvas was perched on a crate. It had been covered up with a piece of muslin but the muslin had slipped and it was obvious that the painting underneath bore some resemblance to the photograph on the bookshelf. The two women exchanged a glance and Jem nodded imperceptibly at Lulu, who crossed the room and unveiled the painting. It was, as they'd both suspected, the woman in the photograph, recreated in painstaking detail. Ralph had replaced the background of palm trees with something resembling a large silver sun and put a sprig of mauve bougainvillaea flower in the woman's hair. It was an exquisite painting, all picked out in shades of white and silver, with the flowers in her hair providing the only colour. It was one of the nicest paintings that Jem could remember Ralph having painted in a long time. Possibly, it pained her to think, since the ones he'd painted of her.

'Fucking hell,' said Lulu, biting her lip.

Jem felt her head begin to spin. Her life seemed to be hurtling through space, untethered and out of control. Could this mysterious blonde beauty be the root of all the strangeness between her and Ralph? Was she the reason that Ralph seemed so distant these days? Was it possible that all these weeks, while Jem had been crawling across the strange landscape of her own emotions, dealing with her adulterous feelings towards Joel, her growing affection towards his son, her sense that maybe there was another ending in store for her than the one she been expecting all these years, that Ralph himself had been crossing the same rocky territory? Was it possible, she thought, that Ralph had fallen in love with someone else, been, in fact, in love with someone else every minute of every day since his return from California? And if that were the case then why the hell had he asked her to marry him? But even as she asked herself the question, Jem already knew the answer: he'd asked her to marry him because he did not want to be in love with the beautiful young girl with the blonde hair and the silver dress. Just like Jem wanted to marry Ralph because she did not want to fall in love with the beautiful young man with the shorn hair and the green eyes. They were getting married to protect themselves from the possibility of a different ending. They were getting married to protect their children.

When Ralph got home from the gallery half an hour later, Jem did not mention either the awful paintings, or the painting of the girl with the buttery hair. Instead she sucked the discomfort back down deep inside her where it turned to mild nausea. She asked him about his interview ('I don't know why these people have to intellectualise everything. You know, at the end of the day, it's some flowers. That is all. It is nothing to do with my childhood or the political climate in America or the price of bloody fish in Beirut, you know. It's just paintings. I am just a painter. Jesus') and reheated some leftover Bolognese sauce for Scarlett's tea. Then she opened a bottle of rosé and poured herself a large glass and took it into the garden where she sat and watched her daughter playing in the afternoon sun.

Ralph didn't join her and by the time she came back indoors, the kitchen was tidy and Ralph was back in his studio.

Chapter 27

Ralph slipped into the Maygrove Centre on his way back from painting at Gil's a couple of nights later, to use the toilets. He peed, washed his hands, examined his face in the mirror and was about to turn and leave when another man walked in. Ralph turned briefly to acknowledge the presence of another person in such close proximity to him. He looked at the man, the man looked at him. There was recognition. A moment's hesitation and then Ralph said: 'It's you, isn't it?'

The man looked at him and squinted. Ralph could tell his struggle to place Ralph's face was pure charade.

'You're Jessica's dad, aren't you?' he continued.

'Er, yeah. That's right. I'm sorry, I er . . .'

'I'm Ralph.' He handed Joel a freshly washed hand to shake. 'I'm Scarlett's dad.'

'Oh, yes, of course, right. Good to finally meet you. I think I've seen you about.'

'Yeah,' said Ralph, 'you definitely have. I would almost say that you've been stalking me,' he continued. He kept his voice amused and his gaze direct. He was channelling Gil.

Joel pulled back, affronted. 'I don't think so,' he countered defensively.

'Yes, you were. Outside the church. A few weeks back. You were there when I went in and you were there when I came out.'

'I was waiting for someone,' said Joel.

Ralph paused. He knew that it was not necessary to challenge Joel's lie. They both knew the truth.

'So,' he continued, the recentness of his afternoon with Gil still fresh in his heart, his head filled with something strong and incontrovertible. 'You're quite good friends then, you and Jem?'

Joel shrugged. 'Not really,' he said.

Ralph nodded and let a silence form. 'You know,' he began, 'we're getting married next weekend.'

Joel gave him a 'good for you, but what's it got to do with me?' look.

Ralph let another silence form and stared at the man, trying to read his blank expression, trying to find the truth somewhere inside that bland arrangement of facial features. Have you, he thought to himself, have you been fucking my girlfriend?

Almost as if his silent thoughts had become audible, the man flinched slightly and adjusted his body language. Suddenly he looked chippy. 'You're very pleased with yourself, aren't you?' he said.

'I beg your pardon?' replied Ralph.

'You. You're very pleased with yourself. Smug is another word that comes to mind.'

'Sorry,' Ralph countered with a small laugh, 'I don't even know you. What qualifies you to make judgements about me?'

The man shrugged. 'I'm just telling you what I see. And what I've been told.'

'Told?'

'Yeah. I get the impression that you're one of those guys who just kind of barrels through life expecting other people to pick up the pieces.'

Ralph threw him a look of amused contempt.

'And I'll tell you another thing. You might be getting married next week, but I don't think she's ready. She's giving off signals. She's scenting the air.'

Ralph stopped and stared at the man. 'Scenting the air?'

'Yeah. You know.'

Ralph frowned at the man, who looked smaller now somehow, like expelling his brash words had somehow diminished him. His choice of words was both revolting and strangely poetic.

'Did you and Jem have an affair?'

The man laughed.

The answer that Ralph had been expecting to hear was wrapped up somewhere inside that laugh, but Ralph waited a beat, just to hear what the man would say. 'No,' he said dismissively. '*We* did *not* have an affair. But that's not to say that *she* hasn't *had* an affair. That's not to say that she's not capable.'

Ralph thought briefly about pounding him into the ground, then, pounding away at him, punch after punch after punch, possibly until he was dead. But then he thought, would Gil hit this pointless little man? And he knew that Gil would not. So he inhaled, deeply, and found his inner peace and then he looked the little man in the eye, smiled, just once, and left.

Ralph had another intense dream that night. He had been dreaming more vividly and more frequently since his encounter with Sarah, Gil and their prayer group. He dreamed that it was his wedding day and that they were getting married in Santa Monica. He dreamed that Smith was his best man and that Jem was very late. He stood inside a beach hut, his shoes were full of sand, people were looking at him anxiously and he was telling them all: it's OK, she's always late. Smith was eating soft-shelled crab at a tiny table in the corner and Ralph found himself thinking: why does he have to be eating soft-shelled crab right now? How incredibly selfish.

Eventually he left the claustrophobic beach hut and strolled across the hot white beach, looking for Jem. His children were not there. He stopped and asked a policeman if he'd seen a small dark woman in a white dress. The policeman said no. And then he saw her, striding towards him, dressed in black. She was cross and had Smith the cat in her arms. Look, she was saying, look. It's all wrong. It's all wrong. I have to go now. And then she passed him the cat and picked up the skirts of her big black dress and strode away from him, purposefully, elbows jutting out angrily. He stood on the hot white beach and watched her walk away from him, her figure becoming smaller and smaller until eventually she was just a tiny black dot on the horizon.

When he went back to the beach hut, Smith had transmogrified into Joel, and Ralph lifted the plate of soft-shelled crab and dropped it on to his head.

Chapter 28

When Ralph announced to Jem for the third Thursday running that he would be going for a run at six o'clock, an alarm bell finally began to ring inside her head. Three Thursdays in a row was not random. Three Thursdays in a row was habitual. Why Thursdays? Why six o'clock? And really, now she thought about it, how localised could a torrential tropical downpour actually be?

She saw him from the house, as brightly and cheerfully as she could manage. 'Have a good run,' she trilled robotically. She gave the children their tea, put them in the bath, put them in their pyjamas and put them in their beds. Then she raced, as she always did, to her computer. She checked her e-mail. A Facebook message from Lucas:

> You need to get some photos up here. I want to see regular updates on my little Blakey! And how is the beautiful Scarlett? And, come to that, how is the beautiful Jemima?

She smiled and typed her reply, keeping her words, as ever, neutral and unflirtatious:

> Working on the photos, apparently I have to download some fancy software, will get round to it eventually. But Blakey is still fat and magnificent and is showing no signs of wanting to crawl. I think he wants to be a Buddha, just sit on his bum, getting fatter and fatter, for the whole of eternity. Miss Scarlett is still the Diva

of the family and I am not beautiful but thank you for saying that I am! How is your dad? I haven't seen him for ages.'

She sent the message and within five minutes he had replied.

Check out the mirror! You are gorgeous! I'm at my mum's, up north, haven't seen my dad for a few days. Spoke to him yesterday, he said he'd seen your husband at the Maygrove Centre? Is he in one of the groups? (Not that I would judge if he was, obviously, given my dad's history.) But Dad's still in an ongoing battle with the bitchcowwoman about taking Jessica. Poor guy. Anyway, mum's calling me down for dinner, then I'm off out with some old school friends. It's good to be home! Take care. I'm back in a couple of weeks, maybe see you at the lido again?

Jem replied again.

I avoid mirrors as much as humanly possible ;)
It must have been someone else your dad saw at the Maygrove. Ralph has his issues but addiction is not one of them! (Unless they have a Runners Anonymous group there?!) Anyway, we're getting married on Saturday so I hope he's not been hiding some terrible secret from me! Enjoy your dinner and being at home. I hope my Blakey wants to come and have dinner with me when he's twenty-four! See you when I get back, fingers crossed for lido weather!'

She pressed Send and then she spent a few minutes perusing his Facebook page, seeing what his friends had been up to and what he'd been up to ('eating Mum's chicken and rice and feeling goooood' apparently). She waited a few minutes but Lucas did not reply. He'd gone down for his dinner, had left cyberspace.

A few minutes later she heard Ralph return. She switched her PC to sleep and tiptoed downstairs to greet him. Once again he was looking fresh and spry, nothing like the way he tended to look after his daytime runs. He was breathing quite heavily and had a glow about him, but not the wide band of sweat down the centre of his T-shirt and the sweaty sheen on his scalp. He looked, it occurred to her, like someone who had just run home from the post box on the corner.

'How was your run?' she asked.

He nodded. 'Good,' he said.

'Where did you run to?'

'Oh, nowhere, just around the park. How were the kids?' He kicked off his running shoes and put them back in the shoe cubby.

'Fine, good,' she said. 'You don't look very sweaty,' she continued.

He shrugged and wandered into the kitchen. 'It's quite cool out.'

'Yeah,' she said, following him, determined to uncover the truth about his strange absences and his chilly demeanour, 'but you've been running for nearly two hours. Even if it was cold out I'd have expected you to look a bit sweatier than that.'

'Well,' he said after a pause just long enough, Jem felt, to fabricate an excuse, 'I stopped for a while. On the way back. To cool down.'

'Where?'

'God, what is this, an interrogation?'

'No, Ralph, it is not an interrogation. It's just your partner wondering where you've been for two hours.'

'And I told you. I've been running.'

'Yes. You've been running. But you stopped. Where did you stop?'

'God, I don't know, just a bench.'

'You sat on a bench? To cool down?'

'Yeah.'

'And then you ran back?'

'Yeah! I told you. Jesus! What is your problem?'

'My problem, Ralph, is . . .' She paused. This was the point at which she could rein the conversation back in or let it run wild. She took a deep breath and said: 'Everything, Ralph. My problem is absolutely everything! You came back from California and it was all lovely and gorgeous and then slowly, day by day, it's all gone wrong. You don't want to have sex with me, you barely talk to me, you've been off painting out of the house and coming back with these – God, I'm really sorry, but I have to say it – these *weird* paintings that look like they were painted by somebody else. And then there's this strange Thursday run. I don't believe you. I don't believe you've been running. And then there's . . .' she paused again, aware that she was about to lob a conversational hand-grenade into the proceedings, 'the girl. The blonde one. I saw her in your studio. You and her. In California. And I saw your portrait. It was beautiful, Ralph, really, really beautiful. But it got me thinking, you know, what happened in America? We never talked about it. I just accepted that you were making more of an effort and we kind of got on with it and I never really wondered what it was that happened in America that made you transform yourself overnight. And was it . . . was it something to do with her. With the girl?'

Ralph had been standing half inside the fridge, about to pluck himself out a beer but stopped statue still as Jem delivered her rant. He blinked as silence fell and then slumped on to a chair. 'No, he said, 'it was nothing to do with the girl. Well, it was partly, I suppose. I mean, she kind of started it.'

'Started what?'

'This sort of change in me. This . . .'

'What?'

'I can't tell you,' he said.

'Can't tell me what?' Jem's heart quickened with trepidation.

'I can't tell you. You'd leave me.'

'What!' she cried. 'Just tell me!'

'It's not what you think,' he continued, 'and in a way, I think it might be worse.'

'Oh my God, Ralph, please will you just tell me!'

'It's . . .' he sighed and pulled his hands across his face. 'It's . . . I've found . . .'

'What!'

'The place I've been going every Thursday night. It's a prayer group. I've been going . . . to pray.'

'Pray?' Jem slumped heavily into a chair too.

'Yes. Group prayer.'

'In a church?'

'No, not in a church. In a hall.'

'You go to a hall and pray with strangers?'

'Yes. I do.'

'But . . . who do you pray to?'

He shrugged. 'I pray to God.'

She threw him a look of unabridged horror.

'No,' he said, 'not that God. Not the man with the beard. Not the man in the Bible. Not the one that people kill in the name of. But just my own, personal God.'

Jem let her head roll back on her shoulders, like the weight of his admission had unbalanced her physiognomy. 'And the girl?'

'Smith's girlfriend,' he said. 'Smith's *ex*-girlfriend. Rosey. She's a Christian. She took me to her church. I thought it was just a passing moment. I sat in this beautiful church and suddenly everything made sense. I realised how crap and useless I'd been at home, I vowed to be better. It gave me some kind of weird strength. After I came home I

374

thought that was it, that I'd just get on with my life. But then after the, you know, the baby, I don't know. I just found myself needing it more and more, that feeling I got from her church.'

'What, you mean after the miscarriage?'

He nodded. 'I wanted that baby so much, Jem. I wanted it so much it hurt. And I couldn't believe how cool you were about it. It was like . . . it was like you'd turned into somebody else. You know. I saw you, Jem, I saw you through the window, reading that magazine, as if you were about to go in to get a tooth pulled or something. And in that moment, Christ, I don't know, I almost felt like I hated you.' He paused. Let the word sink in. Jem didn't flinch. He continued, 'And then you just seemed to blossom afterwards. But it had the opposite effect on me. I kind of shrivelled up. And as for . . . sex, I don't know. It just seemed so wrong. To be there, in that place, where they'd cut out the baby . . .'

'They didn't *cut it out*, Ralph . . .'

'No, I know, but they took it away. And I was scared that it would happen again. That there'd be another baby and another miscarriage or another abortion and seeing you going out and about, so light-hearted, wanting to get drunk, wanting to try and recapture your youth. It made me feel kind of sick, to be honest.'

'Sick?' Jem gulped.

'Yeah. But not just that. More than that. That man.'

'What man?'

'The guy with the little girl, the guy you had a pizza with . . .'

'Joel?'

'Yeah, whatever his name is. I don't know. But I saw him on Monday night. I saw him and I asked him,' he paused for a moment, 'I asked him if there'd been anything between you.'

'You didn't!'

'Yeah, Jem, I did, because I needed to know, because it's been eating away at me, all these text messages and taxi rides, and I know you've given me all these perfectly good explanations but I wanted to know for myself.'

'Oh Christ, I can't believe you said that to him. What did he say?'

'He said exactly what I thought he'd say. He said no.'

'Well, of course he said no,' said Jem, 'I mean, I can't believe you could even have thought that about me.'

'Well, you thought it about me,' Ralph said softly. 'You thought it about me and the girl in the painting.'

The kitchen fell silent for a moment as they both absorbed the new balance of things.

'Why did you paint her, Ralph?' Jem asked in a softer voice.

Ralph shrugged. 'Because she was beautiful,' he said. 'Because she asked me to. Because I wanted to thank her, I suppose, for showing me the light.'

'You've made her look like a saint or something, like an angel. Is that how you see her?'

He shrugged again. 'I suppose I do,' he said.

'Do I need to be worried about her?'

Ralph gazed at her for a moment. 'Are you?' he said.

'What?'

'Are you worried about her?'

Jem blinked and paused to consider the question. 'Yes,' she said eventually. 'I am worried about her. Are you in love with her?'

'No,' he said simply. 'Are you in love with that man?'

'No,' she replied.

'Are you in love with me?'

The question blind-sided Jem. It was a question she'd been avoiding for months. She threw it back at him: 'Are you in love with me?'

'Yes,' was Ralph's immediate response. 'Not in the same way I once was, for sure. But enough to know that my journey stops here. That this is it for me. You, me, the children. What about you?'

She echoed his answer with a nod of her head. 'The same,' she said, 'I feel the same as you.' Jem drew in her breath. It was as close to the truth as she felt she could get for now.

'Why didn't you stop me?' she said a moment later. 'Why didn't you stop me from booking the abortion?'

Ralph shrugged again. 'What was the point?' he muttered. 'You'd made up your mind.'

'I had no idea you felt that bad about everything. I thought you were relieved when the baby didn't come. Why didn't you tell me how you felt?'

'It was too late. What good would it have done to have said anything? Just made you feel guilty. About something we could do nothing about.'

'So you turned to God, instead?' Jem could barely believe she was uttering the words. They sounded bizarre in her mouth, utterly ludicrous. This was Ralph they were talking about. Ralph McLeary. There was no room for the concept of God within her definition of Ralph McLeary.

Ralph nodded and stared at his feet.

'And is this serious, this God thing, I mean, really serious?'

He nodded. 'Yeah,' he said, 'I guess so. It feels real. It feels . . . well, at first it felt really weird, but now it feels just . . . *normal.*'

'And what do you do, at these prayer things?' Jem tried not to sneer as the words left her mouth.

Ralph pulled his gaze from his shoes and squinted his eyes at her. 'We pray,' he answered simply.

'But who to?'

'I don't really know,' he said. 'To myself. To the world. To whatever's out there, God, or whatever. It's fine,' his tone of voice softened, 'honestly. It's nothing to be scared of. It's not Christianity. It's not evangelistic. It's just . . . *prayer.*'

'Yes, I see that, but I still, I just don't understand. I mean . . .' She paused for a moment, trying to find the salient question, until, eventually, she said, '*Why*?'

Ralph sighed and lowered his gaze again. 'I don't know,' he said finally. 'I have no idea. It's just something that's happened to me. And it's something that feels right.'

'And I just need to accept that?'

Ralph sighed again and raised his gaze to meet Jem's. 'Yes,' he said, 'I suppose you do.'

Jem nodded, a small childlike gesture. 'And us,' she asked, in a soft voice. 'What about us?'

'What about us?'

She let her gaze fall. 'Well, are we still cool? I mean, you've said some pretty extreme things tonight. You've brought up some, some . . . issues. And, Christ, we're getting married on Saturday. I mean . . .'

'It's up to you, Jem.'

'No, but it's not. It's up to both of us. This is both of our lives we're talking about. Our future. Our destiny.'

'I know I love you. I know I love myself. That's enough for me. And everything we've said tonight, I feel like I know you better again. I feel better about everything. The final call is yours.' He threw her a pragmatic look and Jem blanched.

She gulped and nodded. 'OK,' she said, 'yeah. I get it. I am a sinner.' She followed this with a wry laugh.

Ralph immediately leaned in towards her, his face full of concern. 'No!' he said, 'No! That's not what I'm saying! I'm just saying, I can deal with the changes in you, but – can you deal with the changes in me? I love you, Jem. I've always loved you. I want to marry you. I want to be with you. For ever. No matter what. OK?'

Jem let him hold her hands in his, but as she looked at his hands she felt something raw and animal deep inside her come bursting to the surface of her consciousness. She wanted to marry Ralph, she wanted to make him happy, she wanted to make her children happy, she wanted to make a secure life and future for herself and her family but she also wanted to run away, open the front door and run through the cool night air, faster and faster, further and further, until her lungs were fit to scream.

But she couldn't run. This was her home. This was her life.

She smiled tightly and she squeezed Ralph's hands. 'OK,' she said, 'OK. It's going to be OK.' But somewhere deep inside she wasn't sure that that was true.

Chapter 29

Ralph and Jem's wedding day dawned pale and watery. There was a suggestion of rain in the air, but also a hint of potential splendour. The weather forecasters were not sure either. It would be a day of mixed fortunes.

Ralph had spent the night in Croydon with his father and would be arriving at the registry office with him at two o'clock. Ralph hadn't wanted to go. 'It's silly,' he'd said, 'we're technically old enough to be going to our own children's weddings, why be coy?' But Jem had never been married before and wanted to treat at least part of the day traditionally. Lulu and her other sister, Isobel, had stayed the night and last night they'd drunk three bottles of champagne and half a bottle of tequila between them. Lulu was now busily frying up a pan of bacon and Jem was popping thick slices of bread into the toaster and all of them were feeling like the last thing they wanted to be doing today was going to a wedding.

Jem sometimes wished it could always be like this, her, her sisters, her children, her sisters' children, no men, just them, cooking, chatting, drinking, sharing the running of the house. It was a strange thing to be thinking on the morning of her wedding, but then everything felt strange about the morning of her wedding. Since their conversation on Thursday night, Jem had been drifting around in a kind of miasmic trance. Life suddenly seemed tinged a different hue, a kind of putrid green. She couldn't quite get a grip on the substance of her life any more. It all felt ephemeral and slightly slippery.

The morning of her wedding passed in a haze. Her parents arrived from Devon at around twelve o'clock and with such a critical mass of people in her small house she shooed them all out into the garden and went into the kitchen to make a pitcher of Pimm's. Her hangover was fading now and she found herself caught between two states: acceptance and discomfort. And as she pushed ice cubes into a large plastic jug, and stared idly through the kitchen window at her family beyond, her gaze was drawn back once again to the orchid on her windowsill; the orchid that had died two years ago and then come miraculously back to life.

Each of the four white flowers that had formed earlier that summer was gone, scattered along the windowsill like cast-off stockings.

The stalk was bare.

Stung by the obvious symbolism, Jem took the Pimm's out into the garden and then, while nobody was looking, she scuttled upstairs to her bedroom.

She tore off her clothes and she peeled apart the clothes hanging in her wardrobe to find a dress she'd hidden in there two months ago, when Ralph had first proposed, snapped up after a frantic last-minute eBay auction. It was a Vivienne Westwood dress, a riotous twisty curvy hourglass affair, printed with snapdragons and peacocks, low across the bust, draped to the calf. She'd tried it on only once, just after she'd unwrapped it. It had fitted her like a dream. She wanted to put it on now. Once it was on, then she was halfway to getting married. Once it was on she could stop thinking all these shady half-thoughts and just get on with it. She would go downstairs in her beautiful dress and everyone would tell her how stunning she looked and she'd have a glass of Pimm's and suddenly everything would seem all right again. But it all started here with the dress.

She climbed into her brand-new underwear – black,

trimmed with lilac, lace-tufted and divine – and then she pulled on the dress and turned to face her reflection in the mirror.

Loose.

The dress was loose.

It hung from her frame like a pair of billowing curtains. Her breasts, which had still been full of milk when she'd first tried it on, sat flat and exposed inside her bra beneath the gaping fabric. Her waist, which had previously been pulled in like a tailor's dummy by the internal boning of the dress had now disappeared. The dress looked wrong on her. The dress looked unhappy. In her mind's eye Jem imagined Vivienne herself, watching her from the corner of her room, shaking her head sadly. No! she imagined the Satsuma-haired one snapping. No! That is not what it is supposed to look like!

The dress hated her. And Ralph was right. She was too thin. She sat down on the bed and dropped her face into her hands. She did not feel like a beautiful bride. She felt like a fraud. An emaciated silly little girl. What would her beautiful daughter say to her when she walked into the garden looking like a mad old lady wearing someone else's designer dress? She would be letting her down. How had she allowed herself to lose so much weight? She hadn't even noticed it happening. It was, she supposed, her way of taking back control after the sadness and confusion of losing the baby. She'd reclaimed her body as her own. And ha! irony of ironies, had ended up with a body that looked nothing at all like hers.

She wiped some tears from beneath her eyes and then she rummaged through her wardrobe for something else. It was only a registry office, something else would do. She had lots of lovely clothes. She would find something else.

And so she walked out into the garden a few moments later in a perfectly nice scarlet slip dress, one she'd worn to a friend's wedding a few years earlier, before she'd had any children. It hung straight and square, neither hugging nor caressing any part of her but showing her elegant porcelain collarbones and her delicate bird-like arms. It matched perfectly the red silk shoes she'd bought to go with her Vivienne Westwood dress and everybody said she looked beautiful, that she'd always suited red, that it was a lovely choice. And none of them, not even her sisters, knew anything about the existence of the beautiful snapdragon and peacock dress now tucked back into the bowels of her wardrobe.

Jem could not shake the sense of sadness and wrongness that possessed her as she and her family headed in a people carrier for the registry office at Camberwell. She looked at her sisters: beautiful, excited, happy for her. She looked at her parents, so serene and so together as they always had been, as they had been since a day like this forty-two years ago in a registry office in Paignton, and then she looked at her children: Scarlett resplendent in her layers of tulle and froth, a small tiara tucked into her curls, and Blake oblivious to the occasion, strapped into his baby seat, dressed like a very small man. Here it was, her wedding day. A day she'd never really imagined before. She was off to get married. To Ralph. Her love. Her destiny.

The taxi dropped them all at the side of the road and her father was dispatched into the building to ensure that Ralph was already there.

'He's there,' said her dad, smilingly, a moment later. 'He's with his dad. He looks very nervous.'

Jem felt something at the pit of her stomach lurch at his words. This was it, she thought, here comes the bride. At two o'clock Jem, Lulu, Isobel and Scarlett entered the building and were shown to their room, the smallest in the building, seating fifteen. Ralph sat in front of the registrar's desk next to his father. In seats to the right were Philippe and Smith's mum and dad.

On the other side of the room sat Jem's parents, Blake on her mother's lap. Jem felt her legs soften beneath her. Her brain needed sugar, desperately. She felt as light and insubstantial as a cloud. Everyone turned to smile at her and Jem tried to smile back but her face was rigid with fear. And then Ralph turned to look at her and he smiled and he looked like he'd looked at the art gallery that night all those years ago: smart in a suit, pale with nerves and handsome as hell.

Beautiful man.

Father of her children

But.

She looked from Ralph to her sister to her mother to her baby. She looked at Ralph's father, her daughter, the registrar.

A silent scream began to build beneath Jem's ribcage.

She wanted to escape.

She couldn't breathe.

She did not want to be here.

She did not want to do this.

Her heart raced and she tried to bring herself back under control.

Of course she could do it, she thought, of course she could do it. She was just nervous, that was all, nervous and hungover.

She moved herself forwards towards Ralph's side and smiled tightly at him. He smiled back at her and clasped her hand. 'You look beautiful,' he whispered. 'That dress looks stunning on you.'

'Thank you,' she whispered back and squeezed his hand for reassurance.

But still it was there, a panicky feeling in the pit of her belly, a feeling growing stronger by the second that she shouldn't be doing this. She thought of the dead-again orchid on her windowsill, the baggy dress in her wardrobe, she thought of the ugly paintings in Ralph's studio and the baby she'd chosen not to have. And then she thought of Ralph in a dank room at the Maygrove, calling out crazed prayers to Lord God Our Saviour.

She thought of the few days she'd spent at the lido with Lucas, that sense that had opened up in her head that there might be another ending for her, not just the one she'd written for herself when she'd kissed Ralph for the first time eleven years ago on a blue sofa in Battersea, but something new, something not already written in the pages of her book of destiny. Another happy ending.

And it was while these thoughts were stampeding through her desiccated mind like barefoot feral children that something altogether unexpected happened: Ralph put his hand to Jem's cheek, then leaned down to kiss her gently on the lips. He smiled at her sadly and he said: 'It's OK. We don't have to do this.'

She looked at him, sharply.

'Let's not,' he whispered, his nose pressed gently against hers. 'Let's not.'

She continued to stare at him, mutely.

'Go,' he said. 'I love you. I can wait. Just go.'

'But I don't want to go,' she whispered.

'Yes,' he said simply, 'you do.' And then he kissed her again.

PART FOUR

13 July 2008

Dear Rosey,

I'm really sorry I never replied to your last e-mail. I've been finishing off for an exhibition and getting ready to get married and also been going to a lot of prayer meetings. I did get in touch with Sarah and I liked her very much. The group is great and the meetings have been amazing. They've really really helped me. I've been going through quite a tough time.

I don't know quite how to say this so I'll just come out and say it: Jem jilted me on our wedding day. Seriously. Well, it's not so much that she jilted me, rather that I let her go. She got to the altar and I looked at her and I just knew. It was all wrong for her. We'd had a big conversation two nights before and I'd told her all about the group and about finding God and she just totally didn't get it. I didn't expect her to. And she didn't. We talked about other stuff too, about the ways we've both changed and how our love for each other has changed. At the end of it, it felt like we'd reached a good place, that we both knew where the other was coming from. Things were fine for the next day or so and then she walked into the registry office on Saturday afternoon and I looked at her and I just knew. I KNEW. She looked trapped, she looked terrified. The funny thing is, it didn't surprise me. It was almost as though I'd been expecting it all along: like a *déjà vu* in reverse, I saw it happening before it did. So I just said to her: we don't have to do this. And she just kind of looked at me, her eyes were full of tears, looked at me and nodded, very gently, and she kissed me and then she went. She just walked out of there, in front of everyone. There was this kind of gasp. It was an utterly shocking moment. Like a soap opera come to life. And as she left I just felt myself saying: Goodbye, Jem. Like I was letting her go. Like I had no choice. Everyone thought I was being so calm about it. Everyone was saying, wow, you're taking this so well. And people were saying that they'd go and talk to her, get her to come back, that it was just nerves, that she'd come round and I was just saying: no, no, don't talk to her, just leave her, she won't come round. And she didn't. So that was a week ago and obviously I've seen her since, I mean, we're still living together. I'm hoping that we can pull back together, that it won't go as far as either one of us moving out. I'm hoping that Jem will find whatever it is she's looking for and realise that it's me.

I can hardly believe it. I honestly thought Jem and me would be together for ever. Everybody thought we would be together for ever. We were one of those couples. But something happened to us, I don't know when, maybe when we started our family, maybe after Blake was born, maybe when I went off to America in April, maybe when I found spirituality, maybe when we lost the baby, the last one, particularly the last one. I don't know when it happened, but it happened. And I have never felt so sad in my life, Rosey. It's the worst thing that ever happened to me. But I think she'll come back. I really do. This isn't just about me and the group, me and God. There's more to this than that. I think there's something she needs to do before she can come back to me and she just needs to find out what it is.

Anyway, I didn't mean this to be quite such a rambling and misery-laden missive. I just really wanted to say that I'm sorry not to have been in touch before and to say a big thank you for introducing me to Sarah. It's been brilliant having them in my life these last few weeks and especially since the wedding fiasco.

Love,

Ralph

Chapter 1

Jem flopped down on to the small beige sofa in Lulu's spare room and sighed deeply. She felt shell-shocked. The children were downstairs with Lulu, and Jem, surrounded by suitcases and holdalls and carrier bags full of toys, was only now feeling the full truth of her situation. She had moved out. She no longer lived with Ralph. Her children no longer lived with their father. This was now their home.

This wasn't, in any way, what Jem had expected.

She had expected to marry Ralph.

Regardless of what he had told her about finding God, regardless of anything that had been said between them that unexpected night two months ago, and in spite of the sick feeling in her gut as she stumbled towards her nuptials, Jem had thought that she would go into that room in the registry office and marry Ralph. How could it possibly be any other way?

But then he'd said those words, *just go,* and she'd known he was right. Because it wasn't just the fact that Ralph had found God that was wrong on that damp July afternoon. Everything had been wrong that afternoon. The dress, the weather, the mood, the nagging, aching suspicion in Jem's heart that she might have another fate. She should not have been thinking of another man on her wedding day.

So she'd gone. Walked out of the registry office and out into the street, her chest rising and falling, hyperventilating, nauseous.

And then they'd gone home and waited. Neither of

them was sure what they were waiting for. Waiting for normality? Waiting for an answer? Waiting for Ralph to change his mind about God? But they waited and they waited and nothing changed. They just felt awkward and uncomfortable. Jem drank more, ate less, Ralph spent more and more time at group meetings and painting with Gil. They grew further and further apart. The moment in the registry office had changed everything and it was impossible at such close quarters to work out how to come back from the shock of it.

So Jem decided to do something about it. She decided to move out.

Maybe, she thought, if we live apart, we can grow together.

It was the hardest decision she had ever made in her life, but she was doing it for them, for her and Ralph, to give them a chance to find a way back to each other.

Now she was here, in her sister's house, the place she used to come to for tea and sympathy, but this time she wasn't going home.

This was her dream come true, living with her sister, a sprawling, unconventional communal family. Here it was. She was in it. But she didn't feel like she'd made her way here in a gentle and measured manner, she felt like she'd been hauled up by the big fat hand of fate and dropped here, unceremoniously, from a great, great height. And she had never felt so miserable in her life.

She remembered Ralph's face as he'd said goodbye to them at the front door an hour earlier, the fake smiles and jollity, and as they tried to keep everything light for the children, pretend they were off on a great adventure. But there'd been one tiny, excruciating moment when their eyes had met across the tops of their children's heads and Ralph had looked so lost, as bewildered as a small boy. At the sight of him, so beautiful, so scared, something buried deep down inside Jem suddenly bubbled up to the surface and she had physically to stop herself from jumping into his arms and saying, 'It's OK, it's OK, I love you, I love you.' But it wasn't the right moment for I Love Yous. Just like it hadn't been the right moment to get married. Jem had tried to smile at him reassuringly, but the smile had faltered and he'd turned away from her, tears shimmering in his blue eyes.

And then they'd gone.

And Jem had not looked back.

23 August 2008

Dear Rosey,

Well, it happened, Jem moved out. I never thought it would come to this. I think I'd kind of assumed that we would get to grips with all this eventually and make it work. But if anything, Jem seems even more distant from me than before.

She's going to stay with her sister and I am going to stay here. And the children will move between us, half and half. It should work out fine. Jem will need more time to herself now anyway, as one of her clients is about to finish his soap contract and she'll be focusing on his career, and then in November she's off to Sydney for one of her other clients who's going to be in a reality thing in the jungle. (Top secret, though – not that you know anyone who would give a shit!) And I guess I can take a break from working crazy hours now that the show's in the bag and I've got some money in my account. I'm not ready to start a new series anyway. Everything's changing so much, not just my life, but the way I feel about everything, the way I respond to the world around me. I've been spending more and more time with Gil. He's this old guy from New Meaning, salty old Scots boy who paints scratchy old seascapes and growls a lot and asks blunt questions. He's very open and real. He

394

reminds me of you in a way (as weird as that might sound) but just in that you don't have to wonder what he's thinking. You can just be with him, just relax. And I feel like I'm starting over with my artwork, kind of regressing back to square one, a little like a Shakespearean actor pretending to be a tree in the wind, you know. It's really liberating and I'm keen to see where it goes. I guess it could just end up with me doing graphic design for travel brochures again, but I just know that I can't go back to where I was. It's time for a new approach.

Anyway, I'm holding up well. The night after Jem left was probably the worst night of my life, wandering all those empty rooms, remembering. To be alone, to know that my family was torn in half. I spent the whole night praying and I got through it to the other end. By morning I was feeling better about things. Feeling positive. Because I have to. Because I have to assume that this has happened because it is the right thing to have happened. I have to assume that, in the end, I will know why this happened and that I will accept it.

Right now I'm just taking one day at a time.

Thanks for your support and write soon.

Love, Ralph x

21 September 2008

Dearest Rosey,

First of all, I'm so sorry I've gone off radar. I moved into my new flat last week and it's taken me an age to get reattached, as it were. Sorting everything out's been a nightmare. We decided to rent out the house. I couldn't stand being there any more, without Jem, without the kids half the week. So we've rented it out and I've got a new place. Two bedrooms, plenty of space for the kids, all their toys and stuff. No garden but they've got a massive one at Jem's sister's place. I feel better for getting out of the house. The flat's pretty cool. It's a conversion in a big house just round the corner from Scarlett's new nursery. She started a couple of weeks ago, such a big girl now! So now it's just me and Blake all day long on the days I have him. He's nine months old now, coming up for ten. Crawling, at last, which is a blessing and a nightmare. It means he doesn't need so much entertainment to be laid on, but it also means I can't just put him down in one place and get on with stuff – he's off in a flash! But he's a lot of fun and it's good for me to have to take so much responsibility for him. I let Jem do everything when Scarlett was little, I regret that now, I really do.

Relations between me and Jem are fine. We see each other twice a week. She looks good. I think she's blossoming – it hurts me a lot to say that. She's got a kind of glow. She didn't have that when were together, not for the last few years, anyway. She certainly had it when I first knew her. I'm glad she's happy, but I can't say that I am. I feel lonely. I really do. x

Chapter 2

It was a dark November afternoon. The streetlights had come on and the pavements glowed dull gold beneath her feet. The children were with Ralph and she was on her way back to Lulu's to get ready for a night out with Lulu and her girlfriends. No nursery run tomorrow, no hungry baby needing porridge. She could drink, stay up late and then lie in bed tomorrow until lunchtime. She hadn't been out at night since she'd moved out of the house on Herne Hill, been feeling too bruised, but she was ready now, ready to make the most of her small freedoms.

She took a different route back from the gym, via a side street off Herne Hill Road. Lulu had told her about a new boutique that had just opened up there. She'd said it was 'very you'. And it was while she cutting through the unfamiliar backstreets that she saw a road name that struck her as familiar. Underwood Street.

She couldn't quite place the familiarity at first. Underwood Street, she thought, why have I heard of Underwood Street? And then she remembered. That was where Joel had seen Ralph going into a chapel.

She saw the small building up ahead, its windows lit up from within. This was the place, she thought, approaching it slowly, this was the place where Ralph had come after they'd lost the baby. He'd come in here and he'd prayed. And suddenly Jem wanted to know, she wanted to understand. The door was ajar and she pushed it open gently. She felt slightly nervous. Not about the prospect of a face-to-face hook-up with God, but because she had no idea what sort of people hung out in quiet chapels on Thursday afternoons. Strangely, she didn't feel quite safe. She scanned her memory for newspaper headlines about women being raped in chapels but couldn't think of such a case. But still she felt unreassured.

She headed through the entrance and walked between the tiny pews. The chapel was empty. She was alone. She sat down on a pew towards the back, closer to the exit, just in case. She rested her hands in her lap and she looked around her. Screens, candles, tombstones, plaques, hymnbooks, kneeling cushions. She shut her eyes and waited for a feeling, a sense of something tangible that she would be able to take away from here, something real and substantial enough for her to begin to understand, even just a tiny bit.

She pulled her eyelids tighter together and she let all her hopes and dreams, fears and fantasies fill her head. She thought about that awful moment in the registry office months earlier, a moment that haunted her every moment of every day, she thought about Ralph's face on the front doorstep when she'd moved out of their home and she thought about the other family now living in that house, a family like hers used to be, a man, a woman, two small children, occupying the space that had once been hers. She thought about Ralph, living alone in his slightly depressing new flat and she thought about herself and her small migrant family staking out the spare corners of her sister's house and she wondered what it was all about. What had stopped her that day in the registry office? Why had it felt so wrong? She found it painful living with Walter and Lulu, with the moment-by-moment reminders that not everyone cocked it up, that not everyone felt too small and too flighty to commit to the concept of a life spent for ever with the same person. Because that's what it felt like now, from her new clearer perspective on the other side of her emotional meltdown. She'd been too small for it all. And now she'd been given space to grow and that was what she was doing, day by day, growing back into herself, and as the days went by she felt more and more that one day soon she might be big enough to walk back into Ralph's arms and stay with him for ever. And as these thoughts went through her mind, the clearest, brightest thoughts she'd had in weeks, she felt it: tiny, but there, a small sense of peace. An iota of release. It wasn't religious, it was therapeutic. But it was nothing to be scared of.

She sat for another ten minutes and did her best to pray.

And then she got up, looked around one more time and headed away from the chapel, away from God and towards the new boutique round the corner.

8 November 2008
Hi Rosey,
Wow, not sure where those last few weeks went. There was half-term and I took the children up to Scotland for the week, stayed with Gil and his sister, who's an ex-nun – yeah, a real ex-nun! The kids loved Gil but weren't that struck on the ex-nun. Scarlett said she had a weird face, which she did, I guess, but think it was more to do with the fact that she had very old-fashioned ideas about children. They always do, people who haven't had any. Anyway, it was a fun week, lots of long walks on the beach and painting al fresco and was a bit gutting having to come back to London and the flat and real life.

And can you get ITV in the States? Jem's client is going into the jungle tonight, big fanfare, big deal. I can't tell you his name, but given that he's only 'famous' (and I use the term loosely) in this country and you'll never have heard of him, I guess I can tell you that his initials, just for identification purposes, are KK. She's in Sydney already, so I've got the kids, certainly for a few days, possibly for two weeks, depending on how long KK spends in the jungle before being kicked out, which is brilliant. I'm finding the time I spend with them more and more absorbing and fulfilling. Blake in particular right now is totally compelling. He'll be one next month. And so much personality. He feels like he's my little buddy, my pal. When he's not there, I feel cut adrift. I hate not living with my kids. I really, really hate it.

And I still keep expecting Jem to walk back in through the door any minute and tell me it was all a terrible mistake. To tell me that she still loves me. To tell me that she wants to start again. On a day-to-day basis, life is manageable. Taken as a whole, though, it's a living fucking nightmare.

Lots of love, R x

22 November 2008
Rosey, shit. Look at this:
www.bbc.co.uk/news/imacelebcontroversy/5480.htm
God, poor Jem. She's coming home with him tomorrow. I'll report back more then.

R x

London DJ Arrested on Reality Show
23 November 2008
London Radio DJ, Karl Kasparov, 47, was today being held in police custody in Sydney after being filmed sexually assaulting fellow jungle contestant, former *Jubilee Road* actress, Melanie David, 27. He was seen on live TV kissing the actress on the cheek and fondling her breasts despite her protestations. He is heard whispering into her ear, 'That'll give the tabloids at home something to talk about.' It is thought that following a conversation earlier on in the day during which the

contestants had talked about the boost to former contestants' careers after forming romantic attachments in the jungle-based show, he was misguidedly hoping to increase the actress's profile. No charges have been brought yet against the Irish-born DJ. His agent was today unavailable for comment.

Chapter 3

Jem dropped her suitcase on to the sofa in the hotel room and began unpacking. She was home. At last. The longest week of her life was almost over. The actress had not brought charges in the end. Karl had been let go with a caution. Jem and Karl had spent three days in a hotel room sorting out the PR disaster and now she was staying in a hotel in Hyde Park for two more nights, just to try to get the whole thing well and truly put to bed before going home and seeing her children. It wasn't fair to bring this circus into Lulu's house. It wasn't fair on anyone.

Karl had gone back to his flat, despite being offered a room in the same hotel. He was adamant that he wanted to go home. The press were camped out on Almanac Road and it sent shivers down Jem's spine every time she switched on the news or opened a paper and saw it, her old home, 31 Almanac Road. The place where it had all started. The house in her dreams. Only now it was in her nightmares. They'd managed to snap Karl only once, leaving the house in a smart black suit that hung a little loose on him. He hadn't left the house again since, and the same photo kept appearing, again and again.

Number 31 Almanac Road.

Infamous.

She placed the photos of her children on the bedside table and then she pulled open the curtains and stared at the view across the park. The air was cold and fresh against her skin through the open window. It was good to be back in London. Sydney had been crazy. Hot, high octane and intense. And that had been before Karl had squeezed that girl's tits in front of twenty cameras and five million viewers.

She shook the thought out of her head. It had spent way too long in her head these past few days.

She replayed it, over and over and over again, Karl's big, shiny face, his lips heading for the young girl's cheeks, sliding against her skin, the girl's look of amused surprise, her hands coming towards his chest, to push him away, but then, almost as though it were in slow motion, his big hands landing on her bikini top, his huge fingers sliding under the tiny triangle of fabric, the girl saying, get off, Karl, get the fuck OFF, but no, he continued, a quick squeeze, his eyes closing for just a split second, the words drawled in her ear as she propelled herself away from him: *That'll give the tabloids at home something to talk about.* Her hand across his cheek. You fucking arsehole, Karl, you fucking arsehole. Karl left sitting there, on a rock, slightly bemused, but worse still, more than a bit amused.

Jem had watched the whole thing in her hotel bedroom on the live feed they provided friends and family with. Within less than two hours Karl was out of the jungle and in a police station. The news had broken worldwide before it had even been broadcast. Jem had not slept for nearly forty-eight hours, because of the time difference. Her boss, Jarvis, had arrived on the first flight over, aware that Jem, for all her years of experience as a theatrical agent, was going to be totally out of her depth handling the fallout from this.

Karl was contrite. He'd given up drink for a month before going into the jungle to help him lose weight. They'd given them champagne that night for winning a task. He'd had three glasses and he'd lost his perspective entirely. He'd genuinely thought that the actress would appreciate the controversy. He hadn't even fancied her, or so he said, though she had won the Most Fanciable Female at the British Soap Awards the previous year so Jem presumed he was being slightly dishonest, not only with her, but also with himself.

He was prepared to face any charges brought against him. He admitted that what he'd done had been indefensible. There had been a desperate twenty-four-hour wait while the producers and the police spoke to Melanie, until eventually she'd decided, after seeing the clip of the assault, not to press charges. She delivered a statement to the press stating how disappointed she had been by Karl's totally inappropriate behaviour, but how she believed everyone deserve a second chance and that she truly believed that Karl had learned his lesson. And then the show resumed.

A moment. That's all it could take sometimes. Just one, brief, shimmering moment and everything could change, just like that. So it had been four months ago when Ralph had told her about finding God. And so it was for Karl Kasparov. It had happened to him once before when he'd lost his mind live on the airwaves after his girlfriend dumped him and the country had been enchanted by his honesty and his emotional realness. Now the country despised him. He was an animal. A pig. A beast. He was fit for nothing. His career, as tiny and as inconsequential as it had been, was effectively over. It would take years to repair the damage. Jem's first client. As good as dead.

And now another moment was about to leap out of nowhere and change things for ever. A beep on her phone. Another text message. Her phone had never made as much noise as it had made over the past few days. Call after call. Text after text. Beep. Beep. Ring. Ring. Hello, Jemima Catterick speaking. Hello, Jemima Catterick speaking . . .

She picked up her phone with a sigh. It was a number she didn't know. She opened it and read it.

'Hi there. It's me, Lucas. I nicked your number off my dad's phone. I just wanted to say that it sounds like you're having a really shitty time and that I'm thinking of you. Take care x.'

Jem blinked and read the message again.

Lucas. She hadn't thought about Lucas for a long time. Well, that wasn't strictly true. She had thought about Lucas. She'd thought about the last time she'd seen him, at the festival in Brockwell Park, back in the summer, the week before her ill-fated wedding day. She'd thought about his confident easy manner, his air of belonging wherever he found himself, that thing he'd said to her, about how anything she did would be interesting. She'd thought about it plenty of times. But not so much now. Life had moved on and other things had happened. Her whole life had been wrapped around a lamp post, written off and repaired. It wasn't the same. It was strange and other. It had different contours and different rhythms. She was single. Thinking about twenty-four-year-old men now that she was free to do as she wished with twenty-four-year-old men didn't feel the same. It felt too close for comfort.

But, here it was. Contact. He had made contact. And not just that but made very mature, very sweet contact at a point in her life when what she really overwhelmingly needed to do was to hug somebody.

She opened up the mini-bar and she extracted a bottle of white wine. She cracked it open and poured some into a stubby wine glass and she downed it. She sat on the edge of the firmly made bed and she stared again for a while through the heavy glass of the window overlooking Hyde Park. Her babies were out there somewhere, she thought, her beautiful babies, over there in the hidden streets of south London. They didn't know she was here. She wondered what they were doing. She had missed them with every shred of her being, slept foetally, aching for them, imagining them in her arms, their scalps in her nose. And now she was home and still a million miles away from them.

A small tear leaked from her left eye and she rubbed it away. She drank some more wine and then she looked at her phone again. She started to type.

'Nice to hear a friendly voice. What a total nightmare! Thanks so much for your lovely message. I hope you're well.' She pressed Send and breathed a sigh of relief. It was neutral. Totally neutral. And it was barely lunchtime. It was hardly a booty call.

A moment later the wine hit her jet lag head-on and the bed called her name and she slept in her clothes for half an hour before her phone rang again and she sprung upright like something automated and answered it and said: Hello, Jemima Catterick speaking.

It was Lucas.

'I just got your message,' he said, 'you're back.'

'Yes,' said Jem, smoothing her hair away from her face, 'yes. I'm back.'

Jem and Lucas slept together that night. They also slept together the following night. When she woke up on the third morning and opened her eyes and looked at him, still half suspended inside her dreams and bleary-eyed, she thought for one bittersweet, twisted moment that he was Ralph. And for one bittersweet, twisted moment, her heart had leaped with joy and relief. On the third night she asked him to leave. She never saw him again.

Chapter 4

A funny thing happened to Jem towards the end of February. Scarlett was at nursery and Blake was asleep in his pram and she was on her way to have lunch with an old college friend in Battersea. She had not been to Battersea since the night all those months ago when she had tried so hard to reignite the pilot light of her bond with Ralph, the night she'd awoken to the fact that they were walking different paths. She felt sad wandering the streets that had once been their home at a time in her life when the possibility of this – separation from Ralph, prayer groups, split parenting – would have seemed preposterous. And it still did.

Jem had finally begun to reconcile herself to the presence of spirituality in Ralph's life. She'd let him take the children up to the Moors with the man called Gil, whom he appeared to revere so much. Scarlett had come home full of talk of a scary lady with a pointy nose who'd told her off for walking on grass and banging her feet against table legs and saying the word 'God' when she was frustrated. But she'd also come home glowing with a kind of a freshness and wholesomeness, like a child from another era. Sometimes Jem took a deliberate detour to the chapel on Underwood Street, usually with the children in tow, to light candles for Ralph's mum and the dead cat on Brixton Hill. She didn't pray but she did think about things in a calm and meditative way, and really, she wondered, what was the difference anyway?

It just no longer seemed to make any sense, this trial

separation. Now that the dust had settled Jem could look back on the last year of her life and see it as a series of separate and poignant moments rather than the blur of confusion, resentment and unhappiness that was how it had felt at the time. From this distance it was clear that she and Ralph had lost their way; after Blake was born, after they'd lost the baby, after Joel had made Jem doubt the very essence of her own true self, after Ralph had found some kind of peace and strength in a room full of prayer, and, she now realised, after the first time she'd slept with Lucas that crazy night at the Hyde Park Hotel all those months earlier. So many moments, so many opportunities to make sense of it all and to find their way back on to the path they'd been sharing. But they'd missed each and every one of them.

She turned a corner towards Northcote Road and saw a familiar face. A woman, tanned to an improbable shade of toast, vanilla hair, long shapely legs, Prada sunglasses, a leather shopper hanging from the crook of her arm. She wore tight black jeans and a fitted sweater in pale apple green. The woman stopped when she saw Jem and squinted at her from beneath her oversized sunglasses. Jem squinted back at her. They both slowed their pace as they neared each other and then Jem remembered: *Cheri*.

The woman's face softened with recognition then too and she pulled her sunglasses from her face and smiled.

'Jem!' she cried.

'Cheri!' replied Jem.

'Wow,' said Cheri, 'wow. I mean, I haven't seen you for, what, ten years, more?'

'More,' said Jem. 'Eleven, probably.'

'Gosh, wow. You look great!'

Jem smiled. She considered the woman in front of her, still beautiful in her late thirties, still glamorous, but softer somehow, prettier. 'So do you,' she said. 'You look amazing.'

'And who is this?' She peered down into the pushchair at the slumbering Blake.

'This is Blake,' said Jem, 'my youngest.'

'Oh, he's divine,' Cheri said, smiling softly. 'You've got more?'

'Yes, a little girl, Scarlett. She's at nursery.'

'Wow – two kids! That's brilliant. And is this . . . with . . . ?'

'Ralph?' Jem nodded. 'Yes. I made these children with Ralph.' She smiled wryly, preparing herself for the next question.

'And how is he? How is Ralph?'

'Oh, he's fine. He's good. We're, er . . . well, we're having a trial separation.'

Cheri's face fell. 'Oh, no!' she cried. 'No. That's terrible.'

Jem threw her a look of surprise. She seemed genuinely distressed by this revelation.

'God, it's just, I know this sounds so silly, but that night, remember, that night at the gallery, when Ralph asked me to help get you two together, that was the most forma-tive night of my life. I'd never really understood what love was before that night. I was lost, you know, going from one unsuitable man to the next, looking for some crap or other, I don't know, money, security, status, what-ever. But after that night, seeing you two together, two people who were so obviously destined to be together. It changed me. It made me want what you had. Something real and meaningful and beautiful and . . .'

Jem was alarmed to see that a small tear was leaking from the side of Cheri's perfectly made-up eye.

'. . . well, I found someone. I did. Someone I'd known for years, but I'd discounted him for being too poor and too nice. And we made it work, we had a beautiful thing together. He was the love of my life. Really. My every-thing. And then, shit, sorry . . .' She wiped more tears from beneath her eyes. 'It's been five years and I still can't talk about it, but he died. My David. He died in front of my very eyes. Some heart condition, undiagnosed, eating a tuna steak at the kitchen table one minute, dead the next.'

'Oh my God, Cheri, I'm so sorry.' Jem put her hand against the soft wool of her expensive sweater, 'I am so, so sorry. That's just awful.'

'Yeah, I know. And we never even got to have any babies. We were talking about it. I often think, if only we hadn't talked about it, if only we'd just done it, then at least I'd have something of him, you know, instead of nothing. So look, you and Ralph – why did you split up?'

Jem looked at her blankly, for a moment. Then she sighed. 'A lot of different reasons,' she said, 'nothing specific. Just the general stress of life, just growing apart, changing, I suppose.'

Cheri shook her head vehemently from side to side. 'Don't get divorced,' she said. 'Please don't. You two are so lucky to have found each other. Two lovely children. The rest of your lives together. Don't throw it away. Imagine,' she said, gripping Jem's hand with hers, 'imagine if Ralph died. Imagine if there was no second chance. How would you feel?' she asked. '*How would you feel?*'

Jem closed her eyes for a moment. She let the question sink in. And then she felt her answer begin to form. She smiled tightly at Cheri. She had no idea what to say.

PART FIVE

Two weeks later

Chapter 1

It is the morning after her visit to Ralph's flat, after Jem found the screwed-up love letter in the bin. Jem drops Scarlett at nursery and then comes straight back to Maygrove Road, walks past her sister's house, past the Maygrove Centre and on to the estate itself. She has left Blake with Lulu, who is going to take him to the skateboarding park, his new favourite place. Not that he is able to use a skateboard yet – he is only sixteen months – but he loves to sit in his buggy and watch the big boys swish and ricochet around the concrete. Ooh, he says, aaah, oh no!

Jem follows the signage until it takes her to a corner of the estate called Sunbury Terrace. Here there are ten or so houses on a crescent-shaped terrace. They are small and slightly unprepossessing, but less foreboding than the towers and blocks that surround them. She finds number fifteen and, unable to find a working doorbell, she clatters the letterbox. The door is opened by a giant of a man in a rust-coloured hooded sweatshirt and combat trousers. He is handsome and tanned and has a paintbrush in his hand.

'Yes?' he says. He has a bristly Scots accent.

'Hello,' Jem smiles. 'Are you Gil?'

'Yes, I cannot deny it.'

'Oh. Good. I'm Jem. I'm –'

'Ralph's sweetheart.'

'Yes. Well, no, not –'

'Come in.' He holds the door ajar for her and ushers

her into a small living room filled with interesting (though not entirely beautiful) antiques and pieces of slightly rough-and-ready art. 'I was just washing my brushes, but now you're here I can take a break instead. Cup of tea?' He claps his large hands together and then cups them.

He is a very appealing person, physically. Everything about him looks clean and strong and healthy. All his proportions are right and in the places that he has aged he has done so very elegantly. Jem feels immediately comfortable in his company and says: 'Yes, a cup of tea would be lovely, thank you.'

'So,' he calls from the tiny kitchen, 'what brings you to my door?'

Jem gets to her feet and replies closer to the door, so that she doesn't have to shout. 'Well,' she says, watching him pour a little too much full-fat milk into her tea, 'it's Ralph. He was supposed to collect the children last Wednesday and he didn't. I spoke to him and he said he had to do something, but that he would be back the next Wednesday, i.e., yesterday to collect them. But he didn't come again and I found a number for a woman called Sarah at his flat, and I spoke to her yesterday and she has no idea where he's gone, but she said that she'd spoken to you, that you'd been with him, that you might know where he is. I'm so, so worried about him. I'm so . . .' she stops, remembering Cheri's words in the street in Battersea. 'I just really hoped you might have some idea where he might be.'

'Right, well, I can see why she'd have thought I'd have an idea about his whereabouts because actually I did spend most of last week with the boy.'

'You did?'

'Yes. Me and the boy went up to the Moors. In Yorkshire. We went to paint.'

Jem nods and takes the steaming mug of too-milky tea from Gil's outstretched hands.

'Yes. The boy was in something of a bother. He came to me on that Wednesday night. I hadn't been expecting him. It was about six o'clock, I suppose . . . and he said – now let me think because I can see that this is important; that's right, he said it was your anniversary. He said that this day a number of years ago you and he shared your first kiss. And then he said that he couldn't face you, not today, not now. He asked me to come away with him, there and then. He waited a moment for me to pack some things in a bag and then he drove me, fast as you like, up to the Moors. I heard him talking to you on the phone. I was concerned then. I could see that this was something out of the ordinary, that it'd have had you worried. But he calmed down once we were there. We found a B&B, we sat and prayed, and the next morning we got up early to paint. But we didn't do much in the way of talking. I could tell he didn't want to say anything so I just let him be. And then the boy said he needed to be home again, home to see his children. So we came back down that motorway, a little slower this time, and he dropped me off at home.'

'When was this?'

'Well, this would've been Saturday. This Saturday, just passed.'

'And he said he was going to see his children?'

'Yes, he seemed quite frantic to see them. I would have vouched that he'd have been straight back around the corner to your place. That's the way it seemed.'

Jem shakes her head.

'Well, then,' the man called Gil licks his dry lips, 'we've gone as far as we can down this road. Although . . .' he pauses.

'Yes?' she almost pleads. She is aching for Gil to tell her something that will quell this sick dread in her belly, to tell her that Ralph is not dead, that she has not *left it too late*.

415

'There was one thing. A phonecall on the way back from Yorkshire. I thought it might be you at first, but from what little I could hear the accent sounded different. Australian. Or maybe even a true London cockney accent. But certainly, now I give it some thought, not your voice. And she was saying I can be there in ten minutes, and he was saying, no, not yet, I won't be home for at least an hour and he sounded a little surprised to hear from this woman. That's all I'll say.'

'Did he mention a name?'

Gil licks his lips again and squints. 'Well, now, I . . . yes!' He slaps his palms against his combat trousers. 'Rosey!'

And at the mention of the name Jem remembers vividly a moment in her fateful conversation with Ralph all those months ago, just before their ill-fated wedding. The beautiful blonde in the photo in his studio. Smith's ex. The Christian with the church that had turned her boyfriend into a man of faith. The woman he'd painted that beautiful portrait of. Rosey.

'Yes,' continues Gil, 'that's what it was. Rosey. And all the while I just thought he was talking to you, I wasn't paying much attention. But he was talking to this Rosey woman. Yes. He was.' He pauses and looks at Jem with almond-shaped eyes of swimming-pool blue. 'Does that help?' he says.

Jem shrugs. One door opens. Another slams in her face. 'A little bit,' she says. 'I'm not sure how much though, because this Rosey girl lives in America.'

'Ah, well, yes. That might well be a problem. Unless of course she is still here.'

Of course, thinks Jem, of course. The bracelet, the cheap pretty bracelet. It belongs to Rosey. Rosey has been in Ralph's bedroom. Rosey has been in Ralph's bed. She is a Christian. She sings in a band. She is beautiful. And it is clear now to Jem that wherever Ralph is, this girl is with him.

Something red and hot and painful floods through her at this thought. It is as bitter as bile. It is deep, raging jealousy.

Who is this irresistible woman who has lured Ralph away from her children? And away from her? Until yesterday Jem had thought that Ralph had a girlfriend called Sarah. From what little she'd heard about Sarah it didn't seem that she was a threat. She sounded dull and pious and unlikely to bring Ralph into a state of paroxysmal love. But Sarah was not his girlfriend. Rosey was. And now this Rosey had appeared from nowhere and air-lifted Ralph right out of his life.

Jem remembers that Sarah mentioned having an e-mail relationship with this Rosey person. 'Excuse me,' she says to Gil, 'I just have to make a quick call.'

She brings up Sarah's number and calls it with shaking hands.

'Sarah,' she says, 'it's Jem. I'm at Gil's. It sounds like Ralph is with this Rosey girl. I don't know where. No idea, no. I just wondered if you could give me her e-mail address. I mean, she might have a BlackBerry with her or something, she might be able to pick it up.'

'I can do better than that,' says Sarah, the tap-tapping of her computer keyboard audible in the background. 'I have her cell. Here. Take it down.'

Jem taps it in, thanks Sarah and then presses Call. Under other circumstances she would feel nervous calling this steely blonde who has possibly taken away her last chance to get back together with Ralph, but she does not feel nervous, she just wants to hear that Ralph is OK and she wants to hear it now.

A female voice answers almost immediately. 'Yes.'

'Hello – is this Rosey?' she begins impatiently.

'Yes, who's this?'

Jem can hear that Rosey is at an airport, or a train station. She can hear the Tannoy, the echo of a high-ceilinged building. 'This is Jem,' she says. 'Ralph's ex-partner, Jem.'

'Oh.'

'Yes. He's gone missing and I'm trying to track him down. I'm with Ralph's friend, Gil, and he seems to think that there's a chance he might be with you?' Please God, she thinks, please, let him be with you.

There is silence on the line, then the ding-dong of another Tannoy announcement in the background. Until, finally: 'What?'

'Ralph,' says Jem, with a hint of impatience, 'is he with you?'

'No,' says the Australian woman, bluntly. 'No. He isn't. I thought . . .' she pauses for a moment. 'I thought he was with you.'

Eight days earlier

Ralph pulled up on Maygrove Road and switched off the engine. It was just after six fifteen and he was running a bit late. The sun had just set and the early evening sky was streaked violet and navy and full of fat, charcoal clouds. As Ralph got out of the car he heard footsteps approaching. He tensed himself as he always did on this street after dark. It was a different place at night, the kind of place where people got mugged.

The footsteps got closer and he turned to face the road. He was about to cross over when a voice, very close to his ear, said, 'Hello, Ralph.'

It was him.

That man.

Joel.

'Oh,' said Ralph, 'hi.'

'On your way to a meeting?' he asked.

'No,' said Ralph, 'no. I'm collecting my kids. And I'm running a bit late.'

'Yes, I heard what happened. I heard that you and Jem had split up,'

'You did?' Ralph replied with raised eyebrows.

'Yes. Seems like I was right.'

Ralph stopped and threw Joel a quizzical look. 'I beg your pardon?'

'Last time we met, I told you, she was looking for

something, she was scenting the air. Well, she found it.'

Ralph closed his eyes and breathed in deeply. 'I'm sorry,' he said.

'Don't be sorry,' said Joel, his voice rich with gratification.

'I mean,' said Ralph, 'what exactly are you talking about?'

'What,' said Joel, 'you don't know?'

'Don't know what?'

'About Jem and Lucas?'

'Who the hell is Lucas?'

'Lucas is my son.'

'Yes. And?'

'And, well, Jem and Lucas, they had a thing.'

Ralph shook his head from side to side, trying to dislodge the wrongness of what Joel had just said. 'A thing?'

'Yes, Jem had an affair with my son. That is correct.'

'But your son is a . . . child?'

'Well,' Joel laughed infuriatingly. 'He *was* a child, yes, a long time ago, but he is now a grown man of twenty-five. Who has been sleeping with your ex.'

Ralph almost stumbled as the words hit his consciousness. 'But, I . . .'

'You didn't know?'

'Well, no, it's bloody obvious I didn't know, isn't it?' Ralph gazed at Joel for a moment. Joel's face was flat and unsmiling, but Ralph could see something gleeful behind his eyes. He had for some reason decided that he hated Ralph and he was now taking pleasure in imparting this development to Ralph, in being the person from whom he heard it first. 'How long did they . . . ?' he whispered.

Joel shrugged. 'No idea,' he said.

Ralph forced a smile. He was not going to give this strange man the reward of seeing him gutted. 'Well,' he said, 'she's a free agent. She can do what she likes.' He dragged the words from between his lips. The thought of

420

Jem 'doing what she liked' with another man made him want to be violently sick.

'Anyway just thought you'd like to know,' said Joel. 'I'll see you around no doubt.'

'Yes,' said Ralph, keeping his tone light and unfazed. 'No doubt.'

He crossed the street towards Lulu's house and he heard Joel's footsteps retreating towards the Maygrove Centre. Ralph let his breath come now as he approached the front door. It came quick and fast and heavy. It came so heavy that he felt his head begin to lose oxygen, his vision begin to blur. He sat down heavily upon the front step and he tried to control his breathing and as his heart rate came down he felt tears coming and he buried his eyes into the heels of his hands to stop them.

Jem had slept with another man.

A twenty-five-year-old man.

His Jem. His little Jem. The sweet, funny, ballsy wisp of a girl he'd fallen in love with in a flat in Battersea. Little Jem, whom he'd eaten curry with and made babies with and thought he was going to spend the rest of his life with. He'd let her go. And instead of bouncing back to him, she'd bounced into the arms of a man of twenty-five. Christ, hardly a man at all. Just a kid. A boy.

The thought of it was appalling to Ralph, in every way.

He appraised Lulu's house behind him. He thought of his children behind those doors. And he knew then that he couldn't face them. He was too crazy to see his children. If he saw them now he would scare them.

He got into his car and he drove. He drove past the Maygrove Centre and he drove through the Maygrove Estate until he reached Sunbury Terrace. He banged on Gil's door with his fist until Gil's face appeared in the crack left by his security chain.

'Come for a drive with me,' he said, 'I need to get away.'

He took Gil to his car and they drove, in silence. He

needed to think and Gil let him do just that. Half an hour out of London the phone rang. It was Lulu. He told her that he was going away for the weekend. He was very apologetic.

'What shall I tell Jem?' she asked.

'Tell her I'll be back for the children next week. Tell her I'm sorry.'

Half an hour later the phone rang again. This time it was Jem. He almost didn't answer it. He didn't know what to say to her. What do you say to the love of your life when you've just found out that she'd had an affair with a man who's almost half your age? What do you say when your head is spinning and all the words you've ever spoken to each other have been pulverised into a grey goo somewhere between your ears? He told her he was sorry. He told her he'd be back for the children next week. And then he hung up before he said something he'd regret.

He took Gil to a bed and breakfast in Yorkshire. He'd been there before, brought the children up for the occasional weekend (if there was something he felt he could give the children out of the mess of his broken relationship with their mother, it was happy weekends in the countryside, some wholesome fodder for their childhood memories), and the owners were happy to see him midweek. For three days he and Gil walked and prayed and talked and contemplated the landscape. They drank cloudy beer in warm pubs and then, on Saturday night, Ralph received an e-mail from Rosey.

'Dear R,' it said, 'guess what? I'm in London. Where are you?'

He phoned her on the number she had embedded into the signature of her e-mails and after three days of virtual silence Ralph found himself talking, too much. He told her all about his conversation with Joel on Wednesday night and she soothed him and she said, it's OK, I'm here. I'm here now. Come home. Come back to London. It's

OK. I'm here. And all Ralph wanted then was to be back in his own bed and to feel someone's warmth against him, hold something in his arms, be with someone who understood. So he hustled his old friend back into his car and they took to the motorway and within four hours Gil was back in his little house on his estate and Ralph was letting Rosey in through the front door of his flat.

Ralph didn't ask Rosey what she was doing in London. He didn't ask her much at all. He gave her a cold beer from his fridge and apologised for the mess and then he put his hand against her face and stared into her remarkable green eyes. She clasped his hand against her cheek with her hand and then she brushed the side of his hand with her lips and Ralph's sleeping lust burst into life.

'I'm so glad you're here,' he said.

'I'm so glad I'm here,' she said. 'I knew,' she said, 'I just knew –'

But Ralph stopped her words with his lips.

It was fast and it was furious. Very little clothing got removed. It was the first time that Ralph had had sex with someone who wasn't Jem since 1996. He barely had a chance to absorb the nuances of Rosey's body, the differences, the feel of her. He was consumed with a desire to get lost in her, he pushed his face into her fine silky hair and he breathed in his own hot, sour breath. He kissed her hard. He sought oblivion inside her. And he found it.

For the seventeen minutes that it took Ralph and Rosey to consummate their passion, Ralph was nowhere; sweet, numb, hot nowhere.

'You know,' said Rosey, falling away from him afterwards, letting her knees fall together again, 'I've wanted to do that with you since the very first moment I set eyes on you.'

Ralph fell on to his back and blinked at the ceiling. He thought back to the first moment he'd set eyes on her, the lightning bolt of her beauty, the shock of his attraction.

He smiled at her. 'Yeah,' he said, 'so have I.' It wasn't strictly true. He'd wanted to do that to her the first time he'd met her and he'd wanted to do it to her just now, but really, he hadn't thought about doing it to her at any other point in between. He'd had other things on his mind. He'd been too busy finding himself to think much about sex with beautiful strangers. And all the while he'd been finding himself, Jem had been too busy thinking about sex with beautiful strangers to find herself. And so they'd passed each other, like night trains, at speed and in opposite directions, blurred and indistinct. He turned to look at Rosey again. Her skin, he could see, now that he was no longer consumed with the business of having her, was smooth and toned and tanned. Her breasts, which he'd barely glanced at, were small and full with nipples like jelly tots. She was firm and young, her body as yet unused by life. She was young. It was good to look upon something so young.

Is this what it was like for Jem? he wondered. Had she too looked upon the half-naked body of her young lover and marvelled at its newness? Had she felt a thrill of gratitude for once more being allowed to have something she thought she'd never again be granted access to?

He turned from Rosey's body then and closed his eyes.

Rosey turned on to her side and let her arm fall across his torso. He was still wearing his T-shirt. She pulled the fabric up so that her arm lay against his bare skin. He tensed slightly.

'You know,' she began, tracing a fingertip across the skin around his belly button, round and round, in a slow circle, 'you know you're the reason why I ditched Smith? You know I've . . .' she paused. 'Well, I've been thinking about you a lot. Since then. Since that very first moment. I knew there was something special about you. Something, I don't know, something magic. And then that night, after the gig, Jesus, when I kissed you, I thought you were going to kiss me back. And I wanted you to, so very, very badly,' she laughed. 'But you didn't. Because you're a good man. And you said you'd paint me. Do you remember?'

He nodded.

'Do you still think you'd like to do that?'

Ralph felt a vein under his eye start to twitch. He kissed her shoulder. He couldn't tell her about the painting in his cupboard, a painting he could never sell, but could never hang on a wall either, a painting that would spend for ever in a cupboard. It would make her think too much about everything. 'Maybe,' he said eventually, 'maybe.'

What would Smith think, he mused as they lay together in silence, what would he think if he could see me here with Rosey? Taking his disillusioned girl away from him, *again*. Being the preferred option. And if this remarkable woman found him preferable to Smith – hell, had *finished* with Smith because of him – then what did that say about Jem? Did it make her remarkable also? Did it mean that she was in fact everything he'd always thought she was? Special? Magical? Enchanted? And that he too was something special? He hadn't felt special for so long.

He stroked Rosey's hair and he smiled down at her. He felt the calmest he'd felt for days, ever since he'd spoken to Joel on the pavement outside Lulu's house. Everything suddenly seemed so simple. Everything was suddenly utterly clear. They'd made a mess between them, he and Jem, but now, blindingly, he knew how to clear it up. It would mean taking himself out of the real world, it would mean weeks away from Jem and his children, but it would also be the start of a new beginning.

He was going to recreate history.

He and Rosey ate takeaway pizza in bed that night and they made love again, this time slowly and gently, and this time Ralph drew everything he could of this perfect young woman into himself, every smell, every texture. He caressed her and he explored her and he lasted as long as he possibly could before he came inside her, because he knew, even as it was happening, that it would never happen again.

In the early morning, while she slept, he packed a carrier bag with pants, a toothbrush, some bananas, a carton of orange juice and a packet of Bran Flakes. Then he rolled together a spare pillow and a sleeping bag, shoved them into another carrier bag and sat down and wrote Rosey a note.

Dearest Rosey.

You are so beautiful. I will take your beauty with me everywhere I go for the rest of my life. You are a pure and sweet and perfect human being. Thank you for coming to me last night. I will never ever forget it.

I have to go now, though. There is something I have to do, something that will hopefully fix the mess of my life. Something that will set me back on the life course I was always supposed to be on. I have to start again. I have to go back to the very beginning and start the whole thing all over again.

Please feel free to stay in my flat for as long as you need it. I'll be gone for a while. Here is my key.

You are an angel.

Ralph x

He left the note on the kitchen table and then he left. The sun had yet to rise.

Chapter 2

Jem turns the words over and over and over in her head, just as Rosey had dictated them to her on the phone that morning.

I have to start again.

I have to go back to the very beginning and start the whole thing all over again.

No wonder Rosey assumed that he'd come home to Jem.

But Ralph is not at home. Ralph isn't anywhere.

Jem walks the streets of SE24 for an hour after leaving Gil's house. She wants Ralph to appear, miraculously, from nowhere. She wants to see him, and to touch him and to know that he is safe and to tell him that she loves him, that she has always loved him and that she is ready now, ready to grow up and move on to the next phase. She trails through Brockwell Park, tears coursing down her cheeks, and she stops at the little chapel on Underwood Street, thinking that maybe he has been there all along, lost in prayer, curled up cold and lonely on a pew. But he is not there. Her Ralph is not there. Of course he isn't. She closes her eyes and she turns the words over again.

The beginning.

When was the Beginning?

Was it Croydon, was it his childhood home? Was it the Royal College of Art, where his career as an artist had begun? Or was it Almanac Road? Did he mean the beginning of them? When was the beginning of them, she wonders, when had 'they' officially sprung to life?

Before she leaves the chapel she lights three candles, one for each of her lost babies and then she heads back to the reassuring noise and brightness of the street outside.

She tries to assess her own notion of their beginning. When did it happen to her – when did she know? And of course, it was that moment. Before she'd even met Ralph, when she'd seen just the silhouette of his head in profile through the basement window. She hadn't known it was his head at the time. It could have belonged to anyone. It was only later that she knew it was him and she knew that it had always been meant to be.

There'd been the night they'd cooked the curry together; the night they'd eaten raw chillies. Was that when it had begun? Or was it the night they'd got stoned and run around Soho sex shops together? Maybe it was that moment, on Pete the Butcher's bed? 'Creep' by Radiohead had been playing in the background. Ralph had looked at her . . . well, she'd known then, known he was falling for her, but she'd tried to ignore it because she was with Smith and Jem didn't want her life to be that complicated. Is Ralph in Soho right now? she wonders. Is he trailing round sex shops, trying to recreate something we lost a long time ago, or is he banging on that door in Chinatown, hoping to get back into that apartment, hoping to get back into that long-lost magical moment when we were young and free and crazy with unrequited love?

But no, she decides, as she heads back towards Lulu's house, those are moments, and moments cannot be revisited. They cannot be started all over again. So what, what can Ralph possibly be doing that he thinks will bring the past back to life? Where can he be? Is he lost for ever? Has she missed her chance to put them back together again? A sense of panic rises within her at the thought, the possibility that this might be it for the rest of her life, this regret, this remorse, this terrible loneliness. And then she remembers another time in her life when she'd felt this way, when she'd let Ralph slip through her fingers and feared she'd lost him. Twelve years ago, just after he'd given her his heart and she'd thrown it back at him. He'd disappeared then, too, for endless painful days.

And that is the moment that Jem knows.

Of course!

She knows where he is. She knows, exactly. She knows now that he is alive, that he is safe, that he is thinking of her and that everything is going to be all right. And she also knows that she must leave him there. Leave him until his is ready, once more, to return.

Ralph returns three weeks later. He stands on Lulu's doorstep, thin and pale. Jem opens the door and stares at him.

'You look fucking awful,' she says.

'I'm so, so sorry, Jem,' he says.

She lets him into the house and immediately the children are aware of his presence. They stream down the stairs in their pyjamas with hair in wet tendrils clutching warm milk and ragged bears. They jump on top of him and Jem watches as they reunite. Their children have missed their father. And so has she.

'I want to explain, Jem,' he says, sitting on the bottom stair with both children hanging off him like baby monkeys.

Jem smiles. 'Later,' she says, 'it's fine.'

'But really, I really need to explain everything.'

'It's fine, Ralph,' she says. 'Really.'

'But it's not fine, Jem. I've left you here, left you coping with everything. I just buggered off without an explanation.'

'I spoke to Rosey,' she says.

Ralph's face falls.

Jem smiles. 'It's OK,' she says, 'don't look so worried. She told me about the note you left her. About starting all over again. And it took me so long to work out what you meant, but then it hit me. I knew where you were. So I called the studio manager at Cable Street and asked him if you'd taken a studio there. Told him not to tell you I'd called.'

Ralph's face softens with relief and surprise. 'You knew where I'd been all these weeks?' he gasps.

Jem nods.

'And you didn't come and get me?'

She shakes her head. 'I didn't disturb you the last time,' she says. 'Why would I disturb you this time?'

Ralph looks at her quizzically.

'The beginning,' she says, 'the beginning of us. The night at the gallery. The night I knew I loved you. We'd got into a mess before that night, hadn't we? You'd told me about reading my diaries, I thought I hated you; it had all come apart at the seams. Then you disappeared. Made me ache for you. Made me pine for you. And then you just . . . came back, quiet as a cat, and fixed everything. Just like now, like tonight.'

'I want you to come and see,' he says. 'There won't be a party. Just you and me. Put the kids to bed. Come and see,' he beseeches.

Jem glances at the time. It is almost bedtime.

'Do you want Daddy to put you to bed tonight?' she asks the children. They squeal and yell their consent.

Half an hour later they are leaving the house. 'Where's the car?' asks Jem, looking from left to right. 'I don't know,' he says, smiling at her, that old smile of Ralph's, slightly lazy, lop-sided, from left to right. 'I assume it's still outside my house.'

'You mean you haven't been home yet?' she asks.

'No,' he smiles, 'of course I haven't.'

'So how are we going to get there?'

He turns his head and he gestures towards a rather elderly moped.

Jem looks at him aghast. 'What, seriously?'

'Yeah,' he smiles, handing her a helmet, 'why not? A guy at the studios sold it to me; he was leaving for Madrid. It's not pretty but it does the job. Come on,' he grins, 'hop on.'

Jem looks at Ralph and then she looks at the ugly moped. And then she remembers, she remembers a girl she used to be. A girl who ate raw chillies and went to sex shops and didn't need half a bottle of white wine just to get her in the mood for life. She jams the helmet over her curls and she mounts the moped. And then they are moving. The moped is loud. She thinks briefly of the parents in the houses they pass who have just put their babies to sleep. She thinks how they will hate the driver of the loud moped with a passion and she thinks, I don't care! She wraps her arms around Ralph's waist and she rests her chin upon his shoulder and she watches London, her London, passing her by in filmic stills: the graffitied, shuttered-down shops of Walworth Road, the stage-set arches and Tudor pubs of Borough High Street, the river beneath them, thick and black as they pass over London Bridge, the strobe of amber lozenges as a dozen empty taxis cavalcade towards them on Lower Thames Street, the sleeping locked-down markets of Smithfield, and then they are there, a place that Jem has never been before, but a place that was the birthing pool of the most romantic night of her life. The artists' studios on Cable Street. The place where Ralph painted twenty-four canvases of her, to tell her that he loved her, but more than that, to tell her that he *knew* her. Better than anyone had known her before.

The building is as dead and as blank-faced as a prison block. It does not look romantic. But as they wander through the turps- and oil-scented corridors, as Jem hears the sounds of people working their crafts, late into the night, the occasional shard of radio noise, of muted conversation, she feels the romance of this place being breathed into her.

'This is it,' says Ralph, 'this is where I've been. Close your eyes.'

Jem closes her eyes and allows Ralph to lead her by the hand across the room.

'Keep them closed,' he says.

She nods her assent and then she hears a noise, a clink of heavy glass, then a dull pop, and a fizz.

'Not yet,' he says. He puts something hard and cold into her hand. 'Champagne!' she says, with delight.

'OK,' says Ralph. 'Now. Open your eyes!'

And she does. And she is in a room that is full of art. But not canvases. A frieze. It encircles the room from one side to the other. It is painted on to cartridge paper, three foot high. And it is beautiful.

She turns, around and around, dizzying herself, trying to decide where to settle her gaze first. There is so much to see. There a child, lazy-mouthed, pulling on a fistful of black curly hair, there is a shred of floral chiffon and a glimpse of pale breast. There is a group of happy women, backlit by flashing Soho lights. There is a baby sleeping at its mother's breast. There lies a woman in the dark of a sleeping house, stroking a smiling cat as it lies in her lap. She sees a swing, a slide, a man watching from the shadows. She sees a shoe, with a tall tapered heel, cast aside on a staircase next to an upturned sippy cup and she sees a woman, smiling at a young man, her face lit with pleasure. It is her life and her dreams and it is joyful! There is not a dark note to be seen. It is a celebration of everything that she wants and everything that she has been through in the last year of her life.

She turns to Ralph and the joy she is feeling spills from her in a smile that she cannot control.

'It's amazing,' she sighs happily. 'Absolutely amazing.'

He walks towards her and holds out his champagne

glass. She brushes hers against his and she takes a sip. 'You like it?' he says. He sounds nervous, uncertain.

'Ralph,' she says, 'I adore it. And I am so, so sorry.'

'What for?' he laughs.

'For thinking that there might be something better for me in this world than you. For not being big enough to make that final commitment to you. For leaving you there in front of your family, in front of our children. I'm so, so sorry.'

'And Jem, I'm sorry too. I'm sorry that I let our relationship get so bad, that I dug such a deep hole for you to climb out of. I'm sorry I wasn't there for you after Blake was born and sorry for running off to California and leaving you when you really needed me. I don't blame you for feeling so disappointed in me.'

'Oh, Ralph, I am not disappointed in you. How could I be?'

'You could be. And you were. I got back from California a new man and just expected you to be all right about everything. I should have known it would take time for you to trust me.' He smiles his lazy smile again and he holds her face by the chin. 'Neither of us has really done anything wrong, you know that, don't you?'

She nods. She has known it for days. All the resentment, all the ambivalence, it has just disappeared. 'I know,' she says. 'It's just, you know . . .'

'Life,' says Ralph. 'Timing. All that shit. But I'd forgotten. Forgotten what this was all about. What *we* were all about. And then I remembered, and it was so simple: we are about *us*. Just . . . *us*. And that used to mean one thing, and now it means something completely different. Us means our children and our careers. Us means accepting that we're not always going to be the same and that sometimes we'll be happy and sometimes we won't, and that you can't look at a year in isolation because one day when we look back on the whole vast, glittering expanse of our relationship, a year will look like such a very tiny little speck of nothing and we'll wonder what all the fuss was about. And the religion thing: I know it freaks you out, but really, it's nothing to fear . . .'

'I know, I know. I know that now . . .'

'Yeah. It's just something I need to do, something to control my creativity, something to keep me positive and focused on the important stuff. And that doesn't mean that I expect you to focus on the same things as me. We can be together and still be . . .'

'Different.'

'Yes.' He takes her face in his hands and looks into her eyes. 'Yes, we can be different.'

'And together?'

'Yes. And together. All four of us. Because I love you, Jem. I love you more now than I've ever loved you before. And if you choose to be with me now, after what we've been through for the past twelve months, I'll know, we'll both know, that this is more than just a romantic dream. That this is destiny. And I mean that in the purest, realest, least romantic sense of the word.'

'You mean we're stuck with each other, no matter what?'

Ralph smiled. 'That's exactly what I mean.'

Jem puts down her champagne glass and covers Ralph's hands with her own. She looks into his eyes and she sees it there, the same tortured young man who painted peonies for her twelve years ago, laying himself open, showing himself raw, asking her to love him. And she does. She really does.

'Good,' she says. 'Thank God.'

And then she kisses him.

Epilogue

Jem walks into the hall and she grips her father's hand. She is wearing a beautiful Vivienne Westwood dress, ruched and pinned in all the right places, decorated with snapdragons and peacocks, and pinned against his décolletage is a single white orchid. She'd felt a shiver of the past as she'd pulled the dress from the back of the wardrobe this morning, taken it from its hanger, smelled the scent of a sad and awful day still lingering in its folds.

'I Want to Stay with You' by Gallagher and Lyle plays through four large speakers, one in each corner of the room. It is a bright, playful song, about long-term love. About wholly unromantic destiny. The song makes her smile. It makes her feel hopeful. That's why they chose it.

It's 5 March, a year since Ralph went missing and thirteen years since their first kiss on a blue sofa in a basement flat in Battersea. Outside it is raining. Jem's red silk shoes are splashed with brown water and the sleeve of her father's jacket is wet. But it doesn't matter. Today is a happy day. Today, at last, Jem is marrying Ralph. And not in a dry room in a registry office this time, not with just the bare bones of family to watch them do it, not with the wrong dress on, not with a hangover and not with a sick dread in the pit of her belly. Today she fits her dress, she is daisy fresh and she knows that she is doing exactly the right thing.

She smiles as she passes the people lining the walkway. There's Karl, big and handsome in a white suit that somehow only Karl could carry off. He gives her the

435

thumbs up and she returns it. He is no longer her client. He took the five thousand pounds to do his redemptive TV interview, redeemed himself, and then retired from the public eye. He does a late-night slot on London Radio now and keeps his face off the telly. He is sitting next to Smith, who arrived on an overnight flight this morning and looks tanned but shell-shocked. Stella, Jarvis and Philippe sit in front of them, Stella's face almost inside out with excitement. Jem waves at her sisters, at her nephews, at her mother, and then at her little boy who is sitting on her mother's lap. Philippe is here with a very beautiful young woman who looks like she has been carved out of fine marble. There is Gil, tall and fine-looking in a brown suit, and Sarah, wearing a feathered adornment on her head that Jem believes is known as a fascinator. She is with her very tiny husband and another couple from the prayer group, whom Jem doesn't recognise. But they look very nice. Jem has accepted that this group and these people are now a part of Ralph's life and she knows that they are good people. Ralph's dad stands at the front, just behind Ralph. He is the best man and somewhere in his jacket pocket sits a box containing two plain white gold bands. He smiles shyly at Jem and moves so that she can make her way next to his son. The hall is decorated with orchids, white ones.

Ralph had expected Jem to want peonies, but peonies were too fleeting, too showy, too yesterday. The old orchid on the windowsill in their new kitchen is in full bloom again today, she checked it this morning, eight fat blooms. That orchid would never die, because it wanted to live.

At the end of the hall, Jem stops and turns to kiss her daughter, who is wearing last year's bridesmaid dress, a little shorter in the leg, a little tighter around the armholes, but still the only dress she'd had any interest in wearing today. 'But I have to wear that dress,' she said, 'it's the dress for your wedding.'

Scarlett slides on to a chair next to Jem's mother and her little brother and then Jem reaches the side of her husband-to-be. Ralph looks beautiful. He is in his Dolce & Gabbana suit, the suit he'd bought for his party in Philippe's gallery thirteen years ago today. It still fits him and if anything, it fits him better. He holds his hand out for her. She looks at him. He looks at her. She wants to cry. She takes his hand. The song comes to an end and silence falls across the room.

The wedding begins.